HOLY ORDERS

Ci Ci Soleil

HOLY ORDERS

A NOVEL

Beach Reads Books

ISBN: 979-8-9850660-5-0

Author: Ci Ci Soleil

Cover Art By: Ruben Fernandez

Beach Reads Books

PO Box 103

Carrboro, NC 27516

BeachReadsBooks.com

Carry On My Wayward Son lyrics by Kerry Livgren

Ghost Riders in the Sky lyrics by Stan Jones

Band on the Run lyrics by Paul McCartney and Linda McCartney

For Erika Lusk and Katie Rosanbalm, with fond memories of cocktails in the yard as we talked plotlines and characters. Thank you for weaving this adventure with me

Prologue

January 1346

"Your Excellency." The arch deacon bowed before his superior as he approached. The clacking of a plethora of clogs stilled to silence, their echoes fading against the hard stone of the church. "Your Excellency: he's not here."

"Gotfried, what do you mean he's not here?" Bishop Eberhard Trōst stared at the man.

The Arch Deacon glanced quickly at the many attendants surrounding them.

Bishop Trōst nodded, took in a breath. He turned to his attendants. "Leave us."

The chorus of deacons and priests that always surrounded the bishop withdrew, allowing Eberhard and the arch deacon to walk together in relative privacy, the retinue following timidly at a respectful distance, as if to ensure that their bishop remained in their sights.

"They're like a flock of pigeons, aren't they?" The bishop rolled his eyes as he shook his head.

"Well, you do offer the spiritual bread of life, your Excellency." The arch deacon suppressed a smile.

"And the actual bread of life. No doubt, they all fear they would starve without me."

The arch deacon glanced back at their trailing entourage. "Happiness, isn't it, that they don't look to be at risk of withering away any time soon."

Eberhard chortled. "Indeed. A rather portly bunch, it is, that waddles ever in my wake." He shook his head, thinking of how his required band of attendants were merely the "spare" sons of the nobility whose parents had paid the required dowry and unceremoniously dumped their extra, unwanted male progeny into the ranks of the church. While literacy was an asset they brought with them, the desire to follow Christ had not generally been among their strengths. Not a man among them was guided by the holy spirit.

But Bernard was different. He wasn't a spare. He was a man of special gifts and talents, even if he shared some of the peculiar habits of his uncle. And he deeply felt the calling, always knowing his destiny was to serve God. If Eberhard had his way, Bernard would be bishop after him, once he'd completed his five years of serving a parish, of course. And maybe even a cardinal one day. Not that Eberhard could admit to that aloud. With Bernard being his nephew, it was crucial that Eberhard played his hand carefully. While nepotism was not uncommon in the Catholic ranks, it was a chess game that must be skillfully engaged, with motives stealthily cloaked. Everything rested on Bernard. "How could Bernard not have come? Today is his ordainment?"

Eberhard suspected that Franz was behind this devilry. An uneasy truce existed between him and his brother. While Eberhard was himself a second son, a "spare" conveniently parked in the church out of expediency, Franz was the cherished first-born and chosen heir of their father, the most powerful duke that Lotharinga had ever known. Eberhard understood his fate was sealed because of his own peculiarities, his "odd little habits", and thus everything—title, money, power, lovers, Hedwig, children—went to his older, and more normal brother, Franz.

"Oh, Sir, Bernard *is* here. It is your brother, the duke, who did not come."

"Did his mother come?" He felt his heart skip a beat, even after all these years.

"The Lady Hedwig is in attendance, along with her other children. She brought these." Gotfried pulled a beautiful golden cross on a very long chain out of his pocket and then a shorter, smaller golden cross on a chain of more typical length, also finely wrought.

"Ordination gifts for her son, no doubt?"

Gotfried nodded. "She asked if you would bless them."

"Of course! Of course I will bless them. It would be a pleasure." He looked at the excellent workmanship of the gold. Hedwig had wonderful taste; perhaps not in husbands, but then again, she didn't really have much of a choice there. Franz was not the one she would have chosen, at any rate.

"And she sent this as a gift for you, your Excellency." Gotfried handed his bishop a small box.

Eberhard looked curiously at the box and opened it slowly. Inside was a gold and diamond ring, a match to the one she had presented to Bernard when he came of age. "She is always so thoughtful." He sighed, his heart full of regret for destinies that did not belong to him.

He stroked his chin and then, as they passed a basin of holy water, he stopped to wash his hands. He always felt the need to wash his hands when he thought of his brother. He'd had basins of holy water installed throughout the halls of the church so that he could wash his hands frequently. He'd heard the snickers that an entire retinue of priests existed simply to bless enough holy water to keep the basins filled and exchanged every day.

An attendant ran up from his trailing entourage to hand him a newly pressed towel. The bishop nodded his thanks and, with a look, sent the attendant back to the gaggle of followers to await his next need.

Once the man was safely out of earshot, he took the ring back from Gotfried and slid it onto his finger. Admiring it, he said, "I'm not surprised Franz didn't come. He always was an ass."

The arch deacon nodded slowly. "Yet even an ass can be essential where a draft horse cannot manage to squeeze his way in."

Eberhard smiled in agreement, but the smile quickly faded. "Now that my brother has successfully exiled the Council of Archbishops from Cologne, not that the greedy fools didn't deserve their fate, we must move carefully and preserve all the ties we have." He gave his senior attendant an intent look. "Gotfried, the balance of power is shifting in Germania."

Gotfried nodded, but didn't look at all concerned as he replied, "The fiefdoms are smaller with every generation. Dukes abound, your Excellency, particularly in the south, where they're all but powerless. Bishops, however, are more rare."

It was true and caused Eberhard to reflect that, in a way, his father had been right after all. By giving the entirety of the largest remaining duchy to Franz and remanding little Eberhard, with his curious habits, to the church, the Duke of Lotharinga had been able to preserve power indeed, for his most beloved son, and, ironically, even his broken one.

"Ah, Gotfried. The battle for Bernard has been arduous. By afternoon, we will have won, but never underestimate my brother. Franz has his own ways of taking back in principle what he's lost through strong arm negotiation. He may have lost his son, his chosen heir to his title, but he will not stop until he finds a way to wrest power from the church."

"The archbishops?"

"Precisely."

Gotfried gave the bishop a serious look. "My reports inform me that the duke is spending more time with the rising powerful who are not of the nobility."

"Yes, I am aware. Hedwig mentioned as much when I saw her last, concerned that she now needs to socialize with those beneath her station. Franz is cozying up with the guilds, sniffing out the most powerful of the merchant class. I wonder what will come of that. My brother is a man of strong ambitions. While today might frustrate some of those aspirations, his gaze will quickly fall elsewhere. I know my brother."

"With all due respect, your Excellency, what possible benefit could he find with alliances with the shopkeepers and warehousers?"

Eberhard gave a slow, small smile. "Never underestimate how those with a desire for dominance can create the realm anew. A new power arises in our world. Some will try to quash it. Others to harness. I've seen my brother play this particular field before. Where some would kill the threat, he captures the wild stallion and harnesses the beast, and brings it under his control. He will do no less now." Eberhard thought for a moment. "Double your spies upon him."

The arch deacon nodded. "It is time, your Excellency. Your nephew's ordainment awaits."

Chapter 1

Everly

"Plague… wow, this is going to be fun!" Everly squirmed in her seat, feeling her heart beating in anticipation.

"Entschuldigung, sie, Fräulein?" the German Uber driver inquired, taking a quick glance at her in his rear-view mirror.

"Schon gut!" she replied, waving away his concern with an *all's good*. She didn't want to try to explain Black Plague to him. He was nice. At least she thought he was nice. He didn't really speak English very well at all, but he had made a valiant attempt to understand her mangled Google Translate Deutsch as she struggled to get all those interconnected syllables to come out of her mouth. She was good at so many things. German was not one of them.

Still in disbelief, she re-read the letter offering her the position: she was going to work with Dr. Trevor Payne. This would make her career. Sure, it was just a dig for a summer, but if she did well, that could turn into fall research assignments and collaborations and those could turn into sabbaticals and new opportunities.

"Wow. A sabbatical at Cambridge." She kept her voice at a whisper so as not to distract her driver again. Academically, it would be the feather in her cap she desperately needed. And if she could impress the famous Dr. Payne, she could be on her way to having serious funding of her own and eventually grasping that ultimate brass ring: tenure. While he was a notoriously prickly old crabapple, having a mentor like him could knock down the walls in the man's world of archeology. If only she could get on his good side. After working her ass off for all these years, what with finishing her doctorate and then toiling away at the fairly thankless job of an assistant professor, she was finally getting the break she needed. The break she deserved. She stiffened at the memory of the condescending and controlling tones of the tenured professors who reigned over her destiny.

"But plague can change everything." She could hear the hope in her voice as she said it.

"Fräulein?"

With a smile, she waved him off again.

After an hour's drive with precious little real communication, the fuel-efficient car pulled up at a barely-there camp site. She looked around, dumbfounded. Mountains surrounded the long, low valley on three sides. She thought she could see a body of water in the distance. If she listened, she was sure she'd hear disobedient nuns singing in the hills.

"Nein, nein!" she said. This could not be the place. This was some Boy Scout campsite. Not an archeology dig of one of the most prestigious professors from Cambridge University. Modern dig sites had trailers, not tents. She handed him the paper with the location and directions.

"Ja, das ist es. Es ist was do wolltest."

She understood the "Ja" part of it, telling her this is just where she was supposed to be. If he had taken her to the middle of no place and missed the dig site, she was going to give him the world's worst review in every language that Google supplied her. It was miles and miles back to the last tiny little town they'd passed through, someplace called Miltenberg. Before she got out of the car, she checked to make sure she had bars on her phone. She didn't.

The man cheerily pulled her huge backpack and her suitcase out of the trunk and set them next to her on the grassy turf. He looked around quickly, shrugged, and then said, "Es ist Schön hier. Viel Glück!"

She roughly translated that as "pretty here… good luck!" but before she could respond, she watched him hop back into his car and drive down the dusty strip that passed for a road through the green valley and disappear into the distance. She felt very alone.

Shouldering her backpack with a grunt and dragging her suitcase behind her, its wheels choking on the thick valley grasses, she made her way over to the semicircle of tents, trying to get her bearings. "Damn wheels!" she muttered, annoyed that a seam on her duffel had ripped wide open at the airport, luckily before she checked it with the gate agent. A regular tourist suitcase was the only short-order replacement she could get. She was acutely aware that real archeologists did not drag suitcases with them at a dig site.

Everly walked around, dumbfounded at her surroundings. Six tents made up the camp. One was obviously for storage, as it was filled with crates, mostly unpacked. Labels advised the onlooker that they held "tools", "equipment" or "specimen trays". The crates were all piled up together and labeled like someone had spray-painted on stenciled words. It looked a little bit like Hollywood's concept of a 1930s dig set—all ready for the director to shout *action* and the explosions to start. She then found a little mess area was set up in the back with a backyard grill, a cook stove, and some small refrigeration units—and more crates labeled "food".

The tent arranged as an artifact and specimen processing lab was evident, being adorned with ample signage about proper attire being required and the admonishment to wear, and then dispose of, gloves properly—no littering. It was the largest tent onsite. She hoped the two closed tents with no signs weren't quarters. She shuddered to think that the taller, circular tent to the back could be some type of showers for personnel living onsite during the dig.

"What is this, the set from M*A*S*H?" she said aloud as she made her way towards a tent in the center of the gathering. The flap was pulled halfway back and revealed tables and chairs inside, cabinets for filing, and an array of computers. A battery center powering everything stood to the far side of the tent with cables running underneath, connecting the battery to a line of solar panels that stood outside.

She thought she could see someone in there and breathed in deeply for courage. It was time to figure out what had happened to the famous archeologist's dig. She stood respectfully outside the door flap and called out, "Hello? Hello?" Her voice didn't carry the confidence with which she'd intended to impress the eminent Dr. Payne.

No one answered her but she did hear a voice, perhaps on a phone call. As she listened, she realized it wasn't talking but rather singing. Surprisingly, it sounded a bit like an East London accent, what she identified from old movies as vaguely cockney.

Masquerading as a man with a reason,
My charade is the event of the season
And if I claim to be a wise man,
Well, it surely means that I don't know.

"Hello?" she said again as she ducked to enter, and once inside the flap, set down her backpack and suitcase. Now that she was inside, she could see the layout of the whole room. There were makeshift tables made of metal storage crates along one side of the tent and other metal folding tables were covered with books, notes, maps, and computers. If there was an organization scheme, she couldn't figure it out. A dark-haired man, likely in his late-thirties to early-forties, sat at the main table in the room which, she was rather surprised to see, was adorned with a fabric blue and yellow tablecloth elaborately decorated with lemons and peacocks. It looked like something that belonged on your grandma's table—but certainly not at an archeology dig. The man sitting there was seemingly absorbed in a thick book, one hand absentmindedly toying with the loose curls his hair made where it was long on the top as he was singing away.

He had maps spread out in front of him and he would read from the book, then excitedly mark on the map in little colored pencils, momentarily losing the beat of his song. He didn't seem to notice that she was there. She looked to the side and saw, to her astonishment, an actual tiny living room set-up on the grass—couch, cushy armchair and even an old-fashioned hutch holding cups and offering a tea service and a coffee station.

"This is the weirdest dig site I've ever seen," she said aloud as she stared about her.

Slowly, as if it took discipline to pull himself away from the page, he turned to look at her. "Hullo. And how might I help you?"

"Hello, uh, yes. I'm Dr. Everly Bergeron."

He looked blank.

"Assistant professor? University of Toronto? I'm here for the medieval research project on the plagues of the fourteenth century?"

"You're who?"

She took in a deep breath to give her more confidence. After all, this was probably someone she would be supervising. "I'm the field director for Dr. Trevor Payne for the summer."

As he sat for several moments, his look of general confusion turned to one of recognition. "Oh yes! Well, cheers! Dr. Bergeron. Everly is it? What do you know. Huh." He looked around, shuffling some papers in the hunt for something, saying to no one in particular, "And here I thought you'd be a bloke." He looked unsure of himself as he turned back to her. "Everly Brothers? Never heard of them? No? Oh, well…" Then he added with a chuckle, "It's nice to have you on board anyway."

"Where would I find Dr. Payne?" She tried to keep it together, after all, this un-named British stranger was going to be one of her dig companions for the next few months and if he was the doctoral fellow, a bit old for the role she added uncharitably, then their writing up of the data would take place over the next couple of years. Like it or not, they were in it for the long haul. Might as well do all she could to get along.

"I suppose I should introduce myself." As he stood up, he bumped the metal collapsible table and nearly knocked it over, computers, papers, garish tablecloth and all. Grabbing frantically to stabilize the lot before disaster ensued, he said, "Oh bollocks! Don't want that to happen! I can be such a muppet!" Centering the large book on the table's surface, he added, "There we go, all's righted now." He took a deep breath and stood up straight in the way a child does after being admonished by his mother. "Sorry 'bout that. Well, hi." He stuck his hand out to shake hers. Everly reached out and accepted the vigorous workout she got from her energetic new companion.

"Hi there. I'm Trevor Payne. *Doctor* Trevor Payne. I always forget that part, but I suppose, it's required, innit?"

Everly paused. Dr. Trevor Payne was a rather ancient professor of archeology at Cambridge University. Everyone studied his work. She had been thrilled have this career-making chance to dig with him for the summer. This was not the Dr. Trevor Payne she was expecting. Could a world-famous professor from Cambridge have even a tinge of a cockney accent? She had assumed he would sound like all those people on the BBC.

Blushing, she realized she was staring at him and still holding his hand. "Oh, I'm so sorry!" she said, quickly withdrawing hers. If this was one of the modern-day fathers of archeology, somewhere he had found the fountain of youth and along the line must have become a cocaine addict, given all that nervous energy.

"Oh, that's all right," he said, one hand rubbing the other and looking a bit pleased with himself. She wondered how often he got the chance to even talk with a woman. "Here, let me show you around." He hefted her backpack, which seemed like a bit of a challenge for him, and she once again dragged her suitcase through the grass, silently cursing the clogged wheels as she fought to make it move.

"So, here's the, uh, women's tent. You'll be in here. Our student arrived yesterday." He set her backpack down outside the tent flap. She lifted the flap and entered, dragging both her suitcase and her backpack inside. There was one cot which had clearly already been claimed.

"You said that there were two of us… staying in a *tent*?"

"Yes, well, given that I thought you were a bloke, I had the other bed set up in the men's tent. We'll move it over. You'll have a bunkmate! How fun!"

She was amazed that he seemed serious. So, this was just a boy scout outing to him after all. While he might be earning badges, she could feel tenure slipping through her fingers. A wasted summer and that tenure clock was ticking.

He showed her the equipment tent, the showers, the trio of port-a-potties rented for the summer out behind the shower tent, and the laboratory. At least the lab was set up as she would have expected from the famous Dr. Trevor Payne. The equipment was certainly acceptable and everything was organized according to the classic Dr. Payne textbook. Her head was spinning as she followed the man who had introduced himself as Dr. Trevor Payne back to the main tent.

He was still babbling on. "And we'll have our team meetings in here and take our meals as well. It's all very nice, innit? Homey-like. At the back of the equipment tent, we've got some cooking gear, coolers, a small refrigerator, but I've arranged to have mid-day meals, hot ones, brought out for us a few times a week. I hope you like brats! Amazing, they have the German version of Deliveroo way out here! That's quite posh, innit?"

He invited her to sit down at what she assumed was the dining table. She fell heavily into her chair, bewildered at this orientation to her next few months of disarray amid the comfortless surroundings. Well, then again, there was that couch looking like it had been picked up off the street, discarded after someone's move. She stared about her.

"Why are the tents so, well…" ratty was what came to mind, but she couldn't say that. "Uh, seasoned? They have a very… classic… design. And, um, like they've seen a lot of active duty?" Nah, ratty was the better descriptor.

"Well, they were made in the seventies, weren't they now? Aw, the history made in these tents. The discoveries uncovered right beneath this canvas! It's thrilling, really. And they're in ace-shape for their age. Lovely. They just don't make 'em like they used to!"

"No, that would be why everyone uses trailers now-a-days," Everly said as she looked at a stain on the wall, hoping it wasn't mold.

"Trailers, that, well, yes. Bugger all funding for that." Trevor mumbled that last part.

"Oh. Just how did you get fifty-year-old tents anyway?"

"Well, my father got them brand new. He got many good digs out of them. Then my uncle, the one on my mum's side, surely not my step-mum's own brother—old Uncle Wilton would never do that! Good gracious, no! Or on second thought, maybe he would. But anyway, Uncle Mac took them fox hunting. That's where that hole up there came from. Of course, my father was sure Mac actually took them to one of those pop-up, off-the-books music festivals. Not really a part of the fox-hunting crowd, Uncle Mac." He looked up at the hole and shrugged. "Good thing it's not where rain will get in!" He seemed honestly excited about the hole not being a conduit for rain. Or maybe it was the fox hunting. Or the clandestine music festival. She wasn't sure.

She followed the direction he pointed at and stared at the hole.

"I can tell you, he never let Uncle Mac borrow these beauties again."

She couldn't stop herself. She finally asked the question that had been gripping her.

"You're Trevor Payne? Of Cambridge?"

"I am."

"Dr. Trevor Payne?"

The man nodded.

"Of Cambridge. I mean the university. Not the city."

"Both, actually!"

"Author of *Archaeology: Essentials of the Modern Dig?*"

"Oh! That would be my dad! I'm Dr. Trevor Payne… Junior."

"Doesn't that figure."

He smiled at her.

"Can you tell me, have you written a book?"

"Oh yes! How perceptive of you. Are you typically this in-tune with people? Impressive! I would expect that of a psychologist, but you know, archeologists are generally more into the dead than they are the living. At least that was always the experience with my parents. On the whole, I've found archeologists themselves to be, well, rather dull people. Much more fun to be out here, in the tents, you know, than in the libraries with them."

Everly was feeling impatient. This was not the shaping up to be the summer she expected at all. "Um, if you don't mind, what is your book?"

Trevor looked like he actually blushed a bit. "Well, I don't have a name for it quite yet, but it's rather exciting. You see, it's about this character who smuggles people from one world into another, a very underground kind of operation, but through space. He's part of secret civilization. And there's this girl, she's a warrior actually…"

"Wait a minute. What you've written… that doesn't sound like a textbook. That sounds like some type of sci-fi romance novel?" Everly looked around the tent and her eyes rested on the gunshot hole blown far up on the side. Or maybe upon closer inspection, it looked more like the calling card of a firework having blown its way through the canvas. "And you got this published?"

"Well, not precisely. I mean, I put it online, chapter by chapter, but it's not published on paper. Very un-environmental, paper, innit?"

She thought he at least had the decency to sound embarrassed. "So, you're not Dr. Trevor Payne, *Senior*." She put her palms to her forehead. "But this is your dig?"

"Oh yes! I love the field work. Any place my dad's not around," he added under his breath and again laughed in that nervous way. Suddenly, a genuine smile came to his face. "You know something, and

I've been meaning to ask you about this, but you don't sound Canadian at all! In fact, you sound like an American. Are you sure you aren't secretly an American? Under cover or something?"

"What?" This line of inquiry caught her totally off guard. "Um… other than a few dropped in *eh's,* there's really not much difference. In fact, people from North Dakota and Montana sound very similar to Canadians."

"Isn't that ace? Very fascinating, that."

She didn't think it was fascinating at all. She was still trying to wrap her mind around the fact that this hyper little chipmunk was going to be running this dig. "You said someone else arrived yesterday?"

"Oh yes! And she *is* an American. But she must not be from North Dakota because she doesn't say 'aye'. No! It's our summer student who arrived yesterday. She turned out to be a woman, too. Nylah, uh, something-or-other. Who would've figured that? Surrounded by women on an archeological dig. Now that's never happened to me before. She's not here at the mo'. Took the car to head to town for a grocery run, but to tell you the truth, I think she's hitting up the Christmas store they have there. Christmas, it's a very big business in Germany. Even in summer. So, anyway, you'll supervise her and I'll watch over the Brandenburg boys."

"The Brandenburg boys?"

"Yes, we'll have some digging assistance from students from the Brandenburg University of Technology. They're young. And not all boys. I mean, they've got some girls too, but 'Brandenburg Boys' just has a ringier sound, don't it? They'll come out quite a lot. We'll be the summer professors for their internships. Old Gunther, Heintzelman, that is, old friend of mine, he's their full-year professor. He'll be here a lot too. But the kids'll get some real-world experience. Move the heavy dirt for us." He gave her a thumbs up. "But for the most part, it will be the three of us. Our little trio and the summer to discover the secret of how the plague wiped this town off the face of the earth! Won't that be fascinating!"

"Yes, fascinating. A barrel of monkeys." Everly's voice was flat.

As she walked back to her new canvas accommodations, she surmised that this experience was going to be *fascinating* in ways she wasn't quite prepared for.

Chapter 2

Nylah

Nylah returned from town on the kind of high one could only get from being on their first trip out of the U.S. and finding themselves in the most picture-perfect little European village imaginable. Without even asking if she had a driver's license, her new boss had handed her his car keys, a small translation dictionary, and a company credit card along with a list of things to pick up. She was surprised when she sat down in the car that it had this funny little handle sticking up between the driver's and passenger's seats. Her research into which international phone plan to get had paid off—she had bars everywhere she went. Google told her that was something called a stick shift. Three YouTube videos later, she felt ready to give driving the funny little car a try. It wasn't that hard once she got into third gear. She just tried to keep it there.

When she finally made it to a little grocery store, she consulted her list. It was full of grown-up things like prosciutto, bottles of wine, and interesting cheeses. Without being asked for I.D. she bought the lot. For good measure she threw in funny looking sausages (it was Germany after all), tons of fresh fruit, boxes of cereal and quirky little boxes of shelf-stable milk and juices. While she was at it, she added a lot of European chocolate to the cart and fresh bread and croissants. If he was surprised at the bill, well, then maybe he'd do his own shopping next time. She was the student on scholarship after all, and not some kind of dig site housekeeper. She found and sent postcards back home to family and friends, which would surprise them. No one did that these days—your postcard was the selfie you texted. But her mother back in New York City would love to stick that actual card to the fridge under one of her dozens of kitschy magnets. While she was at it, Nylah picked up a couple of kitschy magnets too.

It felt very grown up to just run to town and basically buy a charcuterie board for the team for dinner. It made her realize that when you grew up in New York City, you grew up both fast and slow. It was fast, because from an early age you learned how to navigate the subways and busses all on your own. You learned how to pick out who was dangerous and who was safe, what neighborhoods you skirted even if it meant a few extra blocks of walking, and what neighborhoods you detoured to go through because someday you wanted to live there. But it was slow because unlike most other kids in the U.S., you didn't get a driver's license at sixteen. You just didn't need one. And given that parking a car each year cost as much as buying the car in the first place, well, city kids didn't jump behind the wheel and have the freedom to buzz around wherever they wanted across the countryside.

Her first real unpleasant surprise was the car beeping shrilly at her. She pulled over and asked a young man for help. She found out his name was Hans as he drove them to a gas station and showed her how to pump gas. Then he gave her some tips and a quick lesson on how to drive a stick shift, putting his hand over hers so she felt more confident shifting the gears. She'd never really gone for those blue-eyed blonde types before, but framed against that scenic background and so gallantly rushing to her aid, she found herself as intrigued with him as he seemed to be with her. He said he was a botanist, worked at the local botanical museum branch, but he had much bigger plans than that. She said she was from a city that had hardly any plants and that her plans were totally open. She supposed that to one another, they were both quite exotic. Her quick trip to town ended up being a three-hour excursion after they grabbed lunch together and he showed her where to shop. All in all, it was a most pleasant way to start out her work-study experience.

Arriving back to the camp and now feeling like an expert at stick shifts, Nylah parked the car on the grass where she'd found it. "I'm back. Hey, Dr. T, what do you want me to do with all this food? Dr. T?" She looked around. The grass had been trampled and ripped up, as if someone had been pushing around a heavy two-wheeled delivery dolly. "Where'd he go?"

You got used to a lot living in The City. People. Noise. Change. But not being alone. Not quiet. That was a pretty new sensation. "Okay, I guess I'll put these up," she said to herself as she started to haul the bags into the supplies tent. "Hmmmm. Where can this go? Rats and cockroaches back in NYC. I bet they've got bigger, badder shit out here in the wild. Bears." Did they have bears in Germany? Or lions? Surely not. But they would have critters. Everyplace had its critters and every critter wanted human food. "Wild dogs. They'll have wild dogs." She shuddered. Dogs were not her thing.

She dug around, opened a few of the crates and found that some contained what looked like weird metal coolers. She figured those would protect their food from anything, including bears or wild dogs, and filled them up. She stuffed all the perishables she could into the little fridge in the makeshift kitchenette. Inside some crates she found what had to be about a thousand plastic trays, a little bigger than a bento box, and another crate with lids for them, and she wondered what those were for.

After stowing all the supplies, she decided to rest a bit on her cot and text friends pictures of the hot guy who helped her at the gas station. That impromptu lunch date was still giving her tingles. She walked into her tent and discovered that her summer home was not her own: a second cot had been dragged in there, along with an enormous backpack and a suitcase, it's wheels clogged with grass. They were now standing next to her own giant duffel.

"And just who might you be?" She visually inspected the suitcase. The airline tag said E. Bergeron. "Cool, another student for the summer. That'll be fun." She flopped down on her cot, happy to have another woman her own age joining the team. The goofy British dude who was her new boss said a field site director was coming, some flunky from a boy-band-of-brothers that she'd never heard of. She didn't know squat about archeology, but if someone else who'd recently quit their quest for stardom could become a field director, then playing in the dirt couldn't be that hard, could it?

But Dr. T hadn't said that another student was coming. "He probably forgot. Dude's a ditz." And, she mused, it could be really hard to make out what Dr. T actually said at times. Could be the funny accent, which was, she admitted to herself, quite cute. She laughed out loud as she remembered her mother's admonishment to not fall for British accents in Europe. "Yeah, as she swoons over Bridgerton, she warns me off," she said, flipping through pictures on her phone, deciding which were cool enough to send.

She had lain on her cot for ten minutes, enough time to text her two best friends at least fifteen times, sending them the selfie of her and Hans, who they agreed was a thirst trap, when a woman walked into the tent. Nylah sized her up, surprised that she was not the college-age companion she'd been expecting. No, this woman had to be at least thirty. Maybe a little older even. Nylah decided that she was unmarried, which was no crime. That was kind of an abandoned institution anyway. But surely this chick wasn't dating anyone, at least not successfully, and was absolutely a wanna-be, please-respect-me, professor type. Nylah'd had professors like this last year. Women who dressed in that comfortable, relaxed style which was a testament to having no game at all when it came to fashion. The woman had the kind of chin length reddish brown hair that was surely curly when wet, but after having been wind-blown dry, was just haloing her head in frizz. She would be the type who froze up in front of a handsome man, and then she'd go all intellectual around him because she wanted to be appreciated for her mind. Then she'd be disappointed that once again, she was invisible. Well, most men didn't have the apparatus to appreciate a woman in quite that kind of way. At least not at first blush.

"Oh!" The woman sounded surprised, which Nylah found funny since she had to know the tent had a prior occupant. After all, she'd parked her suitcase next to the already resident duffel.

"Hey, whazzup?"

"Uh… hi. My name's Everly."

"I'm Nylah. You, uh, just arrived?"

The woman nodded. "About an hour ago. I just got a tour of the dig site and the church ruins from the P.I."

Nylah sat up on the cot. "The P.I.? You mean this is a forensic site?" Now she was starting to get excited. "Holy shit! I thought I got assigned to some dumb-ass ancient dig but this is a crime scene?" She raised excited fists in the air, "This is gonna to be the baddest summer ever!"

"A crime scene?" Everly looked confused. "No… uh, what?"

"Yeah! P.I. Private Investigator! I haven't met that person yet. Just the funny muppet-man writing the sci-fi novel." Nylah felt like she was on a dope movie set, not a boring dig in the dirt. She stood up and started to pace. There would be news cameras, press conferences about the unraveling of the case. It was going to be so exciting! Dr. T hadn't told her that tidbit, but forensic sites were all about secrets. She loved secrets. And even more so, being in on the secrets.

"P.I. Like Principal Investigator. He's the grantee. He's funded for the dig. And medieval towns aren't ancient, not like the ancient world of Mesopotamia or Greek or Roman-era, but seven or eight-hundred years ago is still pretty old."

"Principal Investigator? Not Private Investigator?" Nylah sat down hard on the cot. Now it just felt like reality TV. Bad reality TV.

"Now I may be crazy, but something tells me that you're not a doctoral student in archeology?" The woman named Everly sounded like her teeth might be clenched, as she looked at Nylah, one eyebrow raised.

"What is it about coming to Germany that everyone adds like a decade on to your age? I bought a half a dozen bottles of wine this afternoon and no one batted an eye. I am happily twenty years old. No, I am most certainly not a doctoral student—I am a dancer. I just finished my freshman year."

Everly looked like she might need to sit down on her cot, the one she hadn't claimed yet, and have a drink from one of those bottles of wine. "You're a… a freshman? And a… did you say *dancer?*" She looked up at the top of the tent and closed her eyes for a second. Nylah wondered if she was silently praying or cursing. She decided it must be cursing.

"They call us rising sophomores, cause, you know, I passed all my classes. Major-wise, I'm in the arts." Nylah looked Everly up and down. "So, what degree program are you in?"

Everly sighed. "I was in the tenure one until I took this nightmare as my summer research. I suppose I can kiss that goodbye. Well, hi. I'm Dr. Everly Bergeron, medieval dig site Field Director for Dr. Trevor Payne."

"You're the field site director? And *you're* here because the band didn't work out?" Nylah gave this woman the once-over again and wondered just how bad her singing really was?

"Band?" Everly looked confused. "Played trumpet in marching band in high school. Uh, but not since. Little bit of guitar in grad school."

"Is it the British accent or just that Dr. T's a total ditz?" Nylah thought that Dr. T was an absolute riot, full of energy, talked a mile a minute, ran off on tangents he found hilarious. He might be adorable, but if she couldn't understand something so basic as the new field director was *not* either a boy nor a boy-band flunky, but rather a new tent-mate for the summer, then just how was she to understand any directions Dr. T gave her? How was she going to make this summer job work? Her scholarship depended on it. She didn't know anything about archeology. She'd just applied because it was Europe, it was exciting, it was a hell of a lot of award money. And it was the pathway to a four-year degree.

"Why do you call him Dr. T?"

"Oh, 'cause after seeing those port-o-potties that pass for our bathrooms out here, I wasn't about to call him 'Dr. P'. And 'Dr. T P' was way worse. So, there wasn't much left to choose from."

"And not Trevor?"

"Ah, no. You don't make the mistake of calling your professors by their first names. Even if they invite you to. Learned that by watching what went down in the dance department. Gets too close to the line. Reflects on your grade or on your references, which you need for jobs and scholarships, like cool work study programs in Europe."

"Oh. I suppose that makes sense."

"So, you're Everly? That's an interesting name. Never heard that before."

"Dr. Bergeron."

"Yeah, if we're tent-mates, we're on a first name basis."

Everly laughed and then let out a deep, audible sigh. "Yeah. Tent mates. First name basis. Absolutely. So, where're you from, Nylah?"

"New York."

Everly pointed to herself. "Toronto. And you're not an archeology student?"

Nylah shook her head. "Here for the summer scholarship and fall semester. I just got assigned to 'an interesting research project through study abroad'. They never asked me what I wanted to study. To tell you the truth, archeology's all new to me. In fact, after I got here I found I've been misspelling the word my whole life. Arch-ae-o-logy."

"Oh, no. That's just because he's British. They spell a lot of words with extra vowels that we don't use as much in the Americas. It all sounds the same though."

"I don't know. I think it sounds better when he says it."

Both women laughed. "Canadian girls really dig the accent too."

"Well, whatever continent we're on, I don't know squat about digging up dead people."

Everly gave a tight-chested chuckle and moved over to start unpacking her huge backpack. "*That* would be grave robbing. We don't dig up dead people either, actually, your love of forensics notwithstanding. We uncover *artifacts*, carefully catalogue them, and slowly figure out what it all means." Everly turned her gaze towards Nylah, who instantly saw that look her mother gave her when she was exasperated and trying to talk some sense into her daughter. "Think of it this way—there's a puzzle here underground. Some of the pieces may be missing—"

"And some of those pieces are human bones. Sounds like forensics to me."

"Well, yeah. But, if we're good enough, we can put the pieces together to see what the puzzle is telling us. It's very rewarding to figure out the puzzle."

"Rewarding? Like there's prize money?"

Everly burst out laughing. "Only if you could put tenure in that category. There's not a reward. It's *rewarding*. In this case, it's a story of people's lives. Of their community. Of how they lived and what happened to them."

"Oh, so we're still solving a mystery! I like mysteries!" Now this was something Nylah could get excited about. Dirt, not so much. The Brandenburg Boys, quite possibly. The Man from Miltenberg, absolutely.

Chapter 3

Trevor

Trevor bounced up and down on his toes. It was exciting, being at a dig without his father standing over him. He could listen to his playlist while he worked. His music. No one ordering him about, yelling at him for not doing it *the Payne way*. This was going to be a pain-less dig as far as he was concerned, and it would be done *the Trevor way*. He was amazed to feel this excited. It was like he couldn't contain his energy.

In the first ten days of working with the Brandenburg boys, they had made terrific progress. The sun had shone and those college kids, ten boys and a couple of girls, could really move a lot of dirt. To be fair, he had moved a lot of dirt himself. It felt great to sweat. It felt great to do something and not sit in a stuffy faculty office all week long.

The medieval village was small but still, getting the basics of it pegged out already was a tremendous accomplishment. His mind spun with the possibilities of what had happened here seven hundred years ago. The whole town wiped off the map, like extraterrestrials had swooped down and lifted them up en masse. "Poor blighters. Black death's what's likely to have swooped down on you. Bad way to die. But something… something's not quite right and I can't put my finger on it."

"Achtung! Herr Doctor Payne!"

Trevor turned towards the voice that had called him. He was trying to get the names straight of all those college students who made up his crew. He thought this was one was Hannah.

"Yes, Hannah?"

"Heidi."

"Oh sorry! Heidi. I'll get it right." *Eventually,* he said to himself.

She looked at him curiously. "Herr Doctor Payne, what were you saying?"

Trevor blushed, having been caught out talking aloud to himself again—and by a student this time. "Well, I was just reasoning out what happened to these poor blighters. Black Plague was a nasty business."

Heidi's brows furrowed. "What was it like?"

"Well, at first they'd feel just fine. Just like you and me. But then they'd come down with a headache. And after that, they'd feel a little bit weak, like maybe they couldn't face milking the cow or rounding up their goats. And shortly thereafter, a fever would set in, with chills." He shivered with the thought of the progression of the plague. "Blimey, I bet most of these poor blokes thought it was just any old cold, wouldn't they? Yeah, sure, until they started gettin' buboes, hideous things. That's like having a goose egg under your skin, mostly in your neck and around your joints. And then," he put his finger to his nose, "their nose would turn black. And their toes as well. Dead in a week." He sighed. "Unfortunate buggers." He paused, leaning on his shovel, quiet for a few moments. "But the Black Death didn't kill everyone, did it? No. It took eight out of ten victims, didn't it? Right! But not everyone. Maybe a half of Europe caught it and most of those died… but not whole towns." He scooped another shovelful and then paused again, saying under his breath to himself, "So, what happened to the rest of you?"

"Herr Doctor Payne, we think there is something you should see."

"Of course, Hannah. I mean Heidi. Of course, mate," Trevor said, trying to sound patient. As Trevor followed Heidi, he had to remind himself that the frequent interruptions were actually good. They were following instructions and anytime they had questions, they needed to find a site director, lest they do unintended damage to the archeological evidence they were beginning to uncover.

"What do you think you've got?"

"We think we've found a mass grave. Just like you suspected."

"Blimey. That's significant." *Damn, I was right...*

"Jawhohl. We thought that as well."

Sure enough, they had staked out the edges of a large rectangular pit. Everly was already there, with Nylah trailing her, as always.

"This looks promising. I must say, Dr. Payne, you have the luck of the devil. I've never heard of a dig that hit the promised land so fast." Everly stood at the side of the pit, shaking her head.

"Oh, I dunno. I think these poor blighters were just beggin' to be found, don't you? And kids, gather round. How do you know exactly where to dig when you arrive at a site? No ideas?"

Otto spoke up. "A Total Station Theodolite? We just learned how to use those in my spring class."

"Good idea, Oscar!"

"Otto."

"Oh! Sorry! Otto. A TST unit helps you survey the site, gives you information about distance, slope, angles, and elevation. And yes, it can be helpful in predicting where to dig. I came out here in early spring and did all that work. But, the biggest clue you'll ever have: blackberry bushes. Take my advice: always dig there." He pointed to the new site and then to a pile of unearthed berry bushes lying many yards away. There were two more large groups of blackberry bushes on slight mounds further down the field.

Heidi looked eager with her pen and notebook in hand. "What is the scientific relationship between blackberries and artifacts?"

"I think you'd say it's more mystical than scientific. Blackberry bushes are the old nemesis of archeologists the world over. Blast it, for how they ruin your clothes and it's hard to find the kind of mountain armor fleece jacket that will stand up to them. For some reason, they absolutely love artifacts. Mark me, it's a safe bet that you'll always find the most important things under a blackberry thicket."

Nylah observed the square rectangle of partially excavated dirt staked out with strings that everyone was gathered around. She looked confused. "Why do you think this is a mass grave and not like a chariot parking lot or something."

Trevor and Everly exchanged looks.

"Chariot parking?" Heidi asked.

"Sure. It looks like a New York City parking space, you know, like for a limo or a bus, all marked off like that. I wouldn't be surprised if we dug up an orange cone. But chariots are what they had back then, right? No? How about a swimming pool? Roman bath?"

Trevor blinked a few times. "Not likely, but skipping that, Nylah, first we used the ground penetrating radar yesterday round the edges of the blackberry thicket, right? And that gave us a good idea of where to dig. We're fairly certain there's people down there." He scratched his head. "Of course, it could also be just a trash pit. And that would be interesting too. Not quite as exciting perhaps."

Everly picked up the lesson for the students. "The radar gives back pretty fuzzy images, so we won't know what we'll find until we actually find it. But since legend holds that the Black Plague wiped out this whole village, we're expecting to find burial evidence." Everly pointed to the corners of the staked-out site. "Mass graves, in ancient Germany in particular, don't show any evidence of grave goods. So, after mass fatality events, bodies would have been deposited in pits quite similar to this one. It was an expedient way just to get rid of lots of bodies when they were piling up. No real ceremony or anything, they would just be all lined up in a row." She pointed off towards the confines of the village proper. "The church ruins stand just over the hill there, so this could have been close enough, just maybe, to be part of their consecrated ground."

"People all lined up in a row? Like in the news about war crimes? Or mass death from outbreaks?" Nylah asked. "Unmarked graves?"

"It's called 'suppressed individuality of the dead'," Trevor explained. "In Viking graves, for example, you'll find their cherished items or other symbols of importance in their lives. Weapons. Jewelry. Household items—those are what Dr. Bergeron called 'grave goods.' But in early European mass graves it's more of burial by panic. Usually they're lined up rather neatly, but sometimes they're all just higgledy-piggledy in there."

Now Nylah and Everly looked at one another. "Higgledy-piggledy?" Everly asked.

"So, students, kindly listen up. I have a few instructions for you before you touch any dirt or artifacts." Trevor gave a brief demonstration to the digging crew about how to carefully, yet efficiently, move the dirt and how far down they were likely to need to dig before they ran into spade and brush work. He was kind but clear that he didn't want any damage done to artifacts they might find. He assigned them each to a spot and they all started work.

Nylah stood to the side of the pit, surveying the young men and women hard at work digging. "You know, field archeology looks to me like a mix of construction work and military deployment. I'm so glad digging wasn't in my job description."

Trevor paused in his shoveling and looked over at her with a raised eyebrow. "You could try moving some dirt, you know. It wouldn't hurt you."

Nylah shook her head. "I'm here to document, keep notes, sort, enter computer data. No one put anything in the agreement about shovels and dirt. I've got the Weatherwriter deep storage clipboard." She gave it a couple of taps as she said it. "A pen, and the digital camera. I'm good. I'm good."

Trevor turned back to his shovel, muttering under his breath, "Bloody school contracts." He wished he'd spent more time writing the student work-study job description, but he'd dashed it off and sent it, never thinking that the funding agency would approve it. Thought it was a waste of time and then boom! The email was in his box that he was being granted an underrepresented minority student from the US to work on his dig, with the option of independent study through the fall semester on a full scholarship for her and at no cost to him. Trevor wasn't quite sure what the underrepresented criteria had to do with it, but he figured that there weren't many women from New York City in archeology, so maybe that's why he'd been sent Nylah. A doctoral student he would have been able to make use of. He'd be able to just point and they'd kick that ball down the field, knowing exactly what he meant and what to do. They'd have ideas of their own, their own research to work on. He had no idea how to use an undergraduate independent study student or a just barely-twenty-year-old work study one for that matter, but he had the strong impression from the funder that he needed to keep her happy and make sure she learned a bloody lot about archeology during her time with him. *It would help if she had any interest in the topic at all,* he thought.

He turned up the sound on the portable speakers, blaring his music, and dug with the Brandenburg Boys for a couple of hours before they got down to spade and brush work. They had a clear squarish pit unearthed and it was looking promising, since it was unexpected for a town of this size to offer a Roman bath, Nylah's suggestion notwithstanding, that it was going to turn out to be some type of mass grave. And Dr. Bergeron was right—it could be a garbage pit. There was no real way to know until you got down there. Radar returned a grainy image through the dirt, and bone could come from creatures other than humans.

He was squatting down, spade in one hand, brush in the other, painstakingly moving dirt, carefully examining each spade full. Dr. Gunther Heintzelman, lucky bastard, had unearthed the first find, pulling out a broken pottery cup. Typical for the era. It caused a lot of consternation because, as Everly had explained to Nylah, grave goods were not found in mass graves. Why would a cup be here? Chalk up one vote for the trash pit. Gunther was so proud of his find, telling the students that it would be placed in the Brandenburg University Museum.

Trevor was expecting to find skeletons and didn't hope for much else. Skeletal remains could be sampled and sent to the lab for testing, finding molecular evidence of *Yersinia pestis,* the organism responsible for the bubonic plague, or "The Black Death" as people had described it for centuries. Of course, to these folks, it was just plague. Horror. Suffering. Loss. Death.

Then his pointing trowel scraped against something hard. "Blimey, here you are! It's about time." It was so hard, he thought this must be his trowel probing bone. He carefully brushed dirt away. It was a big bone. A bloody big bone. "They had a bloomin' Tyrannosaur with them, did they? Bloody hell."

Everly's boots crunched the dirt as she came over to him. "What do you have, Dr. Payne?"

"Here, Dr. Bergeron, help me with this."

She kneeled down next to him and started moving dirt away with her gloved fingers. Together they uncovered a pointy end that grew in size to a shaft. "Not a bone." They both peered curiously at the glint of gold.

"Right. I was expecting that too. Glad it's not though. Wouldn't want to run into anything with bones this size. Careful, any minute now." Trevor had the vague impression that this process was like birthing a baby, but they were birthing an archeological treasure from the earth itself. "No, not a bone but a… it's a…it's a cross."

"Grave goods? Unexpected," Everly replied.

"Oooh, let's make sure it comes out in one piece. Carefully now." By this time, they had a crowd starting to gather round them, everyone clued in that this was a truly significant find.

At last, they extracted the dirt from around the two-foot tall cross, got it photographed and measured, recorded the plot lines in three dimensions for exactly where it was located in the pit, and Trevor made notes on one of his little papers, handing it to Nylah to catalogue and safely squirrel away in her all-weather storage clipboard.

"Herr Doctor Payne. What is it?" Trevor wasn't sure which of the students asked the question.

Trevor turned the relic over a few times and then looked at the assembled crowd. He gently brushed some of the caked-on dirt away, revealing a gold glint. "This artifact was a cross of the Catholic church. It fits the style one would see in Cologne in the early fourteenth century. Or even before. You know, don't you think, Dr. Bergeron, Dr. Heintzelman, this cross resembles the Cross of Mathilde?"

Everly nodded.

Gunther knelt down to look at the cross and then turned to the group to explain. "Herr Doctor Payne is right. Mathilde was Abbess of Essen three-hundred years before this little village disappeared."

"Ooo! Is that her cross?" a student asked.

Trevor shook his head. "Not this one. Hers is in a museum already. But, Gunther, isn't it just classic to the Cologne or Essen style of the time? It's got a figurative sculpture, some filigree here. And even enameling. There were gems." Trevor pointed out the little divots in the cross, "but they're gone now. We might uncover them still but look here… this appears to be a gouge mark."

"Looks like someone dug this up already. And pried off some of the more valuable stones," Everly said.

"Right you are, Dr. Bergeron. But it's odd, innit? Why wouldn't they take the whole gold cross? I mean, this is an amazing find in terms of history, but this would be worth a fortune to them back then. Who would leave it?"

"Maybe they thought grave robbing was as creepy as I think it is," Nylah said smugly from the side of the pit. "I bet they thought it was cursed."

Some of the Brandenburg students chuckled.

Everly said, "Nylah might be right. There were a lot of superstitions that guided life all through the Middle Ages and even up into as late as the seventeen hundreds. But there's a lot of temptation that would go with a cross of gold like this one." Everly looked at the cross more closely.

Trevor turned it over. "If you look here, you'll all see that it's got a hole in the bottom. This cross was meant to sit on a pole and be held up high so that everyone could see it, such as at a big church service or in the street, like when the clergy marched. They did that at times, before an army to bless them as they went off to war, or on a religious holiday, to bring the faithful to service."

"It's so beautiful," Heidi said with a whistle. "I can't believe it's my first dig and this is what we find. I love that I'm majoring in archeology!" There was general consensus from the other students.

"It's a bloody mystery though why something like this would be in a town of this small size."

Everly nodded. "Right. And this is a cross that would inspire some, uh, less than holy feelings, like jealousy and greed. The fact that it's still here kind of makes no sense, particularly if the gems were pried off by grave robbers sometime in the last centuries. Why would they leave something this valuable?"

"I don't know, but this town is full of surprises, innit?" Trevor looked at the group. "Everyone take ten. Before we start up again, I'll give you all some pointers on what to look out for, now that we might be coming across grave goods. It's a very different dig if it's a ceremonial grave. People will be laid out according to plan and they might have their intimate worldly possessions with them, or we might even find small remnants of their clothing! So we want to be particularly careful. When you come back, you'll be needing a set of plastic trays to hold samples. They're in the storage tent. Okay! Time for a break—mind how you go, all. On your bikes, now. Be back in ten!"

The group dispersed with excited whispers, if general confusion, about his instructions about bikes and minding how they went. Where they went was to the big coolers full of bottles of water and sodas.

Trevor turned to Everly and Gunther and rubbed his hands together. "Well, well, Drs. Bergeron and Heintzelman, things are starting to get very interesting around here! Very interesting indeed."

Gunther turned to Everly and softly said, "Bikes?"

With a shake of her head, Everly gave him a shrug.

Chapter 4
Wilhelm
June 1346

Wilhelm stood at the side of the road, more excited than he could ever remember. A pair of drummers had just gone by, watching one another closely and attempting to hit their beats together in time. "Do you hear them, Friar? Aren't they wonderful?"

The friar, a dour man with a frown upon his face, scowled at the parade making its slow way through streets. "It's hot. I hate to be hot."

"These long black robes don't help much on a day like today, that's for sure," Wilhelm replied, his eyes fixed on the procession. "Oh look! They've got the hang of it now!" He bobbed his head up and down to the beat.

His companion gave a grumpy huff. "They probably just figured out that they would be louder if they actually worked in time."

"Oh look! Pipers!" Wilhelm giggled. "I love pipers."

A short string of young people blew away on homemade wooden pipes, not playing any particular tune at all, making a cacophony of sound as they passed.

"Oh Christ in heaven above! He's got *fräuleins* playing in his parade! Girls!" The friar gasped in horror. "Most unseemly."

"Oh indeed. Most unseemly, just like you said, Friar. I guess girls and ladies must be musical in the big city. The new priest must be bringing his big city ways with him to our little village. Who ever thought to see such a thing." While Wilhelm's words were disapproving, the tone of his voice was filled with excitement and his countenance was illuminated with wonder, softening the hard lines scored into him by a lifetime of hunger. He hummed along with a tune of his own, nodding his head to a rhythm only he could hear.

The elders and important folk of the Church of Saint Cyprian started to saunter by, wearing their best, as if they were nobles themselves. It was not a long parade, as parades go, but the villagers of this by-water had never seen its men march off to war. They had never been treated to the sight of the lines of cavalry and pikemen arranged next to the archers, and all gaily encircled by the flagbearers, as they engaged in that prematurely triumphant ritual procession that preceded a grim battle from which few would return. All armies paraded before the battle because, at best, only one would parade after. It was a now or never option. The only other escort those unfortunate souls would know was the one that led their loved ones in grief as they accompanied their mortal shell to its eternal rest.

It was not only Wilhelm who was so excited. Having never seen an actual parade, the townsfolk were in a rapturous state at their objectively poor assembly. If they weren't calling out blessings then they were calling out asking for blessings, all mesmerized by the procession that would soon bring the golden idol to be paraded before them.

"Disgusting display of emotion," the friar snarled. "These misguided peasants don't even understand what they're looking at."

"That mays be true. I don't doubt you're right, oh, but it be lovely!" Wilhelm sighed, not actually paying much attention to the comments. "I've never seen anything like it. Surely, it must be a gift from God himself!"

"More like a gift from the bishop. Wipe that stupid look off your face!" The black robed man growled, which failed to stem any enthusiasm from Wilhelm.

"Oh, Friar Tuckerschade! Do you think so? Really? A bishop in our little village. A blessed day indeed. Mays be he'll come to our church as well? Do you think so, Friar Tuckerschade?"

"He won't." The friar was radiating disapproval with his usual intensity. "He'd like as not see it as an offense to his silks and velvets. Bishops, aye, they've got to keep up appearances. Much like our Brother Bernard will feel pressed to do, like as not, after this." As he muttered this last thought, he ran his hands down the front of his own plain, dark robes.

The two men watched as a priest made his slow way down the street. The man's black robes, the usual requirement of the station for friars, priests, and brothers, were topped with a gleaming white vestment, and over that, a beautifully embroidered red and gold orphrey, like a tapestry in miniature, was draped over his neck and hung down long on each side. Priests were allowed to wear such finery— mere friars and brothers were not. The decorated priest carried a pole in his hands, atop of which rested a decorated golden cross, high enough so that all the gathered villagers could see the wondrous sight. The onlookers were mesmerized. More were joining the parade to follow the cross, not wanting to let it get out of sight as it passed on by.

The friar looked down at his hands and quickly clasped them together. "Besides, that bishop is Brother Bernard's uncle. That's why he's here. That's why he gave the cross to the Church of Saint Cyprian. It's a gift to his nephew, Wilhelm, not to any church in this village. It's all about his nephew. Even St. Cyprian's was a gift to his nephew! Too bad, my boy, if you'd had an important uncle, you might have become something in the church."

For the first time Wilhelm looked away from the parade and at his companion. "But I am something in the church, Friar Tuck. I'm an acolyte!" Pride filled his voice. "You, like the Friar Tuck in the old tales, with that hero band you tell me about, went your own way and established your own order, jus' like you tell me he did. You raised me from a doorkeeper, you did. Said as long as I was your man, you'd raise me up. And you did. And I am." He turned back to stare at the golden cross. "I was the doorman of St. Drogo's and then the acolyte at St. Cyprian, when that church was ours, when we took it over, because it was empty and needed a master. You do good things for the people, to save their souls. And you vint a nice barrel of wine to boot." Wilhelm sighed. "It was a nice church, to be sure, St. Cyprian. But wouldn't it be something? To have a golden cross on the altar of our little church of St. Drogo's, now that we're back there? Humble as we be, that would be a fine thing."

"St. Drogo-Erasmus," the friar corrected. "The name is St. Drogo-Erasmus." Whether attributable to the hot, long black robes he was obliged to wear for his station in life or merely from his frustration and anger, also at his station in life, the steam rising from the man Wilhelm called 'Friar Tuck' was nearly visible. He shook his head, accentuating his clenched jaw. "We're better off, Wilhelm, with our simple wooden crosses. The Son of God was a carpenter. He didn't have gold. Or jewels embedded into that gold. Or a fancy church. No, we're better off without a golden idol, and that's what I'll tell the worshipers come Sunday."

The look of happiness slowly started to bleed away from Wilhelm's face as he turned to his superior and thought through the logic of what the friar was telling him. "Christ would have had a wooden cross to pray upon. That's true."

Friar Tuck looked at Wilhelm and nodded. "Indeed! Christ died upon a wooden cross. Had his hands and feet nailed into a wooden cross. Not a golden one. No gems strewn about his feet. Wood's good enough for us. The small church of St. Drogo-Erasmus is good enough for us." The parade passed them by. Brother Bernard and the miraculous golden cross were out of sight. All they could see were the villagers falling in line and walking behind the procession, their joyful sounds filling the air.

"Do you think more of them will leave us after this?" The acolyte winced at the look Friar Tuck gave him. "I just mean, sir, that people seem to like their worship at a church filled with finery. An music. An that's what Brother Bernard gives them. Not me! Don't look at me like that, please, sir. Not me! I prefer a humble church full of wooden crosses. Wood's good enough for the likes of me!" Wilhelm sighed heavily as he looked fretfully into the eyes of Friar Tuck. His shoulders slumped and he dropped his gaze to the ground. "I will willingly submit, me master, to be punished for me sins."

"We will all submit to be punished for our sins in the end, Wilhelm. Maybe we won't rush into it today."

Wilhelm breathed with a deep inhale of gratitude, the relief visible in the way he stood. "Thank you, Friar Tuck. You're like a father to me. And as high as any Bishop in me eyes. I'm your man."

Friar Tuck let out a heavy sigh, his gaze following the last of the townspeople. "That Bernard will lead his ever-growing flock into idolatry and idleness." He brushed his hands and turned to his companion. "You have no family. I take it as my God-given duty to protect you and see to the state of your soul, Wilhelm Notheisen. I'll not have you fall into sin. Perhaps over dinner we can discuss how the lust for gold can diminish the light of God in the eyes of a man who is lured by the devil himself. And after that, we will pray on this situation."

"Oooh, you sound like you're brewing up a sermon, you do." Wilhelm looked excitedly at Friar Tuck. "I do love it when you preach to the masses. I can see their very souls being saved right before me eyes. It's like watching one of them old saints in the Bible you tell about. Oh, Friar Tuck, I'll bet you'll be sainted one day. You just wait and see. They'll saint you."

For the first time, Friar Tuck smiled. "Oh, I'll never be a saint," he said with a sudden modesty.

The two men started to head back to the poorer side of town where their bedraggled little church stood. Wilhelm had a hard time keeping up with his master, who quickly outdistanced the slighter man. Although the friar was talking to himself, his words drifted back to Wilhelm on the breeze.

"Wouldn't that be something? To be a saint?"

Chapter 5

Father Bernard Trōst
June 1346

Bernard was quite tired from the parade. After handing the pole bearing the golden cross to one of the bishop's attendants, he carefully removed the orphrey, bestowing three reverent kisses on the broad bands of each side of the heavily embroidered cloth.

"I used to do that," the bishop said as he sat down and nodded to another attendant. The man snapped to attention and quickly brought his superior a bowl of water and a cloth. The bishop carefully washed his hands. Then the attendant brought both the bishop and Father Bernard a tumbler of wine. "You may leave us."

The man nodded, kissed the bishop's ring, and left the room making sure not to turn his back to the two remaining men.

"Used to kiss the orphrey?" Bernard asked.

"Yes," the bishop answered dryly, "before I realized how dirty that makes them."

Bernard chuckled. As long as he had known his Uncle Eberhard, the man had always insisted on everything being immaculate. In order. A place for everything. But Bernard understood being different. He and his uncle were cut from the same cloth, even beyond the robes they wore under any other adornments. Bernard lay the orphrey down on the table and straightened it out, carefully smoothing one edge three times and then carefully smoothing the other, again three times. Three was a good number. The holy trinity. Things would be okay if he did them in threes. He looked at the orphrey and crossed himself three times.

Bernard had his peculiar ways, which had always evoked concerned looks from his father, but never his uncle. Eberhard had his own peculiarities which caused eyebrows to rise. As a child, Bernard remembered amused, sometimes scandalous, whispers about cleanliness and godliness as his uncle seemed to hold a fear of dirt, believing it had some type of unholy relationship with sickness. Amused because it was a ridiculous thought. Whispered because it was a blasphemous belief. Everyone knew that sickness was punishment for one's sins. At least, that's what the church taught. It gave Bernard pause, that a man as high as his uncle could have his own thoughts, his own theories, his own odd little rituals, just like Bernard did himself. They were so alike. They even had diamond and gold rings that nearly matched. "There is a great deal of dirt in this village, so I suppose I'm not risking too much in my reverence… at least not that which I don't risk as a matter of daily routine." *Three strokes invokes the protection of the angels,* Bernard told himself.

"You must be careful, Bernard, you'll get sick. And as much as I believe in the power of the Almighty, even I must admit that the Almighty does not always choose to stretch His hand to heal the deserving. No. Many are passed over and even the holiest of men can fall to a sickness. I don't want to hear that you've been taken on the wagon and tossed into a mass grave. That would aggrieve me greatly."

Bernard decided to let the comment pass. His poor uncle lived in such fear of sickness and plague that it made Bernard wonder just what Eberhard had seen in his lifetime. But he knew better than to ask. Bernard finished his gentle folding of the orphrey into thirds and placed it in the ornately carved wooden box in which it came. The orphrey was so beautiful that he felt he could stare at it for hours. The intricate needlework was exquisite. It was an object that could give one hope just by looking at it. He wondered if the women who had spent months, maybe years, making it, fully understood how their embroidery was a metaphor for the wondrous nature of heaven and earth? How it was a meditation on the infinite complexity of the Divine? Of course they must. Doubtless, they would never be able to talk about it, except to one another, yet no craftsman could create an artifact of such rapturous beauty and not have a connection to the celestial realm. Bernard considered these laborers to be holy women, saints in the making, in touch with the divine themselves, to have been able to see and weave and sew these simple materials into such complex patterns.

He turned to the bishop. "Ah, your Excellency, this gift is too fine for me. I am… unworthy of something so rare and precious."

The bishop waved away Bernard's statement. "Old Henry Plantagenet of England, the Second, that is, he collected these things. Spent a fortune on orphreys back in eighty-two and eighty-three, when his sons, young Henry and Richard and his bastard issue, Geoffrey, who became Archbishop of York, and even his wife, were rebelling against him." The bishop reached out to the ornate box but did not touch the wooden structure. "I believe old Henry was trying to buy the favor of the Lord by surrounding himself with symbols of the divine. Keep himself safe. Yes, he spent lavishly, but in the end he lost his son, young Henry, anyway. And Geoffrey. And Richard took the throne after him, but Old Henry could never satisfy the needs of his many sons for land and power and titles."

Bernard looked at the box and nodded three times. "The orphrey has quite a history."

"We owe a lot to Henry Plantagenet of England… and let's see if I remember my history: And Anjou. And Normandy. And Aquitaine." He counted the titles off on his fingers. "Old Henry created the laws that we live by in Germania and all the surrounding lands. He was the

Alexander of our time. And more than a hundred years later, the imprint of his thumb is still on us all. Ah! You're so easy to talk to, Bernard. I forget myself and could go on and on when I'm with you."

"I will cherish it, your Excellency. I am humbled that you would honor a simple priest such as I with a gift worthy of the Holy See himself!" Bernard knew that his smile would please his Uncle Eberhard and the man would not suspect it was mostly at the irony of a bishop's jealousy over power and titles that would never be his to command. He would never be Eberhard of Aquitaine or Eberhard of Normandy or Eberhard of Anjou since he had been a latter son. The only seat open for a latter son was one in the church.

"Oh, yes, fit for the pope, but the Holy See has even more of these rags than Old Henry did." He sounded serious but then he laughed. "It is a rich gift indeed. But a priest whose altar is now home to a cross adorned with gold should have an orphrey on his vestments that befits such a symbol of the Holy Lord." And he laughed heartily.

A cat jumped up onto the table, demanding attention from Bernard. He gave it three quick scratches along the cheekbones and was rewarded with a deep thrumming buzz of the animal's purr. Before it could shed on his vestments, Bernard removed and folded the fine white fabric according to his ritual and set it carefully in the rough cloth in which it had been delivered. He gently laid the package in a drawer.

"You're right to be so cautious with those. Hard to get new ones way out here. A man could really run away from his temptations in a place like this. Hide from almost anything." Apparently seeing that Bernard was not going to give him the satisfaction of taking the bait, the bishop continued, "But I'll include another set when I next send a cart of goods to you, as I'm sure there will be no way to keep it clean out here." He looked around and sniffed. "Why do you keep cats? Dirty beasts, cats."

"I keep three. And they're not dirty for they bathe themselves constantly. I would think that of all animals, the cat would be the closest to your heart, dear Uncle. I even encourage them for my parishioners. In fact, we have become a town of cats since I came to Saint Cyprian. While I try to love all of God's creatures, as the young Saint Francis taught, in my confessions I admit that I struggle to love mice. And rats actually frighten me."

"Is that why you left Cologne? The city's rats?"

Bernard laughed. "Perhaps. Perhaps." He took a sip of his wine and hoped the subject of his father would not come up.

"The Lord works in mysterious ways." Eberhard studied Bernard intently for a moment and then shook his head. "Your mother misses you a great deal."

"How is my mother?"

Eberhard paused a moment. "She is perfect. As always." He gave a heavy sigh. "Your father on the other hand… oh the duke reminds me every time I see him that you were the great hope of your house. Your father feels abandoned."

"Your Excellency, I am doing the duty of my Father. For my Father, who art in heaven, and hallowed be His name," Bernard made the sign of the cross three times, "hath called out mine. In His loud and mighty voice, He came to me, and I have had no doubt from my youngest days that I would serve Him with all my heart. I now answer His call. You can tell my earthly father that I am… content."

"But he is not. He lost his eldest son, who did not choose to follow in his earthly father's footsteps and assume the Duchy, which was rightfully his! But which will now fall to Adolfus. And since he is weak, perhaps even to Dietmar."

"My brother is not weak. He is… misunderstood."

"As much as you love Adolfus, and bless you for your generosity, your brother does not have the mettle to bear the Duchy. He cannot lead an army. The man can barely withstand to sit a horse!" The bishop picked up his wooden tumbler and the cloth he used to dry his hands. He wiped around the rim of the cup several times and, with a grimace, took a sip.

Bernard knew better than to comment on his uncle's peculiar behavior, just as his uncle never commented on Bernard's. He also knew this would be a familiar conversation, as predictable as the western sun disappearing over the horizon each evening or the moon rising to take its place. The only family emissary who didn't deliver the same message was his sister. Adelaide understood him, but then again, she was also meant for the cloth and for her vows.

"Adolfus is a man of music."

"Adolfus is an idiot."

Bernard shook his head. "Not an idiot. He can play the lute, the vielle, the harp and the organ. The man is inspired. He's an artist."

"The second son of a nobleman can be an artist only if the oldest son does his duty by his father." The bishop looked sternly at Bernard. "What good is an artist in leading a dukedom? What useful purpose could he serve?"

"He could keep them entertained," Bernard said with a smile and was happy when the bishop burst out with a laugh.

Both men smiled at their genuine friendship and drank, Eberhard again running the cloth around the rim of his cup. "This is good wine. How do you come by good wine way out here in the bywater? I know you had to serve a parish. It's a five-year requirement. But way out here?"

"Well, Uncle, 'way out here' is where much food is grown, and among the bounty, grapes! And there is another church in town, the Church of St. Drogo, um, something-or-other, run by a friar, I believe. He's been here forever, they tell me. He makes the local wine. I will buy from him, once I finally meet him, and try to make amends for my appearance and mission to re-establish the much-rundown Church of St. Cyprian. Did you know that he had the audacity to move into and take over this building for his own flock, unauthorized by the Mother Church? My arrival became his eviction, and although he had done nothing to actually restore the church while it was his, I am quite sure he was most put out at his removal nonetheless." Bernard looked down into his tumbler, nodding three times. "And I must admit, it is good wine. The half barrel I have is a gift from the butcher in town."

"Friars have the time to make good wine. Brothers and priests they be, but they will never rise above their station. Making wine is a good way for them to spend their time." The bishop snickered. "And in Cologne, they spend their time losing their battle to control the guilds of tailors. The spiritual arbiters of fashion, they have made themselves. Ridiculous they are, trying to control the guild though their mathematical principles." He shook his head. "The guilds have outsmarted them. The guilds will outsmart us all, mark my words!"

"This friar does not seem to dictate how the local craftsmen do their labors. But I hear tell he also gives sermons on Sundays."

"Sermons? In that bedraggled, dirty, little sad excuse for a church? The one on the other side of the town? You told me there was a swamp a few miles away in that direction. I was sure I could smell it when we went by."

"Oh, you would probably be smelling the tanners. It's also just out of town on that side. And it seems that throwing one's night pot into the street in the morning is common on that side of town as well."

The bishop's nose wrinkled. "Well, I'm glad I've not received an invitation to St. Drogo-something-or-other, or I'd have to go. I'd probably never get the filth or the smell out of my vestments."

"Erasmus! That's it. Saint Drogo-Erasmus." Bernard was proud of himself for remembering.

Eberhard gave Bernard a look. "What a name for a church! You know that St. Drogo is the patron saint of the unsightly and unattractive. And St. Erasmus, well, you pray to him when you suffer abdominal pain!" He picked up his tumbler and ran his cloth around the rim again. "In truth, I think this is as close as I want to come to the church of St. Ugly Stomach Discomfort." He took another sip. "But bless that friar, this is truly drinkable, as unattractive as he must be."

Bernard laughed heartily. "I will be on the lookout for this ugly man of the cloth with mighty belches and farts."

Eberhard laughed with his nephew, and said, "This wine may be the only redeeming part of your tenure here." Then he sighed. "I will report back to Cologne that you have done an admirable job in refurbishing the structure. It's a nice church. Small, but it has a good feel to it, Bernard."

"Thank you, your Excellency."

"You're good at building things, Bernard. You could serve the Lord well in Cologne."

"I cannot serve the Lord and serve my father's ambitions at the same time." Bernard said calmly. "I had hoped that he might see and accept the truth of this. I am called to the cloth. To the people themselves."

The bishop looked thoughtful for a moment and then, with a tentative tone in his voice, said, "You could be a man of the cloth in Cologne. Coming back to the city would not necessarily mean having to assume the title and report to the king."

Bernard looked curiously at the bishop.

"You know, as a bishop, I can choose my attendants. The deacons. The priests. Bernard, listen to me. I have influence. You have intelligence and, yes, yes, goodness, bless you! I am old now and won't rise higher than my station, but you! You could become an archbishop. Maybe a cardinal. We consecrated the eastern wing of our great cathedral just twenty years ago. Bernard, come back to Cologne and let me help you become what you are meant to be! You are my nephew and you are meant for better things than this by-water of a village. This pigsty of a town is so small that it's practically not on the map! You'll never become anything here up in the hills."

"Uncle, Uncle, you sound like my father now." Bernard gave his uncle a look. "You yourself would have made a good duke."

"Humph! Indeed, I would have, but it is not the destiny for a latter son. There was no other road for me than the church."

"And your ambition has served you well! You're a bishop!" Bernard hoped his smile looked approving.

"Bernard, your problem is that you have no ambition. A little ambition is very good for a man, even a man of the cloth."

"Indeed. My father insisted that I would never become anything if I turned to the church and look at me! I'm a priest," he said proudly. "I have my own church and flock of the faithful that I tend as their shepherd. They are a quaint and rustic people here in the mountains. Amusing in their local mannerisms and dialect." Bernard chuckled. "Oh, I have great ambitions for these people. Many a civic-improvement project planned."

"Rustic people! Bah! You'll tire of them soon enough. You need to think of yourself as well."

"And as for myself, I live in the light of the Holy Lord and I walk the path of Jesus."

"That's what I'm afraid of. He didn't live to be an old man. He didn't have a pleasant end."

"I'm not praying for a pleasant end. I'm praying that I might be of use in the Lord's great plan. He has a plan and there is an end for me, as there is an end for each of us. His will be done." Bernard surprised himself with how calm he felt. Men didn't stand up to their betters. Priests didn't stand up to their bishops. Nephews to their uncles nor sons to their fathers. You did what you were told. You lived the destiny you were born into. And that had been true for him until a higher calling pulled him into a different river of life. He relinquished the riches, the titles, the betrothals to eligible noblewomen. He relinquished the esteem of the educated and the adulation of the masses of poor who owed their livelihoods to his family and the feudal system that everyone lived by. He relinquished his ambition... and as he did so, it relinquished its hold on him as well. And he was free. Finally free.

Chapter 6

Trevor

Trevor found himself called to multiple sites at the dig, which, while exciting, prevented him from being able to concentrate on any one aspect of operations, much less settle into his playlist. Music was a big part of a dig site; it kept the work rolling along, but with being called hither and thither, he really couldn't get into the flow of the work. He was normally what people called a "big picture person", so on any given day this would have been his preference, but after finding that gold cross, now the thrill of the find, the magic of the discovery, rather consumed him. He was afraid of missing out on the next big thing as he got called from site project to site project—but that's what his role was, wasn't it? After all, this was his dig. Trevor sighed, positive that Dr. Trevor Payne, Senior, would have ensured that he himself unearthed every important relic. But of course, every find would have been an important photo op for his next book. Trevor shuddered to think what his father would've been like had social media been a thing in his day. "Probably would've had a million anoraks following him."

"What's an *anorak?*" Nylah asked, dogging his heels like a self-appointed administrative assistant.

Trevor jumped, having forgotten she was trailing him again, anything to avoid actually getting in the dirt, and not realizing he'd fallen into his bad habit of thinking aloud, which was only slightly more preferable than his habit of singing aloud. "Technically means a warm jacket, but in British-speak we call odd people obsessed with niche peculiarities anoraks. I think in American-speak, you'd call them' nerds' or something like that."

"That's your best idea today, Dr. T! I'll set it up. No problem." She started making notes on her clipboard.

"Set what up?" Trevor felt a shiver at the thought that Nylah would arrange for his father to come for a photo op. "He's recovering from hip surgery. He can't make the trip."

"Hip surgery? Who?"

Trevor stopped walking. He had to get a hold of himself. He was too scattered, even for him. "Let's hold on a minute. What are you talking about?"

"Your idea to put what we're finding out there on social media. I'll create a site. I can make us a webpage and we'll post pictures and blogs. I'm really, really good at TikTok. Instagram is a snap."

"Oh gods. I'll have to Facebook friend my mum and dad?"

"Facebook? Ummm, wasn't quite thinking of that one. But followers, geeky followers, uh huh, I think I can get you that." Nylah returned to making notes on her ever-present clipboard.

Trevor had to admit that while Nylah was the most unlikely person to be on the dig site, she was just what they needed. She thought differently. She certainly shopped differently, making sure they had food on site that made this trip feel more like a junket in Bavaria than work. She asked questions no one with any background in archeology would ever ask. Sometimes that no sane person would ask, he was sure. *Chariots indeed!* She wasn't at all flustered at his note keeping system, or rather, lack thereof. She'd just pick up the little random sheets he'd scribble on, catch them sometimes as they were blowing away on the wind, and paperclip them to a family of ideas she assigned them to. She had little clusters of paperclipped scraps safely stowed in her case with the built-in all-weather clipboard on top. And now she was talking about setting up a social media presence? Where did she come up with ideas like that? He had to admit, maybe it wasn't a bad way to go. Could it be good to have followers? It would certainly please his father, he was sure of that. "Maybe that will impress the funders, right? Sure, well, let's run it by Dr. Bergeron, shall we?"

Nylah gave him a sideways look. "Do you even know her first name? Like, you never use it."

"Of course, I do. She's named after those singing brothers from the nineteen-sixties. *Wake up, Little Susie, wake up!*" he started to sing, although not quite on key. His hips spontaneously moved in a little dance as he did so. "Oh, you don't know it? How about *I've been cheated, been mistreated. When will I be loved?* Still no? Linda Ronstadt did an amazing cover of that one after the Everly Brothers made it a big hit. You should check it out. Not an audiophile, are you? Well, I suppose you can't be good at everything, right? We all have our limitations." He shook his head and continued to walk on, hoping that would successfully change the subject.

"Ev-er-ly. Everly. You can't even say it, can you? Why you both so stiff round each other?"

Trevor made a face and looked anyplace but at Nylah as he continued walking and thinking that she could sound just a New Yorker in the movies. "Stiff? I have no idea what you're talking about." His father was *stiff*. That was the opposite of Dr. Payne *Junior*. How could he be stiff around Dr. Bergeron? Or anybody?

"How two people can get so down and dirty with one another and be so weirdly formal, I tell you, I don't get it. It's like you think she's the queen or something."

"What? No!" Trevor could feel he was stammering. "The queen was... the queen! Dr. Bergeron's very professional, that's all. I'm, yeah, respecting her, uh, professionalism." *Down and dirty with Everly.* For some reason that made him all higgledy-piggledy feeling inside. "She's a highly competent woman. Uh doctor. Yes, a female in our field. That's very important. Glass ceilings and all that."

"Yeah, whatever. All my professors were on a first name basis with each other unless something was going on between them. Just saying. You *look* like you're trying to cover something up."

"What? No! Oh, uh, let's just focus on the dig, right? Or maybe I'll start calling you Miss Anderson all the time?" Trevor headed over to the potential mass grave site. At least they were sure it wasn't Nylah's chariot parking lot, although it could still turn out to be a dump of animal bones and trash. That would be somewhat disappointing. Despite yesterday's excitement, there had been no further discoveries, deepening the mystery of the gold cross. They had dug quite a bit further down but hadn't hit any more "paydirt", as Nylah called it. He hoped those gems missing from the cross would show up. He'd like to see the golden cross restored to its former glory before it went into a museum someplace. He hoped it was the The British Museum. That way he could take his dad there, hear him say how proud he was of his son. Achieve something the old man hadn't himself. Trevor Senior didn't even have anything in the MOLA, much less the British M.

"Nah. He'd probably choke on those words." Trevor reminded himself to stop thinking aloud. "Dr. Bergeron!" Trevor called out as they arrived. She'd been lucky enough to be at the mass grave site all morning. "Any developments?"

"Not yet, Dr. Payne. I'd have radioed you if we'd found anything more than dirt." She held up the ancient walkie talkie Trevor insisted the dig leaders clip to their belts given the unevenness of their cell phone coverage. "We're going slow, but we want to be precise in our recording. I'm taking soil samples as we move down through the layers." She pointed to a rather large pile of dirt some twenty-five feet away with a cluster of students standing around low tables. A power washer was standing to the side "I have the boys screening the removed dirt over there."

Trevor nodded. "You do love your soil samples, Dr. Bergeron."

Everly looked at Trevor with mild curious confusion while Nylah audibly sighed and rolled her eyes.

They were interrupted by a young student assigned to the other side of the village who seemed nervous as he approached the dig site leader. "Herr Doctor Payne?" he called out.

"Yes, Matthew?"

"Matthias."

"Oh, sorry, mate. I'll get it right."

"I think we've found something. Can you come over?"

Trevor nodded, sighing at the reality that he would never get the chance to actually focus on anything today. He put down the shovel he had just picked up, and followed.

Nylah looked at Everly and raised her eyebrows. Everly crossed her arms and shook her head, but in a good-natured sort of way, and with a smile said, "Oh sure, I'll follow him. Not much happening here after all. Maybe it'll be interesting."

By the time the three of them reached the far side of the dig site, a little crowd had gathered, curiosity pulling the students away from their assigned tasks. Trevor referred to this side of the ruins as the Tower Hamlets of the village, indicating his suspicion that this had been the section where the poor people lived. He jokingly referred to the mass grave end of town as Knightsbridge, given the ruins of the nicer church and evidence of what would have been actual buildings for merchant shops and posher homes.

Trevor smiled as he walked up to the little group. "I see the excitement of finding the gold cross has gotten everyone keyed up about possible treasure, hasn't it?"

A few *jawohls* were mixed in with general laughter. A dig always went better after the first exciting find, which was usually some small bone fragment or a nearly worn away coin. He'd never been on a dig where one of the first artifacts found was something actually worth getting excited about, something that might actually make it into an archeology textbook someday.

A tall fellow with brown hair said, "Dr. Payne, we have found two footings of a small building and curiously, what appears to be another hole."

Trevor held out his hand and one of the students handed him a brush. "Well, let's take a closer look, Horton, uh Horst. Uh, right, mate?" He squatted down, glad he wasn't corrected on the name and hoping he'd gotten that one right and started to examine the footing stone. He pulled a small measuring tape out of his pocket and on a pad from the same pocket, noted down the numbers. He measured the hole and asked for a metered stick, and one of the college crew brought it to him. He carefully tested the dirt around the hole and then in the hole, finding it to be much softer. He poked into the dirt a couple of times with the metal pick he always had clipped to his breast pocket.

"What is it?" Nylah asked the question on everyone's mind.

Trevor looked about him at the expectant faces. "Well, given the measurement from point A to point B, between the footings, I would expect that if you dig here," he marked a space with the stick, "and here, that you'll find evidence of where other footings sat once upon a time."

Immediately two of the Brandenburg University students started to work with their tools on those spots. Before long, an excited cry brought cheers from the group, as evidence surfaced that a footing stone had once stood there, exactly as Trevor had predicted.

"What is it?" Horst asked.

"I do believe that you'll have a terrific term paper this fall, Horst. If I'm right, you've made an important archeological discovery here. This, my friend, is a toilet. A latrine, to be more specific."

"A latrine?" The look on Horst's face was anything but excited.

"Yes! And if you get really lucky, it will turn out to be a cesspit. It'll have walls made of brick or stone and it will expand, to usually about a meter square. Interesting finds, cesspits. A little sludgy sometimes."

All the students were snickering and poking poor Horst, who did not look proud of his find. "A cesspit?"

"Right you are! Probably not a toilet because we haven't found any evidence of running water in this town or any kind of rudimentary plumbing."

"An outhouse? You found an outhouse?" Nylah was visibly trying to hold in her laughter. "Now that *is* the find of the century!"

"Actually, it's pretty significant," Everly said. "It says that this town had some degree of sophistication to it, which is saying something given how small the village is." She looked around at the mountain tops that distantly encircled the valley on three sides. "And where it's located. In this era, it was common for people to use a pot to pee in if they had to go during the night. During the day, they would kind of just go wherever. Maybe walk to a field or behind a bush. Maybe on the side of a building. But the night-pots would pretty much just get dumped out in the street in the morning if the local tanner wasn't collecting urine for the leather-making process."

"Eeeewww!" echoed from several students.

"They threw their shit in the street?" Nylah asked.

"Language, Nylah," Everly said. "Yup. Right out the door. Disease was a significant concern, many thanks to their handling of fecal matter in particular in the Dark and Middle Ages."

Trevor nodded. "Dr. Bergeron's right. It was unusual, but not unheard of, for a town to have dug out latrines. Given its location here in the Tower Hamlets part of town, I would imagine this one was for, uh, well, general use. We'll have to look for evidence of these around the village or see if they just put the little building, which would have held an easily identifiable smell, on the shoddier side of town. Knightsbridge might have more sophisticated and larger cesspits."

"If it was a public privy," Everly said, "and if it tuns out to be rudimentary in nature, then this might be the side of town where such places as tanners were located."

Nylah looked puzzled. Hannah held her nose. Nylah nodded in understanding. "How could a place... like this... have public bathrooms? I thought that was a more modern century kind of thing?"

Horst jumped into the conversation. "The Romans had them. And their public toilets had running water!"

"Yeah, but were the Romans… here?" Nylah looked around at their remote location. "I thought you said 'no chariots?' Will we find a temple to Zeus or something?"

"Jupiter," Horst corrected. "Zeus was Greek."

"Whatever." Nylah waved him off.

"I admit, it does bring a new light to what this town was, don't it?" Trevor nodded.

Everly looked over at Trevor. "This village might be full of surprises, if we're finding evidence of public toilets. Any gut instinct on an explanation, Dr. Payne?"

"Well, let's see, uh, Dr. Bergeron." Trevor looked up as he thought and tried to not sound nervous. "Anyone who had tutors and had been classically trained, which would most likely be the nobility, would have had at least a chance of learning about such things. They would've studied a lot about ancient Rome. And it's not hard to replicate, innit? All you need is a shovel, and *those* have been around since truly ancient times."

"People studied Roman stuff in the Middle Ages?" Nylah asked.

Trevor gave Nylah a smile. "Oh, the nobility, sure! Makes me wonder why anyone of noble birth would have come to such a faraway place, you know? Come here and stuck round, not just swing by to collect taxes and the like. But you have to remember, Nylah, that in your part of the world, the Roman era of history is a topic you study in class, but over here in Europe, it's the basis of our laws, much of our culture, our architecture. You see old Roman ruins just all over the place. It's easier to keep the ideas alive when the history surrounds you. So yes, it would've been quite normal for the nobility to have learned about the greatness of Rome from its temples to…" he used both hands to point to the circular depression in the excavated earth.

"It's shit pits," Nylah said and the local college crew snickered again.

Everly rolled her eyes but was laughing.

Trevor scratched his head. "Well, the Romans were an earthy bunch. From what we can tell, they might've called them that indeed."

"In Colonial times in the U.S.," Everly said, "outhouses were convenient dumping holes, as well as places to relieve yourself when you needed to go. Towns didn't have garbage pick-up or a city dump outside their borders, so people just threw their broken items down the outhouse hole." With a smile she added, "And anything they wanted to hide the evidence of."

Now everyone leaned over to look curiously at the depression in the ground, as if it had been carefully dug out already and held unimaginable and mysterious treasures.

Everly continued, "So, in addition to being able to find out what kind of foods the population ate, because so much evidence is analyzable in the pit using modern chemical analyses, researchers of colonial America also learned a great deal about the tools people used, the types of housewares they had, even some about the jewelry they wore or the coins they carried. People drop all kinds of things, I'm sure not all on purpose, down the hole."

With a smile, Horst said, "And it would have to be a very special object indeed for someone to go after it!"

Many nodded or chuckled at his comment.

Trevor said, "Horst, take your team and use the medium-sized shovels. I'm sure you've got a ways to go to reach through the dirt that's collapsed in the hole before you get to any artifacts or, shall we say, interesting soil samples."

Nylah groaned at Trevor's joke.

"Dr. Bergeron, perhaps you'd be so kind as to be in charge here? Feel free to come and get me if you'd like when the dirt texture starts to change. You can supervise the switch to the pointing trowels and brushes." As Trevor started to walk away, he shouted, "Horst, make sure you photograph each step. You'll need the documentation for your term paper."

"*Jawohl*, Herr Doctor Payne!" several voices said in unison.

Everly leaned on her shovel. "Sure, I'll stay around. And guys, when we get to the 'interesting soil' part," she snickered, "I'll show you how to put specimens in the sample vials. We can send them out to the lab at the end of the week. See if we can get some insight into the diets these people ate out here seven hundred years ago."

Trevor called out to Nylah, "C'mon. Let's head back to the 'not-a-chariot-parking-lot' on the other side of the village."

"I'm never going to live that down, am I?" she said as she caught up with him.

"On your gravestone, I'm sure! Your epitaph will be all about discovering Roman chariots of Zeus in the Bavarian highlands."

"Ha! Ha! And hey, Tom Sawyer, you got that crew excited about digging up a shit pit. That was clever."

"What was?"

"Sure, look so innocent. C'mon, no one, and I mean no one wants to dig up poop. Even hundreds of years old poop!"

"Dr. Bergeron does."

"Okay, maybe Everly does, But no one else. But mention hidden evidence or accidentally dropped treasure and suddenly you've got those students lining up to dig up a latrine. A possibly 'sludgy' experience. Very clever."

"Thank you. I'm glad you approve!" Trevor chuckled as he said it. "But I'll be glad to get back to our Knightsbridge site. I've got a funny feeling about that hole in particular."

"Yeah? Why?"

"Those blackberry bushes were just vicious."

It was only an hour before Everly found Trevor showing Nylah how to use the small spade and brush in a technique that removed excess dirt quickly but wouldn't damage the objects of interest hidden beneath as he carefully worked in Knightsbridge. He was trying to get her to hold the metal pic and poke it into the dirt.

"Remember, I do the organizing. Not the dirty work," she reminded him yet again.

Suddenly they were interrupted.

"Hey, you two. I think you'll want to see this," Everly said.

"Did you find some interesting dishware?" Trevor asked.

Everly shook her head.

"Cool ancient coins?" Nylah asked. "Maybe some Roman ones?"

Everly smiled and shook her head.

"You found poop, didn't you?"

"Not exactly, Nylah. But we did find something quite interesting. Unusual. Unexpected."

Nylah stood up straight with interest. "Ah, so the smoking gun?"

"Not quite. But still, you have to see this to believe it."

They both looked at her expectantly. Trevor asked, "And the shit pit held?"

"A hand. And well, well… you know, you just kind of have to see it for yourself, I mean, given the location of the body."

"The location of the body?" Nylah asked with some excitement. "We have to check this out!"

As they walked with Everly, Trevor said to Nylah, "You know, Nylah, if archeology's not your dream field, you might like police work. I could see you as a smashing detective!"

When they got to the latrine dig site, Nylah was the first to speak. "Damn! Damn! That nasty!" She pointed to the bones emerging from the ground and looked around at the other workers. "Y'all see that! Damn, that like something that came out of a Stephen King novel. One that Jordan Peele done made into a movie. Shit!"

Everyone stared at her as she paced about, taking quick, shallow breaths. Trevor turned to Everly and asked, "Why, uh, why is she talking like that?"

Everly shrugged. "I think it's a New York thing." She nodded a couple of times and added. "Yeah, scared New York thing."

Sure enough, the team led by Dr. Bergeron and Horst had carefully unearthed a skeletal hand, which was reaching up through the dirt and pointing towards the sky.

"Oh, right. So, Nylah, we all see it. And you can calm down. He's not moving. Not gonna move. Trust me. Maybe you should head to the mess tent and get things set up for our evening review, right? You don't have to stay here. Hannah, could you maybe, uh, escort Nylah? Make sure she's okay?"

Hannah was frozen and not moving to help Nylah. "Herr Doctor?" She gestured rapidly at the bones.

"Yes, Hannah?" Trevor asked, a bit impatient with the crises his students were seemingly having.

"It just moved!"

Everyone stood frozen in place as their heads turned towards the pit. The fingers which had been pointing skyward were slowly falling toward the earth as if the hand was making a fist.

"Oh, I just don't know if I can un-see that," Nylah said as she started to walk away with a nervous-looking Hannah at her side. "That dude about to come right up through the earth and whup your ass! Oh my God! Get me outta' here!"

Everly slid over to stand by Trevor, whispering calmly, almost with amusement, "Nylah's right. That's the creepiest thing I've seen on a dig."

"Right. Un-see that. Right." Trevor said, trying to hide the nervous tone in his own voice.

"Why would a person be in a latrine?" Everly still sounded calm and objective.

Trevor thought that perhaps nothing could really shake that woman, but then he gave a little giggle and said, "Maybe he had a killer crap?" He looked expectantly at Everly, but she wasn't laughing. He cleared his throat and said, "Yeah, right. It's like they died trying to crawl out. That's our mystery to solve, innit?"

Two days later Everly and Trevor were working in the specimen tent while the onsite team continued the dig of what now everyone referred to as the 'shit pits'. Everly had obtained her specimens that would lead to clues about the dietary habits of the villagers, and the remnants of several ancient, broken tools were starting to be carefully extracted.

Nylah walked into the tent. "I just downloaded the photos from the sim card. Man, we take photos like my mama at Christmas time. Just who's gonna go through all of these anyway?"

"If you were my doctoral student instead of my work study student, it would be you!" Trevor said teasingly while he remained focused on the skeleton in front of him. "Could still be an independent study in the fall."

"Lucky me!" Nylah snorted. "What's up with, uh," she coughed, "Dude A?"

"Well," said Everly, "*Specimen A* died a long time ago. And he's still dead. Going to stay that way, so no worries, Nylah."

Trevor sighed with satisfaction while he worked. "Accounting for why there's only bones left, and a few bits of this gray cloth. I must say, we're bloody lucky to have any of this at all!" As he held up a scrap of ancient, fragile cloth with tweezers and carefully stuck it into a plastic specimen container and screwed on the lid, he started singing in a rather chipper tune, *"Dust in the wind. All we are is dust in the wind. Everything is dust in the wind."*

Everly shot Nylah a look and shrugged. "Hey, he's in the nineteen-seventies now. Just go with it."

"So, he'll start rappin' soon?"

"Not so sure we should be encouraging him…" Everly said under her breath.

Nylah moved over to the specimen table and took a long look at the bone fragments.

Trevor glanced up at her. "You know, for someone who's so passionate about forensics, detective work, and mysteries, you're a little bit squeamish about bones!"

"C'mon man, you have to admit, he was pretty damn scary when he trying to climb his way out of the latrine and whup everybody's ass. And threatening us with that fist? Nah, that wasn't detective work. That was some poltergeist shit!"

"Language, Nylah."

"Sorry, Everly," Nylah said over her shoulder, not really meaning it. "But lying there like that, it's like he trying to disco in a garbage disposal! That's definitely not as scary. In fact, that's kinda interesting. How come so many pieces of the dude are missing?" Nylah looked at Trevor with sincere curiosity, then she shuddered. "I sorta thought when the hand was reaching up through the pit, that the rest of him would be right behind. Not to mention righteously angry."

The bones on the specimen table weren't laid out in a skeleton shape. There was the hand and part of the forearm, once again pointing upwards, at the top of the specimen table, and the rest of the body was a complete jumble below, laid out to recreate exactly how it had been found in the earth. They were what Trevor would have called "higgledy-piggledy". Scattered among the bones were a few small clumps of dirt.

Everly carefully attached a label to the piece of bone she was working on. "Nylah, even in a burial excavation, where you have a coffin of some type, you might not have an intact skeleton. More likely if the person is entombed in some way you'll get a really complete sample, but this guy we found in 'interesting circumstances', you might say. And take a look at this." Using a pair of tongs Everly pointed to the small dirt globs. "You know how the dirt we remove goes over to the screens to sift for smaller artifacts?"

"Yeah, the boys love using that power washer. You should see what they do with it when you aren't there to supervise."

Everly shook her head and decided to tuck away that bit of extra information. "Well, we found these while you were running errands in town."

"More like while you were on your date with Herr Hans!" Trevor's voice was filled with mirth and he gave her a teasing look.

Nylah laughed back at him. "One dinner out and I miss the good stuff? You've got to be kidding? What kind of broken up trash was thrown down the latrine?"

Trevor grinned, even though he was pretty sure that Nylah found any time spent with Hans far more engaging than time spent with dirt.

Everly's face glowed with excitement as she brushed some of the crusted soil away and revealed a grimy blue object. "Digging way down, yes, we did find some broken up discarded tools and such, as would be expected. But this is different. This is exciting: it's the gems. We found the gems that we think belong to the golden cross!"

"In the toilet," Nylah asked. "No shit!"

"Not shit! So right!" Trevor said with a cackle.

"Language! Both of you!"

Trevor ignored her. "But gems! The cross wasn't vandalized by grave robbers, tossing the cross itself away like a piece of junk."

"Junk!" Everly looked up sharply. "In no time in history would that gold cross be considered a piece of junk!"

Trevor gave Everly a smile, putting his index finger to the tip of his nose and then pointing at her with a nod. "So, someone didn't want to be found with them, now did they? And that must have been a heartbreaking choice for them, now right? Get caught and maybe have your hand cut off, or some other type of old-world justice, or lose those gems forever. I guess it turned out to be forever."

"Someone probably got caught paying off their debts to the local brothel with stolen goods," Nylah said, her voice dripping with disgust. Then she brightened. "Ooh! That's actually a great theory! No chance that shit pit was located in the local brothel or something? Wait a minute." She drew back. "Is that a dude or was that a woman?"

"It's a 'dude', as you called him," Trevor answered. "Not a woman. But that's an interesting hypothesis. A brothel. What do you think, Dr. Bergeron?"

"Hard to tell. From the footings, we think the little outhouse was free-standing. But the town could have had a brothel. They were popular even back in the thirteen hundreds. Called 'city tolerance houses' by the populace and they appeared on the local tax rolls, so they were important businesses."

Trevor chuckled. "World's oldest profession, innit? And it was a business that never quite went away. Back then they believed that tolerance houses had to be tolerated because men couldn't control their urges!"

At this Nylah snorted and Everly rolled her eyes and shook her head in agreement with Nylah.

Trevor continued, "So while it wasn't discussed in polite society, like the Knightsbridge side of town, they had them on nearly every block in the big cities. From what we can tell of the writings at the time, it was a place where men socialized by getting drunk and looking for 'exotic' experiences. The more exotic the more enticing—and the higher the revenue for the city. Cologne, which was a big city even at the time our poor friend here lived, was a hotspot for tolerance houses. Much like Essen."

"But a little village like this? I don't know," Everly mused. "A whole house? I would imagine every town had at least a prostitute or two, the kind who would pick up and follow an army and then settle down in a town or city for a while, taking up trailing the army again when they got restless or needed to escape their unpaid taxes."

"Always business of that type at the back end of an army in those days," Trevor said. "And probably in these days too. But back to our friend here and to his untimely demise."

"Untimely?" Everly looked over at Trevor. "I peg these bones for about mid-thirties. Maybe as old as mid-forties. That's not quite untimely for someone in the fourteenth century."

"And I agree with you. Whether this bloke would have seen sixty and been a ripe old gent, I can't say. But this skeleton is only partial for a good reason." Trevor bent down with the magnifying glass and then took a picture of the bit of bone he was studying.

"And?" Nylah looked at him expectantly.

Trevor looked up at his companions. "This fellow was eaten."

Chapter 7

Father Bernard Trōst
August 1346

The spectators called out loudly to one another, jeering at poor attempts to catch the ball and cheering the clashing players as they knocked one another down. Bernard leaned against a fence which stood to one side of the field and watched the competitors, puzzled. "What is this game?" he asked an older man who was shouting encouragement to one team and disparagement to the other.

"Oh, Father, don't you know? This be Shrovetide football."

"And the object of the game is…?"

"Each team tries to get the ball across the goal line of the other team. Other than that, not many rules. Try not to get hurt too badly… There you go!" the man suddenly shouted at the play on the field. "Run 'im over! Kill him!" He was surprisingly loud for his advanced age.

Bernard watched for a while as the men threw and kicked their cloth ball around the pasture sparsely speckled with grass. He couldn't really tell who was on which side and wondered how the players could. "Ooo," he said and turned to the elderly man, "does that happen often?"

"What? Losing the ball? All the damn time!"

"No, I meant slipping in the cow pats."

"Oh that. Right, that. Sure." The man seemed unconcerned.

"It doesn't seem that many people in this village are overly concerned with excrement."

"Excre-what?"

"Excrement. Uh, well, uh… shit."

"Part o' life, right?" the elderly man said, much more absorbed in his spectating. "Besides, we gots to shoo the cows outta this field in order to have a place to play."

Indeed, the cows were just off in the distance, chewing their cud and also watching the humans scamper about. As the teams and the spectators betting on the game's outcome got frustrated with the play, their pleas for divine intercession evolved into mild cursing and eventually became quite elaborate blasphemies:

"There is no God and Jesus doesn't live in heaven!" one of the goalkeepers shouted as he stomped on the ground in anger after letting a goal pass by him.

"The eternal soul be damned! If such a thing existed, then that pass wouldn't have gone so awry!" another spectator muttered and then looked at Bernard guiltily.

Bernard just gave him a beneficent smile and turned to the old man standing on his other side, who was engrossed in the game. "Do they actually believe what they're saying?"

The older man turned and looked Bernard up and down. "Well, you bein' a man of the church and all, I would suppose that God does show up in your life, don't He? But, don't you know, the men out here don't see much of Him at all."

Bernard looked with wonder at the horizon. "But the majestic mountains? The expanse of the sky?"

"Ach! If there were a God, the winters wouldn't be so cold. Those mountains send us harsh rain and deep snow. Take it from an old man like me, there's nothing but this world. No heaven. No hell. Nothing but what you make it of it on earth. And none of your preaching can amend that. But there is always a having a nice girlfriend and plenty of food to eat!" The man elbowed Bernard in the ribs.

A couple of people who had wandered up to enjoy the sport laughed at the old man's comment, calling out, "So right, so right!" and "Never spoke a truer word, that one."

Bernard felt he had no choice but to laugh at the man's comment, as he could not tell whether it had been made in jest or earnestness. He was new and wanted to fit in. He certainly didn't want to drive parishioners away from St. Cyprian's as he was just getting it started. It was one thing to parade a golden cross through the streets to bring them in, but in order to keep them there, he had to build real relationships with the people of the village. Even the doubting Thomases.

A few of the players groaned, causing the spectators to turn their heads as well. Bernard turned to see a man standing on the other side of the pasture, watching the game with a scowl on his face. One of the men muttered, "Look out blokes, for Tuckerschade has arrived, his dark cloud in tow!'

"Oh my!" said another, "Old Friar Tuck, back to frighten us! Got a whip with him? Whip us into shape?"

The man looked to be wearing a worn *vestis talaris*, or a "cassock", Bernard thought, as the country folk commonly called them since clearly no Latin was spoken here. As a couple of the men got into an argument about whether the last ball played was fair or not, Bernard made use of the time to meet another fellow of the cloth, walking over to where the man called Friar Tuck was standing.

"Good day to you, Brother," Bernard said pleasantly. He was somewhat surprised that this man was not much older than himself. He smiled inwardly that the friar didn't look at all like he suffered from stomach pains, nor did he look like the saint of unattractive people was his spiritual guide, the bishop's speculations notwithstanding. Actually, this Friar Tuck was rather handsome in a rustic and rugged kind of way, with a strong jaw line that made for a somewhat imposing face.

70

"Lovely to be out and enjoying the sunshine." After being given no answer, Bernard added, "I'm Father Bernard. I've been sent to reawaken the Church of St. Cyprian."

"I know who you are. I saw you parading about that golden cross." The man looked at him sternly. "Moses was enraged at the golden idol paraded before the people."

Bernard was taken aback at such recrimination upon first meeting. "Yes, that is true," he said slowly. "But this is a cross blessed by the Holy See himself, to call the masses. You would be the servant of the Holy Orders for the church on the far side of the village? St. Drogo's, if I'm correct?"

The man gave him a flat look. "It's St. Drogo-Erasmus. I be Friar Karel Tuckerschade."

"Friar. Yes then, Friar, of course." That made sense to Bernard. This was obviously a man of lesser education and in a tiny village such as this, it was understandable that they had only a friar to attend to their spiritual needs. He had probably been born and raised in this village.

One of the spectators called out, "Oh Father, watch yourself. Friar Tuck believes in hell for sure. Don't know about heaven though!" A few of the men laughed.

Friar Tuck scowled. "These be blasphemers. The non-righteous. Not a one of them comes to service at St. Drogo-Erasmus. Nor did they show their hides in St. Cyprian when I was a-preaching there." He turned to the players on the pitch, yelling and wagging a finger. "You'll all more than likely burn in hell lest you start to repent for your sins!" Turning a more peaceful face to Father Bernard, Friar Tuck added, "They little understand the moral peril their souls are in, but I remind them, I assure you."

"Oh, yes, I see. I'll have to see what I can do about that as well."

"Some people are beyond redemption. I've tried. They're a lost lot. 'Tis all about games and wine with them."

"We have many in Cologne who feel the same. I'm familiar with the type."

Friar Tuck gave a hard look at the men who had joyfully resumed their play on the field. "It be hardly appropriate for a man of the cloth, in a station such as yours, to be engaging in… games. You weren't betting on the outcome, were you?"

Bernard shrugged and laughed. "I can hardly bet on the outcome when I can't even understand what they're doing on the field, now can I? But I think there's no harm in spending time with one's fellow men, getting to know the people of this village. And what better way to know them than to engage in their pastimes, for I wouldn't expect them to join me in mine."

Friar Tuck looked rather suspiciously at Bernard before he asked, "And just what be your pastimes?"

Bernard gave a hearty laugh. "Why, I thank you for asking, my good friar. I enjoy reading."

"The holy word?"

"Yes, of course. And books. I brought a few with me from Cologne, imported from Hapsburg. Of course, the Hapsburgs love courtly poetry as well as the increasingly popular *Schwankliteratur*, and I have to say, I myself love a good fools' literature! Very comical indeed. I get a good laugh every time I read it! I could loan you a copy if you'd like?" Books were precious to Bernard and rare to come by, so he rather hoped his fellow clergyman would be uninterested and not take him up on his gesture of goodwill. He was not disappointed.

"A clergyman's eyes should be for the Lord's word alone."

"Oh, I don't disagree with you. But I also find that the Lord inspires men to write who are not of the clergy. And I have a book by a woman which is particularly hilarious." At this Friar Tuck paled, so Bernard decided it might be best to break away from the subject of literature. He strongly suspected that Friar Tuck had memorized the required parts of the Bible and might have a very limited capacity, supporting his very limited interest, to actually read. "But the everyman enjoys his games more than the writings of others."

"The everyman enjoys his wine, or rather *my* wine," Tuck said, shooting a look at the drinkers.

Bernard looked at the friar with renewed interest. "So, you are the famous wine-making-friar I've heard about? I have been gifted with a half-barrel of your wine. Even the bishop himself praised it. You have a true gift, bestowed by God no doubt, for your craft."

Tuck seemed to flush and not quite know where to look, as if such praise was a novel experience to him, but he managed to give a quick, if awkward, nod.

"Well, I am indeed lucky to have met you. Might it be possible for my little church, my *kirch*, St. Cyprian's, to purchase some of your most excellent vintage for our holy communion? Yes? That's wonderful. I'll pay you half again the price you give others in town, as a gesture of goodwill amongst our sister churches, for, shall we say, four barrels?"

Tuck nodded dumbly and then stammered, "I'll, uh, I'll have Wilhelm, my acolyte, bring them round."

One of the players called out, "C'mon there, Father Bernie! We need you!"

Tuck looked at Bernard. "Maybe you can save their souls from the playing pitch." He grunted, gave Bernard a respectful nod and the men a disapproving stare, and then stalked off.

As Bernard rejoined the spectators at the wall, the players took a break and joined them. A man named Olaf, muttered, "He's a fun one, ain't he?"

"Did you not go to mass at St. Drogo's?" Bernard asked the group.

Several of the men shrugged and nodded. "Tried it," one said, "but he's all doom and gloom. It's all about sin and never about the blessing of a sunny day!"

"Right!" said another. "If I'm gonna burn in hell for what I done, which is what the good Friar Tuck assures his people from his pulpit, then I'd rather actually do something to earn me punishment! For him, all you need is to be breathin' in order to be sinnin'. No good deed will get you into his heaven, so the way I see it, it ain't worth the try. Might as well enjoy a sunny day, which to him is sin, have fun playing some Shrovetide with me friends, which to him is sin, and live your life as you choose."

"Which is also a sin to him! You should live it as *he* chooses for you," cautioned the first man.

A third man joined their circle. "Don't worry about Old Saint Tuck. He gets his jollies shouting and threatening from his grimy little pulpit in his dirty little church. Sure, he's got his followers, but Good Father, I hope *you* have a message the people want to hear. Life's already hard. We need to hear about the joys of heaven, or," he said as he elbowed Bernard in the ribs, "even better, the joys of Earth, and not the fiery torments of hell that await us. Now the good friar makes a tasty wine, and if he would keep that as his purpose, his reason for being born would be right fulfilled!"

"I'll uh, keep that in mind. I hope you'll come to mass at St. Cyprian's. I just ordered wine from him for our service."

The group of players all looked at one another. One of the men asked, "Will you bless the magical transformation of a whole barrel? And can I bring me own cup?"

"Of course, you may, but for what?" Bernard asked.

"For the wine! If I can get more than just a taste of salvation, I'll come, for a man like me, dear Father, needs a whole cup of salvation!"

Bernard stammered and nodded mutely, wondering if this technically counted as a bribe to get the not-so-faithful to come to church. He wondered if he would need to confess it as a sin, and suddenly knew in his heart that he would never go to confession with Friar Tuck as the fellow clergyman standing in as the steward of his soul.

The men, completely unaware of Bernard's momentary ecclesiastical crisis, looked at each other, big smiles breaking across their faces. They all started nodding. "We'll be there! Bring your own cups, boys! It's gonna be Sunday!"

A slow smile grew on Bernard's face as he had an idea. "If you do show up for holy mass, then I'll have another opportunity for more than just a few swallows of wine. Whole tankards full for those who engage in general good deeds with me."

Now he had the attention of the men.

"Whole tankards full? Of wine?" one of them asked. "Not just cups?"

"Aye!" Bernard nodded. "For I have in mind that this village needs a formal cesspit or two and some latrines for the benefit of the general populace."

The men looked at him, confused.

"It's not hard, my fellows. All it takes is some shovels."

The men looked at one another and Olaf said, "I don't know what those contraptions are that you want built, but I've got a shovel and I'll sign up for helping you benefit the general populace for a tankard or two of salvation!"

◆━◆━◆

Bernard sat down at his table after a long day. His head was full of thoughts and confusion. He had stretched himself a bit far today in order to build relationships with the people of this little village. The people were as rough as their football pitch, to put it politely. It shouldn't surprise him how the folk here lacked the sophistication and education of those he had rubbed shoulders with back in Cologne. While that was to be expected, in truth he had not anticipated their free-thinking ways. In Cologne, the people loved the mass as though it were the highlight of their week, but perhaps strict church teaching was a religion for the elites? Now he was running into what he could only call "the peasant religion" and their unorthodox interpretations and beliefs. His Bishop Eberhard would call it *disobedient*, he was sure.

Bernard mused on how the elites accepted the church's teachings and navigated its powers, and yet the country folk expressed doubts or even disbelieved in startling ways. Perhaps it was that empty bellies and hard circumstances gave one a different relationship to God. *No,* he thought. *Not to God but to the mediator of God. To the church itself.* He spent a long time contemplating the possible outcomes in a world where the Church caged the serfs and held peasants down, just like the nobility did with their laws and rules, rather than enlightening their hearts and minds. If he was going to minister to the souls in this little town, perhaps he needed to listen to what their souls needed? Perhaps their local priest might be able to see that more clearly than even the Holy See in Avignon? The pope was over six hundred miles away, after all.

Scratching his head three times, Bernard reached for a pitcher and poured himself a glass of water, tapping it three times on the table, seeking refuge in the holy trinity, reflecting on his experience that afternoon. He hadn't anticipated a rival church, certainly not from the rather bedraggled little building on the impoverished side of town. Still, he had done a good deed today in offering an exorbitant price for four barrels of wine. That would help the good friar out and Bernard was sure he could win the man over in time through simple acts of charity.

A knock at the door caught his attention. "Sir? Father? With the trading carts that came, there is something here for you."

"Enter."

The serving girl gave him a quick curtsy and entered the room with a scroll tube. She handed it to him. "Can I get you anything else?"

Bernard shook his head and she curtsied again before she left.

He could tell from the seal that it came from his family, and by the way the seal was done that it came from his sister. Adelaide was a woman of letters. She loved to read and write more than anything. While her enthusiasm for the written word never seemed to dull in the slightest, he did wish her inspiration for what she wrote about would expand somewhat. He took a deep breath and then fetched himself a small tankard of wine to bolster his courage before he immersed himself into what was sure to be a passionately written missive.

So far, she was entirely correct: this family news was absolutely what he would expect. As he read, he absentmindedly tapped his hands on the table in three beat sets.

Bernard sat back and thought that his sister was re-making the world to be as she wished. Their father had not accepted Bernard's choice. The two men had not been speaking when Bernard returned to visit the family home after taking his vows. The duke had not accepted Bernard's blessing as a priest, nor had he offered a father's blessing to his son. Bernard remembered how the duke had called him a Judas for this betrayal. It was a bitter memory to bring to mind. If Duke Trōst of Lotharingia could not come to terms with his oldest son becoming a man of God, then he would certainly never accept it of his only daughter. Those paths were only open to the third or fourth daughter or son. Older daughters were to marry to enhance the family's political power. That was their purpose. First and second sons owed their ancestry successive generations to carry the family title. Third and fourth sons were given to the military or the church. He mused on Adolfus. No sons were ever given over to be artists. He turned back to his sister's letter:

Bernard let out a heavy sigh. "My dear sister—your wish isn't marriage, that's true. It's martyrdom." While he adored his only sister, he could not indulge in her fantasy that she could control her own destiny. That was not the fate of women. She was wrong that their father saw her as cattle. Nothing so crude. She was silk. Her connections were valuable. No one could help her become a nun. Bernard had barely been able to navigate his way to his own calling.

He vowed to reply to Adelaide and advise her to be more sensible. More realistic. One had to accept one's destiny. One's duty. He separated the hand-written letter from the blank page behind it. Adelaide always included a page, sometimes two, blank. Mostly she expected him to write back, which he often did. The other blank page was a gift.

He retrieved his ink and quill and pondered on how to respond. "Humility," he said aloud. "Humility and destiny and duty."

Chapter 8

Nylah

For days, Nylah stood patiently at the side of what was now becoming a pit. There was no other word for it. Poor Dr. T. He'd been so excited for this exhumation, waiting for the legions of the dead to arise.

That man's got some real daddy issues, Nylah thought to herself. She'd made a gorgeous website, not quite as slick as she'd made to support her dancing career, but of course, she'd worked on that for about six years. The dig's website she'd put about six hours into, but still, it was cool. She'd posted amazing pictures of Dr. T and Everly in action, with all their full academic *blah, blah, blah* at their insistence. "Your average follower isn't going to care about that stuff," she told Dr. T.

"Maybe so, but Dr. Trevor Payne, *Senior,* is not an average follower."

"And neither is the committee evaluating me for tenure." Everly had looked defeated as she said it.

Nylah had been amazed at how stricken they both looked. Haunted even. So, she gave in, smeared their credentials all over the site, and decided that whatever she was going to be when she grew up, it was not going to be an academic. Still, she used every trick up her sleeve to make the site come to life with an energy that would not have been wasted on a Broadway production. And now she had very specific ideas for the photographs she needed to really make it pop and make archeology into something other than mind-numbingly boring.

Getting the right shots of Dr. T turned out to be easy: the man looked better in pictures than he did in real life, but she figured that was because the photographs didn't translate his utter goofiness the way his tone of voice, the turn of his head, or the ridiculous way a smile broke across his face did. In a still shot, there was no excited wiggling. No, he looked like a serious archeologist. More important to Dr. T, he looked like someone his father could respect. It was easy to make him into the star of the production.

Now Everly… she was much more of a problem. That frizzy hair and "I got no game" style was a challenge, but Nylah had a plan. She'd already gotten Everly's size from the discarded clothes in the tent laundry pile and placed the order online, all on Dr. T's credit card, of course. She had broken the news to Everly a few days ago as they were lying on their cots at night after a long, hard, and disappointing day. Everly had put up a good fight.

"But the clothes I wear on site are fine! My God, Nylah, it's a *dig*. We're in the *dirt*. It's about finding clothes that will be durable with all the wear and tear. It's about protecting yourself and not getting hurt."

"All right! You're gonna make me do it. I'm gonna tell you what they look like."

"Like I'm getting old ahead of my time. Like I'm an old maid. Like I'll never get a date. I know, I know. Like I haven't heard that before. It kinda comes with the profession, you know?" To Nylah's surprise, Everly's voice sounded flat. Emotionless. Full of acceptance.

"No. Not that. Not at all. You look like you're in boyfriend clothes."

"What are boyfriend clothes?"

"You know, boyfriend clothes. When you stay over but you didn't plan to… and you aren't serious enough to have a stash at his place. So, you have to wear his clothes the next day, and they don't fit but they do, kinda. You wear his big shirt and it's loose and baggy and it has his scent on it, not 'cause it's sweaty or anything but just because everything at his place feels and looks and smells like his. And then you feel and look and smell like his, too."

"I… I… I look like that?"

Nylah ignored her. "And the jeans. His jeans, I mean, they don't fit because he's bigger than you are and all, but they do, kinda, really loose. It's just so damn sexy to be in his clothes. And he thinks it sexy. Yeah." She punctuated that last word with a big sigh.

"That's how I look in front of everyone? Like I'm in boyfriend clothes? Oh my god." Everly rolled over and stared at the ceiling of the tent. "This is awful. It's like ten shades of gray or something."

Nylah rolled over on one side and propped up her head on her hand. She was working hard to stay serious. "Uh huh. Yeah, right. You do look like you're in boyfriend clothes. And the hair, Ev, it so looks like you just rolled out of bed."

"But that's what I do every morning. I roll out of bed and hit the dig."

"Yeah. And you look so happy. And you look like you're in boyfriend clothes. You look like you're having the best summer ever. For, you know, a lot of reasons."

Everly's eyes were huge. Nylah knew she was winning. "I *am* having the best summer ever."

"Well, that's too bad, but that's a different problem. Anyway, I just want you to try a different look for the website pictures, so you know, the whole *world* doesn't think something different about you and Dr. T."

"Me and Dr. T?" Now Everly's voice held a tinge of alarm and Nylah knew for sure she was going to win this round. For one, Everly hadn't called him 'Dr. Payne.' She never called him anything but Dr. Payne.

"Well, uh… yeah. I mean, you look so cute and truly happy out on the site, but you do kinda look like you're on a summer-long date. And that you're looking pretty damn sexy in his clothes."

Everly was quiet for a few moments like she was thinking. Nylah thought *probably panicking*. "I'll wear whatever you tell me to for your photo op, boss. That's not a look I want my colleagues back in Toronto to see."

"No problem. I got you covered. New threads should be arriving tomorrow. I had them shipped to Hans's place, since we don't have an actual address to deliver anything to. I'll pick them up when I make the supplies run."

"Okay."

Nylah was surprised at how much Everly sounded like a little girl. "And I think I've got something for your hair."

"My hair?" Everly's hand went to that frizzy mess on top of her head.

"Yeah, you White girls just don't understand frizzy hair. But I can help you there. Now there's nothing wrong with your hair, but for the pictures for the world to see, let's give you a more professional look, just for the photo shoot, and something that isn't screaming out 'sleepover!', okay?"

"Yeah, okay." Everly's voice sounded weak.

"You need product. And a sister. I got you covered, girl."

Everly was quiet for a while and then she said in a soft voice that Nylah had never heard before, like the Everly that existed under all the harder, more professional, I've-got-to-make-it-on-my-own crust, like the Everly you'd really want to be friends with, "Thanks, Nylah."

"No problem. I got your back."

"I'm glad for that. Grateful for that. Glad you're with us."

"Yeah. Me too," Nylah said. And she meant it.

The next night, Nylah spent the evening working with Everly on how to manage curly, frizzy hair. Now it was framing her face in gorgeous ringlets in a way that actually enhanced the color, giving a reddish glow to the natural brown. She'd even gotten Everly to put on some makeup, explaining that the photos were likely to just blur out her face without some help, and those professors back in Toronto needed to know beyond a doubt that this was Dr. Bergeron managing this ground-breaking dig site! She'd dressed Dr. Bergeron in all three of the new dig outfits she'd ordered, pleased with herself that they all looked good. She picked the dark blue pants and the teal-and-dark blue long-sleeved shirt. They had shape. They had game. She needed Everly to look part academic and part like a young Meryl Streep would have, if she'd played Everly in a movie at this point in her career.

Nylah couldn't make an artifact appear out of the dirt for her perfect photo, but she could dress her players for the moment. And if no dead people or their belongings wanted to come out to play then they could all fake some really interesting shots if they needed to. No use in wasting the hair or make up or new clothes.

As the time came for the shoot, Nylah was standing at the edge of the pit of the damned, as she had named it.

"Damned because we're not finding a damned thing in here." Trevor grumbled as he worked. "I hope Dr. Bergeron is having better luck at her new project. I haven't seen her all day."

"Well, you did find a gold cross, and that probably counts for something," Nylah said. She wished he'd find something. She had plenty of pictures of him in the pit of the damned, looking frustrated, surrounded by endless dirt.

"Five feet down and nothing but that, which, yes, good, all that, and half a broken cup." He knelt down again and pulled out the metal rod from his shirt pocket. He held it up to the sky, as if in prayer, and then started poking the ground methodically, three pokes in each location, moving over a few inches, three pokes into the dirt there, until he would cover all the ground within his reach. Being reassured that no artifacts were located in that immediate area, he would start to dig away the dirt to the next layer that had not yet been probed. "C'mon! Get lucky. One, two, three!" Suddenly he froze. Then he moved slowly and carefully and repeated, "One... two... three." He bent down as if to listen to the ground. "Nylah, would you please go and find Dr. Bergeron? I think we might have something here and I don't want her to miss it."

Nylah took off at a run to find Everly, who was overseeing a new discovery of a cesspit on the Knightsbridge side of town, a real structure with bricked-in walls. She'd been very excited about it, going on extensively about all things related to ancient poop and soil samples.

Nylah ran up, a bit breathless. "Everly! Dr. T needs you!"

"What? Is he okay? Did he get hurt or something?" She picked up the walkie-talkie, a questioning look on her face.

Nylah shook her head. "He's not hurt. It's just that his poker rod struck something. He didn't want you to miss it. If it's something, he wants you to be in the pictures for the website. Today's photoshoot day."

Everly's hand went up to brush her hair away from her face and Nylah grabbed her phone and snapped some shots. "Those were good! The new clothes look really good, Ev," Nylah said as she checked out the shot while they made their way over to the pit of the damned.

"They're really comfortable. I have to say I love them. I just hope they hold up. They're more like hiking clothes than dig site ones."

"They only have to hold up for the right pictures," Nylah said dismissively.

"Wait!" Everly stopped in her tracks. "He doesn't want me to miss it?"

"Yeah. If it's anything, he wants you in the picture."

"He does?"

"Uh, yeah. Said just the other day that it's your dig, too. C'mon, while he's a totally decent guy he also has like zero impulse control."

"It's my dig too... that's so... decent."

"I dunno what you were expecting, but c'mon."

"He's just not like any archeology professor I've ever met before."

"Let's be real, Ev: he's not like anyone *anybody's* ever met before. Dude's unique."

As they arrived at the pit that now required a ladder to enter, Trevor was excitedly prodding the ground with the rod, saying, "Oh my! Well now, that's interesting. Can only imagine what that can be…" and then, "Oh, Dr. Bergeron, you're here!" He stood up and looked at her, total confusion crossing his face. "Dr. Bergeron? Everly?" He looked her up and down.

"Uh, yes? Something wrong?"

Trevor caught himself and looked quite awkward. "Oh no, no, not at all. You just look different."

Involuntarily, Everly touched her hair. "Oh, that. Nylah's trying to create an image for the website photos. Do you think it's working?"

Trevor nodded, his mouth open a little bit. "Yes, I would say it's working."

"So, um, what did you find here?"

Even Nylah thought Everly sounded awkward. "Oh my god, it's like they're in high school," she muttered under her breath.

Pulling himself together, Trevor said, "Dr. Bergeron, I think we've got a live one!"

Everly burst out laughing. "Well, don't say that loud enough for Nylah to hear you or she'll run away!"

"I heard that!" Nylah called back.

"I think, just maybe, we've found our first skeleton. Which means…"

"It really could be a mass grave!"

"Right! And we're that much closer to solving the mystery of what happened in this little town." Trevor looked like a little boy at a county fair.

"Yes! And once we solve that… oh, then we'll return to our… lives." Everly turned away slowly and looked at the dirt at their feet. "And our universities."

Trevor's face fell. "Oh, right. Bollocks that. It's the beginning of the end, innit?"

"Pictures! Your fans are waiting!" Nylah called out impatiently from the side of the pit.

"Right, right!" Trevor said, pulling himself together. "Uh, won't you need to be closer to get good shots? How can you take them from way up there?"

"I don't do dirt. And I ordered a telephoto lens for my phone. It's really dope. Thank you, by the way."

Trevor blinked a couple of times. "Well then, Dr. Bergeron, shall we? For posterity's sake?"

They got down in the dirt and started working, with Nylah calling out instructions to them like she was photographing them on some type of Mother Earth catwalk.

"Just ignore her." Everly brought out her own probe.

"Right here," Trevor said as he put his hand over hers and they inserted the probe together. "Do you feel it?"

"That feels like bone!"

Trevor nodded, excitement filling his face. They carefully removed the dirt from around the harder structure, gradually revealing a skull. "Are you getting this, Nylah? This is specimen B, our second skeletal remain of the dig. Very exciting."

"I'm getting it, I'm getting it."

"Let's dig a bit more around here and see if we can reveal the neck and at least a part of the torso," Trevor said. They worked diligently for the next half hour until they uncovered the head, neck, and part of the shoulders.

"Oh my god, Dr. Payne, we've got clothing remnants. It looks like Specimen B is wrapped in some type of, well, being from Canada, I would call this seal cloth."

"Right, it's an impervious sort of a blanket or a rain cloak he's wearing." Trevor looked wide-eyed at Everly. "Maybe a linseed oil-impregnated skin? It's definitely some kind of skin. I mean, not many seals here in Bavaria. But that means there's a chance that it could have afforded some protection to his clothing, even during all this time. Do you think we could get so lucky?"

"Only one way to find out!" They dove in with their pointing spades and brushes. Everly gently pulled away the thin shell of the ancient waterproof remnant and they peered underneath. "Oh, my word. Look at that."

"It's heavily damaged but, I say, that's embroidery."

"That's what I thought."

"What do you have?" Nylah called down.

"We found an embroidered cloth. It looks like it might be hanging around his neck?" Everly called back up at her.

"So fancy dress! Was this dude one of the upper class, then?"

Trevor sat back on his heels. "It could only mean one thing. He was a priest."

"Oh, that is interesting. I'm switching to video."

"Let's just focus, shall we?" Everly said to Trevor. They got the remains uncovered down to the waist, and with Nylah taking video, they gently pulled back the waterproof cloak to reveal the man beneath. While the clothing was much disintegrated, the remains were clearly that of a man of the cloth, with long black cassock, once-white vestments, and a badly decayed orphrey around his neck. His arms were stretched down long in front of him, with hands clutching a metal cross, looking like it also might be made of gold, and hanging on a long chain around his neck.

They chatted away happily, giving one another directions and sharing hypotheses. Trevor moved back up to the head to do some more close examination, not realizing that Nylah was still taking video. "You know, he's got really nice teeth for someone in the thirteen-hundreds." Then he froze and said, "Oh no! Oh gods! I just pulled his bloomin' head off!"

Everly turned to him. "You what?"

"I just pulled his head off. It just came off in my hands." Trevor sat back and the skull went with him, leaving the rest of the body behind. "That won't be on the website will it? Me decapitating this poor man, this poor priest, who's already suffered enough, I mean, look at him, he's dead. Likely of the plague and now all this indignity seven-hundred years later."

Trevor looked up at Nylah with fear on his face, the skull still in his hands.

"Dr. T, it's not live news. It's a website. We can put up whatever we want." Nylah put one hand on her hip and looked skyward. "I can't believe I'm doing this."

"Doing what? I'm the one with a man's head in my hands!"

"I'm coming down there. You all need me to channel some serious Steven Spielberg here and give you some direction." She climbed down the ladder with the grace of a dancer. "Now, Dr. T, you lean back in there and pretend his head never came off, right? Ev, let's make sure you're in the shot. And then I'm gonna interview you both about the find. We'll get some good website footage and I can pull stills from the video. Now remember, Dr. T, your daddy's gonna be watching this."

Trevor blanched but turned to the camera and when Nylah pointed to him he spoke with a polished British accent, "And you see here we have evidence, rarely found, of the kind of ecclesiastical costume worn in the mid-fourteenth century. Dr. Bergeron, my esteemed colleague, what do you observe about our medieval friend here?"

Everly seemed to miss a beat but quickly recovered, and the two engaged in jargon-filled banter about different aspects of the find—his clothing, his posture, the exciting elements about the dig, which was likely to be a mass grave from the Black Plague.

Trevor looked back up at the camera and with his new accent said, "Yes, what a lovely way to be introduced to Specimen B, who is obviously 'Father B'. Isn't it interesting that he was buried here, in a suspected mass grave, as though he is still, after all these centuries, watching over his flock. What a good, good man."

"Aaaand cut! That's great!" Nylah called out from behind her phone as she finished their interview. "We'll make Father B into a star, if only posthumously. And you guys, you look pretty good in here too. I'm headed to Command Central to work on this footage. I'll send over a few of the college kids to help you. I'll bet they'd enjoy this seeing dead people stuff."

Everly turned to Trevor. "Um, what's with the accent?"

Trevor looked at her, confusion written all over his face. Sounding just like his everyday self, he said, "What accent?"

Chapter 9

Adelaide Trōst
September 1346

Adelaide put down her quill and re-read her letter. "Well, maybe that will move your heart," she said as she studied her writing. She wondered if she should put more emphasis on suffering, but then when she really thought about Bernard, suffering wasn't what came to mind. It was solitude, study, and structure. She rolled her eyes.

"Maybe I should give him *three* reasons why he needs to intervene! It's always a triad of everything with him." She tapped her finger on the table, pondering his strange obsession with three. And cats. How a person could be so attached to animals, she couldn't imagine.

She returned her gaze to her letter. "You should be more concerned with your sister and less concerned with yourself! You're a man of the cloth now, dedicated to the service of our Lord, as I should be. You should have no concern for yourself." It was what she wanted to say to him directly, but she didn't dare. There was so much she wanted to convey but it was not a woman's place. Not in her father's household.

Firstly, women were to be beautiful.

Secondly, they were to be quiet.

And thirdly, they were to be useful.

Useful, as in being sold off in marriage to gain wealth, relationships, or military power. So far, she was safe from being "useful", but she was always wary in case her father's greedy gaze fell on how he might place her on his personal chess board, moving her about, sacrificing her if need be, so that he could advance his ambitions.

A sharp knock on the door to her apartments startled her. "Come," she called out as she stood up and smoothed her skirts.

The doors flew open and her mother swooshed in, youngest child in her grasp. Little Dietmar had a toy soldier in his free hand, still playing out his fantasy even though his mother had him in tow.

"Thank you for knocking, Lady Mother," Adelaide said with a slight curtsy.

"You're a grown woman now. Your door should be knocked upon before entry. That's one of the many privileges of leaving childhood behind."

"When will you knock on my door?" Dietmar asked.

His mother ignored him. "I more than half expected I'd interrupt you at your prayers, but I see you've been writing letters." Lady Hedwig nodded approvingly towards the desk with its papers, ink, and quill.

"Yes. To Bernard."

"Hooray Bernard! I want to see Bernard!" Dietmar squealed.

"Yes, Dietmar. We all would like to see Bernard, but he's far away now." Hedwig gave her son a smile and readjusted her hold on the hand of the squirming lad.

"He has a vo… vo… a vocation." Dietmar flushed with satisfaction when he got the word right.

"Yes," his mother groaned. "Please don't remind me. There's been no end to your father's complaints about Bernard defecting from the aristocracy to become a priest!"

"But he was called! Mother, he had no choice. When the Lord calls you, you must follow." Adelaide was shocked that her mother could deny the power of the call of the Holy Lord.

"When your father is a lord and he calls you, *then* you have no choice."

"Mother!"

"Oh, don't lecture me about blasphemy, Adelaide. You only became an adult this year and even though you've nearly worn out your Bible already, your *life* experience is rather thin to start lecturing me. I am twenty-eight years older than you. The Holy Lord only calls you twice in your life: to be born and to die. Everything else is just in-between and up to you."

Adelaide's heart jumped. This was her chance. "I'm so glad to hear you say that, Mother. Since I'm now an adult and this in-between is up to me, as you say, I know just what I want to do with it. I know exactly what I feel called to be. But I need your help. I want to become a nun. That is my place in life and…"

"Don't start with that again, please, Adelaide!" Lady Hedwig put her hands over her ears, dropping her hold on Dietmar, who instantly began running about, making the most of his freedom. She followed him briefly with her eyes and then seemed to give up, letting him engage in his boisterous play. When she spoke her voice was full of forced patience. "Adelaide, my dear, your piety is a credit to you. It's a credit to our whole family. Your devotion is remarkable."

"The Lord needs me as a part of his army."

"Your father needs you more. You are born into a life of privilege, Adelaide. The nobility. You need to be a shining beacon to the people, because of your goodness, *but not as a nun!* Oh, and now that I'm thinking of that," she pulled a small bag of coins out of a pocket of her dress, "the next time you go to market, make sure you are seen giving alms to the poor. Use this." She handed Adelaide the bag.

"The poor?"

"Yes, the poor. Your reputation for piety is a great asset to your father, but he needs our family to be seen as generous and you're just the person to fulfill that duty. So, tomorrow, when you go to market to buy those ribbons you were talking about, hand out the alms to the poor."

"But they're so dirty."

"You can wash the coins if you'd like. It's a little like what your Uncle Eberhard would do…" Hedwig gave her daughter a hard look, peering at her as if to see whether she was also going to manifest some of the more bizarre traits of her husband's family.

"What? I mean the people. The people are so dirty. The last time you asked me to do that, they touched me. One of them smudged my dress." Adelaide shuddered at the thought of having to get close to those people again. They smelled terribly. They pawed at her. Touched the fine braids in her hair. Always begged for more, as if what she gave them was never enough. *And their teeth!*

"Of course, they're dirty: they're poor. In fact, the dirtier the better! That will help your father's reputation. But, darling, try to smile."

Adelaide tried to force a smile to her face while simultaneously suppressing a shudder at the thought of what her mother was commanding her to do.

"You look like you're about to bite someone," Dietmar said seriously. Then his toy soldier knocked over a vase of flowers.

His mother gave a well-practiced leap and caught the vase before it hit the table. "Now, Dietmar, I've told you: your soldiers can't attack the house. And that includes your sister's apartments."

"How come she gets apartments and I'm still in the nursery?"

"When you are older, you'll have a set of rooms of your own, just like your sister. Just like Adolfus has. But while you're still a child, you will stay in the nursery where everything around you is not quite so breakable!"

Adelaide looked about, trying to think of a solution to entertain Deitmar. Books weren't the answer. Unlike his two older brothers who would happily lose themselves in any book there was to be had, Dietmar was an active child, a physical type. "Here, brother, look at this!" She threw several pillows onto the floor. "Look at this mountain!

This is a hill for your soldier to take—if he can…" She smiled at him as his face lit up, accepting the challenge.

"My darling daughter, try to smile like *that* when you hand out the alms to the poor."

Adelaide stared at her mother. "I have no idea what you mean. I always smile just like that. That's my smile."

Hedwig gave a deep sigh and looked to the heavens as she shook her head. "On another matter, we will be having guests to dinner in three weeks' time. As a woman of the household, you will have two duties. First, you will plan the dinner with the steward. I will be available for consultation should you need me, but this is your moment, Adelaide. It's an important dinner and your father is generously allowing you to show off your talents."

Adelaide felt her heart skip a beat. "I have talents in hosting? But I've never planned a meal in my life."

"Yes, I know. That's why I will be available for consultation. I want you to impress your father and he wants you to impress his guests. So, impress them, Adelaide."

Adelaide looked down and gave her mother a curtsy, smoothing her skirts. "Yes, Mother. And what is my other duty?"

"It's a festive dinner. The mood should be upbeat. Happy. Adelaide, I expect the menu to reflect that and not look like it belongs on some monk's meager table. And you should be festive. Social. Entertaining."

Adelaide gave her mother a sideways glance. "If it's entertaining you want, perhaps you should ask Adolfus?"

"Most amusing," her mother replied, not sounding at all amused.

"Who will the guests be?"

"Your father has invited the Engelhaft household. All of them," Hedwig said with a sigh.

"They're merchants. Oh! That's why I'm being allowed to plan the evening. Because they *aren't* nobles in rank."

Lady Hedwig gave her daughter an appraising look. "Merchants, perhaps. But wealthy. And well-connected. Influential, maybe not because of station but because of skill. Your father wants the Engelhafts on his side. This dinner is meant to lay the foundations for his plans in the future."

Adelaide could feel the tears welling up in her eyes. She felt the dam of emotions break over her. "It's always about his plans! His goals! His needs! What about what I want? When is it my turn to have what I want?" She stamped her foot. She was startled by the sharp slap across her face that stopped her tears and the shriek in her voice. She looked at her mother's face and began to tremble.

"You *will* remember your place. You will remember that you are a daughter of the Duke of Lotharingia. You are third cousin to the king. You are niece of a bishop. And that given your exalted station in life, you will be respectful of the important opportunities your father gives you. You will plan this dinner and it will be festive and light-hearted and fun. I don't want any crosses decorating the room. I don't want any talk of suffering. If the men drink, smile and offer them more. No sermonizing. Do you hear me, young lady?"

"Yes, Mother," Adelaide answered weakly. Her mother scooped up Dietmar from the pile of pillows and swooped out of the room, just as she had come into it. Adelaide threw herself on her bed and cried.

Chapter 10

Everly

The evening was still young and the Brandenburg students had retreated in their little touring bus to their host families in the town of Miltenberg. Trevor and Everly were going over the day's notes as Nylah uploaded content to their new website. Trevor moved over to the computer table, located conveniently close to the solar powered battery block, and leaned over Nylah's shoulder to study the computer screen. "I like what you're doing, with the website and all. It's very posh looking. Exciting."

"I'm so glad, boss! Here, look at the new pictures I uploaded."

"Who is… oh my."

"Let me introduce you to Dr. Everly Bergeron, titles, credentials, blah, blah, blah, and Dr. Trevor Payne, Junior, academic hoo hah, yah, yah, yah." She turned to Trevor. "All smarty-pants sounding, just like you wanted. Huh? What's wrong? What's the matter?"

"I, I just, well…" He was stammering and looked like he couldn't help himself. "That bloke?"

"Yeah, that's you."

"I mean I know it's me. Nylah, what did you do to these pictures? Just how crazy did you go with photoshop?" He got very close to the screen, scrutinizing it.

Nylah put a hand on his shoulder and gently moved him back. "Dr. T, you can blow up the screen, see. You don't have to get nose prints on the computer, geez. Just make the image bigger."

Trevor blinked a couple of times and shook his head while Nylah used two fingers and expanded the image on the screen. "Nylah, the alterations you've made are…"

"What alterations? What're you talking about?"

Everly put down her pen and came over to the screen.

Trevor looked at Everly with consternation and pointed to the image. "I don't look like that."

Nylah looked at the screen and then at Trevor and then back at the computer. "You're not happy with how you look?"

Everly looked at the shot, unable to figure out how Nylah had altered it. Given the way Dr. Payne was reacting, she initially wondered if Nylah had added forty pounds and gray hair to him as a joke.

Trevor was still flustered. "Happy! Yes. Who wouldn't be happy to look like that? I'm wondering who you got to stand in for those pictures. I mean, that bloke only vaguely looks like me."

Nylah looked at Everly, who shrugged back at her. Everly couldn't imagine what he was upset about. She knew there would be pictures of her, too, on the website, but those would pale in comparison to Trevor's.

Nylah shook her head, a bit confused. "I hate to break it to you, Dr. T, but that is you. That is what you look like, on camera and off."

Trevor chuffed. "You need to be a photographer. Clearly that's your calling." He shook his head. "Wait 'til my old step mum sees this."

"Oh, she's left like a dozen comments already. She's a huge fan of the site. Asked me to send her the original digital images. Oh, and you're supposed to call her back."

"What? *She* called?"

"Yeah. She's great to talk to. Nice lady."

Trevor turned to Nylah, wide-eyed. "And my dad?"

"Has yet to comment. Or give us a like. Let's scroll a bit, see more of the pics. And then you can call your mom."

"Not mum. Step mum. Um, anyway, sure. Right. Oh look, there's Dr. Bergeron. She looks very…"

"Fabulous! Ev, the new hair, totally hot. You got game, girl!"

"Professional! Professional! Dr. Bergeron looks *intelligent* and, yes, smart."

"Uh, Dr. T, 'intelligent' and 'smart' are the same thing," Nylah corrected.

Trevor gave her a look. "Oh, this is one of those cross-cultural moments, innit? I meant it as *snappy* or *posh,* as we say in the U.K."

"Oh. In the U.S. it means stuff like *you do well on tests.*"

"I'm sure she always did that!" Trevor said with a nervous smile. "And it can mean that too."

Everly leaned into the screen, rather amazed at what she saw. There she was looking like herself, only enhanced in some way. She reached up and touched her hair, feeling the tight ringlets.

Nylah's hand came up and pulled Everly's down. "No touchie. That's the secret. No touchie once it's perfect."

"Yeah, right," Everly answered. She'd seen pictures of herself on digs before, sure, but she always looked like a blocky Minecraft character, given the traditional clothes one wore on a dig. Digs were rough places and the tough clothes that were perfect for the work just weren't made for women—there weren't enough female archeologists to create market demand. So women were stuck wearing the smallest men's clothes they could find, which, of course, never actually fit. *Boyfriend clothes,* she thought with a blush. Nylah had dressed her in completely inadequate attire, done her hair and makeup so that she could get shots that looked more like they came from a movie set than a historical dig. And now the features on her face stood out. Usually, she looked kind of blurry and indistinct.

"Oh, hey, if you all like this, check out the video blog!"

Trevor and Everly leaned down in unison to watch the video of them uncovering "Father B", conversationally narrating the find for the camera.

"Don't worry, I didn't include the footage of you pulling the head off."

Everly was all smiles. "This is good stuff. Nylah, cancel you being a photographer. You should be a producer. It looks like it could play on the BBC."

"And, for some really weird reason, Dr. T, you *sound* BBC-ready, too." Nylah had a smirk on her face.

"I'm sure I don't know what you're talking about," Trevor said, still sounding comfortably East London. "Wait a minute… what do you mean by *Father B's Bad Ass Blog?*" He pointed at the screen and then turned to Everly, a look of incredulity on his face.

"Hey, I told you I'd make him a star! Wait 'til you see this! I animated his head so he looks like he talks. He's such a badass!"

"Oh no, Nylah. You can't do that. It's not respectful." Everly's eyes were wide. She knew that a twenty-year-old would probably need to be coached about how to treat the physical remains they uncovered, but she'd never actually thought of having to talk about the reputation of the remains.

"But he gives the hot dirt from the dig."

"Do we have hot dirt? Do you mean news? From the dig? Did I miss something?" Trevor sounded astounded.

"Course we do. All the finds. They just needed an angle."

"Why would they need an angle?" Everly asked.

"Everything needs an angle. And let's face it, the world's not gonna get too worked up about a bunch of old bones, even if one of them's a newly-headless ancient priest. What? I got my inspiration from him." She pointed over Trevor's shoulder at the skull sitting atop a tall metal filing cabinet. "Uh… just how long are you going to keep his head over here in Command Central anyway?"

"What? Oh, that. I dunno. I just like him." Trevor turned around and picked up the skull. "Don't know why. Just felt right. Like one of the ancestors looking over the dig. Being a part of the team, right? Like he's included and one of us. Part of the local community right here, cheek to cheek, as it were, while we discuss our findings." As he spoke he held the skull up next to his head.

"That's weird." Nylah shook her head and looked at Everly.

"Yeah, I thought that was weird too… until you just explained it that way. Now, I'm not so sure."

Trevor gave one of those characteristic little wiggles he did when he was excited or nervous. "I dunno. It seemed respectful." Then he held the skull, looking like Hamlet posing with Yorick, and addressed the relic. "What do you think, Father B? You were the shepherd of the flock to these people, with them right 'til the end, black plague and all, not that you called it that. Blue sickness it was sometimes called. By the end, once you started to understand the toll it was taking, it was dubbed *The Great Mortality*." He turned back to Nylah and Everly and shrugged. "Seemed right, somehow, for him to help oversee bringing them all back to the light. Like he'd want to be here. And, well, he's got such nice teeth."

"Still weird." Nylah shook her head like her boss was a lost cause. "But I know how close you feel to him, so I gave him his own byline." The animated image of the skull was moving around, nice teeth and all. "Ta Da! A star is born!"

Everly snickered, "I think you should say 're-born'."

"Born again?" Trevor said but he moved the skull as if Father B had offered the idea.

Everly crossed her arms and thought. "If he's the spokesperson for the dig, then Father B would be talking about his holy orders…"

"That's it! *Father B's Holy Orders*! Perfect!" Nylah nearly shouted with excitement, did some quick typing and clicking, changing the title of the blog.

"Can you make that dancing animated gif into a still? I mean, he's a priest and not a tap-dancing pirate." Everly thought how they represented the man was important.

Nylah typed and clicked for a bit, working on the computer. "There, that isn't nearly as fun, but it's got class and style."

"Uh, Nylah," Trevor asked, "don't you think that maybe Father B should tell them the truth about the gold cross? I mean, he is a priest and all."

"What do you mean? This is all accurate."

"Well, in a manner of speaking it is. Or it might be. I mean, we don't really know if the Holy See of the time actually blessed this cross," Trevor said.

"Okay, wait a minute. There. Now Father B only says it was *worthy* of the blessing of the pope," Nylah said as she nodded at the screen.

Everly pointed to the page. "And the pope at the time wasn't Francis, that's like the last pope. Or maybe the current one. I lose track of the living, to tell you the truth. Back then it was Clement the Sixth. No, no. You do the sixth in Roman numerals, a capital V, and an I. And he didn't live in Rome at the time. He was in France. In a place called Avignon actually."

"Okay, all correct now!" Nylah announced as she finished typing.

"You do leave a lot to the imagination." Everly muttered as she bent toward the screen to read Nylah's creative fiction.

"Right, and that's what I'm worried about," Trevor finished her sentence. "Just maybe we should tell the truth about the cross and the dig…"

"I hate to break it to you, Dr. T, but archeology is b-o-r-i-n-g."

"Well, that's quite crushing to hear from your scholarship work study student." Trevor said it as though what he'd heard didn't surprise him at all.

Nylah sat up poker straight and assumed a perfect BBC-style British accent. "Today we dug in the dirt and found nothing. Just like yesterday. But the day before, we found more dirt, interesting soil samples, and most fascinating, a broken cup! And under that... more earth."

Trevor looked at Everly. "Blimey, don't tell me I sound like that?"

"Not... very... often." She still couldn't figure out where that "posh" accent had come from as soon as Nylah started filming. Apparently, it was still on Nylah's mind as well.

"Guys, it's yawning-dull dirt and a few broken cups. It needs a little help."

"A little help? Is that what you mean by 'legions of the dead awaiting to be resurrected from the pit of the damned'? No wonder my dad hasn't even given us a like yet."

"Nah, that's brilliant," Nylah said. "But this cross is just crying out for a name. How about 'the golden cross of... of... hey, what was the name of this little village anyway?"

"Haven't I told you? So sorry, you should know where you're working, even if it hasn't been on a map for centuries. From what we know, it was called *Dreibergtaldorf*."

"What?"

"*Dreibergtaldorf*." As Trevor said it, it rolled off his tongue.

Nylah leaned back in her seat, one eyebrow raised. "Yeah, uh, if you did tell me that, there's a reason I didn't get it."

Trevor smiled. "The Germans do like their long words. But for being a people who make smashing good sausage, excellent beer, and some quite passable chocolate, I have to admit they aren't very creative when it comes to naming things. Tell me, Nylah, if you were going to found your little dream village here in this lovely spot, what would you call it?

"Sun Valley or maybe Mystic Mountain Town."

Everly said with a smile, "I'd call it Eden. Yeah, if Eden were located anyplace, it would be here. This spot is gorgeous."

Trevor stared at her for a moment. "Well, that's quite lovely, innit?" Missing a beat, he turned back to Nylah. "Um, maybe you should be in advertising as your calling. But no, the early Germans didn't do anything quite so poetic. A very literal lot, the Germans. The name actually means 'Three Mountain Valley Village'. Highly descriptive, innit? Three mountains, count them: one, two, three. *Drei*, that's three. *Berg's* a mountain. One valley, which is the *Tal* part, and then their village, or *Dorf*. While that's long, it's a real stretch of creative license that they didn't name it Drei-Berg-Eines-Tal-Eine Kleine Dorf Stadt! It could almost be its own haiku."

"Yeah. Uh huh. It's not going to be *The Cross of Eine-Kline-Dorf-Stadt*. I'm calling it *The Cross of the Holy Order*. That sounds medieval and it goes with Father B's new blog. Most importantly, it sounds like a movie title. And *that's* what we're going for."

Everly pointed to a map on the page. "Nylah, this map isn't right. The dig site isn't located here."

"Oh, I know that. I'm from New York. Duh! You never put your *real* personal information online. That's why everyone has a handle." The confused looks on their faces led to her giving a heavy sigh. "A fake name. Since we didn't have any name at all I went with a fake location. Lest you want, you know, tourists here."

Everly shook her head. "No tourists at the dig site. No, no, no. It's a liability."

"They're a bloody nuisance!" Trevor said. "Walk all over. Pick up artifacts. Take 'souvenirs'. Good thinking to give us a fake profile, Nylah."

"Agreed," Everly said. "How about going with 'Sun Valley' as the location? That way it'll sound like we're out in Utah or Idaho or someplace with lots of ski resorts, and people will show up there instead of here."

"Good idea!" Trevor said. "Because the way you've described this gold cross is pretty spectacular. I wouldn't want anyone to get the wrong idea and decide they might like it in their own private collection, if you know what I mean."

"Like steal it? Like rob from a dig site?" Everly asked.

"It's been done before." Trevor shrugged. "I mean, just ask the Egyptians."

They moved to sit around the table and talk about the next day's schedule and as Trevor sat down, Nylah brought him the phone.

"What am I supposed to do with this?"

"Duh. Call your mom, I mean step-mom, remember?"

"Now?"

Nylah just gave him a look and Trevor's eyes darted around guiltily, and then he started tapping in numbers. He moved over to the squashy chair while Nylah and Everly huddled over the site map and schedule directives.

Trevor wiggled in the chair a bit, listening to the phone. "Nobody home!" he announced, the relief evident in his voice. Then suddenly he sat bolt upright and with a perfect posh British accent he said, "Oh, hullo, Amelia. My team said that you called? Oh yes, very nice, smashing dig. Lovely time… Father would love it." He got up and proceeded to walk outside the tent. "I'm glad you liked the photographs. Yes, Nylah's very talented…. Oh, she enjoyed talking with you as well…. And how is Father doing? Up and walking about yet? Oh, that doesn't sound good…."

Nylah's eyes flew open. "The dude code switches!"

Everly shook her head slightly, her brows furrowed.

Nylah looked towards the tent opening and then back at Everly. "You know, code switches."

Everly shrugged.

"You know, like how you talk with your friends in one way but then you straighten up your language to talk with your momma, 'cause she's not gonna brook all that street talk. She'll lecture you, 'a lady doesn't talk like that', and don't get me started on Grandma! Man, she's a stickler, but Dr. T does the same thing! He talks with us like he got some character role in a Disney flick but then his momma gets him on the phone and he goes all BBC suddenly. That's the British version of code switching!"

Everly nodded. "Hey, you talked with his, uh, stepmom? What does she sound like?"

Nylah shrugged. "Like the royal family."

"Ohhhh. Yeah. He can't talk around her like he talks around us." Everly looked out the flap of the tent to where Trevor was pacing and talking on the phone. "That must be weird, to have an accent that's not the same as your parents."

Nylah nodded. "Sounds like classic dysfunctional family shit. Did you see how stiff he got as soon as she got on the line? Like he was a little boy in trouble."

"Well, you never know what's going on with someone, do you? It's complicated. Relationships are complicated." Everly turned her attention back to the documents on the table. "And messy. Really messy."

"Huh," Nylah said, staring up at the ceiling of the tent, thinking.

"What?"

"I bet Dr. T talks like the family he identifies with… and that's *not* his parents. Unless… hmmmm. I wonder if Dr. T's dad… the documents in the filing cabinet say he works at Cambridge University."

"Yeah, that's right."

"What's that like?"

Everly thought for a moment and then answered, "Old world posh. Not East London like the Dr. Payne we know sounds."

"Uh huh. You think old daddy-O might actually have come from a low-born life, sounding a lot like Dr. T does, but he well, he re-made himself so that he'd fit in with, what did you call it? Posh? Posh society. You know, so he could pass for a professor at Cambridge University? Amelia," she jerked her head toward Dr. T and his phone call, "in our conversations, she was that period-drama kind of genteel. I imagine that fitting in with her parents would be, well, you know, would be something. But our Dr. T, man, he just doesn't jive with all that. Bet he feels it's phony."

Everly stared at Nylah. "Give it rest, Sherlock Holmes. Who knows why he's the man of many accents? Let's work on the dig plans."

After several minutes Trevor returned to the tent. He picked up Father B and brought him over to where the women were sitting, setting him down next to the golden cross which sat on a stand at one end of the table, much like it would have on the altar of the medieval church.

"Must he?" Nylah asked. "I'm sure he wouldn't approve of today's tablecloth."

Back in his usual accent, Trevor said, "Of course he would! You know, it's my dad who always insists that a tablecloth is laid out properly on this very table. No dig should be without it. Civilization brought to our Command Central tent!"

"This tablecloth may be fancy fabric and not picnic plastic, but it's an image of a giant-headed cartoon guy holding a toilet plunger." Everly gave him a sideways look and wondered if this was actually a rather petty way at getting back at his overly-controlling father who also sounded like British royalty.

"Well, what daddy doesn't know, won't hurt him." Trevor poured Father B a small glass of the sweet German wine they were drinking. "There you go, mate."

Nylah looked askance at the glass. "Not very generous are you? I mean, he's got to be almost eight-hundred years old and I'm underage, yet I get a bigger portion than he does."

"Trying to be respectful of his lower body weight," Trevor answered. "And in Germany, you *are* of age."

"Have I said lately how much I love Germany?"

"Only when Hans is around," Everly said with a laugh. "So, team," she nodded to Father B, "extended team… okay, well, let's get the dig schedule planned out for tomorrow."

They worked for another hour, with Trevor regularly asking Father B to ring in with a "You like this, right? Sure, look at that smile." After calling it quits the women retired to their tent and Trevor stayed behind at Command Central to finish up a bit.

When Everly headed to what she euphemistically called "freshen up central", the port-o-potties and tents that served as their bathroom and showers, she heard talking. Curious, she followed the sound, discovering it was Trevor's voice, like he might be on a phone call.

"But he's never happy. It's never good enough, is it? So, what do you think I should I do?"

Everly wondered if he might be talking with his stepmother but then realized this was the normal sounding Trevor, not the stiff sounding one.

"Right, right." His voice sounded distracted. "You could be more explicit. No? I mean, you're just a bit vague. Well, thanks for listening anyway. You've got a real talent for listening even though you're missing ears."

Everly scooted along to brush her teeth. It was late and she wanted to hit her cot so she'd be rested for their big day tomorrow.

Hours later, she was dead asleep when Nylah shook her arm with an insistent whisper.

"Ev! Wake up! Wake up."

'Huh? What is it?" She asked sleepily.

"Shhhh! Someone's out there. Listen."

Everly sat straight up and listened while she tried to pry the vise-like grip of Nylah's frightened hand off her arm. Sure enough, there were rustling sounds like people were moving around, trying, but not quite succeeding at being quiet. The sound of indistinct whispers and grunting-like signals gave her a chill. "Oh my god, do you think…"

"It's my fault."

The moon was bright, giving a dim nightlight effect through the walls of the tent. Everly shook her head with incomprehension and looked at Nylah.

Nylah leaned right into Everly's ear and said, "The website. The golden cross. They found us. I think someone's come to steal it! Just like we were talking about tonight!"

Everly felt her heart race. "We can't let them do that! We have to do something!"

"Everly, it's a thing. A hunk of eight-hundred-year-old junk. It's not worth it. Let it go."

Everly shook her head slowly. "It's everything I've ever worked for. It's my career. Promotion. Tenure. Security. I'm not letting anyone take that away from me."

"Well, whoever is here to nab it is thinking it's their security too. Look, I lost a friend in high school, shot over a three-hundred-dollar pair of sneakers. Not worth it. It's stuff. Really cool, old stuff, but still, stuff."

Everly would have objected, sure that Father B would have told them to save his cross, but the shushing and snuffling sounds of the search reached the walls of their tent. The two women stiffened and froze and before long the steps moved away. Everly tried to figure out what she could use as a weapon.

Suddenly she heard a voice shout: "Who's out there?"

"He sounds really scared." Everly looked at Nylah.

"Duh. Dude's not an idiot."

Everly took Nylah's hand. "We have to help him."

Nylah looked at her a moment and then gave Everly's hand a strong squeeze, nodding. The two women stood up and approached the flap of their tent, slowly lifting it to look outside. Seeing no one, they moved stealthily through the grass, trying to make no noise, and they headed for Trevor's tent. When they reached his tent flap, Everly flicked it a couple of times with her finger.

"Who's there?" Trevor's frightened voice came from inside.

"It's us," Everly hissed and then ducked into his tent, dragging Nylah behind her.

There stood Trevor with a shovel in his hand, ready to strike. "Oh blimey, it's you," he said at full volume. "You scared the living daylights out of me." He lowered the shovel. "What are you doing out there?"

Wide-eyed, Everly and Nylah shook their heads slowly. Then they all heard it again, the shuffling and grunting-shushing sounds.

"They're after the artifacts!" Trevor whispered and raised his shovel again. He pointed to the side of the tent where a few other tools were lined up. Everly and Nylah each selected one and raised them up over their shoulders, readying for a fight. As a group, the three of them inched toward the tent flap. "On three," Trevor whispered.

"One… two… three!"

They all ran from the tent screaming, hoping to scare off would-be robbers and get to Command Central before valuable relics disappeared. As they crashed through the flap of the meeting tent, they yelled and waved their make-shift weapons about.

"There's no one here," Nylah said, breathlessly.

"It's still here!" Everly and Trevor said simultaneously as they dropped their tools, with Everly running to grab the cross and Trevor running to grab Father B's skull.

"He's safe!" Trevor sounded markedly relieved.

Everly looked over at him. "You were running into the face of danger to protect the *skull*?"

Trevor looked abashed, but said, "Shh! You'll hurt his feelings."

Everly shook herself to get a hold of her fear. "We are going to search the campsite and see if we can find our thieves. Arm yourselves, troops!" She took command. "Nylah, throw the switch for site lights. Trevor, follow me."

Nylah ran over to the control box and flipped up the switch for the floodlights, which illuminated the surroundings. With dig tools raised above their shoulders once again, they exited the tent, all following Everly. "No one is going to take tenure from me. No one," she said to herself through gritted teeth. With hearts beating wildly, they systematically searched the grounds, finding no intruders. No sign of anyone at all.

"Aw man! The perps got away. Why do the perps always get away?" Nylah threw down her shovel.

"Well, they didn't get away with anything valuable." The three of them looked at one another. "But they'll be back. We've got to find a better place to keep the cross. It's not safe here." There was a tinge of panic to Trevor's voice.

Everly nodded and Nylah looked numb. "How about Brandenburg? Can Gunther help us? Can they keep it for us at the university, at least for a while?" Everly asked.

"I'll speak with him tomorrow. Until then, I'll hide the cross."

"We might need to think about security measures," Nylah said. "Yup, we need bodyguards."

"Nylah, this is a dig site, not a movie set," Trevor said. "Not a bank. Not a diamond mine. We stay in the tents and not in town, so someone's here to discourage the curious. *We* are the bodyguards." Trevor looked thoughtful for a moment. "Well, at least Everly is. She's obviously the brave one among us."

Everly felt something curious. Something she'd never felt before. She'd always been rather timid, never speaking up at faculty meetings, lest she incur the ire of the powerful and particular interests who held sway at her institution. But now she felt... brave. She stood up straighter.

Trevor looked at her. "You're like a warrior. Like a Knight of the Cross, you are."

Everly struggled to fall asleep that night. When she did at last, she then dreamed of herself as a knight, a Joan of Arc character, full of the bravery she had never experienced in real life. She woke up ready to take on anything the world could throw at her. She felt her shoulders square as she moved about the camp and greeted the Brandenburg students as they disembarked from their little transport bus in the bright light of morning, ready for another day of work. They had their usual twenty minutes of what she called "playtime" and then she started to call them to order. Her little army. She was their Joan.

Dr. Gunther Heintzelman, along with Hannah and Heidi, joined the group, laughing and passing Trevor's leather hat between them.

"What are you doing with my hat?" Trevor asked them, snatching it back.

"Oh, Herr Doctor Payne, you can't drop your hat on the ground. Not overnight. It is not safe."

"Not safe? What do you mean? And I didn't intend to drop it. We had some excitement last night and it sort of got lost."

"*Jawohl.* And it got eaten," Gunther laughed.

"Eaten?" Everly asked.

"*Ja!* Look at the bite taken out of the brim!" Heidi was giggling and said in a teasing tone, "You have to be careful. They are very hungry when they come out at night."

"What are?" Everly asked.

"Wild dogs?" Nylah asked, her voice tight.

"Marmots," Gunther said with a broad wave at the mountains. "These hills are full of marmots."

Hannah looked at her summer professors. "And just what was the excitement last night?"

Trevor and Everly looked at one another. Everly looked back at the students and shrugged. "Nothing. It, it was really nothing."

Chapter 11
Friar Karel Tuckerschade September 1346

"Welcome, my friends," Friar Karel Tuckerschade said from the entrance of St. Drogo-Erasmus. It was going to be a small mass today. Maybe fifteen people. Others were heading to St. Cyprian's in droves. Not that the friar himself had ever had much of a following—even when he was the only clergyman in town and no matter which church he inhabited. He told himself that at least *he* didn't need to lure the people in with golden crosses and offers of free wine. He preached to the faithful. His people lived with a fear of missing their mass, the communion and lessons from him, and the repentance that saved their souls each week. He made sure they did. That was the role of the clergy, after all.

He closed the doors and as the entrance song started, Friar Tuckerschade walked up the aisle and bowed to the altar and started the mass. He particularly liked the Act of Penitence, reminding his small flock to recall their sins of the week, that the confessional would be open after mass, and that he, as their shepherd would relieve them of their sins. He found great comfort in that part, where he relieved the spiritual burden from these fine and faithful folk. After confessional, they would come to see him throughout the evening or some on the next day, and he would take the time and the care to remove the sin, each to his or her own need and circumstance. It was his pleasure, as their shepherd. It was his power, as a man of God. The divine power worked through him.

The service would move through the Gloria—a praise and adoration of glory to God in the highest, and then the Collect—the opening prayer that gave context for the mass and the upcoming homily. The Liturgy of The Word gave the people the word of God from the holy Bible—at least the memorized passages that he could recall—and they would sing the Responsorial Psalm. And then came the part he loved the most: the Homily, the part of the mass that helped each of the faithful live a better life and grow in their own holiness. He'd always thought about his homilies during the week, taking inspiration from even the smallest events that might happen during a day. But since that dratted Father Bernard had come and usurped his St. Cyprian's, the friar found that he perseverated on his homilies for the greater part of each day. They consumed him.

"Today, my friends, I bring you a story you well know, for we have talked on it many a time in these humble walls and under the blue sky of the Lord. The tale of Robin of Locksley, not a nobleman but a yeoman, my friends, a man who worked to earn his living, as do you and I. He wasn't a highborn son of a duke, come to seek his fortune among his lessers, to rule them and lord over them in the Lord's name. Among good Robin's friends, his Merry Men, was a man of the cloth, one of my own forebears: Friar Tuck. These simple men focused on the needs of the poor, the downtrodden, the faithful. Not the corrupt, wealthy barons of the major cities. They were the good shepherds and caretakers of the simple people, as I am your shepherd. I am your Friar Tuck."

"Friar Tuck! Friar Tuck!" the people shouted out, led by Wilhelm.

Good Wilhelm, thought Tuckerschade, *he knows his place and his cue.*

"We are the chosen. We are the repentant. And they will not replace us. Don't stretch your hand to them, for they will bite you. They mean to take what is yours, like they took Cyprian's from us! They cast us out and mean to hold us down. I call them the *warped*, for they are worthless, arrogant, rich, pompous, elitists who are damned." He looked at his small crowd, so proud of his cleverness, and so disappointed to see that not a one among them understood his wit. It was beyond the edge of his own literacy, but he remembered it from his days as an acolyte. With a sigh of acceptance of the dim wits of his followers, he continued: "We do not associate with the warped. They speak like the crazed, touting free education for all. What blasphemy! It is not the place for the common man to read. That usurper has set up a school and is even allowing girls to learn their letters and numbers! But then, I ask you, who will then spin the wool? Will you?" He pointed to one woman. She shook her head.

"Or you?" He pointed to another.

She shook her head as well. "I hated the combing and spinning even as a child. I'm a grown woman and I'm not doing it again! That be child's work."

"Right!" The first woman yelled back. "It's for them to sit in the corner and spin, not talking, but working!"

Friar Tuckerschade smiled. They may be too stupid to appreciate his cleverness, but their anger was easy to rouse. "While girls learn to read, who will fetch water for their families? Are we all to run naked and cold, with the winter coming on? Are we all to go thirsty?"

Grumbles of, "No! No!" started to echo around the room.

The friar surveyed his audience and saw that he had their attention bound as tightly to him as Christ was nailed to the cross.

"That apostate is warped, he is not one of us. He should be preaching not teaching! I ask you: what do you need to read for? It will make you indolent. It will lead to starvation, for who will work the fields, bake the bread, butcher the animals if they are off reading? Adventus, the Forty Days of St. Martin is nearly upon us. Do you want your feasting tables to be bare? Would you all look at a bare table covered with what? Pages? Books? Words and letters cannot feed the body. He would have you starve! Because he's of the warped. And soon comes Christmastide, for your quiet prayer on that day, do you not want to have hot soup? The leader of St. Cyprian's would have you reflect. But reflection does nothing to save your soul! You need to repent! Confess your sins and repent so that you may be forgiven and know that the kingdom of heaven awaits you."

"Save us, Friar Tuck! Save us!" resounded from the pews.

"Those folk from far off lands, from Cologne and Bonn, those warped people are not us! The warped are coming to destroy you and your way of life. The warped are coming to take your freedoms after *you* built this town. This should be a homeland just for us, just for those born and raised in Germania, right here in our mountains. In our valley. Not for the warped. Not for those who refuse to worship and repent and suffer for our God, but for *we* who show Christ that *we* suffer as He did. We don't want the warped outsiders here in our town. The three mountains surround us, ever to remind us of the holy trinity. Anyone who doesn't believe in the trinity and suffer the three-fold repentance, which is a part of us, then they aren't right for us. We loathe them and their ungodly ways, for they are warped, surely as the wood left in the rain bends and twists and becomes unusable."

"Ungodly heathens! Them and their fancy cesspits! They want us to shit in the pit and not on the street!" shouted one.

"The street is good enough for me!" called out another.

Friar Tuckerschade smiled at them. "If you do choose to go in the street, you might try the one behind St. Cyprian's, my friends, and show them what you think of their unrighteous ways and innovations." He said the word *innovations* with particular distain.

The crowd called out its approval of his suggestion. He was more than satisfied with his homily as he always enjoyed sermonizing his flock. Even if they completely lacked the capacity to appreciate his wit, his clever depiction of those not in his flock as unrighteous warped outsiders delighted him to no end. His sheepish followers responded with the passion and anger and enthusiasm that he coaxed out of them, week after week. These unwashed and downtrodden folk were now veritably growling at their village neighbors as they passed in the street, hardening a rift between them and the "warped" of the tiny burg.

Later, after the service, his people filed into the church for confession. This was his favorite part, learning about their weaknesses and falls from grace during the previous week. It gave him insight into how to help them willingly comply with his guidance and direction, for their Friar Tuck knew best.

A man named Cuonrat came and confessed how he'd lost his temper and taken it out on his cow, beating the poor beast. And when that didn't satisfy him, he searched for his son, who was wise enough to be nowhere to be found.

"He who would beat will receive the same," Karel said, feeling a sense of anticipation.

"Aye. You're right, Friar Tuck. Ah, the good Friar Tuck. You know what is best for our souls. I thought you might recommend that. And I willingly submit."

Tuckerschade had taught them to say *I willingly submit* to the atonements he prescribed. They were pliant as sheep. His sheep.

"And, you being my holy father, you'll surely be sainted one day, like Wilhelm always says." Cuonrat nodded solemnly. "Good father, I brought something you might smile over."

"And what is that, my son?"

"Just a brick of cheese."

"Cheese? What kind of cheese?"

"It would be a Münster, Good Friar Tuck."

"Oh. I do love Münster." Karel had a smile on his face, which then faded to a frown of suspicion. "Not Quark? You're sure it's not Quark?"

Cuonrat shook his head.

"A whole brick you say?"

"Aye. It be a small stone's worth, a respectable weight," Cuonrat said. "I wondered if maybe, just perhaps, that could figure into my redemption, now?"

"And it comes from the cow which was beaten?"

"Aye, in part."

Karel was silent for a short while. "I think the sacrifice of a brick of cheese is sufficient repentance for your sin, Cuonrat. I could allow it, as an… indulgence. 'Tis a discipline to make that sacrifice, and so the strap is not needed this week. You may leave your brick with me and go in peace, my son, for your sins are removed from your shoulders for this week."

"I thank you, good Friar. You are the shepherd we all need."

"So right. And just remember. I also like the white cheese with the holes in it."

"Hard to come by that, but I will remember." Cuonrat began to stand. "For a time when my sin is mightier than I can bear, I will bring the cheese like the Helvetians make, with the nutty taste and the small holes."

"Well, the next time you fall into bed with your brother's wife perhaps you'll bring a good size stone's worth of that and avoid the atonement that you'll meet otherwise."

"Aye. I will remember, as you always remember my past sins, and remind me, lest I forget."

The confessional followed a similar pattern and while Tuckerschade was given a spate of goods he sorely needed, as he produced little of his own food, it also left him feeling unsatisfied with the atonements for the week. There was much deprivation to be had, but very little in the way of true suffering. The last person to confess was Wilhelm.

"Father, I have come to confess my sins. Firstly, I looked at a woman today in a most unholy way. She smiled at me and I had impure thoughts."

"Hmmmm," Tuckerschade answered, not really listening. Wilhelm's loneliness drove him to desire women, but his poverty meant he would never have the courage to actually talk to one of them. It was the often the same, having to listen to Wilhelm's frustrated desires for the touch and affection of another.

"And I must confess, that I used the cesspit today."

This caught Karel's attention.

"And I must confess that I liked it. I didn't get shit on me shoes when I squatted down. I got to sit, like on a chair, but there be a hole in the chair! And when you make water it goes down the hole, but of course you have to point yourself in the right direction. I learned that the hard way. But the shit disappears! And while it smells, it's nothing like that from the street. And I must confess that I was uncomfortable with the idea of taking a piss behind a house of God. Any house of God."

Karel started to feel his temperature rise. "You were disloyal!" he uttered with a low growl.

"I confess that I had thoughts of disloyalty. And I willingly submit to me atonement."

Karel nodded, his anger raising in him at this betrayal. "We will meet in my kitchen after all have departed. I will minister to you before bedtime tonight."

"Thank you, good Friar, for relieving me of me sin."

"It shall be done. Go forth and sin no more."

That evening Friar Karel Tuckerschade stood in his kitchen, his strap in hand. Wilhelm was before him, naked, kneeling on the little pile of his clothes. "I am ready to submit, my father. I thank you for taking the sin from me." Wilhelm bowed his head, waiting.

The friar swung his arm a few times to warm up and then started to strike his acolyte.

Wilhelm cried out, "I suffer as did Christ! May the Lord forgive me of me sins!"

"You may say your rosary after I finish with the strap." Friar Tuckerschade let out a long slow breath. This was improving his mood. Removing the sin from the sinner, stripping it away through his sweat and the sinner's blood was always a path back to himself, a way to calm and center himself. The cries of pain never failed to quell his inner demons, which at the moment were tormenting him with jealousy and avarice for all that had been taken from him.

He swung his arm back again, poising for another blow. "I will not let him bleed the faithful away from me. They are my people. I will not let him re-make this village into his own warped image. Putting him into power." Under his breath he said, "Just like that damn bishop."

Karel Tuckerschade had been denied elevation in the church, been told he was unfit. Was stuck in this backwater village of nothing, living in poverty. Preaching to the few faithful, teaching them to be frightened and to repent, punishing those who showed any signs of questioning his authority. And then one day this Father Bernard showed up, with holy orders to set up his church on the other side of town. "A man could get into real trouble in telling the truth," he explained to Wilhelm as he sweated. "But from the altar I have no choice but to speak the truth. Men who told the truth in their day later became saints at the hand of the Holy See, that's the pope, 'cause that's the punishment for telling the Lord's sheep the truth. But the holy men who tell the Lord's truth are rewarded in heaven. So, I will embody the bravery of heaven most high to tell the truth that gold is the devil's weapon. He uses it to put lust and avarice in the hearts of men. It may be cleverly carved to look like a cross, but 'tis a golden idol. And as we know, it was a golden idol that kept the wicked out of the promised land. You want to go to the promised land, don't you?"

"I do! I do want to go to the promised land."

Karel shook himself out of his reverie and looked at Wilhelm's back. He had gone further than he'd meant to. Wilhelm had sinned but this punishment was meant for a greater sin yet, one greater than Wilhelm would have the capacity to commit at any point in time.

Karel took a deep breath and shook himself, wiping the sweat from his brow. "Your sins are washed from you, Wilhelm. You are now made pure. You will be rewarded and heaven's gifts will shower down upon you, both here and in the hereafter."

"Oh, Friar Tuck, you're a good man. A holy man, just like your forebear you're named for! They'll saint you someday for sure," Wilhelm said in a shaky voice as he slowly stood and started to pick up his clothes. "I feel shriven, for sure I do."

The friar looked at his back. "Aye, you have been, my son. You have been." He thought for a moment. "Why don't you sleep in the small room off the kitchen tonight."

"And not in the barn with the beasts?"

"Not tonight. I'm sure they will be fine. Sleep there and know that you've been forgiven."

"Is that one of the rewards you said would shower down upon me?" Wilhelm looked stunned.

Karel thought and then nodded.

Wilhelm gave him a grateful bow and as he was retreating to the little room he turned, still naked and said, "I hope you make a sermon about what you were saying. Powerful that was. *Gold is the devil's weapon. Telling the truth is dangerous business.* It gave me shivers, it did."

Karel nodded. "I will. You're right. It is powerful. I will give it in a homily."

He poured himself a glass of wine and cut himself a slice of his new brick of cheese, but a knock at the door interrupted him before he could enjoy any of it. It was Jezzie.

"And what would the likes of the town prostitute want from the good Friar Tuck?"

"Well, I missed the mass today. Had business to attend to, if ye know what I mean, and I never got to confess or receive the holy communion."

He looked the brazen woman up and down. "I'm surprised that mass and confession mean enough to you to show up at my door at this time of night."

She shrugged. "Night's me time, ain't it? And given my line of work, confession and absolution are the most important part of my week, the way I see it."

Friar Tuckerschade snorted. "But atonement doesn't get you to change your behavior. Why should I absolve you of your sins?"

She gave him a level look. "And what man or what woman changes their behavior? Don't they come and confess the same old sins to ye? Why, old Cuonrat sleeps with his brother's wife every time he gets the chance. That never changes. It's all right with his brother actually, because his brother doesn't like his wife that much and he'd rather be off with the milkmaid. Or with me, iffen he got any coin! And Cuonrat will beat on his cow if it's not giving as much milk as he'd like it to, not that that helps the cow milk any better. But they come and confess to ye and they never changes. People don't make changes. So why should I? And why should ye care? Ye got something to sell: absolution. I got something to sell: meself. And I'm here with a mind to buy."

Friar Tuckerschade started to get an idea. He felt he owed poor Wilhelm for his inattentiveness at his absolution earlier.

"I think we can strike a deal. I know just the atonement that 'tis right for you."

◆━◆━◆

Friar Karel Tuckerschade knelt down on the floor of his own humble bedroom, naked as Wilhelm had been. His discipline in hand, he started his own ritual of abasement and humility before God. Of suffering as Christ suffered. Of penitence. He had confessed, both to God and himself, although he had struggled to find worthy sins to admit to and lay before the Divine. As a man of cloth, he strove to live a life beyond reproach.

"Christ suffered and forgave us all."

He was sure that suffering atoned for any sin and righted you with the Lord in heaven. What he didn't anticipate was hearing all the noises from the other room. It was distracting and surprised him just how loud Wilhelm was with the reward being rained down upon him at the moment.

"It could be the cheese," he said aloud, thinking of how Wilhelm reacted to his rare bites of quality food.

Friar Tuckerschade resolved to strike himself until the prostitute left and all was quiet again, but he didn't anticipate how long that was taking and it disrupted his usual rhythm. Quickly he realized that his back would receive perhaps four times the blows as his typical pattern and that he needed to go much slower, but disrupting the pattern made it difficult to complete. Rhythm was important for making it through the practice. It meant he had long pauses between his strikes where he was forced to listen and wonder what was happening in the other room.

"This is suffering twice over!"

In the end he lay his discipline on the little table long before he met his goal and lay down on his bed.

The next day Wilhelm was moving slowly but with a smile on his face.

"Wilhelm, how are you today?" Karel asked.

"I be sore, to be sure, Friar Tuck. But I am a happy man. I slept well in that little room off the kitchen. I think the rewards you spoke about started to come to me already!"

"Oh really?"

Wilhelm blushed. "I was trying to fulfill me role in the church and you weren't there and I know to never bother you after you've retired for the evening. If you'll believe it, that Jezzie woman came to my room. That little one off the kitchen. She had a generous slice of *cheese* in her hand and she shared it with me. And then she… she… well, she said it was the Lord's own work that I needed to do so that she could be shriven of her sins, since I was a part of the church of St. Drogo's and all. And I couldn't say no to helping someone atone, now could I? She even told me that you'd said she should come to me for help. I be the one who could help her."

Friar Tuckerschade shook his head. "It's Drogo-Erasmus. And no, you couldn't turn her away. You must do as you are called upon, even as a mere acolyte in the church, to help the parishioners in all their needs."

"That's what I thought." Wilhelm was quiet for a moment and looked up at the sky with a small smile on his face. "Today I feel like a man with a clean conscience and a restored soul." He exhaled deeply. "Today, I am a happy man."

Chapter 12

Nylah

"Hey, Everly, what're you so excited about? Don't see you this animated usually!" Nylah enjoyed teasing her tent-mate, even if Everly was more than ten years her senior. Nylah was starting to think of Everly like the older sister she never had or maybe a really young aunt, also someone she'd never had. She found it funny that you didn't know how much you wanted a certain type of relationship until unexpectedly it was there and suddenly you understood just what you'd been missing. Nylah had wanted an older sister. She'd just never known it.

"Oh, I suppose I *am* pretty stoked. Look here: these are clothing remnants! Good ones. You know, there's this tomb in Prague that has really good samples of clothing from the same era. I went to see it. It was like a religious experience. And now we've found them in the most unlikely place." Everly gestured with the tongs holding her sample. "Right here. Right here in my forceps." She looked up towards the ceiling of the tent. "Thank God for clay soil! That's all I can say."

"You are such a geek. Wow."

"Nylah! These will be in a museum someday."

"But there's nothing to see. They're just torn up scraps."

"Maybe. But it's a lot of material for seven hundred years of wear and tear. These are the garments of a priest, and it's pretty interesting he was buried in his vestments."

"How so?"

"Well, it's what they wear during mass," Everly answered.

"So, like he dropped dead during a mass? Or he just wore them, like, all the time? Married to his work?"

Everly gave a chuckle. "Hard to say. It could be that for some reason, he was put into his most special clothing, his holiest attire, for his burial. But while a cassock, that's the black robe that you see priests in all the time, would be the norm, you just wouldn't expect an ordinary priest in an ordinary tiny town to be buried in his vestments *and* the church orphrey. Those weren't personal possessions—they were the church's. And he was quite purposely buried. Look at this: this was a sealskin cloak, and he was wrapped in it. Someone loved and cherished this man." Everly breathed out a heavy sigh. "I do hope we find some ordinary people and that we're lucky enough that they have clothing remnants too. No one knows that much about what people wore up in the highlands during that time. I mean, not much has made it through the ages unless you were a king or a queen—and those remnants have usually been found in royal tombs."

Nylah's eyebrows furrowed. "Did they dress that differently than in the cities? I mean, when I was in Hamburg everyone looked just the same as those who live in that totally dope village of Miltenberg where Hans lives."

Everly looked so animated that Nylah had to remind herself not to laugh.

"Oh, yes! Quite different. The mid-thirteen-hundreds turned out to be a revolutionary time in fashion history. Right here in Germania just before the Black Plague hit and spread throughout Europe, the clergy—the friars to be very specific—started to micromanage the fashion world. Back then there was a very clear distinction between bishops, priests, and friars. It was much more regimented. Sharing power, it seems, was just as difficult among the clergy as it was among the nobility. The bishops gave the friars the duty of regulating 'the morality of clothing', mostly because they had to give them something to do."

"The morality of clothing?"

"Fashion police of the worst type," Everly answered. "The friars prided themselves on their mathematical talents and they decided to control the guilds that made clothing by tight prescriptions on exactly how garments must be measured and cut and sewn. Of course, they didn't know squat about how to make clothes themselves, tailoring and seamstressing being carefully guarded guild secrets, so they gave really stupid directions."

Nylah blew out a breath. "I bet that was frustrating. I mean, I remember when the principal of our school got involved in the dance team uniforms. Oh my god, said we were showing too much skin. I remember asking her, 'have you even looked at what the girls wore to prom?' Yeah, she didn't much appreciate me sharing that information. No, she called it 'talking back', can you believe it? But those girls showed more skin than fabric. Uh huh. It was so unfair."

"Well, the guild felt similarly as offended as your dance team. And they fought back."

"Fought back?" Nylah wasn't actually interested in history, but she had to admit that Everly had her attention now. "How did a guild fight the clergy?"

"Oh, you'll like this: they followed the prescriptions to the extreme! To a ridiculous extreme. They made clothes that were so tailored that the outfits were nearly painted onto the people! There was nothing left to hide for the fashionable. Surviving paintings and drawings from the time show that highborn ladies wore off the shoulder dresses to fine occasions, and those dresses were so low cut they could just about walk a Hollywood red carpet today and fit in. Their uh, let's call it 'their modesty' would have been saved by fuzzy fur trimming!" Everly danced her fingers across low across her bosom. "And the young men wore tight leggings and body-hugging tunics that stopped just at the hips, which meant the tight leggings left little to the imagination. Think of full-legged speedos."

"Oh! That's just not right!" Nylah said as she wrinkled her nose.

"I'm with you. And as embellishments, the men wore large, heavily decorated purses. Hopefully for strategic coverage in the front, and quite often a dagger hanging down the back"

"Oh! To hide their butt cracks!"

Everly nodded. "Like I said, not much left to the imagination!" She laughed as she shook her head. "Clothes were really complicated back then if you were anything but a serf. The serf class basically threw on a single tunic—and nothing else. You know, I bet you'd be amazed at how rayon, elastic, and spandex revolutionized the world for us. But back then, nothing, and I mean *nothing* could be just pulled up—it all had to be tied onto you. So, people of any means at all wore a type of base clothing, think of a central rag tied around your waist, that the next items got progressively tied to. They were a bit like a ball of string by the time they were done dressing with everything tied onto everything else. Eh! Must have taken them forever to get dressed and undressed! Even the painted-on ones."

Nylah's lip curled. "So, old fat dudes and young skinny ones would parade about in painted on clothes? Oh! That is so not right."

"Ah… maybe right now isn't quite a teachable moment about judgey comments?" Everly gave Nylah the raised eyebrow look, "so we'll just keep focusing on history."

"Whaaaaat?"

"From paintings we have of older, more seasoned nobles, some also wore the tights, but more often what would look to you and me like pantaloons."

"What's a pantaloon?"

"Larger pants that came down to about the knee, with elaborate tunics that came down far past the hips, sometimes to mid-thigh. They were quite modest."

Nylah digested this information. "So, the old fat dudes looked like Henry the Eighth and the young, handsome ones looked like Robin Hood?"

Everly gave a wry smile. "I'm kind of afraid to endorse that idea by agreeing with it, but in the very largest sense… uh huh."

"So, did Robin of Locksley ever hold up Henry the Eighth?"

Everly nodded slowly and looked like she was thinking hard. "So, I'm guessing that maybe you, um, haven't taken in course in medieval English history? No, not yet? Watched any of the History channel on cable? No? Never read a book by Philippa Gregory? No. Okay." She scratched her head. "I would guess that Robin Hood never held up Henry the Eighth, given the four hundred or so years between their times. Henry the Eighth lived in the early fifteen hundreds and we know a lot about him, being one of the most infamous monarchs in English history. Robin of Locksley, however, is a more mythical being. Most think the stories are pointing to an Earl—the Earl of Huntingdon, who lived in ten-sixty, in what in modern times is Loxley in South Yorkshire, but there are real problems with that, partly because that earl was a noble and nobles weren't archers. Never, never. Archers were commoners. A noble would not draw a bow in battle."

"Never, never?" Nylah asked.

Everly shook her head. "Seven hundred years ago, they only had oral tradition, you know, storytelling around the fireplace kind of thing. There were a lot of ballads and folk tales about 'Robe Hood' all throughout the twelve-hundreds. These anti-heroes were general bandits and outlaws, but someplace in the early thirteen-hundreds these stories started to coalesce into a, well, rather mythical figure, who, with his band of thieves, was a hero to the common people who were tired of the oppression they faced from the nobility. Sort of like how today people obsess about superheroes. But these merry men made it into folklore originally for being infamous and only later on, through the generosity of entertainment, became the heroes."

"Sounds like infamy is the way to get into books and movies," Nylah said.

Everly chuckled. "Aren't you so right! People don't want to read a book or watch a movie about a happy life, do they? They only want the drama about a life they would never want to live themselves."

"Makes you worry about the TikTok challenge, doesn't it?"

Everly looked confused. "Just how are you making that link between medieval people and swallowing cinnamon and Tide pods?"

"It's just that people are stupid. They do anything that gets them attention. I'm surprised a whole lot of people didn't try to become the next Robin Hood, you know, just so they could say the tale was about them."

Everly nodded. "Hmmm. You're onto something, Nylah. They probably did. That's probably why the legends were still around until somebody turned them into a written tale. Actually, just after the time of this little village, in thirteen-seventy-seven, the first known literary reference to Robin Hood and his little band of merry men was created. Who knows what kind of people propagated those stories until then? Or what kind of tales they told? I bet there were those who used the legends to get attention for themselves. But I don't think anybody would want to be the next Henry the Eighth."

"I don't know. People are pretty stupid. If he were alive today and on social media, who knows how many people would swing through eight wives with an executioner?"

"Just six. Six wives. Two executions. But yeah, I get your point."

"How do you know all these details? How do you keep them all in your head?"

Everly paused. "I guess I should say that minor in medieval history, and of course, writing my dissertation in archeology, but really, I just love the medieval era. I find it all quite fascinating."

Nylah chewed her lip and nodded, using a pair of tongs to pick up one of the fabric scraps. "Huh. I'm sure glad I'm living now and not back then. The living looks pretty darn hard back then."

"It was. It was."

"Hard life. Bad death. Weird clothes." She looked at Everly. "Honestly, I'm not sure which was worse."

Chapter 13

Adelaide Trōst
October 1346

After their most necessary help in getting Adelaide into her new dress, she dismissed her servants and knelt on the floor in front of the large cross that stood prominently in her room. She clasped her hands, bowed her head, and prayed for strength to make it through the evening. She asked for forgiveness for her failure. She had tried to put her hair shirt on under the dress, but it was so tight, according to the new fashion, that she was left with no alternative but to wear nothing at all under the garment. She figured the difficulty breathing would have to suffice for her suffering. In particular, she asked for special blessings for Adolfus, who might never be a knight but who had come to her rescue, riding on the power of his white steed of party planning, which apparently he loved to do. She didn't know quite what to make of it, but when she had gone to him, tears flowing, throwing herself at his feet, begging for his intercession with their parents, his response had been completely unexpected.

"Adelaide! My sister, rise! For there is no call for intercession to change the minds of our parents. This is a problem with a willing solution! Lift your heart, my dear." He took her hands and pulled her to her feet, wiping her tears as he spoke.

"I cannot but fail at this task. I know nothing of menu planning. I fast three days a week for the Lord. What do I know of food? I know nothing of festive gaiety. I spend my time in prayer or reading the Holy Writ. If I fail father, he will beat me again. I will live in fear each day of the next three weeks."

Adolfus looked at her with great compassion. "He will not beat you this time, my sister. I will protect you."

"How? He beats you, Adolfus."

"Yes, but he's trying to toughen me up, not punish me." Adolfus crossed his arms and then tapped his fingers against his lips, thinking. "If you trust me and do just as I say, I'm quite sure I can save you. I'm quite sure I can glorify you in the eyes of our parents. And whomever he's inviting over this time."

"The Engelhafts," Adelaide said. Even she could hear the despondence in her voice.

"Ooo, really? The family of Gerung and Wolfgang? Hmmm. Handsome lot, they are."

"Yes, I suppose so."

"I hear they're quite fun. Clever. Witty. Like games. Like music. Gerung was a friend of Bernard's, you know. I always wanted to know him much better. Or Wolfgang. Either one."

"Oh, I didn't know that. Really?"

"Yes. They used to like to talk philosophy together."

"Philosophy?" She had no idea what he meant.

"Yes, church stuff."

"Oh!" Adelaide felt her head spin. These were people who shared her interests… they would be her allies! Impressing them, winning them to her side, could be a solution to her predicament with her father. "Adolfus, I want to throw the dinner party of the year. The most fabulous event Father has ever seen."

"Oh, I can help you there, little sister. I can help you there."

◆━◆━◆

And now the big night was upon them. She prayed for Adolfus to have whatever his heart desired in recompense for all of his help. Help wasn't quite an adequate description. This was his show, from the first decoration to the final custard. She had memorized her part well for the evening. Done her hair just as her older brother had instructed. Dressed exactly as he demanded, wearing the new gown at the peak of fashion he had ordered for her, after taking her to the tailors for rather elaborate measurements. She was grateful for the fur trim as it gave her some grace from the discomforting new fashion of bodices that were far strangers from one's neck.

A knock on her door startled her. She stood, smoothed the skirts of her sleek new gown. She had to be careful how she breathed, for her dress was so tailored to her waist and tight across her embarrassing bosom that she was afraid if she moved too quickly, she might cause unforgiveable mortification to her family. Her shoulders were completely bare and while the front of her hair was done up in elaborate curls and braids intertwined with ribbons, the back hung down, blonde tresses waving across her back. She pulled her long locks around to the front to give her more seemly coverage. "Come," she called.

The door to her apartments opened and in strode Adolfus, adorned in what she could only describe as ridiculous attire. For starters, his liripipe dangled from the cap on his head down to his waist. Then he had a savage looking dagger hanging from his belt down his backside.

Adolfus was effusive. "You look marvelous! I was sure that new style of dress would be just the thing for the evening. Here, let's keep your hair down your back. Yes, you look absolutely fetching!"

"I feel nervous. Undressed, Adolfus!"

"Ridiculous!"

"Yes, that too," she murmured, but he was too excited to hear her.

"It's the fashion of the day! Thank the friars! I would think you would love this gown, Adelaide. All this new fashion is because of them. In their endeavor to serve as the guardians of our morality, they demand strict measurements for clothing. So, the guilds have done all they can to comply—and just look at the wonders of their works! It's revolutionized fashion in the thirteen-forties!"

"Well, these clothes don't leave much to the imagination, dear brother." She gave her brother a once-over. "On either of us."

"I know! Isn't it wonderful? I always suspected the friars were against the imagination in general, and now we know that to be true with their new edicts on fashion. *Follow the precise measurements of the body*, and just look at what the algebra of the friars' becomes in the hands of the guilds! Inspired."

"Somehow, I don't think this is quite what the friars meant…"

Adolfus ignored his sister's concerns. "Tell me, do I look dashing? Handsome? Don't resemble my esteemed father too much, do I? Not that he'd be caught dead without his poofy sleeves, billowing tunic to his thighs and those ridiculous high boots! Please tell me I don't look like I've become old and fat before my time?"

"What? Adolfus, you are twenty-four years old. You're lean as a weasel." She couldn't imagine what he was concerned about as he preened and posed before her. The man was practically a stick to her mind and the new fashion celebrated that long and lithe look.

"Oooo, lean as a weasel! I like the sound of that. Well, it's time for us to head downstairs so that we can greet our guests." He held out his arm to escort her.

Adelaide smiled weakly and took his arm.

"Remember to smile and be brilliantly entertaining this evening, my sister."

Adelaide squeaked in anxiety. "I don't know how to do that!"

"Then listen well with a smile on your face. In that gown and looking as you do, all you have to do is smile and listen, my dear. Smile and listen."

They went to the door to greet the Engelhafts, a contingent twelve strong, overwhelming the Trōst party's mere seven members.

As the guests entered, everyone was formally introduced and then led into a large drawing room where they would drink before dinner. Frau Engelhaft, in particular, seemed taken with the finery set out for the evening's entertainment.

"Oh! Look at your decorations, Duchess Trōst! Beautiful! Most unusual use of peacock feathers. You have a daring sense of taste. I am most impressed."

Duchess Hedwig Trōst smiled graciously. "Thank you, Frau Engelhaft. I must confess that I had nothing to do with it." She looked about her with an expression that betrayed some trepidation when her face was turned away from her guest. "My daughter, Adelaide, took command of the evening. She is quite the… accomplished hostess. She didn't ask my advice on… well, anything."

Frau Engelhaft peered across the room to where her sons Gerung and Wolfgang were in animated conversation with Adolfus and Adelaide. "Your daughter is a ravishing beauty, as anyone can see in that gown."

"Oh," the Duchess caught her breath and gave a nervous laugh. "The fashion of the day, they assure me. Please, call me Lady Hedwig."

"But of course, Lady Hedwig. The young people and their fashion. Were we not the same at their age?" She smiled generously. "Although I must admit, looking at my sons, that their outfits seem ridiculous to me. Handsomeness such as theirs can be quite offset by the choice of clothing, don't you think? Tunics, so short and tight. It gives me pause to wonder how our children breathe in those costumes?" She gave a laugh and shrugged. "But to be young and at a party. 'Tis a thrill for them. And if our boys want to wear a large purse at their hips, so be it."

"Pray tell, what do you think they keep in those purses? My son as well! All three of them look like peas in a pod with those showy buckles on their belts. I told my Adolfus that it looked like he was wearing a horse girdle."

Frau Engelhaft gave a laugh like little bells ringing in the wind and she winked surreptitiously at her companion. "My own sons confessed to me that the fashion *is* daring, and is supposed to suggest comparisons to a horse!"

Lady Hedwig smiled and nodded, obviously not following her guest's train of thought.

Frau Engelhaft continued. "It's like the new fashion with the long pointy beards—my boys assure me 'tis to make them look fierce!" Here she laughed, as if that goal were ridiculous, which it was, given that the outfits cladding all the young men made them look more like willowy flowers adorned with bright buckles rather than military fighters or men born to administrative rule. "But we all know what's really going on! Ah, men and their foolish games. They are too obsessed with the size of their members. I wouldn't be surprised if someday one of them builds a house worshipping the phallus and collecting examples from all across God's creation!"

"Oh! Really?" Lady Hedwig squeaked, her face turning a bright shade of pink as she finally understood Frau Engelhaft's meaning. "You have such a, such a… daring imagination."

"I do hope so, Lady Hedwig. I do hope so. But those daggers hanging from their belts on their behinds are likely to make eunuchs of them all, if they aren't careful how they sit! We'd best get them all married off before it's too late if we'd like any heirs, shouldn't we?"

Adelaide walked up to her mother and the lady of the visiting household and curtsied.

"Oh, my dear, you are ravishing! Just look at you. Lithe and lovely yet shapely and womanly. How can it be that you are not married?"

"Thank you, Frau Engelhaft. I have only recently come of age, but my desires for my future are to serve my Lord…"

Hedwig cut her daughter off, "Yes, my daughter has great ambitions. She is a great reader, you know. And her design of the evening's menu will be most delightful, I'm sure." Hedwig turned to her daughter. "What is on the menu for the evening, Adelaide?"

Adelaide took in a breath, not too deep, and tried to resist looking down at her bodice to ensure that her dress was still providing her any modesty at all. "We will start with a pottage soup to whet the appetite, and then a course of meats will include roast goat, and blancmanges of chicken and fresh fish in spiced almond milk, roasted fowl including black grouse and a slow roasted peacock."

"Oh! Grouse and peacock!" Frau Engelhaft nodded at the array of opulent feathers standing in place of flowers in vases. "Oh delightful! And you found such a good use for the feathers, my dear."

"Uh, yes." Adelaide nodded, thinking that the Frau must mean what she was saying. She wasn't sure, and that made her feel nervous. "And then we'll have a course of tarts and fritters and custards."

Frau Engelhaft nodded knowingly. "You are a young woman with real talent. I wonder, would you be so kind as to share a messer at dinner with my oldest son? Poor Gerung is so shy. It would be good for him to have your adept guidance as he navigates all the finery of your vast manor. We are but humble people and I fear he might need the gentle guidance of a beautiful young woman such as yourself, dear Adelaide."

Adelaide blinked a couple of times and glanced at her mother, who surreptitiously nodded at her. "Uh, yes. I would be, um, happy to."

Frau Engelhaft smiled at Lady Hedwig. "So modest. Such a credit to your family." She took Hedwig's arm and started to stroll about the room. As they walked away, Adelaide could hear the woman say, "…and she's so generous! I heard about her giving alms to the poor…"

Adelaide let out her breath, not realizing that she'd been holding it. Adolfus came up from behind, surprising her and making her jump. She had to quickly readjust her bodice and wiggle back down into her dress as she turned around to him. She was absolutely mortified to find he wasn't alone: Gerung was with him, smiling rakishly at her predicament.

"Sister! Gerung thinks your decorations are fantastic. Just wait until he tries your menu!" Adolfus gave her a wink.

Adelaide wasn't sure how long she was supposed to take the credit for all of Adolfus' work or whether by his gesture he wanted any revelation that he was the true mastermind behind the event.

"Why don't you tell our guest about the entertainment for the evening?" Adolfus said, raising his eyebrows.

"Entertainment? Oh yes! The entertainment! Of course. Well, my brother Adolfus is going to play and sing for us." She tried to sound bright as she said it, but worried what her parents would say.

"So!" Gerung turned again towards Adolfus, "are all the members of your family just bristling with such talent? Or is it just the two of you who are so very blessed?"

"Ooooh!" Adolfus gave Gerung a playful punch in the arm. "You're too kind, but don't stop. I like your style. Perhaps, if I do well, maybe afterwards, Gerung, we can share a messer together at dinner?" He had a happy, expectant smile on his face.

"Oh! He's sharing a messer with me."

Both men turned to look at Adelaide.

"I am?"

"Yes. Um, your mother…"

"Oh, of course, my mother. Well, if you're not opposed, dearest Adelaide," he said as he kissed her hand, his gaze lingering far below her eyes, "and believe me, I am not opposed, I would be most pleased to share a messer with you."

She gave him a small curtsy and blushed, knowing she had no say in the matter at all. She had hoped to share a messer with her brother, who now looked rather disappointed at this turn of events.

Gerung leaned into Adolfus and whispered in his ear, but Adelaide caught his words. "Wolfgang would be, heh, thrilled to share a messer with you, regardless of whether you sing like an angel or a devil." He gave the man a wink. "He might prefer the devil actually."

Adolfus leaned back and put his hands on his hips. "Well then, I'd better scuttle over there before another becomes his dinner partner, hadn't I?"

Gerung watched Adolfus dance his way over to Wolfgang, who greeted his host with matching enthusiasm. "Ah, a dangerous game they play." He turned to Adelaide. "But no worries, my lady, for I would rather dine with you than the king himself." He gave her a look up and down her body, a look which made her blush again. "You are fetching and much more to my liking." He stared at her deeply, almost hungrily.

Adelaide wondered how much of the spirits the boys had imbibed already if the young men were acting in such a flagrant and foolish manner this early in the evening. Spirits were being liberally poured along with the platters of various cheeses and sausages which served as appetizers before the courses of dinner started. She thought she should try to make some conversation with this stranger she was now consigned to share a platter at dinner with. She comforted herself with the relief that she would never need to see him again after tonight. She could just smile her way through the evening as her mother had commanded her. She hoped the man didn't try to share bites and actually feed her from their shared messer. "Um, what talents do you possess, Gerung?"

"Me? Talents? Oh, none I suppose. I mean, I'm very good at making money. Very, very good at it. I suppose that's a talent, however I hardly think that's what you mean, is it?"

She opened her mouth and drew in breath as if to speak, but couldn't think of an appropriate thing to say, so she smiled in what she hoped was an indulgent way.

"And I'm very good at persuading people to get on board."

"On board? On a ship, good sir? My father tells me that you are a merchant family and own a great many ships for trading."

"Yes, of course. But I mean just on board. It doesn't matter much with what. It's the persuasion that counts."

She nodded and smiled, not knowing what to do or say.

She was saved by the announcement of Adolfus's musical exposition. He played three pieces, all on different instruments, singing when allowed by his instrument of choice, and all to rousing applause and stamping by the Engelhaft clan. Afterwards they enjoined at dinner, where she was forced to sit all too close to Gerung, who did indeed feed her and give her repeated sips from a shared cup, which she found supremely embarrassing as it brought their mother's heads together constantly during the meal. She rarely drank wine or ale, and his cup was full of strong spirits. She kept a smile on her face, although she was mortified inside and afeared of the talking-to her mother was sure to give her after the evening concluded. Wolfgang was sitting on Gerung's other side and was indeed sharing with Adolfus. They did not feed one another bites, although it looked like they desired to do just that. The drink was going to Adelaide's head and she found the evening to be confusing and the lightning quick discussions between the three men to be unnerving. She didn't know what to say so she simply smiled and nodded and tried to take tiny bites of the morsels Gerung seemed so intent on feeding her.

◆ ▬ ◆ ▬ ◆

The next day she woke up with her head throbbing and her stomach nauseated. Her once flat midriff, a sign of her sacrifice for Christ from her days of fasting, now had a small bulge from the feasting. She thought she looked like a snake who had consumed too large a victim and now needed to let it digest in her belly. It felt repulsive.

Her mother came bursting into her room near to midday. "Oh good! You're still alive!"

"Oh, Mother! I did my best. And I'm sick from all the effort. Don't let Father beat me."

Hedwig laughed. "You're sick from all the spirits and wine you drank, Adelaide! And I've never seen you eat so much! But why would anyone beat you? You were perfect last night. Perfect. And for the first time I can remember, you looked like you were actually having a good time."

"A good time? I was suffering…" Adelaide choked out the words.

"Were you? Excellent, since it's what you like the best," her mother said in a sarcastic retort. "As I said, you looked like you were enjoying yourself immensely. So sleep all day if you like, my love. And I'm going to buy you a new dress. Maybe one that keeps your ample bosom in better capacity than what you wore last night, but you deserve it. Ribbons galore, all the ribbons you want."

Adelaide wished she could have been happy about this pronouncement; on any other occasion she would have been thrilled at the prospect of a new higher cut dress with ribbons, but she found it too bewildering at the moment, when her head was spinning.

"I have great hopes for you my dear. Now, why don't you rest. I'll send up a servant with some willow bark tea, and that should lessen the pain I imagine is tormenting your pretty little head. I advise you to not be a martyr and drink it."

"I'm sure I don't know what you mean," Adelaide objected in a weak and miserable voice.

"Hmmm. Sleep well, my daughter." And her mother left her rooms, leaving Adelaide in the peace and darkness she desired.

Chapter 14

Father Bernard Trōst December 1346

Bernard wrapped his seal skin cloak around him to block out the wind. He was amazed at how effective it was in keeping him warm and thrice blessed his Uncle Eberhard for sending it to him. "His generosity knows no bounds. I have always felt he loved me even more than my own father." The latest wagon load had arrived bearing incense for the censers and candles for the church. Yet another set of clean vestments. Money—he always sent money. For Bernard, some lovely sausages. A generous amount of dried fruit. A barrel of mead, which excited Bernard a great deal. And this magnificent cloak. "May the Lord bless you and keep you, dear Uncle Eberhard." But for right now he needed some bread. That couldn't be shipped by wagon over long distances. He needed to go out into the cold to visit the baker's. He decided to make the rounds to the shopkeepers who regularly attended his mass, and some of those who didn't. He would keep it at three establishments to visit: the baker's, the chandler's and the cobbler's. He had other errands to run, but he felt he could manage the task if he kept it to just three parts. He hoped he didn't run into anyone who tried to upset his pattern.

Padding his way down the street, he wished the cobbler's was the closest to him, but it was going to be his last stop. He was relieved to enter the baker's shop. "Hello, Beatrice! It's so lovely and warm in here! What a blessing of a place to work!"

"In the wintertime, sure, a right blessing it is. But in the summer, 'tis so hot that I imagine it's like having a job in hell. Though I hope to never find out if I'm right! Good Christian, I am. Never miss your mass."

"Yes, you've been most faithful and the rolls you bring to give to the hungry each week are very generous of you. I know the angels in heaven are smiling down upon you, Beatrice."

"I hope so. I hope so. And what can I get for you today, Father?"

Bernard placed his order and when she handed it to him, she put up her hand to refuse his money. "I couldn't take funds from a man of the cloth. Not a good one like you!"

"No, no, Beatrice. I cannot let you support both the church and me. I want to pay you a fair price. And what's more, I intend to pay you for the bread for the next family you see who cannot afford your wares." He handed over the money and made arrangements for her to bring bread for the feasts he would hold for the poor during the Christmas season.

"You're a right generous soul, Father."

Bernard shrugged. "It goes with the profession."

"And I wanted to say how much I appreciate your cesspit project!"

"Oh! I'm so glad! Thank you for mentioning that." Bernard couldn't help but smile.

"Right! Not having to step over as much shit in the streets is quite an improvement. Town smells better too."

Bernard mumbled an uncomfortable thank you and made his way along the blustery street to the chandler's, reminding himself that these were country folk who used more rustic language than what had been common back in Cologne. But he needed to keep moving if he wanted to be home before the winter sun set. Uncle Eberhard sent special beeswax candles for the church but the manse needed light too, and he would soon run out of light if he didn't replenish his candle supply.

"Good day to you, Adelman. I'm here to purchase some of your excellent candlesticks."

Adelman looked at Father Bernard a bit warily. "Are ye now? I see you've been at Bernice's. I hope you won't be asking for a baker's dozen from me, good Father. I know you in the clergy are important folk, but I'm just a poor man. You know, wax isn't like wheat flour. Wheat flour Bernice has in abundance, but bee's wax is much harder to come by. I can't see how I can slip ye some free ones. Of course, I can get ye tallow candles, as many as you need. And if I can skip confession, I'd be happy to throw in some of those." Adelman leaned on his counter and gave Father Bernard a level look.

"I wouldn't dream of asking you to give me any of your wares for free, Adelman, and it would be against church teaching to trade confession for goods and services. One is the province of the holy soul and the other of mortal incarnation. You need your soul to be well tended, which I try to do in church. And I need my house to have light, which I take care of when I come to you to purchase candles… just like all your other customers. I'll take a dozen beeswax and a dozen-plus-a-half tallow, please." Bernard paid the man.

"Humph!" Adelman chuffed as he counted the payment, nodding that it was fair. "Ye know, I wanted to say that at first I thought all your new ideas weren't right for our Valley Village."

"Oh really? Not a fan of the cesspits, are you?" Bernard tried to keep his voice light and friendly.

"Oh no, them's fine. I thought that was a great idea from the start. To tell ye the truth, I got tired of seeing all those fat asses takin' a squat in the street!"

Bernard nodded, thinking to himself, *rustic language. Would be the same in any village.* Nevertheless, he was glad his uncle wasn't here. After a few more pleasantries, which were much more pleasant once Adelman realized he really was going to be paid for his wares, Bernard moved on, curious why the shopkeepers seemed to believe that giving clergy free goods was expected. He'd never asked any of them for that. While it concerned him, he was pleasantly distracted by Adelman's appreciation for Bernard's small classes teaching any willing young ones to read and write.

"Me daughter's good at sums. Never thought to see the like of that," Adelman had said. "Looking forward to her doing all the counting and accounting. I'm never sure I've got it all right. No one ever taught me. I had to figure it for meself!"

As Bernard walked down the street, he started to compose his next sermon in his mind. "Maybe something about the meek inheriting the Earth?" he said as he contemplated the talents that could be unleashed with just a little bit of education and enlightenment. "Meek as the wee ones may be, they can change everything."

As he walked down the street, he passed the man called Wilhelm, who smiled and waved in a friendly manner and then headed over towards the new cesspits. Bernard smiled and waved back, grateful for a friendly face and a kindly gesture. There was a contingent of the villagers who always seemed to growl and scowl at him, and he could never discern why. But not Wilhelm. That man exuded friendliness and kindness and an innocent sense of joy. Bernard paused and watched Wilhelm as the man walked off.

The priest's final stop before the sun set was at the cobblers, to pick up his hopefully repaired sturdy shoes that he was quickly wearing out given the rugged new location in which he lived. Before any suspicions could be raised that the priest might request free services merely because of his status as a clergy, he was clear that he was there to pay the full price for the repair of his shoes.

"Ah! You be a fair one. Don't think I ever met a clergy quite like you. Maybe I should come to St. Cyprian's for mass once in a while and give me back a break from old St. Drogo's."

"Uh, your back? You would always be welcome at St. Cyprian's, my good man. I'm afraid we also have pews, which may not be any better on your back."

"Tis not the pews." The man shook his head. "Tis the penance! But here're your boots and I hope they serve you well."

Bernard was confused, but as he took the shoes he noticed the man had a basket on the shelf with a chew hole in the side of it. He shuddered. He hated mice. "Good cobbler, what keep you in the basket there?"

"Just vittles. Me shop is out front but I lives in the back." The man jerked his head toward the rooms behind him. "Why? You hungry?" He had that suspicious look again.

"No, I'm well stocked." Bernard pointed to the breads in his basket. "It's just I was wondering about the small hole in the side. And I see you don't have a lid on the top of your basket."

"Don't right know where the lid got to. But Friar Tuck says that lids aren't necessary."

"Does he now?" Bernard blinked a couple of times, trying to digest this information. He'd met Karel Tuckerschade once or twice now and come to the conclusion that the man wasn't very learned or sophisticated. That poor Wilhelm who followed the friar around looked like one of the poorest men Bernard had ever seen. His shoes were in a deplorable state, but the man was probably grateful to have any at all.

"Friar Tuck tells us to leave a gift for the angels on the table. A bite or two in gratitude for all their protection. And in the morning, you can see where they come and you know you been blessed. I don't bother leaving anything out on the table though, because the angels just find their way into me basket."

"The angels are coming and eating your food?"

"Oh aye! Friar Tuck says so. But me grandma always said it was the fairies. And if you didn't want them to steal your child and leave you with a changeling, then you'd better pay off the fairies." The cobbler looked at Father Bernard more closely. "Say, you're a clergyman. Are angels just bigger fairies with bigger wings?"

Bernard felt quite dumbfounded. He'd been forewarned by his father, threatened was a closer descriptor, that these mountain people would be primitives. He ran into their rough language at every turn. Their unsophisticated ways marked their every move. Their lack of reading skills made learning-by-doing an utter necessity. And now… fairies. Fairies and angels being the same thing.

"Actually, I don't think that either angels or fairies are visiting you."

"No? So, I'm not being blessed? Friar Tuck assures me I'm being blessed."

"Be that as it may, I would guess you've got mice."

"Well, don't tell Friar Tuck your mouse theory. He'd call you a warped for sure."

Bernard was confused again. "What is a… *warped?*"

"You know…" The man took a breath and looked up. "Well, it's…" He stopped again, one finger raised as he was about to answer. He lowered his hand. "I don't rightly remember. But he likes to say it all the same: *those are the warped,* says he."

Bernard went over to the basket and picked it up. Sure enough, the telltale black scat lined the shelf. "See here, man. Angels don't leave behind excrement."

"What's excrement?"

Bernard let out a little breath. "Shit."

"Oh. I never thought of that. Angels don't shit, do they? What do they with it then? They can't keep it in 'em."

"I, I, I…" Bernard stuttered and then started again. "I think you have mice. You might consider a clay pot. One with a lid, a clay one that can't be chewed through, to keep your vittles safe."

"Right. I'll think about that. But I like the idea that I'm being blessed even more." The cobbler nodded, looking satisfied with the system he had in place.

Bernard shook his head and gave up with a sigh and a smile. He put down coins for the price of a good pair of boots. "I will pay you this sum if you will make a pair of boots, good ones, for that Wilhelm fellow."

"Wilhelm? The rag tag that runs behind Father Tuck?" the man said as he happily scooped up the coins. "Surely I will, but why him? He's not your acolyte."

"No, but he is in need. And he's kind. Just think of it as the angels blessing him."

The man nodded. "He's a man who could use a blessing, that's for sure!"

Bernard left the shop and made his way back to the manse, happy to have completed his three-fold set of tasks, his head full of plans to start his next improvement campaign. Tomorrow he would visit the potters to see about how the church could support the creation of vermin-safe food storage pots, lids included, that he could ensure made it to every household in the village.

Chapter 15

Adelaide Trōst Engelhaft
January 1347

Adelaide went through the ceremony like a person drugged. The priest had to ask her twice to repeat the words after him. She could barely process what he was saying. At some point, a ring appeared upon her finger. It was made of two golden intertwined bands centered on an inverted diamond, its head sticking up like a little pyramid.

At the feast afterwards, she took only a few of the bites that Gerung fed her and would sip nothing other than water.

"My wife, my dearest Adelaide, for that is what you are." He lifted her hand and kissed it. "Won't you have a glass of wine? I have been told that on a wedding night a new bride might appreciate a glass of wine."

"My mother said the same to me." She would have said "my lord" to her husband, but he wasn't a lord, was he? No. Her father had married her off to a merchant. Wealthy. Powerful. But below her station. She wasn't about to call him *my dearest Gerung.* This was the man who had stolen her life from her, removed any hope for her to become a nun. Would despoil her in just a few hours. She didn't want to call him anything at all.

"Do you not love your wedding band? Did you see the inscription on the inside?"

"No. I mean it's lovely. What inscription?"

"It reads, '*ieo vos tien foi tenes le moy.*' It is the language of Franconia, the very language of love. It translates as, 'I hold your faith, hold mine'." He kissed her hand. "Smile, my love! This is your party, after all." He gave her a kiss on the cheek. "I know the day has made you terribly nervous, but my dear, now the ceremony is over and tonight is all about the fun! Enjoy yourself. Everyone here loves you, and no one more than I."

She endured and managed to smile from time to time. Gerung certainly acted like the party was for him. He talked to everyone, hugged everyone, smiled and laughed. After their required dance as a newly bound couple, he continued to frolic about, pairing up with anyone who was available or stood by the sides with that longing look on their pathetic faces. He wanted to include everyone. Adelaide was shocked that he couldn't seem to understand that not everyone wanted to be included. Some people just wanted to be left alone.

As the evening's celebrations came to a close, her parents approached to take their leave of the couple.

"I know you'll take good care of my daughter. If you treat her half as well as you did your guests this evening, she'll be spoiled rotten by springtime!" The old Duke laughed as he embraced his new son-in-law. "Ah, the joining of our families. There's nothing we cannot do together!"

"I'm looking forward to being part of your family and conquering new ventures as father and son," Gerung said with real warmth. "And Mother," he turned to Duchess Hedwig. "I hope we bring you grandchildren to love and dote upon." He gave her a wink.

"The only thing I want at this point in my life!" she exclaimed with a laugh. Hedwig turned to her daughter and embraced her.

As her mother held her close, Adelaide whispered in her ear, "Don't leave. You cannot leave."

"Adelaide, drink a cup of wine. Maybe two," her mother whispered back. As she pulled away, she said, her hands still holding Adelaide's arms, "When I see you next, you truly will be a woman, Adelaide."

Adelaide did as her mother bade her and drank a cup of wine.

Gerung led his new wife upstairs in the immense house that would now be hers. "I have something to show you. Come, my wife." As they went up the staircase, he said, "You gave me your wedding gift earlier, but I wanted to surprise you with mine. And, uh, it was so thoughtful of you to give me such a large cross."

"I thought we could hang it on the wall of the dining hall, so that we never forget whom we honor as we feast."

"That is an idea. I will have to consult a mason about how to install it. It could suffice for a church itself. It must weigh several times what I do. And it certainly is as tall as I am."

"Our guests should have no doubt as to the faith our house stands upon."

"Indeed, yes. Ah, of course." He led her into a small library, the walls and shelves filled with books. Such a collection was truly priceless. Adelaide looked about her, eyes wide. While she was skilled at reading and writing, she had never seen so many books in her lifetime. The room was something Bernard would love. He might give up his calling if he could live his life inside a room like this. She smirked and thought that Adolfus would enjoy many of these too, as long as they held no serious thoughts. She walked around and looked at the leather bindings.

Gerung smiled at her like a little boy full of anticipation. "This is my library. Now our library. And as a wedding present, I bought you these." He led her over to a table where a dozen books were laid out next to a very comfortable looking chair.

"You bought me these, my husband? Books?"

"Yes. Here is a comedy, quite funny actually, and written by a woman. I know your brother Bernard is most fond of that one. It's a laugh on almost every page! And this one is poetry. Most gallant, I assure you. And this one…"

"And which of them are the Bible?"

"What?"

"Which of these books are the Bible? Or illuminated manuscripts? Or hymns?"

"Um." Gerung looked around him. "I believe you keep a Bible by your bedside?"

"I do."

"Then that would be where the Bible is. The books I sought out for you are rare and precious works that cover a wide range of topics, from art and poetry to comedy to drama. They come from Franconia and England and Genoa. This one," he said picking up a volume, "is about the Roman gods and their mythology."

Adelaide looked at Gerung with astonishment. "Why would you think I would fill my mind with such heathen trash?"

Gerung looked stunned and took a small step back. "My lady, you are a great reader. You are ever with a book. A woman of letters and literature."

"I read only the holy writ," she answered stiffly.

Gerung crossed his arms and gave a slow nod, as if to surmise this new development. "Well, I apologize, my lady wife, for I did not know that your taste in the written word was so… singularly devoted."

"Yes. I am singularly devoted. It's time you learned that about me."

"Well, perhaps I can find you a different wedding present."

"Yes. I think that would be in good order."

He led her to their chamber. Adelaide wasn't sure what she was supposed to do, so she just stood there, as tall and as proud as she could.

"My lady, will you not come to bed?"

She nodded and walked over to the bed they would now share.

"My lady, will you not take off your wedding gown? Would you sleep in that? Your mother left you a nightdress. It is lying on the chair hence." He pointed to a gauzy, white gown trimmed in lace that graced a chair a few feet away.

She felt frozen, not knowing what to do and not wanting to put that thing on. She had elected to wear her mother's wedding dress. Old fashioned, to be sure, but it was bulky and voluminous and completely opposite to the costumes of the day which looked to be painted onto their wearers. She felt she could hide under all that fabric.

"Here, my love, let me help you." Gerung patiently undid the many buttons up the back of the dress. He untied the ribbons that connected the sleeves and bound the bodice. "My wife… what is… this?" There was concern in his voice. "What are you wearing under your gown?"

"It's called a hairshirt. The righteous wear them. I am pure and I abase myself before God."

"So, I see. I am only your husband. You never need to abase yourself before me." A look of concern crossed his face. "Oh my! Your skin! Look what this thing has done to your skin! You poor thing! Here, let me wash you. You are covered in rashes and sores. My love, no wonder you've been distracted tonight and did not want to dance— this could not have been comfortable for you!"

"It's not supposed to be comfortable. It's supposed to be suffering. I suffer for Christ."

He blinked at her a couple of times and took a step back. "I knew that you were a righteous woman, Adelaide. You have a reputation for giving alms to the poor. For being generous to the church. But I did not know that you were quite so devout."

"Then you did not take the time to know me at all." She felt stiff. Annoyed. If he didn't appreciate her passion, he shouldn't have married her.

"But when we met, at the party your parents invited my family to so that we could see if we were a match… you seemed so different."

"And how was I different?"

"Well, you certainly dressed differently."

"Oh, that humiliating costume? Adolfus had it made for me."

"And you ate and drank and were merry."

"My stomach ached all the next day. Believe me, my new husband, I fast three days a week for my God. I do not eat and drink like a pig at a trough."

"Oh. I see. And you laughed at our jokes. You smiled, I thought with agreement, at our philosophies. You joined in the discussion."

"I don't remember any of that! I might have had too much to drink."

"Well, whatever it was, you were funny and intelligent and delightful. I knew then you were a rare and talented woman. The party you designed. The decorations were inspired. So artistic. And your menu!"

"Oh, that was all Adolfus' work. Maybe you should have married him." She thought she probably shouldn't sound so bitchy to her new husband but then again, if he was going to bind himself until death to a woman, perhaps he should get to know her first.

"Tell me, Adelaide, do you honestly believe that women should speak their minds to their husbands?"

"Women can do that?" She said it before she realized it came out of her mouth. Certainly, her own mother never told the duke what she thought, at least not in front of Adelaide. Lady Hedwig would extoll at length about her opinions to her daughter, but Adelaide thought of that more as an outlet than as a rehearsal.

"You seem to do it with me quite frequently."

"Do I? Surely not! You must be mistaken."

"Hmmm. How about women having an equal say in the decisions of the household?"

"I don't know what you mean." What decisions were there in a household? What to serve for dinner? A steward took care of that. Whom to employ as servants? Again, that was the Chief Steward's role. As far as she had experienced, the household simply ran itself.

"All right then. Hmmm. What say you about women having a voice in the politics of the day?"

"Never!" she said, and then realized she was quoting her own father. She didn't know how she felt about that, in part because she didn't know what the politics of the day were. Certainly, the King of Germania had been elected, but he was such a weak leader that what did it matter who voted for king or not?

"My lady, on the night I fell in love with you, you had many opinions about these issues."

She stiffened. "My Lor—" she stopped herself. He wasn't a noble. She couldn't call her husband *my lord*. She wasn't quite sure what to call him. 'Gerung' seemed far too familiar. "Well, when you're ready for me to have an opinion, I'm sure you'll give it to me." That was what she had heard her own mother say countless times. That was all a woman was born to, wasn't it?

Gerung paced about the bedroom for a few moments, his hand on his chin, deep in thought. "My lady wife, I would be most pleased if you had your own opinions that evolved from reading widely, discussing ideas openly with other educated people, and engaging in serious self-reflection."

"Self-reflection. Bernard always prattled on and on about that. Adolfus isn't quite so enamored of it however."

"You certainly know your brothers. Hmmm." Gerung took a long look at her. "You are my wife. No changing that. That is where we are. But I must confess I find myself a bit surprised that you are so different after we said our vows as compared to who you were before that happy moment."

Adelaide found it interesting that he said the word *happy* but he didn't sound happy.

"I know that you are an intelligent woman. I know that you have ideas, opinions, hopes and dreams for your life, Adelaide."

"My dream is to be a nun."

"A nun?" Gerung was quiet for a moment as he reflected on this information. "I confess to feeling a bit duped. I had not realized that I was betrothed to a would-be nun?"

Adelaide stiffened. "I was wearing a golden cross around my neck."

Gerung pulled out his own cross from under his shirt. "Everyone wears a cross about their necks, Adelaide, from the poorest serf to the king himself." He sighed deeply and paced a few steps. "I would never have suspected that the woman who threw that dinner feast would consider herself as a nun. What do you want out of life, Adelaide? What is your purpose, particularly now that you are a married woman?"

"My purpose is the same as everyone's purpose."

"And what is that, my lady?"

"We are born to suffer."

Gerung paced a few more steps. "And is there no happiness allowable in your world?"

"We are not born to happiness."

He nodded, still deep in thought. At last he said, "Well, my lady wife, I cannot make you be happy. That is your choice. But still, we have our duty to perform. And if you choose to suffer, I will be sorry for you, but I do not choose to suffer."

She nodded.

"Do you choose to wear the night dress your mother provided for you?"

"I do not."

"That is fine with me, my lady." Then he added with a chuckle, "Actually, I prefer it that way. We will do our duty and you are welcome to suffer as much as you feel duty calls for. Or you could join me and have a pleasurable evening."

Adelaide chose to suffer.

Chapter 16

Everly

Everly wiped the sweat from her brow. Digging was hard work. She was back in her "boyfriend clothes" since the photo-shoot duds, snap-worthy as they might have been in Nylah's creative world, would never stand up to the rigors of a day of real archeologic excavation. But they were good for post-shower evening "nosh", as Dr. Payne called it, and the team meetings where their little trio went over the day's progress and planned for tomorrow's attack on the dig.

Yesterday had been full-on war with the blackberry bushes, and the now-vanquished stems lay torn asunder, their thorns still angry and unaccepting of their loss. The earth they had once covered lay naked, stretched out before Everly and looking vulnerable and timid by comparison. A third stand of blackberry bushes stood on menacing guard, just yards away.

"And how is today's work progressing, Dr. Bergeron?"

She looked up. "Oh, good morning, Dr. Payne. I think we're off to a good start here. I guess we'll test your theory about the relationship between blackberry bushes and artifacts." She was glad he was comfortable with good natured teasing.

"Not just real… but sinister!" He chuckled and looked over at the torn-up blackberry stand. "Those Brandenburg girls had far too much fun yesterday. Heidi and Hannah: terrors on a bobcat."

"They did seem to like working with the heavy machinery. And I see you've gotten their names straightened out at last!"

Trevor blushed slightly and scuffed the toe of his boot in the dirt. "Secret? Not really. I just always assign them together 'cause then I don't have to worry about it. It's just Heidi and Hannah. The Double H's. But they don't seem to mind." He looked around uncomfortably. "So, Dr. Bergeron, would you be so kind as to work with me in Pit A today?"

Everly blinked a couple of times. "I can. What's up? I mean, we want to make progress here in Pit B as well. I thought the goal was to discover if this is a construction by the townspeople?"

"Yeah, right. I know. I just have this sense… this intuition you might say, that something big is going to happen today." He looked down at her as she stood in a flat area just six inches deep. It was still the starting stage of the excavation of the second discovered pit. "And I think you've got time here, not to mention dirt, but I… I *feel something* in Father B's pit. Will you help me?"

"Feel something? Like with the probes?"

"Not that kind of feel."

Everly dusted off her hands and walked over to the edge of Pit B and stepped out. "Sure, of course. I'll ask Gunther to oversee the students in this dig, shall I?" She looked around and spotted him. "You know, I think he'd really like the chance to oversee a pit of his own."

"What every archeologist wants, right? A pit of their own. A place to call home. An army of students and a really old bone."

Everly couldn't help but burst out into a laugh. "Where does that come from?"

"I don't know. It just seems to pop out of my mouth."

She nodded and wondered if he really should have been a writer. Or a poet. Or maybe just a lyricist for a local pub band in a small college town. Still chuckling, she found Gunther and asked if he and his team of students would take over Pit B. He was delighted at the opportunity.

She caught up with Trevor at Pit A, the former home of Father B's remains. The floor was now about eighteen inches below the depth of where Father B had been laid to rest. If they didn't start to find artifacts in the next eight to twelve inches, then there might not be any others to be found. But then why would a clergyman have been laid to rest in a field with no marker? No headstone? In unconsecrated ground? In a huge, excavated pit? There were so many mysteries to solve with so few clues to guide them.

Everly picked up some tools from the supply bucket and went down the ladder to join Trevor.

He got up from where he was working in the dirt. "Why don't we start at opposite ends and make our way to meet in the middle?"

Everly nodded and went to her corner, dropped the tools on the ground and pulled her probe out of her pocket. She started making a four-step pattern of probing the dirt, moving down a few inches, probing again. It was like listening to the earth, only with your hands and fingers sensing the resistance of the dirt and discerning if the probe hit a change in character of the soil. Once the prodding indicated the area was clear, she could gently start with a spade or a pointing trowel to move a section of dirt, progressively clearing an area. She was on her fourth round of her pattern when she felt a click at the end of her probe. She froze. Gently, she probed again. The tiniest *click!* that she could imagine vibrated through the metal rod and tingled in her fingertip. She could feel her heartbeat start to pick up.

Could just be a rock, she told herself. It was a mountain valley after all. They had a lot of clover and an abundance of rocks. She picked up her trowel and using the two tools, she carefully pulled the dirt away.

"Dr. Payne?"

"Oh my."

"Dr. Payne, I… I think I might have something." She looked over at Trevor. He was staring down at the area in front of him.

"Me too."

She left her probe and trowel in the dirt and came over to him. "Okay. Let's, uh, take a look at what you've got." She thought he looked terribly excited. But then he took a deep breath and set down his tools.

"No. You first. You spoke first. We check your discovery and then we'll check mine. See if either of us got lucky."

Everly didn't know what to say to him. She wasn't used to such generosity on a dig team. They went back to her growing hole in the dirt and got to work. In minutes they had unearthed the bones of a foot.

"Dr. Bergeron. What a find." He pulled the walkie talkie off his belt. "Nylah, Everly's just made a major find in Pit A. Can you please come to document?"

The walkie talkie in his hand crackled as it came to life. "Sure thing, boss. On my way with the camera."

"Great. We'll capture Dr. Bergeron with her discovery."

Working together, it didn't take long for the next bone to emerge, but in removing the dirt to trace the foot up the leg, they uncovered a hand. In tracing the hand to the elbow, they discovered a head. In tracing the head down the neck they quickly uncovered a pelvis.

"Oh my! They're all higgledy-piggledy in here, aren't they?" Trevor said, his brow starting to bead sweat with the hard work.

"At least they don't look like they've been eaten!" Everly whispered back. "Or else Nylah would have run away already."

"Right, whole, but jumbled they are." He shook his head as he looked at the tangled skeletons starting to emerge from the dirt.

Everly looked at Trevor. "I think we need to call in the calvary. This is starting to be too many for just the two of us."

"Right. Nylah!" Trevor called out. "Hey Nylah? Can you please ask Gunther and company to come to Pit A?"

Nylah appeared at the side of the pit. "Yeah, sure. Oh, look, you found so many more of them." She snapped with her camera. "This will be great for the website! Our followers will love it! I mean, these dudes look like a fun-loving lot: it's like they died playing Twister!"

◆━◆━◆

Everly lay on her cot unable to sleep. There was something bothering her, but she couldn't put her finger on it. This should be the most miserable research assignment ever. They lived in tents. Old, slightly moldy ones. When they showered, it was in cold water. The dig director's organization scheme could have been written by a drunk donkey: it made no sense. It was everything that just six months ago would have described her nightmare research assignment, but the funny thing was… she was not living a nightmare. She was having fun. The work was not only thrilling, it was a blast. Yes, she was having the most fun she could remember. She had never thought that working with someone like Dr. Payne could be a pleasant experience, but in reality, their styles complemented one another quite well.

And nice bonus, she thought, *he seems to appreciate what I bring to the team too.* That was definitely not how she felt around the other faculty back in Toronto.

Another surprise: she was grateful for Nylah, despite the fact that the girl knew nothing about archeology, history, or frankly, science. Having a third person to help organize and run the dig changed the tenor from what might have been awkward had it been just Everly and Dr. Payne, even with their army of local students. Nylah had quickly taken on the role of Girl Friday, making sure everything was organized. And she had a great food sense—their little trio's working dinners always felt like they should be written up in some "locavore" magazine. Of course, Nylah had Hans to help her navigate the food finds, from local farmer's stands to specialty meat and cheese shops to the wonders of European chocolate and pastry. Nylah would disappear with the car, often for overnight, and return with veritable foodie feasts for the week.

Yes, it would have been awkward without Nylah. Dr. Payne was not the typical archeologist. He was what Everly previously would have referred to as a "creative type"—rather derisively were she being honest—except now that moniker came with an aura of appreciation. And yet he was strangely proper. He always referred to her as "Dr. Bergeron", not just in front of the other students, which was probably appropriate, if a bit unnecessary, but it was how he addressed her even when they were alone. That really left her no choice but to call him "Dr. Payne", which she thought must rankle a bit since his father didn't leave much space in that realm. With a father like him, there could only be one true Dr. Payne. She'd been on plenty of digs, but never one where she felt like all the adults were teachers in some highly specialized British boarding school.

Good morning, Dr. Bergeron, I hope you're well this morning? Looking forward to a good day of digging in the dirt?

Good morning to you, Dr. Payne. I'm quite well, as I hope you are.

It was so weirdly formal, as if he didn't know how to talk to her like a real person.

"So, you're tossing and turning." Nylah's voice broke into her thoughts.

"Am I?" Everly asked, trying to keep her voice sounding innocent.

"Uh huh. Yup. So, what's bothering you?"

"Bothering me? What should be bothering me?" Everly could hear Nylah sit up on her cot.

"I don't know. But nobody tosses and turns like that unless they've got something bothering them."

"Not bothering me. I'm not bothered. I'm… excited. Yeah, that's it: I'm excited."

"It was *exciting* to find out that Twister was invented in the Middle Ages?"

"Nylah! We found forty people today. Forty. Just by way of clarification, that's a *lot*. I mean, we never could have recovered those artifacts if we hadn't pulled just everyone into the project."

Nylah nodded. "You know, at some point, you're going to have to admit it."

Everly was confused. "Admit what? That Dr. Payne has an uncanny sense of where to dig?"

"What? No! That I was right. Me! I was right. *Legions of the dead just waiting to be found.*" Nylah shook her head and Everly could hear her laying back down on her cot. "I pegged it. I told you so. Man, this is gonna be so great on the web page."

"The archeological find? Or your victory lap?" Everly couldn't suppress a snicker.

"Victory lap all the way, baby! All the way! Nah, seriously, it's gonna be a great write up: you and your find. I got such awesome pictures of you with them. They're your legions of the dead, you know."

They sat in silence for a while, then Everly said, "He gave me the find."

"What do you mean, gave you the find? When I got there he pointed to his corner with more dirt in it and then to your corner with three bodies already starting to shout with joy at seeing the light of day."

"Nylah, you do know that you can't put on the website that the skeletons were playing Twister or shouted with joy, right?"

"You take all fun out of this job, Ev, I mean, really!" Nylah was snarky right back at her. "Tell me something about archeology, writ large. You're from a university, like he is. Do you think he's a good dig director? I mean, are all digging people like him?"

Everly thought about that. "All archeologists, you mean? I don't know that I've ever met anyone quite like him."

"Yeah, I know what you mean. He's… unique."

"Uh huh. For him, talking seems to require full body engagement. I've never seen anyone so… wiggly."

"Wiggly?" Nylah asked.

"Uh huh. Does he ever talk without using his hands? Or shaking his hips? I mean, he's so, well, I should say 'animated', but if I'm telling the truth, he's wiggly."

"You're right. I got a friend like that. But he's not a professor."

"No? What does he do for a living?"

"Evan? He's a drag queen."

Everly turned her head to look toward Nylah, although it was so dark in their tent that she couldn't have seen her under any circumstances. "You don't think…"

"That he's secretly a drag queen? Nah."

Everly couldn't help but giggle.

Nylah surprised her when she said, "And I don't think he's gay either."

"I didn't ask that!"

"No, but you were thinkin' it."

"No, no, no, no, no. I was not thinking it. Nylah, he's my boss. He's a nice guy, I'll grant you that, but might as well be already married, even to another nice guy, because he's my boss on this project. And those are lines you just don't cross: already taken or your supervisor." She paused for a moment, surprised that they were even having this conversation. "I don't want to know about his personal life." Everly thought that Nylah had a world of hurt waiting for her if she held romantic fantasies about dating a work supervisor. Those were messy hashtag moments that careers didn't recover from. Either person's careers.

"He's not your boss."

"Of course, he is. He's the dig director. He's the big wig. We all report to him."

"He doesn't treat anyone like they're inferior. Not me, not you, not the students, or that Gunther guy, their professor. He defers to your judgement all the time."

"He's very egalitarian. Very good at sharing the credit. But, Nylah, a little bit of mentoring for you here: don't confuse creating a really nice team culture with actually being friends. Or any other level of interest. You never cross that line with a supervisor and he's both of our supervisors."

"Not officially. Not on paper."

"What? Of course, he is."

"Nope. The dig project is in his father's name. Some old dude who's apparently recovering from a hip replacement and secretly stalking our Instagram site is technically everybody's supervisor. You and the young Dr. T are listed as equals on all the paperwork."

"I am? But I'm just the site director."

"Well, I don't know, maybe he promoted you or something? He probably forgot to tell you, knowing him. He's a real muppet isn't he? But no, I've seen the files. You work for Dr. Trevor Payne. Senior, that is."

Everly was glad she was lying down. If she'd been standing she would've sat. Even so, it was as if the earth spun for just a bit. So, *the* Dr. Trevor Payne, the father of modern archeology, was actually listed as her supervisor? That was a career-making connection. In her world it was like saying, *Oh, Einstein? He's my uncle…*

"Yeah, there's an org chart and everything. You guys are shoulder to shoulder. Heck, half the time he tells everyone you're in charge! I guess that's probably because you actually are. I mean, why do you think he's handed off the last three press interviews to you? And those got good traction, I mean, you were like trending on Twitter for about four minutes. And he mentioned something about a tenure that he didn't need, but you do."

"Whaddya know?" As Everly lay there, she thought about how he treated her. He did defer to her judgement. He did direct the students to her. At her worst moments, she'd fleetingly thought he was dumping work on her so he could be in his head, entertained by his theories, fantasies, or more likely, that stupid novel he was enthusiastically trying to write, but no—he'd been acknowledging her expertise. Accepting her as an equal. It helped explain the press interviews. He'd been so generous as he directed the reporters to talk to her, saying:

Dr. Bergeron's really the one you want to speak with. She's really in charge around here.

Everly couldn't imagine the faculty from her own department ever doing anything like that. Sharing the credit? Promoting the ideas of a colleague? For them, everyone else was competition and the fishbowl they lived in was filled with piranhas.

"He's a nice guy." She lay there and listened to the frogs and insects making their nightly chorus and she started to feel warm all over, but in a good way.

Nylah let out a heavy sigh.

"Now that sounds like you're pondering something over there," Everly said.

Nylah was quiet for a bit, but then asked, "Did you always know you wanted to dig up dead people and their broken trash?"

Everly burst out with a laugh. "I actually never thought about it that way, but I can see where there's a ring of truth in that statement." She moved to lie on her side with her hand supporting her head. "The things we find are quite fascinating. At least to me."

"Like the old scraps of moldy, dirty clothing?"

Everly chuckled again. "Yes. Today's discovery was a huge find. And it's through discoveries like today's in particular that I feel like I get to know these people who lived hundreds of years ago. All that 'broken trash' is full of clues about their lives. Putting the puzzle together is just fascinating. Better than solving the New York Times crossword. On a Saturday."

Nylah yawned.

"Nylah, clearly archeology is not your first love. What is it that you want to do? What do you want to be when you, you know, grow up?"

Nylah sighed deeply. "I always knew exactly what I wanted to be when I grew up. I was gonna make it. Be a star. Be on stage. Be everything I ever wanted as a little girl."

Everly looked over in Nylah's direction in the darkness. With a puzzled tone she asked, "Then… why are you… here?" While she couldn't see Nylah, she knew the girl was playing with her twists, twirling the clusters of hair between her fingers, just like she always did when she was pondering an idea.

"I think it had a lot to do with my best friend. We'd always danced together. Taken ballet as little girls. Modern dance and tap as tweens. We were on the same dance squads all through high school. Shared the same dreams. Swore we were both going to dance in *Rent*. And then in *Hamilton*. And whatever next big thing that came after."

"And what happened?"

"Not what we'd planned. She went off to college, the traitor! Her dad's a college professor so she didn't really have a choice. You know how it goes."

Everly nodded. She'd seen a lot of kids at college with no idea what they wanted to study or what they wanted to become. They were there because it was an expectation. It was just the path you followed. But when a kid was trying to find themselves, figure out *who* they would become, it could be hard for them to focus on *what* they would become—and the subject matter they were supposed to study. College was hard work. It wasn't for everyone, and it certainly wasn't for those who were too distracted to put in the time and effort on coursework.

"My mom likes to call it *my gap year*," Nylah said with a chuckle, "but I was going to dance on Broadway! Or at the worst, join a traveling company that played all through Europe."

Everly put her hands behind her head and lay back on her pillow. "Wow. That really does sound like a dream."

"And it was. But a dream that, you know, never came true. I auditioned but never made a call back. All I could get was on a squad that did drill team kind of stuff during halftime at basketball games. Meanwhile, my best friend came back from her freshman year so excited about her fun new life. She was learning all kinds of stuff.

Meeting all kinds of people. To be honest, I felt left behind. I mean, I worked in a coffee shop and spent my life in tryouts."

"That must have been less than fulfilling."

"Yeah, it sucked. She was so wrapped up in her new life that she didn't even notice that I wasn't that into it. Then her dad caught me alone a bit later on and he asked me what I was waiting for. It was a big question. And the only thing I could think of was: halftime."

"Halftime?"

"Yeah. My life was basically about waiting for halftime. Waiting for that moment that I was going to dance and be on stage. He told me I was better than that and offered to help me find something more engaging. More fulfilling. And with more of a future."

"And so, you're here."

Nylah looked over at Everly in the dim light. "Yeah. He nudged me into a community college and then he learned about the scholarship. They're trying to move unlikely kids like me into four-year degree programs. I applied and got matched with Dr. Payne's project for the summer and fall semester, all expenses paid. So, you see, I made it to Europe after all, even if I ended up not on a stage but in the mud in Southern Germany. And come spring semester, I'll transfer into a four-year college with one year of community college basics behind me and about seven months of research experience."

Everly blew out her breath. "What an opportunity! Wasn't it a little bit daunting to think of all that change?"

"Nah. Once I'd mastered being a barista in New York, I knew I could do anything."

Everly laughed. "That's probably true, Nylah. That's probably true." As she lay on her cot, she felt a growing sensation inside of her. Like *she* could do anything. Just a fleeting sensation and then the reality of her past would flood in and swamp that little boat of hope, sinking it back to the dark depths. But for right now, for this moment, she clung to that feeling, wondering what it would be like to live like that. To live feeling like you could actually do anything.

Chapter 17

Father Bernard Trōst
May 1347

Bernard walked in the sunshine, enjoying the warmth on his face but distracted by the letter he had received a fortnight past. It was old and had been much delayed. He'd read it a few times since it arrived and now pulled it out of his sleeves, unfurled it, and read it yet again.

November, the year of our Lord, 1346

My Dearest Brother, Bernard,

I write you now to implore you to help me, not as a Brother of the cloth, but as a man previously born into a role assigned by God to be my own brother of bloodline. You know more well than any man on the face of this earth or in heaven, save be for Jesus himself, that I am committed to take my vows and serve our Lord. But our lord father, and here I mean our earthly father, has done the unthinkable. Bernard, Father has betrothed me! And to none other than Gerung Engelhaft. There could not be a worse fate. I would dispose of this mortal flesh except for it is a sin in the eyes of Heaven. I cannot believe that God would let it come to pass that I be wed. And to give me to an Engelhaft! They are merchants, not nobility! I cannot bear to dwell on the blasphemy of this man who I am to be sworn to as a wife, until death do us part. Bernard, I heard him say to his own brother that "hell and paradise are simply specters to frighten us". He said they are the Avati coco, nothing more than a bogeyman, that scare the children into behaving. When I challenged him, told him that I was in a state of despair over his soul, he had the audacity to think I was making a joke! He laughed as though we were sharing this humor, and he actually made the claim that: God will save the good Jew; God will save the good Moor, for He loves all His creation.

Much to my shock, he predicted that he and I would be in good company, being broad-minded men and women. I was so insulted, I laughed at his absurd ideas. Bernard, how can I be wed to such a heathen? You must intervene with Father! Both as a Brother of the cloth and as my brother of blood. This simply cannot be borne. I cannot be the wife of an apostate!

I have prayed and worn my hairshirt under my clothes daily to mortify my flesh. I had to cut and re-fashion the one you left to make it fit so that no one knows it's there. Mother would have a conniption if she were aware. But God knows. He knows my suffering and I pray that it may please Him. I cry each night, dear brother,

Bernard rolled the page and slid it up his sleeve for safekeeping. He resumed his walk to meditate on the developments at home. It was most interesting. "Ahh, my sister. I hope you will find some fulfillment in sacrificing yourself to be a dutiful wife." He knew his sister: she was far more persuaded by sacrifice and suffering than by duty. Or even happiness.

But Gerung? He remembered Gerung quite well. Good man. Good mind. Well educated. Fun. They had been friends at one point in time. Merchant class, yes, but fabulously wealthy. It was obvious that their father wanted influence and Gerung's father must want legitimacy. Yet it surprised Bernard that Gerung would have agreed to the match with Adelaide. While Bernard could see where it was a good match in the parents' eyes, he did wonder whether he should intervene on behalf of Gerung?

He shook his head as he thought of his father. "The old Duke cannot understand his own lack of influence, but it probably has something to do with the volume of his style of persuasion: if you don't agree with him, he simply gets louder and louder until you do. And his fists come into it at some point in time. Ah, my Pa." Bernard released a heavy sigh. "He might be figuring out that there are other ways, if he's trying to make an alliance with the Engelhafts. I would suppose that they persuade with the vast amount of wine and spirits they pour into other people's cups. That seems to go far in the field of influence."

Bernard smirked at the words he heard himself say aloud, for it was precisely what he was doing to promote the creation of public works for this town. "I guess I learned more from Gerung than I thought. He's a good man."

He wondered how a match between Gerung and Adelaide would work out. "Happiness is not what matches are about, are they? No, they have other purposes. The match will bring Gerung's family much more power."

It was true, the merchant classes had risen far beyond what anyone ever could have imagined. Particularly after the archbishops had been banned from Cologne, a fate they well deserved for how they had been abusing their power, and were currently exiled to Bonn, from where they continued to meddle. But the merchant class and the guilds now held equal sway with the nobility, a fact only true in Germania. For too long, fathers had divided their duchies amongst all their sons, resulting in tiny fiefs and an excess of dukes throughout the lands. The king was elected and weak, the aristocracy of the church claimed a more than equal stake in rulership, thus each fiefdom felt entitled to go its own way ignoring them all. It created a ripple effect as small towns sprung up in the South unallied with a noble family, tiny bastions of unauthorized freedom. Lack of unity within any group created ripe circumstances for previously unimaginable, yet productive alliances across them: hence the highly logical and advantageous betrothal of his sister to his old friend.

Bernard was not surprised at what Adelaide reported in her letter. Gerung believed in the equality of men, no matter their religious background. Bernard had heard similar thoughts from the more free-thinking inhabitants of this town. Gerung also believed that women had good minds and stout spirts and thus should be respected and honored; allowed to make decisions for themselves. At one time the thought had left Bernard speechless, but now that he lived in this small town he understood: women made up half the population and that meant that half the shopkeepers, half the merchants, half the craftsmen, half the farmers were actually women. There was no possible way a small-town society could function without the efforts, intelligence, and sweat of the women who lived there. Indeed, the quite successful butcher who had gifted him with the half-barrel of wine upon his arrival had been a woman.

Bernard clasped his hands behind his back, deep in thought as he walked. *I am grateful for the lessons bestowed upon me, the gifts of wisdom granted, and the evolution of my own enlightenment, my Lord,* he prayed in three parts. The experience had stretched him, that was certain, but it had changed his mind and reformed his opinions in ways he had not anticipated as remotely possible. He had failed to understand what it meant to be the firstborn son of one of the most powerful dukes in Germania until he gave it up. And now he understood that his previous life of privilege meant not understanding the strength and the ingenuity and yes, even the charity of the common folk.

"Father Bernard! Father Bernard!"

He turned to see a young lad running across the field towards him. "Konrad! What is it?"

The boy caught up to him and put his hands on his knees, breathing hard.

"Catch your breath, my son. Take your time."

The boy stood up and took a few more deep inhales. "Father Bernard, the diggers sent me to find you. I've looked all over. Why are you out here in the hillsides?"

"Because they are beautiful."

"But they're dangerous, Father Bernard. And no one wants to lose ye to the demons who live here in the wilds. You're popular! People like ye! You're nothing like the old grim friar."

Bernard laughed. "Well, I do ply the people with wine when they engage in good works to make our little town prosper. I do reward their charity to one another, and their willingness to learn and try new things."

"True. I've heard me own parents talk about your generosity. Says it makes them feel generous as well. People like ye. They like themselves when you're in the pulpit. They would all cry if they lost ye to the hillside demons."

Bernard took the lad's hand and turned towards the path back to the town. "I have had a good stroll, a lovely time talking with the Lord, some time to contemplate family matters. It is of the hour to return to the town. But tell me more of these 'demons of the hills'? What wildlife lives here that frightens the people so? For I have only seen the slow-moving Black Grouse and his mate. And quite a few overly tame marmots."

Konrad stuck out his tongue. "Marmots! Bah. Taste awful, they do. Me Pa has sworn he'll never bag another, no matter how nice their fur might be. Better to just breed the rabbits, tired as we get of their meat."

Bernard laughed out loud and spoke with comical drama to the boy, "Yes, we will leave the dreadful marmots to their wild and dangerous hills."

"Aw, you tease me, Father Bernard, don't ye? But it's not the marmots I'm afraid of, not unless they're on me dinner plate and then I'm greatly afeared indeed! It's the wild pigs. I'm dead frightened of them."

"Wild pigs. There are… boars in these valleys?"

"Oh, aye, there's one. He's the king of the wild pigs. Has his family right with him in tow all the time. He's a giant. A devil pig they say. Bigger than me. Almost as big as ye are, but much, much wider. I've never seen him with me own eyes, which is probably why I'm still Konrad the boy, and not poor dead Konrad, eaten by a herd of wild swine, nothin' left to gather up and bury."

Bernard started to pick up their pace. He expected foxes in the hills. Birds of all manner. Admitted there could be a lone wolf, but in truth anticipated that the great number of birds and rabbits and deer to prey upon would more than satisfy such a creature, who would not then be tempted to target a man as a potential source of food. These animals did not hunt for sport, they hunted to satisfy hunger, and then, like water, they chose the path of least resistance, the easiest catch that could be made. But wild pigs were different. They were herd animals. They would trample you at the slightest provocation. And boars had reputations as cantankerous, nasty lots who would gladly assume any moving object was a challenger to their dominion. He did not want to run into a wild boar guarding his harem.

"Let's look lively there, Konrad. We don't want to meet this devil you describe."

"But I haven't told ye about the devil yet, sir. I've only told ye about the big pig."

Without breaking stride Bernard said, "What could be out here that would be more frightening than a giant wild boar?"

"Well," Konrad said, "there's the devil himself. Or his henchman. We aren't quite sure and believe me, no one wants to find out. Ye see, a dark gray devil has been spotted in these hills. He comes from time-to-time and if he's seen, ye know one of the herd is going to disappear: goats or a sheep. Once even a cow!"

Bernard gave a chuckle. "Konrad, I think what you have is a thief, probably from another village or some remote farmstead in the hills, who doesn't want to be identified, mostly because he's stealing our townsfolk's livestock."

Konrad shook his head. "No. No. Ye might think that, but he's a devil. Big he is, a big old gray wrap about him, blowin' in the wind. A huge, tall head. Not shaped like a man. Eyes, red and glowing. He's the grim reaper to be sure. And when he takes a beast, he leaves a pool of green slime behind him."

"Green slime?"

"Aye. Blood of the devil, we call it. Ye can't touch it. We dig it out from the dirt and carry it out to a pit we've dug deep in the ground outside of town."

"How curious. Why do you do that?"

"If we leave it and an animal eats it, because, ye know, dumb, animals are, well then, they die. And it burns, it does. We've learned to not touch it. It will take your skin right off. Me own father has a scar something fierce on his hand where some of it once splattered. He shown the devil's blood to me now, so that I'll recognize it when I see it and never make the mistake of stepping in it, maybe losing me foot if I did so. We've got special shovels to move it with, because it burns through them too, but I'm not allowed to help 'cause of being so young."

"What is this pit?"

"Most people call it the pit of the damned. Some throw their trash in there, broken things, tools, discarded animal bones after a feast and the like. Me Pa says some fools get a thrill from the danger of going near the pit, but most don't stand close. Most hurl their refuse from as far away as they can throw it." Then Konrad's tone lightened up quite a bit, "But of course, now that you're building cesspits and latrines for our village, people won't have to go close to the pit of the damned no more. They can just put their refuse where they take a shit! Oh, yes, you're very popular! Some are calling ye The Piss King."

"How, uh, quaint." Bernard tried to digest this new information. He started to think that creating formal trash pits outside the town area would be a good idea and help preserve his public 'neccessariums'. "Konrad, have you seen this devil-man?"

"The grim reaper himself? Just once. I was tasked with bringing the goats back, sometimes the sheep, from grazing up in the hills. And I saw him a stridin' across the valley, heading towards the swamp."

"What swamp?"

Konrad pointed to a low pass between two of the mountains. "It's supposed to be there. But me dad'd beat me somethin' fierce were I to go a-lookin' for it. These hills got a wolf or two, the wild pigs, and the devil. Dad tells me it ain't no place for a boy like me. And I think me dad is right!"

"Has anyone gone to check this out? To see if there is a swamp?"

Konrad shook his head. "A group of the men went once, carrying pitch forks and rough swords and the like, but halfway there, they ran into the wild pigs. The great boar killed one of them. Ran him right over. It was all they could do to get the body back."

"That's terrible!" Bernard wondered if they could possibly move any faster. Ecclesiastical robes were not made for speed, and neither were a young lad's legs. "No wonder no one else ever tried."

"Oh, one man did. That old Friar Tuck said he wasn't afraid."

"And what happened to him?"

"He came back from his try, said he didn't make it, and that he was now very, very afraid. Said he'd run into the devil himself. Saw his glowing eyes, burning red like hot coals in a fire. Old Tuck had a burn on his arm, he did. Bad one, too. Said he barely got away with his life and that he's not going back there and he forbid any of the villagers from giving it a try. Said he'd say special prayers and make sacrifices to protect our village from the specter. Said he and his could suffer and Christ would grant them special protection and the specter would never set foot in our town."

Bernard looked at the boy, astonishment written all over his face. "Through his suffering, he will protect the town from the devil's servant?"

Konrad nodded seriously. "A lot of people went to his little church after that. Me parents did, but they couldn't stay. Said it wasn't for them. Don't right know why but they were right glad when ye came to town. Breath of fresh air ye were. Brought the Holy Spirit back, so they said."

The village was now in sight and Bernard felt he could moderate their pace a bit. His head was spinning both from their quick walk in the hot sun and from the stories Konrad shared.

"And what was it that you wanted me for in the first place?"

"Oh, the diggers, they've run into a question. Never built a cesspit before, have they? So, they don't know what's next."

"Oh! Yes. Fine," Bernard said with relief as he looked over his shoulder at the hills, wondering if the specter was lurking there someplace. "Take me to them, Konrad."

◆━◆━◆

Hours later, Bernard returned to the manse, only to learn that a trade wagon had arrived earlier in the day, bearing with it more church-related shipments and a few barrels of gifts from his uncle. Among the items that his servant had laid on his table were two scrolled letters from Adelaide. Both of them were months old.

"Oh Adelaide! It does no good to write me in winter as there are no trade wagons until all the snows melt." He started with the scroll on which the wax seal was chipped, as it looked far older.

January, the year of our Lord, 1347
Dear Bernard,

Today my world and my dreams ended. Today I was traded by my father for his political gain, sent like a sheep to slaughter, and forced to become Adelaide Trōst Engelhaft. I am a married woman. There is no mortification of the flesh that will reinstate my innocence in the eyes of the Lord and I shall never now be allowed to become a nun. My calling is denied me and for me, the sun shall never shine. I will continue to pray that I may learn to forgive you for turning your back to your only sister and allowing her to rot in the prison of marriage to a faithless man who would defend Jews and Muslims and turn his back on the one and only true faith and true path. My very virginity, that which I dedicated to the Lord, has now been taken by this man whom I am forced to call

Bernard returned the letter to the table. His sister went on for some additional pages in this vein, blaming him for her fortunes. Blaming her father. Blaming Gerung, who Bernard had always found to be a congenial fellow, perhaps a bit overly fond of wine and a warm fire, quick with a clever retort, but he was an intelligent and deep thinker. A philosopher. Bernard remembered many a late-night debate with Gerung and his friends about whether God loved diversity in all things and if he had indeed made man around the world, did he not love them though they were different than the men who might live in Germania? Or who might live under a rule that was not Christian? Or live in a wild place to which Christianity had never been introduced?

Bernard wished his father would write to him, but apparently the old goat was still too angry. He had never known his mother to write a letter in her life, but there were always items in the barrels that were tied up in ribbons of her particular colors, so he knew they were gifts from her. She was thinking of him. She still loved him.

With some trepidation, he opened the other scroll and eagerly scanned it for news of his mother and father, of little Dietmar, or the talented and fun-loving Adolfus.

report to him on the count of the ducks and chickens in our estate? Women of esteem weave and sew. They do not count ducks. Women of measure embroider richly to adorn the wardrobe of the household. They do not collect eggs. He would reduce me to the role of the house steward! It is demeaning and humiliating. Perhaps I should bear this torment with grace since it must serve as my mortification. My husband, in his great wisdom, as he puts it to me, has taken my hair shirt. Can you believe that, Bernard? He has removed my path to the divine and my road to supplication of the Lord! I can only believe him to be envious, as he is a man of leisure and pleasure, and cannot bear to suffer for the sake of the Lord. As part of my penance, I pray for his deliverance, but I am afraid that the Lord God hears the hollowness of my petitions upon my husband, for I struggle to be whole of heart when the rote words fall from my lips.

This man whom I must call husband has the audacity to tell me that if I choose to suffer as a dutiful wife, that he will happily provide me with all the suffering my heart desires, as he satisfies his desires of quite a different nature. Oh, my brother, why am I not delivered from the indignities of marriage? I have been devout all my life. I can only try to be like Job and suffer in silence while my faith remains unblemished. The Lord will deliver me. He has a miraculous plan. He will show me the way. I have a destiny.

Bernard set the letter down and rubbed his temples. All in all, given his choice he thought it would have been more pleasant had he spent this last hour at the cesspit project. That hairshirt. He had forgotten to pack it and had never thought of it again. Even Clement the Sixth wasn't a proponent of them and Bernard found their itchiness didn't bring him closer to God. It just distracted him with all the scratching. But Adelaide had found it and now claimed it as her own. Or did until Gerung took it from her. "Good man."

Maybe it had not been a good idea when their father had insisted that all his children learn how to read and write. As a duke, the man wished to brag about the intelligence, accomplishments, and obedience of his offspring, and so tutors were brought in for each of them. Adelaide had latched onto learning the Bible, which had been an early sign of her obedience as a good and faithful Christian daughter. Suddenly, Bernard couldn't suppress his laugh.

"Intelligence and obedience. Father, your insistence on our education made each one of us disobedient. My education led me to the cloth. Adolfus' mastery of the musical arts became his disobedience. Dietmar, the son meant for the vows, learned about bearing arms and ever plays with his toy soldiers. And even Adelaide, who cannot choose her destiny, is surely trying to rebel by using up all of the paper in the entire city of Cologne!" Bernard pulled out the wooden box in which he kept correspondence. He filed Adelaide's missive with the others. Paper was too precious to waste, even if it was filled with the words of a whining woman.

"Oh Gerung, my brother, if only dear Adelaide understood that had you become a clergyman, you would most assuredly have risen to become pope, then indeed, she would love you." Bernard wondered briefly what kind of man Adelaide could ever love? She was so young and already so jaded. "Bless you, Gerung. Bless you for being the husband to my sister." He thought his friend would need all the blessings he could get.

Chapter 18

Adelaide Trōst Engelhaft
May 1348

Adelaide walked next to Gerung through the street, glad she had been allowed to come along on his business. He seemed distracted and his thoughts far away from her, or anyone on the street for that matter. She'd had to steer him away from bumping into people more than once. Not that there were that many people out and about. Since the Blue Sickness had come, great mortality followed in its wake. Few now ventured into the streets. Taking care of the sick and the dead was an all-consuming process. Few in her own household volunteered to go out. While that was a disappointment, she was happy that none of them had been visited by the specter of illness as yet.

"Do you hear that, my lor-, um, my husband?" She had heard her mother call her father *my lord* so many times that she found it nearly impossible to erase the words from her tongue when she addressed her own spouse.

"What, my lady?"

"I hear cries! Like, like a processional!" She stopped and turned her head towards the distant sounds of *Make way! Make way!* "Do you not hear that, good sir?"

For a moment, she was excited, remembering the joyous processions that would march down the promenade and through the streets before the plague had come. She used to love the events and tried to be on the streets as much as possible so that she wouldn't miss them. She felt a pang of guilt at the memory. To hold any joy during times like these felt unseemly. Even the recollection of joy.

"A processional?" Gerung grunted. "Haven't seen one of those in all too long."

"Yes! I remember most fondly the processionals that would call the faithful to mass for the lesser holidays."

With a smile Gerung replied, "The lesser holidays. Quite right, for then the churches would be looking to fill their pews and use the procession of priests and monks to entice the people to give up their sunny afternoon for one of worship inside a cool house of stone, not attending to either business nor pleasure!"

She ignored the sarcastic tone in his voice. "And at times a bishop himself would be in the parade!"

"Ah, such days to remember," her husband said, but that tone lingered in his voice.

"Come, my husband, let us away to the side of the street so that we can have a good view." She was happy that he obliged her. In past times she had often been pushed against the buildings themselves by the crush of people, making it challenging to see the excitement. There would be no such challenge today. "Perhaps Pope Clement the Sixth will have given a rich gift to one of the city's cathedrals? You know, I remember one such processional for a quite a large cross. It took three men to hold it up on the poles for the people to see."

Gerung smiled at her. "Cologne's churches enjoy a healthy rivalry in attaining the Pope's good will. They certainly enjoy showing off their riches in order to entice the membership of the city's populace."

"I was amazed to see such a cross! And I'm not ashamed to confess that although the church was not my regular, I did attend a mass so that I could witness the glory of that gold cross shining above the altar. It was well worth the visit."

"And did you leave an offering? A nice one?"

"Of course, I did!"

"Nicer than you usually left in your own house of worship?"

Adelaide looked around a bit uncomfortably, thinking back. She was annoyed at what she suspected was one of his logic traps, his little debates that left her feeling slow and stupid. No matter how she answered, yay or nay, he would make a comment that made her feel silly. It was damned if you do or damned if you don't. Carefully she answered, "Yes. I believe I did. But there is no sin in that!"

"Oh no. No sin at all! It's just proof of the pudding that the processional had its desired effect."

She decided to change the subject. "I even liked the parades that celebrated the changing of the drapes to signify whether Christ is suffering, crucified, or resurrected." She sighed audibly. "The purple were always my favorite."

"Christ suffering. Of course, they were. My dear, maybe you should leave the suffering to men."

She looked resolutely down the street and wouldn't meet his eyes when he looked at her. "Before the Blue Sickness, some of these processions had been pageants. They taught Biblical lessons or recounted the history of the world to the people. Those were the days! I wonder if this procession will be something like that, something to remind the people of the great plan of God, even during these dark times." She felt so hopeful and internally pleaded that he wouldn't mock her.

"I share your passion, my Adelaide, for I, too, loved those guild-sponsored stages. The pageant wagons with the guild members themselves as the actors!" He burst out with laughter. "Such memories. I will take you today to the house of a good friend of mine who designed some of those wagons and wrote one of their plays. You'll like him. And his family."

"Is that where we're going?" She lifted her skirts to keep them out of the muddy section that lay between them and a place they could stand where the sun wouldn't be in their eyes. She hoped this would be a pageant with wagons and a theater for the masses and not just a processional celebrating the betrothal or a marriage of the city's elite. Her own such processional had been her least favorite of all.

As they stood at the side of the street, they listened to the cries which were getting louder. She could almost make out their words. Suddenly, they came around the corner.

"Make way, make way! Make way for the suffering so that Christ may know we share in His. Make way! Make way!" resounded from the pole and flag bearers at the front of the line and a chanting-like singing came from the group of men following behind. She was in shock. The men wore black hats of various shapes and hooded drapes of somber colors partially covering their shoulders, but their chests and arms were bare and the wraps of once-white cloth around their lower extremities did little to cover them.

"Why! They are naked! And so many of them!" She reeled in her astonishment and grabbed onto her husband's arm to steady herself.

"Half naked. And about thirty, by my count." He looked grim as he watched the men make their slow march past them, their chant like a dirge. "Smaller numbers than reports I've heard, but still..." His expression turned to worry.

Adelaide could not look away. She knew it was unseemly to stare so blatantly at the nearly naked men walking and singing in unison down the street, but she could not help herself. Neither could any of the other observers.

"What is that?" she asked, staring at the red streaks running down the backs of some of the men. As she looked harder, she noticed that all the men were covered with welts and cuts, most of which were swollen. Most of the men were bleeding and surely all would be soon.

Suddenly, one of the men cried out: *"For Christ!"*

The others returned the shout in unity: *"For Christ!"*

Then they started to sing. Four at the front would call out a line of their *Geisslerlieder* chant, then the others following behind would repeat it. At the end of each echoed line, as one, the group would swing their right hands over their shoulders, where a scourge with three tails, each with knots and a tiny, barbed cross within, would then strike their backs. Many cried out in pain. One screamed in agony. Blood was spattering as they sang:

> *Now here comes the wave of evil*
> *Now here comes the wave of evil*
> *Flee from hot, hot hell.*
> *Flee from hot, hot hell.*
> *Lucifer is an evil companion.*
> *Lucifer is an evil companion.*
> *Whomever he catches, he smears with pitch.*
> *Whomever he catches, he smears with pitch.*
> *Therefore, we intend to flee him.*
> *Therefore, we intend to flee him.*

"What are they singing?" Adelaide whispered to her husband. "I do not know this hymn."

"It's a called a flagellant song. A *Geisslerlieder*. It's not a good thing that they are here. At least there are so few."

"So few?" She looked around her, stunned. "They seem to be so many."

"Other cities have as many as five hundred. An army of naked, bleeding men whipping themselves with their scourges. Tournai is particularly bad."

Adelaide stared keenly at the men, finding this whole business to be quite fascinating in a macabre sort of fashion. She could not tear her gaze away.

"Who are they?" Adelaide whispered to her husband. She took a step closer, but Gerung pulled her back.

"Careful. They'll spatter on you. They are called flagellants. They beat themselves to illustrate to Christ how they suffer. They seek God's forgiveness and to end this plague through their suffering."

"They suffer so that the people of Cologne will not? That is so noble!" She could feel her heart beating faster in her chest.

"Adelaide, it is highly doubtful that one man's suffering, no matter how well-intended, will prevent another from becoming ill and dying. It is a false nobility."

"What are they doing now?"

"Something useless, I am sure."

The men lined up into three columns, with the man at the head of each column lying prostrate on the ground in a shape of a cross. The next behind him in line would step over his prostrate fellow and strike the man with his scourge as he did so. After each follower in the column had struck the flagellant lying in the road, the next man in line would take his place, lying down prostrate, and the ritual continued until each man had been struck by every other in his column. Then they all stood up and replaced their caps and reformed their lines.

Adelaide looked about her. Blood was spattered on the walls of the building. It was all over the men. It was all over the ground. She felt the whole street had been washed in redemption. She had been washed in redemption just to be in their presence. "These are holy brothers! Saints!"

Gerung snorted. "They'll join the saints soon. Like as not these fellows will so weaken their humors that they'll not have a chance of surviving the sickness when it visits them. There is no purpose to this. You cannot suffer for another or redeem another's sins."

"Christ did. He suffered for us. And we are forgiven of our sins because of it. They are noble. They are holy men to take this on, on our behalf." She was insistent.

"These men are not like Christ, Adelaide. They also blame the Jews for the plague."

Adelaide looked at her husband in horror. "The Jews did this to us?"

He gave her that exasperated sigh and rolled his eyes. She was so accustomed to that look from him. "No, Adelaide. The Jews have nothing to do with this plague."

A man standing within earshot of them leaned over and said, "I heard it whispered that they poisoned the wells!"

"Come, Adelaide. We are late for our appointment. And no one, but no one, poisons their own children. The Jews are dying of the Blue Sickness just like the rest of us." Gerung bit off the words as he passed the man and pulled Adelaide away.

As they moved away from him, the man added, "I hear they have secret protections and do not take ill as do Christians. They must be blasphemers for sure, or they would be suffering just like the Christians!"

Adelaide was astounded. She asked Gerung, "What protections could anyone need other than their cross and their Bible?"

"Yes, Adelaide. Those are very powerful totems for you. When I've given you money to give to the poor, you've instead handed out wooden crosses on leather thongs to them, to make sure they wear the symbol that they follow Christ. My God, woman, I've even seen you give them to the Jews."

"Well, they need them the most of all!"

Gerung rolled his eyes.

The pole-bearing leaders resumed their cry of "Make way! Make way!" and then the men started up their chanting again as the entire party moved on down the street and eventually out of view. When she heard the singing stop, she could hear the cry of "For Christ!" ring out in chorus in another square and knew what was about to happen.

Gerung quickened his pace and she took hurried steps to keep up with him.

In another half hour they came to their destination in a merchant district of town. With prosperity, Gerung's family had purchased homes that had formerly belonged to noble families now facing thinned out fortunes, or in Gerung's case himself, the home of a former archbishop who had been exiled to Bonn and forced to give up his property. Adelaide was surprised to see that the Jewish merchants lived in such nice homes. They weren't anything to rival the nobility or the clergy, for certain, but she had expected their homes to be more like the shopkeepers who lived above their stores. Those were adequate to the station of the people.

"These shopkeepers must be a prosperous folk to live in such finery. I didn't know these guild fellows were merchant kings like your family."

"When you import silks and precious ores, you are not merely a baker or candlestick maker. It is important to guild leaders that they show off their riches, since no merchant wants to do business with an unsuccessful one! It's a principle of business begets business. You and I live as we do because it is important that all these folk see us as kings of the merchants."

"Not only the merchants! The nobility and the clergy too. Humph! It sounds like pride and vanity to me."

"Well, if the clog fits, it fits," Gerung said with a wry smile.

"I'm sure I don't know what you mean," Adelaide said, feeling confused.

He stopped in front of a large, well-kept house and knocked on the door. It was answered by a servant, and Gerung announced himself and his wife.

The man invited them in and said, "I bid you to kindly wait here," and then disappeared through a set of doors.

Gerung turned towards his wife. "Now Adelaide, I want you to smile and look lovely and welcoming, do you understand? No matter what you hear, I want you to be pleasant and look pleasant and more than anything, I do not want you to speak until I ask you to. And then I only want you to agree with me. Do you understand?"

She nodded solemnly. She was never asked to come along on his business ventures, so she was excited for the secrets of trade that she was going to learn. If he wanted her support, she would gladly gift him with that.

"Good. Now keep to your word." He turned as their host came into the entrance hall.

"Aahron!"

"Gerung! My friend. I am so happy to see you." The middle-aged man came over to Gerung and gave him a kiss on each cheek. "You are looking well. I see married life is suiting you."

"And so it is. Please, let me introduce you to my wife. This is the Lady Adelaide Trōst Engelhaft." Adelaide gave the man a small curtsy, not sure of how far she should dip to a merchant and wondering if his wealth might require her to bend her knees a bit more?

"Lady Adelaide, wife of Gerung, you are welcome in our home." The man gave her a little bow and invited Gerung and Adelaide into a chamber clearly meant for entertainment and pleasure. There were comfortable chairs about and small tables, musical instruments which looked like they were well loved and regularly used, embroidery set up by a window, and several books lying about. Within moments of being seated a woman entered, wearing a dress made of richly embroidered fabric with a lace kerchief upon her head. She was accompanied by a servant, bearing glasses of mead.

Their hospitality rivals our own, Adelaide thought, and felt a slight twinge of injustice, for such finery was not meant for people of business. She reminded herself to stitch a smile onto her face and hold it there, as her husband had ordered.

"Please allow me to introduce my own wife to you. This is Rivkeh. Rivkeh, you remember Gerung? And this is his bride, the Lady Adelaide Trōst Engelhaft."

"It is lovely to meet you," Rivkeh said, adding, "You are welcome in our home." She also gave Gerung a kiss on both cheeks and started to move toward Adelaide, but after seeing the look on Adelaide's face, she seemed to settle for a politely deep curtsy instead. "Please, do sit. Be comfortable."

After some discussion about who they each knew who had died of the Blue Sickness, and then the weather—the only point at which Gerung turned to Adelaide for comment—he became more serious. "Aahron, Rivkeh, I'm afraid I have come with news of developments in the North. Tournai has seen violence. I fear for what might happen here in Cologne as well."

Aahron nodded, a sad look on his face. "We live caged lives. We can only work as the pope or the local nobility gives us licenses. We can only live where they will allow us. And then we are blamed for all ills that befall mankind."

"Oh, by the saints! You're Jewish!" Adelaide stared at Aahron and Rivkeh, who just smiled awkwardly. Then she stared at the house around her. She never thought to set foot in the house of Jew. She wondered what she might be seeing that would have given her a clue, but she realized that she knew nothing about these people that she hadn't heard whispered at church or at a dinner event with other nobility. She was amazed at how lovely their home was and how it attested to the talent of those who lived within. Her mind felt like it was full of bees buzzing and she felt dazed and confused at such contradiction. She could hardly comprehend the words of her husband as he spoke with their hosts.

"I have come, with my wife, bearing an invitation. A plea, actually. Aahron, I beg of you to bring your wife and children to our home. I had thought to merely try to persuade you, but today my mission has become all the more urgent."

"Come to your home?" Rivkeh asked.

Adelaide was stunned that this woman would speak as though she were an equal in this conversation. She could feel herself getting hotter. Women were not to venture opinions in such a manner.

"Yes. We can keep you safe there. Both of you. And the children. And your two servants. Bring what you wish but we must be quick and we must be discreet."

"My work? My business? My life here..." Aahron sounded devastated.

"Your lives are worth more than your business. I know, I'm asking you to leave everything, it must feel like I'm asking you to lose everything, but indeed, you must come when I send a wagon for you tonight. Please my friend, you must come and live with us. Hide with us."

Again, Rivkeh spoke. "Hide with you?"

Gerung nodded, a grim look on his face. "The flagellants have come to Cologne."

Both Aahron and Rivkeh took in sharp breaths.

"They are still a small band, but their numbers will swell. And they will be hit with a religious fervor. And they will come for you. For your kind."

Aahron swallowed hard. "I have heard of some of the attacks. People being burned alive. Slaughtered."

"That is why you must come. I can keep you safe until either this madness passes or we can figure out what to do. Our household is large enough. My wife will give up her apartments to your family."

"I will do what? Where will I sleep?" Adelaide felt breathless and could hardly form the words.

Gerung turned towards her. "With me, of course."

Adelaide swallowed hard and nodded demurely. This is why he had told her to not speak. He knew she wouldn't agree with his plans.

Gerung turned back to Aahron and Rivkeh. "Will you come? My friends, I do believe all your lives depend upon it."

They looked at one another and then back at Gerung. Rivkeh wiped a tear from her cheek, but it was Aahron who answered. "When your wagon comes, we will be ready. We will be quiet. Discreet."

Gerung nodded. "It will be a Christian cart to keep you safe in passage. I have enjoyed your acting in the processionals in happier times. There will be serious roles for all of you to play in the days ahead. I am sorry to have to ask it of you. It is about being... discreet."

"We understand." Aahron took his wife's hand. "We thank you."

"Our community…" Rivkeh's words were broken with tears.

"Tell them to prepare. I know not what choices they will make. I don't know what they should do. I wish I could help them all. But it is in our power to help you."

"Bless you, my friend. Bless you," Aahron said. "You are a righteous man."

The couples said their goodbyes, or at least everyone did but Adelaide, who was too dumbstruck to say anything at all.

As they walked the streets back to their home, Gerung said, "Not a word, my wife. Not a word until we are in our own bedchamber."

They saw no more flagellants as they made their way through the streets back to their residence. Adelaide didn't think she could have spoken on any account. Her head was spinning with thoughts of giving up her apartments and having to share her husband's. She shuddered. And just how did her husband know that Jews didn't start the plague? Someone had to start it. *It's not like it was coming from animals! They aren't dying,* she thought furiously to herself.

An entire month passed before she and Gerung had a heated argument.

Adelaide was pacing. "You take away my freedom, to take my rooms away from me. Now I just shelter like a spider in your apartments." Alone with him was the only place she could ever say what she truly felt. Or at least a part of it.

"You have no less freedom now than you did." He looked exasperated. "You just have… more guests."

"More guests? We have *no* guests since they have been with us, lest someone recognize who or what they are. I can't believe the servants aren't whispering about it when they run the errands. We'll be lucky if we don't have a horde of armed citizens out for blood at our doors as well." She was wringing her hands. She knew he hated it when she did it, but she couldn't help herself. The anxiety was tearing her apart. The only thing that would make her feel better would be to wear her hair shirt, to suffer for redemption, but he had destroyed it.

"The servants won't talk. I guarantee you they won't talk."

She wondered how he could sound so confident. "There is no way you can make such a guarantee! All servants talk. It is in their nature. That is why the nobility send them away when we talk about anything important. And still the walls have ears."

He walked over to the table and poured himself a glass of wine. "They will not talk, Adelaide. The servants all have ties to that community."

She turned to stare at him. "You have secretly filled our house with these people? And then you brought more here?"

"They are good people. They are safer here."

"But are we safe?"

There was a pause before he answered, "No one is truly safe these days. Don't fool yourself, my dear. There is nothing that can protect us from this blue sickness and the ills it brings through superstition and belief in magic."

Adelaide was tempted to pour herself a glass of wine to steady her nerves. She thought that Gerung must have seen the look on her face because he put down his and poured her a glass. As he handed it to her, she said in a small voice, "What if they are responsible? What if they have brought this down on mankind?"

"Brought this down on mankind? What? How? Think about what you're saying. This plague came from God. Not from any man, woman, or child. From God."

"Well, if the plague came from God then maybe He is mad that not all men are Christians! That must be what he is trying to teach us!" She couldn't believe that Gerung had no capacity for logic at all in this matter. "They cross our borders, coming from... well, wherever they come from. They aren't us. They aren't like us. They are coming to displace us, to take over our good Christian lives and take away what we have! Just look at how prosperous they are. This is a Christian country. It's meant for Christians!"

Gerung sighed heavily. "Oh, Good Lord above, please bring me something much stronger to drink!" He clasped his hands in mock prayer. "For you have saddled me with a cow for a wife!" He turned to Adelaide. "Listen to me, my Lady: you will show them all kindness and decency. Not only did this plague not come from the Jews, this family did nothing but live their lives in peace and quiet. And now, since they have been with us for the past month, many of their friends lie dead. Their lovely house was burnt to the ground. Those massacres won't stop. This is the only place they are safe. They will continue to live their lives in what peace and quiet they can take solace in here, in your apartments, which, while nice, my Lady, are not truly sufficient for eight people! Yet I do not hear any complaining from them. Despite their grieving and losses."

In the end she made no headway with her husband, unable to help him to see reason. He made her swear upon her cross that she would show them every mercy and never speak a word of their presence to anyone. She went to bed that night without a word to him, glad he seemed to have no interest in any nightly pleasure. In truth, he did not even seem to want to look at her and he stayed up late in other parts of their manor. *Probably with his Jewish friends,* she thought uncharitably. She didn't know what to do, but Bernard would. She would write to Bernard.

Chapter 19

Trevor

Trevor put his leather fedora on his head and tamped it down. He felt like Indiana Jones in the wilds, free from the clutches of his university and oversight of any government minders. For Trevor, this dig had been a way to get out from under his father's scrutiny. At first, "Old Senior" was slated for this adventure and Trevor was looking forward to a quiet summer in Cambridge, both Dad and his wife on the road. Then the doctors told Daddy that he just couldn't put the hip surgery off any longer or he might never be able to walk again. With a look of unbearable frustration, "Old Senior" gave his son the nod and "Junior" knew he was the one heading off to Germany.

So here he was now. Trevor breathed in the crisp morning air of the mountains. The days might get hot, but the nights never were, and you could always count on mornings to carry the same quality as a perfectly ripe and cold green apple—so fresh when you bit into it that your whole body reacted to the crunchy texture and sweet-tart flavor. He was grateful to be here, even had the dig turned out to be a dud. Of course, the idea of a quiet dig in the beautiful mountains was a long-lost dream now.

"Hordes of blokes about these past two weeks. Not a moment's peace. Daddy would've loved it. TV cameras. Interviews. Web pages.

Trending." Trevor made a mental note to check in with Nylah to see if his father had left any comments on the webpage yet. Amelia commented nearly every day, sometimes saying all-too-motherly things, not quite realizing that not only Trevor could read them—and that she wasn't his mother—but the whole world was potentially in the audience—and might actually think she was his mother. He found the doting act very awkward, but since she had never been able to have any children of her own, she clung to little Trevor. He'd had to ask Nylah to remove one from a fortnight ago before it got snapshotted and Tweeted out:

Oh darling, I'm so proud of you! A dig of your own. I'm sure it's just like when you were a little boy playing in the sand pit in the back yard. And now you're all grown up!

But it had been too late: a reporter mentioned it in a story, gushing over the total cuteness of a mother's never-changing love for her little boy, even when that little boy was now commanding one of the most interesting digs in the history of modern European archeology, no longer digging up little plastic toy soldiers, but rather unearthing victims of the Black Plague. *Human interest* they called it.

"Supremely embarrassing." But it had upped their web traffic by a thousand percent. Nylah was thrilled.

"Don't tell me you're still on about that reporter's story?"

Trevor jumped. "Dr. Bergeron! I didn't hear you come up."

"If it helps, Dr. Payne, I don't think it hurts your reputation at all to have a mother who adores you."

"Stepmother."

"Okay, stepmother. Still, it's endearing in a profession that most people probably see as rather boring and dry. And besides, Nylah's thrilled."

He couldn't believe that Everly had the audacity to laugh.

"Yes!" Her voice was filled with mirth. "She told me last night that you're starting to trend. A couple of websites have added your name to their 'Most Eligible Bachelor' lists."

Trevor felt the sudden sensation of his stomach leaving his body and hitting the ground. "Oh. Please don't let Amelia know that. Not that she wouldn't be thrilled to bits." He put his hands over his face.

"Dr. Payne, what's wrong? Are you okay? You look… pale."

He shook his head and dropped his hands, crossing them over his chest. "I'll be all right as long as mummy Amelia doesn't post anything about me maybe being able to get a date now." He winced. "Have your mum and dad posted? Do they make every attempt to supremely embarrass you in front of the whole bloomin' world?"

"Um. No, actually. Never. I can safely say that won't happen."

"Lucky you. Let me know if you want to trade." He blew out hard, puffing out his cheeks. "Well, keep a stiff upper lip and all that. On to business now, shall we?" He gestured to the path and they started walking towards the dig site. "I think maybe two more days of the total circus and then we'll be able to say goodbye to our new guests. Just look at how all the grass is trampled. And I thought the Brandenburg students were bad."

Everly nodded. "True. But we certainly needed them. I think it was right to follow Gunther's advice and contact the other universities around Europe. How else could we get thirty-plus more volunteers practically overnight? It was like a miracle when they showed up."

"You're right. When you're right, you're right, Dr. Bergeron. Your little find in Pit A, as Nylah dubbed it, 'Legions of the Dead playing Twister', unearthed so many more relics than we lot could have handled, even with Gunter's revolving band of summer students."

"Agreed." Everly nodded her head. "And beneath all those bodies was the trash pit that we were afraid would be our only find!"

"Trash pits. A treasure trove for archeologists. And their students. And their volunteers." Trevor shuddered. "How many people have been on site?"

"Uh, fifty? Nylah would know for sure. She organizes the volunteers."

"Circus." Trevor shook his head. "It's been a circus around here."

Everly nodded. "Also true, but face it: we never could have gotten those forty remains moved out, tagged, boxed up and stored without them."

"Right. I'll give you that. Those Brandenburg students are good, but they aren't that good."

"Extra hands make light work, my mother always used to say."

Trevor noticed that Everly didn't sound as chipper as he would have expected, but she brightened up as she said,

"And now we can get down to business and figure out the puzzle of why they even had a trash pit and just what happened here. Fascinating, absolutely fascinating." Everly brushed her hair back from her face and surveyed the scene. "You realize that at least thirty doctoral students will have their dissertations based on your dig."

"Our dig, Dr. Bergeron. Our dig."

"You're one of a kind, Dr. Payne. One of a kind." Everly shook her head but didn't make eye contact with him.

"You know, I think that's my dad's problem with me. But here we are. Say, how about we tackle Pit B today? I think the volunteer team is well on their way to confirm that Pit A is complete, and to tell you the truth, I'm more than ready to not be surrounded by people or cameras or reporters. Pit B is so much quieter."

Everly nodded. "Gunther is certainly living his dream, taking over the excavation and directing the final exhumation of Pit A. And to tell you the truth, pulling out the first thirty bodies was enough for me. I was happy to share the glory with good old Gunther."

Trevor chuckled. "And he certainly likes to talk to the press! Hmmm, maybe they'll put *him* on their Most Eligible Bachelor lists and forget about me."

"Yeah, uh, maybe in *Out Magazine*."

Trevor stopped and looked at Everly. "No! Really?"

Everly nodded.

"Dr. Bergeron, how in the world do you know such things?"

"Oh, Dr. Payne, I'm learning just about everything from Nylah."

Trevor marveled at how such a young person could be so in-the-know about everyone else's business. He started to wonder what Nylah had figured out about him, but then shrugged it off, given that he already had such a TMI problem. He had too many words and had to admit that at times those could reveal more than even he was ready for. He looked up and saw Gunther walking towards them.

"Man of the hour, aren't you? How are all the press interviews going?"

"Schon gut!" Gunther answered. "You know that girl Nylah who runs this dig? She just told me that I was named to a most eligible bachelor list! I think that might not be a good thing for my university, jah?"

"Do you have tenure?" Everly asked.

"Jah, I do."

"Then don't worry about it."

Still looking at Everly he shrugged and said, "Nylah said any press is good press. I am not so sure. Anyway, I think today I shall oversee the doctoral students in the specimen tent."

"Yes, that would be great." Everly gave him a nod. "We wanted to start extracting samples to send off for testing for *Yersinia pestis*."

Gunther returned with a curt nod of his own. "Ja, I can oversee that if you would like. I have two students who need to learn how to draw such samples."

"Fantastic. I never really liked working with all the vials and reagents anyway," Trevor said. "I'm more of a dirt man. Dr. Bergeron and I are going to move forward with Pit B, if that's all right with you."

Gunther waved them off. "There is nothing in that hole. It's a waste of time. We dug and dug and dug. I am skeptical about your blackberry theory."

"I suppose we'll know soon enough," Trevor answered jovially. Gunther left them and he and Everly made their way to the second pit.

"What do you think about Gunther's opinion that there's nothing here?" Everly asked as she looked into the yawning mouth of the excavated dirt.

"Dead wrong. I can feel them down there. I know they're hunkering down." He turned to stare at the pit. "Legions of the dead, just waiting to be found. That's what it says on our website, so here we go." He jumped down into the pit, feeling even more like Indiana Jones. Everly climbed down the ladder into the three-foot deep excavation.

They worked for two hours, each starting on opposite sides of the hole and working their way towards one another in the middle, chatting as they worked. He felt the pace pick up and wasn't sure if he was sensing competition or if they both seemed to like the part when they came together. They would work a bit more slowly then, spending time talking about the quality of the dirt and clay and the finds they had made thus far this summer. He thought it was a new kind of fun to so casually talk shop with a colleague. It didn't feel like work at all. In fact, he was thinking more about Everly than about the task before him when he suddenly felt his probe meet resistance. His mind stopped, his focus now solely on the mission. He slowly pushed the probe back into the dirt. Sure enough, there was something there. He took his spade and started to work carefully, pulling the dirt away.

"Well, well, well. And here you are." He sighed with satisfaction. It was a hand emerging from the earth. And even more special, there was a ring on one of the fingers. "Dr. Bergeron? Would you be interested in seeing another example of jewelry from the Middle Ages?" Trevor was particularly excited about the personal adornments of the time. In fact, when he would sit late at night and work alone and occasionally chat with Father B's skull, he would often pull out the ring they'd found on the priest's skeleton. Trevor had tried it on and found it was a perfect fit. It made him feel close to Father B. It made him feel Father B's humanity. As though he was there with them in spirit.

Everly looked over at him and left her probing line. "Jewelry from this time is exceedingly rare. We found a gold ring set with a diamond on Father B."

Trevor immediately felt a pang of guilt, as she named what had been on his mind. Archeologists didn't typically wear the adornments once belonging to the human artifacts. He'd never told Dr. Bergeron that he'd tried the ring on. She already thought it was weird that he included the skull and talked with Father B, treating him like he was still alive in some way. "Uh, right. Right you are! They believed at the time that diamond warded off plague. And it's a sure indication that Father B came from a powerful noble family before he became a priest. I mean the gold too. Hard to come by, gold."

Everly squatted down next to Trevor and examined his find. "I would say this is bronze and is that a sapphire? It's hard to tell for all the grime." She looked deep in thought. "Commoners weren't allowed to wear gold or silver, so this person was likely a well-to-do merchant. They were allowed to wear copper and bronze."

Trevor thought for a moment. "Sapphire. What did that mean to them? Oh, I think I remember: they thought it had magical powers and could detect fraud. Humph! I wonder if this was a merchant? Maybe someone who delt with caravans and traveling salesmen and the like? They'd need to believe they could detect a liar."

"I think sapphire was also believed to ward off witchcraft. There's a whole history behind gems and jewels and adornments at that time that I find just fascinating."

"Yes, me too." He loved that look on her face when she was totally concentrated on an object. Then he realized that he was staring at Everly with the same intensity that she was staring at the ring. "Yes, um, well, let's see. This brings up a good question of whether there was nobility here other than our Father B, who clearly came from that kind of lineage. I mean, how to explain the sapphire?" Trevor carefully pulled the ring off the skeleton's finger in order to examine it more closely. He rubbed away some of the centuries of grime. "Right, yes, this is a sapphire. Here's a theory: from what we know, people in the small towns kind of broke away from the rules imposed in the big cities. They were a freer lot out here, in the hinterlands. Did what they liked. Believed what they liked. Held more to superstition and magic—that was the old ways to them." Gently, he handed the ring to Everly and instantly felt awkward. Men had handed rings to women for centuries as they huddled close and whispered of important things, but then again, those men and women weren't covered in dirt and the rings that passed between them were generally new rather than hundreds of years old.

She didn't seem to notice. "So, it's possible that being set in bronze, and not in gold, followed the laws enough that this person could see their way clear to using the stone to protect or guide them? That's an interesting theory, Dr. Payne."

"That's just what I was going to say…"

"Well, let me help you free the rest of him or her. Better call Nylah." Everly put the ring back on the finger of the dead. "She'll want to document this as well."

Trevor picked up his walkie talkie. Before he switched it to on, he turned to Everly and said, "You know, old Gunther won't be too keen on the fact that we dug for two hours and hit pay dirt, now will he? I mean, a fourteenth century ring and all that. It's a museum piece, that is."

Everly waved Trevor off. "He'll be in pig heaven as soon as those samples all test positive for the Black Plague. And this is a lucky find. It's not like it's a whole pit of this."

Nylah showed up with her camera and extra site flags and snapped away. "Ev, you get back to work and let me get more action shots."

Everly worked to remove the dirt from around the newly discovered body, but she quickly ran into the bones of another finger. "Oh my God."

"What? What?" Nylah asked. "Wait, wait. If it's you two doing your magic in the dirt, then let me switch to video. You know you're about to find something big."

Everly picked up her pace. "I think. I think. It can't be. It can't be."

Trevor joined her and together they freed the fingers. Then Trevor sat back on his heels and blew out his breath, puffing up his cheeks. "Blimey." He looked over at Everly. "You found another ring." Then he looked over at Nylah. "And not just any ring." His accent was suddenly back to his "on camera persona".

"Yes." Everly looked up at Trevor and then back at the find, blinking a couple of times. She pulled the ring off of the finger and tenderly cleaned off the dirt. "Do you know what this is? It's a Jewish wedding ring."

Trevor leaned over and examined the ring. "Look! It's a miniature dome. You know if we can get some of the dirt out of here, I would wager there will be little arches under that dome."

"Arches? You mean those tiny little lines?" Nylah asked. "I bet that means something. In archeology it always means something more than just looking cool."

Everly's brows furrowed. "If I remember, I think it's the imagined form of the lost Temple in Jerusalem. Oh! How lovely. This would connect the Temple to the newlywed's home. Dr. Payne, this looks to me like red and green enamel? What do you think?"

"Aren't you astute! This is absolutely exquisite. And look at this, does that say, oh, I'm a bit rusty in my Hebrew, but that's a pretty traditional inscription? Wait, wait: I bet it says, yes, *mazel tov*."

"*Mazel tov*. Good luck. Just the thing for a wedding ring." Everly sat back on her heels. "So, there was a Jewish community here. Wow. That will blow the socks off of medieval historians!"

"Hopefully we'll find evidence of a community here! Wait a minute, oh bugger! That could be really devastating." Trevor sat back and gave Everly a sad look and turned to Nylah. "Nylah—turn off the video." He blew out a breath and then added in his regular accent, "If so, we'll have to prepare the students. That can be the traumatizing side of archeology, innit?"

"What do you mean by 'devastating' and 'traumatizing'?" Nylah asked.

Everly looked sad and glanced at Trevor. "It's awful to explain. During the Black Plague, the people had no idea what was happening to them, no idea of contagion, of course. Anyone who held those ideas would have been considered heretical. The cause of your sickness was sin or your unbalanced humors or the devil. And when nothing made sense, they looked for a scapegoat."

"A scapegoat?"

Trevor took a deep breath. There were parts of history that were wonderful and fascinating and a delight to talk about. And then there were those parts that made you lose faith in humanity and that you wish you could forget. But it was important to never forget. The story had to be told, lest it be lost to time, and ugly history repeat itself. "Nylah, this is hard to share, but the people of the time formed bands. Roving bands of young men, crazed out of their minds, who tried to suffer in the place of the populace. When that didn't work, didn't end the plague, they blamed the Jews. Said they poisoned the wells, engaged in black magic, you name it. They stormed the ghettos where the Jewish people were already forced to live and committed horrible crimes against humanity." He felt nauseated.

Everly put a hand on his shoulder. "It's okay. It's long in the past." She gave his shoulder a squeeze and turned to Nylah. "We would have to prepare the students and allow those who might not be able to take it to excuse themselves."

"Traumatizing stuff. Just what would we see?" Nylah asked cautiously.

Everly bit her lip. "Well, what happened seven hundred years ago included locking people in houses and burning them alive, stabbing them in the street, and throwing whole families down wells. Anything they could think of. It was awful. By the time it was done, two-hundred-and-ten Jewish communities had been wiped out. Most never recovered."

Nylah looked thoughtful. "Like the dude who was in the latrine? Do you think he was Jewish? Was he killed by a bunch of fanatics?"

Everly and Trevor looked at one another. Trevor shrugged. "He was nibbled on. Bones crunched by teeth." Trevor looked up at Nylah. "Not human ones. I'm no expert on this, but I would say he was eaten by a large animal. We'll likely never know if the poor bloke was Jewish or Christian or a fairy follower, but I don't think the signs point to genocide in his case."

Everly nodded. "But if we do find signs of genocide in this pit, particularly against the Jewish people, particularly here, in Germany, we are going to need counselors."

"For the students or for us?" Trevor asked quite seriously.

"Can we back up a minute?" Nylah asked. "Lovely as this conversation is, what did you say about the roving bands trying to suffer for… for what did you say?"

Trevor grimaced. "Flagellants. They were called flagellants. They roamed the streets of the major cities, but we don't have any records of them in small towns. They would beat themselves with a thing called a discipline."

"What's a discipline?" Nylah asked.

Everly said, "It's a whip. A personal whip. Usually with three tails on it. Often with spikes." She gestured to explain. "The flagellants would beat themselves, step on one another, beat one another. They believed that if they could suffer enough, they could end the plague for humanity."

"That's sick. And I mean that in not a good way," Nylah said, her lip curled.

"Right. It didn't do them a lot of favors either. Massively injuring the body is not a great strategy during the plague. Laters! You know. See you on the flip flop—the ultimate one." Trevor drew his finger across his throat. "And for them, it was all the more reason to kill anyone they could blame. And the Jews were an easy target. An all too easy target. Same old story."

"That's awful." Nylah said. "So, this pit might be full of genocide? Is that what you're saying."

Everly breathed heavily. "It's not likely. Possible, but not likely. A more plausible scenario is that a few Jews found ways to live and hide out in small towns like this one. They didn't advertise and in the relative freedom of a small town, people didn't ask. There were probably more than a few people in the town with something to hide."

"And what better place to hide than in a place no one is looking?" Trevor said. "What we find will tell us. For example, their jewelry will help tell their story. Just like this person's wedding band." He sighed heavily. "Much more to go, much more to learn. Time to plunge in."

They continued their work with Nylah documenting. It turned out that Everly had been wrong in her prediction that it wouldn't turn out to be a pit full of wonder. From an archeological standpoint, the finds were stunning. It was a whole pit of the fairly well-to-do who had been decked out in their finest for the day they died. Nylah snapped the photos, took video, and gathered more interviews with Trevor and Everly about the fascinating discoveries. Just like in Pit A, one body led to another, which led to another, which led to another. It was a seemingly endless trove of death. Gunther was green with envy.

They found no more rings or other artifacts indicating anyone of Jewish heritage. The single wedding band remained a mystery.

"You guys are gonna have to tell me way more about life in the Middle Ages," Nylah said, back to snapping stills. "This looks like these people rocked."

Trevor looked at the tangle of skeletons and then at Nylah. "Nylah, what about these bodies makes you think there's something different to tell than everything we've said before?"

"Are you kidding? These people look like they're fun, and I mean a lot of fun. Just look at them. You're telling me that those little shards of cloth were from nice clothes. So, they're all dressed for a party.

You've got different kinds of what used to be jewelry on about a third of them. So again, dressed for a party. And they all dropped dead. Together. Dressed for a party. This isn't a burial pit. It's more like a mosh pit where they all got crushed in a stampede."

Trevor gave Everly a quick glance and then picked up the walkie talkie. "Gunther, can you examine the remains for broken bones and fractures? We need to know if anyone in the pits was crushed."

◆━◆━◆

Later that evening as the three of them were fresh from showers, they drank wine and discussed the day. Trevor raised his glass. "I must say, team, that you bring better luck to any dig than I've ever had the pleasure to be a part of. Today was bloody phenomenal." He poured a little glass for Father B. "Museum pieces. We found relics worthy of being museum pieces. Never in my career did I expect to find that. Hoped, yes. Expected, no."

Nylah shook her head. "Right, because who's buried wearing their jewelry? I mean, all that stuff is left to your kids."

Everly sipped her wine. "You're right, Nylah. Even in the Middle Ages, bodies were prepared for burial. Only a few of the nobility might have been buried with very specific pieces of jewelry."

Trevor said, "Right. The Egyptians might have believed you could take it with you, but the Christians generally believed just the opposite. So, you're right, Nylah, it's highly unusual for grave goods to be present. Lucky us."

Everly nodded. "Extremely lucky. That's the good news. But all good news is balanced out by bad. You know what this means, don't you?"

Trevor didn't want to think about the bad news. He'd had so little really good news in his career that he just wanted to sit and soak that in for a few minutes.

It was Nylah who answered. "Yeah, it means I have to cancel the pickup of the five additional port-o-potties. And I have to extend Esther's contract for at least another month. Ugh, the paperwork. But I have to say, I really love having an assistant. I mean, really? What other twenty-year-old has an assistant? I tell her to arrange for lunch for the crew and she has to do the dirty work. It's awesome. You know, I think I've figured out my life's goal. What I'm really waiting for!"

"If not halftime, then what?" Everly asked.

Trevor was confused. "Halftime? What's halftime?"

Nylah ignored him. "CEO. Yeah. I like the CEO role."

"What are you both talking about?" Trevor asked.

Once thirty-some additional students and volunteers showed up on site to help with the excavation and processing of the finds in Pit A, Nylah had gone out and hired herself an executive assistant, a middle-aged woman she loved to give orders to, but this discussion about port-o-potty pick-ups baffled him.

"Dr. T, today you uncovered the legions of the damned Part Two. All the volunteers and students… we need them. They can't leave or you'll never get all those bodies out of that pit."

"Oh, that's right! Bollocks! More of the bloody circus. I tell you, I'm starting to miss the quiet days of our little dig. Just the three of us before we woke the armies of the dead."

Chapter 20

Friar Karel Tuckerschade
August 1348

"Friar Tuck! Wait! Friar Tuck!"

Karel gave a heavy sigh and turned around. There was Wilhelm. Again. "Yes, Wilhelm?"

"Where are you going, Friar?" Wilhelm looked anxious.

"I am going up into the mountains." After a lengthy silence he added, "To pray."

"Can I come along?"

Karel sighed again. "What is wrong, Wilhelm?"

Wilhelm looked about, eyes darting back and forth nervously, and struggled to form words. "It's just that, well I, I…"

"Have you finished your chores, Wilhelm?" Karel made sure his voice sounded calm and reassuring.

Wilhelm brightened up considerably. "Oh, yes! I picked up the eggs and fed the chickens. And the ducks. My, they are loud, Friar Tuck! And they always sound like they're laughing. Haaaa! Haaaa! Haaaa!" Wilhelm was all excitement now, as he enthusiastically imitated the sound of the hungry ducks. He waddled about, imitating their movements, flapping his feet in his new boots.

"Yes, go on…"

"And I fed the pig. I turned the goats out to graze. You might see them up on the mountain. I could come with you to keep an eye on them." Wilhelm looked most eager. "Then you wouldn't be alone."

"Ah," Karel said, understanding. "But you see, Wilhelm, I am trying to be alone. I need to be alone so that I can hear the voice of God." After a lengthy silence, he once again added, "When I pray."

Wilhelm puzzled this statement out and then became animated again. "The goats might disturb you. I could keep the goats away so that you can be alone with God! Right! I could do that."

Karel tried to relax the line of his lips into a pleasant, understanding smile. "That is so kind of you, Wilhelm. I am always amazed at what good care you take of me. Did you wash down the pews in the church? Or the altar? That would be a godly action, for sure and certain."

Wilhelm looked downcast. "No. I didn't think of that."

"My friend, I think that would be an honorable task, and I would appreciate it if you could attend to it. There is no one else I trust to attend to the altar. 'Tis an important job and only someone of your stature could be allowed to touch our sacred space in such a way."

Wilhelm looked puzzled again. "Was old lady Prinzel of the same stature as me?"

Karel jumped a little in surprise at Wilhelm's reasoning. "Before she died, that woman had the light of the divine in her cheeks."

"Was that the light of the divine? I thought she had a fever!"

"Well, uh, yes. The light of the divine. That's how I know that the task can only be done by someone who has dedicated themselves to the Lord. And since I, like Moses, need to climb up the mountain, *alone*, to find God, to pray, the task of preparing our little vestibule to receive our holy orders falls to the most capable and worthy man left shining in the light of our Lord."

Wilhelm looked about him, curiosity written across his face.

"That would be you, Wilhelm."

Slowly, a huge smile broke across Wilhelm's face. "Me? I have the light of the divine shining in me cheeks?" He quickly put a hand to his cheek to reassure himself that he hadn't been taken by a fever.

Karel coughed slightly. "Uh, yes. I see the glow and I'm sure that's what it 'tis. Pray as you scrub the church, Wilhelm, and maybe God will speak to you as well."

"Speak to me? Heavens! As low as I am…"

"For the meek shall inherit the earth, so it is written." Karel raised his hand in blessing and made the sign of the cross over Wilhelm. "You attend to your chores, attend to our holy church, and I will, like Moses, ascend the mountain, *alone*, to seek the voice of God." Karel turned and took a few more steps on the path.

Wilhelm nodded vigorously. "And, uh, are you sure you don't need any help? In case the path is uneven?"

"I am counting on the path being uneven, Wilhelm. 'Tis part of the test. I will be fine."

"It could be dangerous. Remember, we lost Elvina. There could be wolves. Or, or worse things!"

"I will be under the protection of our Holy Lord. You show your devotion as God has commanded you and I will show mine as God has commanded me. I will see you at dinner and for evening prayer and songs."

"Oh, yes, all right. I'll have dinner ready when you get back."

"That's a good man. I will count on the church being scrubbed and dinner being ready when I return." Karel looked at Wilhelm standing expectantly before him. "You'd better go and get started, Wilhelm. There's much to do before Evensong."

"Oh, yes! Right! Until Evensong then."

"Until Evensong." Once again Karel raised his hand in blessing. He didn't move until Wilhelm had turned and started to walk away. After he was nearly out of sight, Karel finally turned and resumed his trek up the mountain path. The goats certainly had made their jaunty way up this path in the previous hour, for not a flower was left along the trail, their roots and all pulled from the ground by the many greedy mouths. Karel had to pay attention to where he stepped to miss the little balls of their dung. They would be skittering about the highlands during the sunshine and find their way home to safety as the dark fell.

Karel followed the trail until it rounded a large rock formation and took him out of sight of the path that Wilhelm had followed back to the village. Stopping, he looked around to make sure that no one was in sight. From under his dark robes, he pulled out a cloth satchel. Hiding in the lee of the towering stone and out of sight from the world, he then unfurled his satchel revealing it to be a lined, long gray cloak. From a cleverly disguised hiding place in the rock, he extracted a roughly made high, spiky wooden crown and placed it upon his brow. Karel then threw the cloak over his shoulders and transformed into a gray, ghost-like figure as he raised the voluminous hood over his head, spreading it across his high, ominous crown.

Looking like a minion of the dreaded reaper of death, the eerily tall specter with the enormous head looked up and down the path as it emerged from the stone and struck out across the green valley towards the lowlands between the peaks. He was careful to not reinforce any trail he had previously taken, lest a course be carved in the green grasses that would lead anyone to his secret destination.

After an hour of walking, he came to the first signs of the highland swamp he referred to as the *Hohes Venn*. Little coneflowers dotted the land here and there. If you didn't step carefully, you could easily end up ankle-deep in a muddy quag. He'd nearly lost a shoe there once and quickly learned that every step had to be meticulously planned out, but that was all right. If there was any quality that he felt described him, meticulous was a good fit. It was like the tall crown on his brow, a good detail he had created to ensure that no one would ever associate the gangly specter with himself. That wouldn't do at all. And it kept the hood from touching any part of his head.

His steps flushed a family of black grouse from some low-lying scrub as they made their slow way in front of him, the blue and green breasted Blackcock male with the fancy black plumed tail leading the way with his Greyhen, a gray-and-white striped mate-for-life, herding the juvenile chicks from behind. "Lazy bird. Yah! Move on!" He kicked his foot at the sedentary bird which was unruffled by his presence. Black grouse heavily populated these upper hills. You could nearly trip over them if you weren't paying attention. "Damn birds! Someday you featherbrains will all be dead if you don't get out of the way!"

It was the red wattle that encircled the eyes of the male in a broad and wrinkled disc that always unnerved Karel. He thought they looked like demon birds with huge, looming, bright red eyes. But of course, demon birds would live along the path to where he was headed.

Pink swamp heath started to greet him, standing proudly with its spiky pink and white flowers looking almost like a mace used in war. He always marveled at how nature sheathed her violence with beauty. Many flowers dotted the swamp—and sharp thorns protected those blossoms from the hidden vantage point of their stems. Butterflies flitted about, but bog lizards and wall lizards were abundant in the *Hohes Venn* of the high fen land, and they preyed upon the fragile, brightly colored butterflies as the strong took the meek.

"This world isn't corrupted. Some of nature's creatures are meant to be eaten," he muttered as he stopped to study the blooming hollyhocks, which were themselves being visited by busy bees. One might lean in to explore the smell of the flowers and if subsequently unlucky, could get far more up one's nose than bargained for. But that was the *Hohes Venn*, wasn't it? Everything was more than bargained for. A simple glance attested to barren peat with scrub pines and scraggly flowers. Closer inspection revealed a landscape teeming with the odd and the ugly or the awkwardly beautiful hiding vicious defenses. This was the kind of place that Saint Drogo would surely bless. And Saint Erasmus, the patron saint of sailors, and of course, abdominal discomfort, would see the *Venn* as a kind of an ocean of its own.

As he penetrated deeply into the fen, he stepped carefully on large flat stones, many of which he had dragged over himself to create a safe and swift path through the dangers of the swamp. He could walk this path night or day now; he could recall each step in his sleep. Then he came upon it: the upside down cross next to the off-kilter X of a cross lying on its side. A few minutes down the path a bird skeleton was nailed to a tree, its bony wings outstretched and its long beak and empty eye sockets staring down anyone who dared to come hither. Karel knew the people of his village would see these as signs of the devil and run screaming in fear from this place. But of course, that was why he had set these protective totems along the path. He had done all he could think of to scare them off. This place was too special, too extraordinary for the people of his village. He picked his way along the path and finally arrived at the most secret heart of the fen: the apple grove. It was guarded by the rotting head of a goat, hideously piked onto the trunk of a thin, scraggly tree.

"Hello, Elvina," he said casually to the remnants of the animal. He had liked Elvina. She was a good milker. But she had become too attached to Karel and had followed him here too many times. She might have been one of God's creatures, but she risked everything with her devotion to him. She had started to beat a path through the grasses, and where a path emerged, the curious would follow. He was right to make Wilhelm manage all the animals now. He couldn't risk them becoming attached and following him around, like chicks chasing after their mother hen.

He took a seat on a stone at the perimeter of the little circle of dwarf apple trees. He was careful to keep his distance. Through painful exploration, he had learned of the burning that came from proximity to these green fruits. Even sitting under the leaves of the trees in the rain would give you a severe rash. Nothing grew beneath them. The lined cloak was his protection. After burning his fingers, he had meticulously sewn himself thick gloves of hide, so that he could harvest the fruit and oh-so-carefully distill down the powerful juices within. But today was not a harvest day. Today was merely observation and prayer. He had an experiment he needed to check on. The wild boar that roamed the fen was a violent and dangerous beast. Worse yet, he was destructive to the delicate climate of the *Hohes Venn*. If the townspeople caught the trail of a wild boar, some brave fools would surely hunt it down. Or worse, distant lords would come for the thrill of the hunt with their army of fools in tow. And his miraculous secret would be discovered and probably destroyed. This place was his. God had given it to him. Only him.

"No. No one can know about this," he said as he surveyed the fen about him. "Whoever would have thought that it all started here? Right here. This corner is all that is left of the Garden of Eden." He looked lovingly on the cluster of tiny apple trees. "And to think, at the dawn of mankind, Eve walked up to one of your forebears and as the Great Serpent whispered in her ear, she plucked your grandsire's deadly fruit from its branches and enticed noble Adam to eat of wisdom not intended for his pure and innocent spirit."

He was quiet for a while. "Forbidden knowledge, distilled down over the eons, has made you what you are." He looked over at the rotting head of the goat, posted far enough to keep the stench at bay. He shook his head. "Poor Elvina was also expelled from the garden of Eden, or the remnants of it, when she partook of the apple."

Of course, unlike Adam, Elvina hadn't greedily consumed the fruit. No, she fought Karel most desperately to avoid it. No matter how he tried to conceal the poison apple, she could detect it until he put the juices in wine mash. Those goats were a disaster for the vineyards, crazy for grapes. Fermented ones turned them into nearly uncontrollable locusts, voracious in their hunger. The townspeople fed the used, fermented mash from the grape harvest to the goats every year, and then were entertained by watching the poor beasts fumble around in their drunkenness. The milk, and cheese from the milkings the next two days, were prized for their subtle wine-like flavors. Wagon trains in search of trade would come all the way to the Valley Village of the Three Mountains for the wines and cheeses made here. Elvina had slurped down the mash with the ground apple in it, as the wine had a curious way of concealing the taste. Before she realized what she had eaten, it was too far into her.

Her death had been interesting to observe. Of course, he would have preferred it had she just slipped gently away, but given the burns he received on his hands when he first discovered the toxic fruit, he imagined the process from the inside would be rather searing as well. It certainly looked that way, and in a little less than hour, it was done. Her form had been grotesquely twisted as an aftermath of her spasms.

Of course, her milk and flesh would be poison, just like the apples themselves. There was nothing he could do to reclaim any use from her body, until he decided to make her the guardian of the Garden of Eden. "That's a redemption for you, Elvina! You're the angel of the back door," he called out cheerily to her dead head. "I'd better go and see to the rest of you."

He walked about a half an hour before he got to the far end of the *Hohes Venn* and its high swampland. This was where the boar had been rampaging lately, tearing up the ground and destroying everything in its path. "I'm sure you're the devil's emissary, wanting to stamp out all that's left of the Holy Garden. Your master's been bent on destroying it since the dawn of time. But not on my watch." He had put the rest of Elvina's body on the boar's stomping grounds. Boars ate everything with greed, even carrion. If only he could get the devilish beast to devour Elvina's remains. If only it could slow the boar down, there might be a way to trap it, to finally weaken it enough to kill the beast before he drew the attention of powerful lords wishing for a tusked head to mount on a wall.

He could feel his heart quicken as he approached the peat flat. The tracks of the boar were everywhere but more important was the smell. It was overpowering. Nauseating in that particular way the smell of death owns. Karel cried out in victory and raised his arms in celebration, even while he wrinkled his nose in disgust. He followed the foul smell until he found the beast.

"Now you look like you got the death you deserved!" He felt the flush of satisfaction as though he had just personally slaughtered the spawn of the devil himself.

"I am the guardian of the Garden of Eden," he shouted to the sky, standing over the decaying beast, his fists raised to the heavens. Pride filled his heart. "I am the appointed of God." He fell to his knees and prayed. He never walked to the top of the mountain but he had found his god indeed, kneeling by the rotting, poisoned carcass of the great boar.

◆━◆━◆━◆━◆

At Evensong that night, Karel was distracted by his euphoric thoughts of being the guardian of the Garden of Eden. He might not have been named a Father. He might never be a bishop. But somehow, he was sure he had a better title in the eyes of God. A more noble calling. And surely the rewards of heaven would be heaped upon him.

Later, during dinner, Wilhelm kept trying to talk to Karel, but the friar had to ask his poor assistant to repeat himself. Karel's mind was on the boar and just how powerful the juice of the little apples was. Knowledge was power. Too much knowledge was poison. It had gotten Adam and Eve kicked out of Eden. He wanted to be careful of how he handled this knowledge, since its power was immense. But a serving killed the goat. The dead goat poisoned the boar.

"What did you say, Wilhelm?"

"Oh, I wondered if you heard me. Your mind must still be with God! It's no wonder that you can't hear my little voice. I said that I got the chores done so quickly that I went up the mountain path to make sure you were safe. There's wolves out there, I'm sure of it. And there's that big boar that sometimes makes his rounds. And don't forget the specter. Maybe no one should be walking by themselves. So, I went up to find you, but I didn't see you nowhere. I did find the goats though and brought them back down. I sure do worry about what happened to

Elvina. The rest of the herd keep going up the mountain, but I don't think they're looking for God. I think they're looking for Elvina."

Chapter 21

Everly

Everly was enjoying some time alone. By day the dig site was absolutely crawling with people—students, visiting faculty, volunteers, reporters. It was hard to ever get a moment to think. It felt like she was asked a million-and-one questions, first by site personnel needing direction and then by the press. The days seemed endless. At least everyone cleared out at dinnertime.

Of course, by night she was sharing a tent. Back at home she lived alone in a nice little house in Toronto. She was used to being alone, and the circus crowds by day coupled with the whole canvas-roommate thing at night wasn't helping. The only time she was by herself was in the shower, and since that bordered on the unpleasant in that little M*A*S*H-like set-up, she made the experience as short as humanly possible. With so little time to process and think, she could feel a sense of pressure building up inside her.

But for right now, Trevor was on a trip to Brandenburg University, having been invited to give a talk about their dig. Nylah was spending the night with her German boyfriend. Everly was glad to be alone, even if it was only for the evening. Blessed Solitude! She walked around the quiet yet eerie emptiness of the camp and found herself at the Command Central tent, but she felt antsy and didn't know what to do with herself, as though she'd somehow gotten rusty in the art of being alone.

"What the hell. Catalogue the field notes. There's a boatload of those still outstanding." She walked through the tent flap and after picking up the field catalogue, she took a seat at the desk. She couldn't sit at the long table—it had some hideous tablecloth with winged unicorns on it. Her mood continued to feel heavy and distracted. Trying to focus, she called up files from the computer and transferred notes from the pictures stored there to the notebooks on the table. It was slow work. Some of this Nylah could do but a lot of it required an actual archeological historian. Sighing, she spied a plastic bin lying haphazardly on a metal crate to the side of the tent—the bin was jammed full of random papers. Every day when they came back from the dig site, they would collect any paper notes Nylah had not already clipped to a family of ideas, moving the orphaned insights from the all-weather storage clipboard and dumping them into a big plastic bin of papers that needed to be processed. Trevor would sometimes dig through the bin and, in the process of finding what he was looking for, he would leave random discarded field notes all over the place. It drove Everly crazy.

"Honestly, how can he be so organized in the specimen tent and such a disaster here?" She snorted at the irony of calling it "Command Central" when "Chaos Central" was more like it, but she knew the answer to her question: the specimen tent was his father's space while the central working tent was Trevor's head space. Everything here reflected how his mind worked—everything all over the place and yet interconnected and somehow making sense, if only to him. An explosion of ideas. Brilliant, but disorganized. The uncomfortable thought crossed her mind that organization could make up for a lack of brilliance just like disorganization could obfuscate the quality, but she quickly dismissed the thought. With a heavy sigh, she pulled the plastic bin of field notes closer to her and started to shuffle through them, organizing them with color-coded paperclips so they could be transcribed into both the computer-based notes and the paper notebooks of field catalogues. The dual recording system was absolutely necessary. There were days without power—and without computers—so old-fashioned notebooks were crucial. But all the data would eventually be analyzed and written up on a computer when they returned to their respective universities.

After a half an hour of work, she sat back and studied a clipped together set of Trevor's scratches.

> Plague still likely suspect. Many simultaneous co-mortalities questionable. Presence of grave goods atypical for plague times.
> Possible culprit: Algae blooms?
> Possible culprit: Well water poisoning?
> Possible culprit: Milk sickness?
> Possible culprit: Military action?
> Possible culprit: Food poisoning?
> Mass death in close time proximity sufficient to overwhelm the cemetery. Use of mass graves required. Why would bodies have jewelry, be dressed for formal burial, and yet be higgledy-piggledy?

And finally, a sticky note that said:

> Possible culprit: Mosh pit dance rave?

Everly groaned and rolled her eyes. "Of course, it was the plague. They didn't die all at once, Dr. Payne. Those poor people didn't magically bury themselves." It was accepted fact that of the many tiny towns springing up in the relative freedom of southern Germania between the eleventh and early fourteenth centuries, a good proportion were wiped out by the mid-thirteen-fifties. Mass graves were all too common, a tragic necessity of the times. Burial rites abandoned in the rush to rid homes and streets of dead bodies.

"He's brilliant. I'm sure he's brilliant. But no question: it was the plague." She snorted and shook her head. "Mosh pit dance rave, indeed!"

She looked around her, spotting one set of field notes that was so random, she wasn't sure how to classify it. Still, the completed and organized notebooks were piling up. The whiteboard was covered with erasable pen depicting the site and Trevor's color-coded yarn strings made obtuse connections between the findings, as if a private investigator was dissecting a crime scene.

She had never been a fan of his approach, but she nodded as she studied the tangled webs of interrelationships that stretched out before her. "I can't believe I'm saying this, but our little skeleton crew is actually making headway. We're starting to make sense of all of this." Then she looked back at the current conundrum in her hand. "Despite field notes like you. Who would've thought?" She tossed the paper aside in frustration. It drifted over and came to rest against the skull of Father B, who had yet again been moved from his perch-on-high atop the filing cabinet to once more join a teammate at a table. Feeling a little guilty for hitting their resident holy man in the head, she retrieved the paper but kept looking at the skull as it sat on the small table. Trevor talked to him all the time, included him like he was a member of their tiny crew. She was pretty sure she'd passed by the tent at night and heard him having actual conversations with the priest's remains. Either that or he was phoning some late-night tele-therapist.

Facing away from the entrance flap of the tent, she leaned back in her chair and stared at the quiet chaos of their Command Central, which served as a haven for the three of them. "Well, four if we count you, Father B." She reached up to brush her hair back but then remembered Nylah's admonishment of *no touchie*. She sighed and leaned forward, resting her arms on the table. "So, Father B, now that you're the patron saint of our dig, do you have any advice for me?

Trevor certainly seems to talk to you a lot." She looked around at the papers and then around at the tent. "If I were being truly honest, and if you truly were a priest, then I would want to ask you how you could possibly believe in God? So many awful things happen. Just look at your village. The whole thing got wiped out in what looks like a tsunami of infection. Must have been the septicemic phase of the plague. How could any kind of God allow that?" She crossed her arms, still looking at the skull. "Or what happened to my mother? Or to me?"

The skull looked back at her through empty sockets. Silence filled the tent.

She chuffed. "Surely, no kind or compassionate God would let fifty million people die in fear and agony. A third of the population," she snapped her fingers, "just gone. Only took a few years. And your loving God hasn't changed much seven-hundred years later. As a thirteen-year-old girl, I had to watch my mother be mowed down by a car. What we endured after that! At least it was fast for you. Get sick on a Monday, be dead by Thursday night. You were a man of the cloth. Faith might have steered you through your epidemic, but my faith was destroyed by the back bumper of a cheap compact. Do you know how many years it took me to go back into a grocery store parking lot? I'd have to fight off a panic attack every time I passed a Loblaws."

She looked harder at the skull. "Why am I talking to you?" She shook her head. "I must be going crazy. Even if you were alive today, there'd be no way to explain a grocery store to you. You probably never saw that much food in your entire lifetime."

Everly went back to work cataloguing field notes, which kept her occupied for a while, but soon enough her attention started to falter and she stared off into the distance. "Mom was never the same after that." She chewed on the end of the pen for a moment, lost in thought, staring up at the gunshot hole in the canvas. After a heavy sigh, she laid her chin on her hands down on the table and pulled Father B over so that she was eye-to-eye with him. "We'd see glimmers, you know? Like she was there. She'd have a good day and inside I'd be shouting, 'Mom is back!' and I'd have faith that a thirteen-year old's prayers had been answered. Everything was gonna go back like it had been. But then it didn't. The next day she wouldn't know who I was."

Everly blinked back tears. "Traumatic brain injury is tricky like that. Did you ever have a TBI?" She picked up the skull and examined it. "You don't look like it. For being eight-hundred-years-old, you actually look like you're in pretty good shape. If you'd met my mother, you probably would've said her mind had been captured by fairies or something. No, wait, you were in Germania, not Ireland, so you probably blamed demons and angels instead."

She set the skull back down and then reached for the hand sanitizer. Trevor might feel free and easy with the dead bodies, but for her part, she tried to never touch any of the relics without wearing gloves. With the permafrost melting, there were fears of ancient plagues springing back to life after millennia, tormenting humanity's overly pampered and weakened immune system. With a grimace, she took another pump of the sanitizer and started to work it through her hands.

"TBIs cheat you in a way the plague doesn't. You can have a good day when the neural connections are working, and that gives you hope. But it's a false hope. It's not progress. It's not healing. You just lose them again. Over and over again. I cried an ocean and where was God in all this? I never felt more alone in my life." She took in a deep breath, blinking to hold back tears, and her voice cracked when she spoke again. "All her memories were jumbled up… just like Trevor's stupid disorganized notes from the dig! Arrgh! But unlike my task now, there was no way I could sort them out and put them back in the right places again." She felt overwhelmed by the weight of the memories and the chaos of the unattached ideas surrounding her. She let a handful of the post-its rain down on the table as she said, "You know what, Father B? It seems to me that time slips right through our fingers during childhood, but in the end, our loved ones slip past our fingers through time. Was it like that for you too? Just seeing them all slip away? Like I watched my mother slip away?"

"Everly... I'm so sorry." Trevor's voice came from the door flap of the tent.

Everly jumped out of her chair, knocking Father B a few inches in the process. "Trevor! How… how long have you been standing there?"

He looked at her empathetically. "Long enough." He came into the tent and walked over to the table, picking up Father B from where Everly had sent him scooting across the surface. "He's a very good listener, isn't he? I find him so easy to confide in, but then, he's had about eight-hundred years of practice, hasn't he?" He gave Everly an unsure half-smile. "He's really sorry that you had to go through all that. And your mum. I mean, that's a lot to put on anyone, but as a child? Me too. I'm really sorry, too, Everly. I'm sure if he were here, he'd give you a hug."

Everly felt frozen. She'd used Trevor's first name automatically in response to him saying hers, without thinking about it or even realizing it, and suddenly they were on a first-name basis. She wasn't sure what to do. Now he *knew*. She'd only told Father B, confided to a dead priest, what had to be the safest confession in the world, but now Trevor knew. It was like some door had opened between them… or more like the whole house had blown away. She felt unsheltered. Vulnerable. And Trevor looked like he knew that, too.

Trevor looked about the tent, clearly unsure of what to say or do. "I could…" He scratched his head. "I could stand in for him, since his body is over in the other tent. And it's all full of tags and labels. And you know, not very hug-able." He held up the skull. "I mean he's dead-on handsome, right? But not someone you'd want to get cheek-to-cheek with, is he?" He shrugged. "I may not be much. But I am alive. And I am here. And I have, well you know, arms."

The feeling started welling up from deep inside Everly. She couldn't control it. It surprised her: she began to laugh. It wasn't the emotion she expected to feel after her tirade to the ancient skull and the sudden unveiling of her own tragic and pathetic past, but it was a relief to be able to see the humor in Trevor's clumsy and completely awkward sincerity. "You have too many words, Trevor. Too many words."

"Yeah. I've been told that. I'm sorry. Can't really control it, you know. Built that way, I guess."

"Don't be sorry. You're a kind man, Trevor. You mean well." It still felt somehow strange to be on a first name basis with him after all these weeks of formality.

He looked around, again unsure. "Does that mean… does that mean you'll be wanting that hug or does that mean the words…"

"Sure. I could use a hug. I haven't talked about that in so long. Haven't felt all that in such a long time."

Trevor shrugged in his awkward way and held his arms open, looking for all the world like he didn't know what to do next.

Everly gave a soft chortle and with equal awkwardness, stepped into his embrace.

As Trevor closed his arms around her, he patted her back gently and whispered into her ear, "I'm here. For whatever you need. For all that you had to carry, I can bear that for a while. Right, you just breathe. It's like Father B's here to give you comfort, after all you've done for him."

The upswell of emotion again caught Everly by surprise, but this time she didn't laugh. This time she started to cry. At first gentle, slow tears but they quickly grew into sobs. Trevor didn't shush her or say "There, there" like her father had, wanting to hurry the emotion along and get through the uncomfortable moment. Trevor just held her and rocked her oh-so-gently as she stood in his embrace, and he let her feel whatever she needed to.

At last the sobs subsided. "Oh my God, I'm a mess," Everly could barely speak. She wiped the tears from her cheeks.

Trevor pulled out a clean handkerchief from one of his many pockets and handed it to her. "Not a mess. You're perfect. A little wet maybe, but tell you what—how 'bout we rehydrate? You lost a lot of moisture there. And maybe a little bit of snot."

"Oh, I'm so sorry." She wiped her nose again with his handkerchief.

He just shrugged. "I'm an archeologist. I'm always covered in goo. Say, I've got a lovely bottle of Riga Black Balsam that the Brandenburg folk gave me as a gift today."

"A what?"

He went back to the tent door, where a little gift bag was sitting. "It's a type of a kräuterlikör." Seeing the confusion on Everly's face, he added, "It's liquor! Who cares what kind it is. This evening calls for something strong to sip. We'll even pour one for our good friend here. He's so parched, he looks dead. Just look at him. If I looked like that, I'd need a drink for sure."

Everly gave a small chuckle and wiped her cheeks again.

"There you go. There's my professor. C'mon. A good stiff sip of Riga will do all three of us some good."

They moved over to their little living room set-up and Everly flopped into a squashy chair while Trevor retrieved three shot glasses from a cupboard and gathered up Father B. He brought everything over to the table and, from the gift bag, pulled a tall, cylindrical black bottle with a silver and purple label. "This one seems to be blackcurrant. I always thought those were meant for scones, but hey, when in Rome." He poured out the little glasses. "Bottoms up!"

Everly squinted as she drank. The liquid burned as it went down but felt soothing after her emotional storm.

"Oh, that's not a happy face, is it?" Trevor looked at his half-empty glass. "I thought it was pretty good actually. The flavors are as advertised!"

Everly's eyebrows furrowed. "Like what?" She was surprised that her voice was so raspy.

"Oh ho ho! It's getting to you already!" Trevor laughed. "Take a tiny sip and roll it about on your tongue. Yes, that's the stuff! You'll get a combination of birch, lime, and ginger."

"Birch? Like the tree?"

"Oh." Trevor looked about him. "I don't know. I was just reading the label. Yes, that does sound like a tree, don't it? It's also got licorice, oh gods! I usually hate that stuff. And spices and blackcurrants. Complex, innit?"

"It's something." Her voice was surprisingly hoarse. It wasn't that she didn't like the flavors, it was just that it was awfully strong. She coughed and thumped her chest once or twice and managed to choke out, "So, how did the talk at Brandenburg go?"

He shrugged. "Same as always, I guess. They introduced me. The assembled crowd applauded. And then I had to get up there and sadly disabuse them of the notion that they'd invited my esteemed father there today. No, they were stuck with little ole' me, now, weren't they? *Not* the father of modern archeology."

"And they hadn't figured that out? I mean, they're sending their students here. Of course they know they're working with you! The faculty there, they've met you, like, a dozen times at least."

"You might think so, right? But maybe they thought we kept old Daddy-O in a sarcophagus round here someplace, 'cause he's ancient now." Trevor drained his glass and gave a breathless cough. "I mean, not as ancient as you, Father B, all due respects." He tipped his head towards the skull. "I s'pose they thought maybe we'd drag him out for the dog and pony show. But alas, they just got me telling the crowd that this town died out dramatically but even though Black Plague surrounded them, we aren't confident it was that which did them in. It was possibly some other mysterious undetermined evil."

Everly took a sip of her Riga. It got better as you got used to it. In fact, she was starting to think it was pretty good. She totally got the ginger and blackcurrant. She still wasn't sure what a tree tasted like. "And were they excited about *your* new hypothesis?" She tried to sound supportive even though she was not a fan of his belief that Black Plague might not be the cause of the village's demise. She persisted in her theory, despite the fact that they had yet to get a positive test result returned for *Yersinia pestis*. Like skeletons, bacteria also broke down over the ages and finding some remnants whole enough to positively identify was a tough proposition.

Trevor grimaced at her. "Not really. They seemed like a 'give us Black Plague or give us nothing' kind of crowd." He shook his fist in the air, mimicking the mob he'd faced. "All that press going on about 'the Black Death' has been great for our ratings but not really in helping the audience be very objective." Slumping back into the couch, he continued, "And we don't have any proof yet, right? To be truthful, they weren't too keen on my hunches. Probably because my dad isn't a man to follow his gut. 'Follow the trail, son,' he always tells me." Trevor sat up very straight and spoke in a deep, resonant tone when he mimicked his father, once again sounding like a broadcaster on the BBC. "Follow the facts. The facts will lead you to success!" Trevor then seemed to ease back into himself as his shoulders relaxed and his chin fell back more into his face. He resumed talking with his higher pitched, East-London accent. "But despite the name and the fact that I look dead-on like him, well, 'cept he's gone all silver you know, I'll never be the man my father is."

"Still," Everly said, "to not know which person you've invited to give a talk is just astounding."

He shrugged.

"Trevor. What do I not know?" She was trying to get used to using his name and this new familiarity. *Well, I suppose getting snot all over a person does make you much more familiar.*

"Oh bollocks. You're a perceptive one, aren't you?" He sighed heavily. "It's Daddy's dig." Trevor poured Father B's Riga into his own cup. "Here, let me help you with that, my friend."

"Daddy's dig?"

Trevor poured another serving into Everly's cup as well, but from the bottle. "Dr. Trevor Payne, *Senior*, is really the Principal Investigator. And the funder. It's his name on the paperwork filed in Germany. He doesn't think he's too old to come, of course, but his hip surgeon and post-op rehab team disagree with him, so he sent me. It's not an unreasonable mistake to make now, innit? I mean, it's in his name and all. And the mistake benefits us. You know, if anyone looked up my publications, well, I'm sure they wouldn't send their students to *my* dig."

"Trevor, I don't think you have to worry about that. I mean, everyone under the sun is coming to your dig. Guest faculty. Their students. Volunteers. Despite Nylah's attempts to make us look like we're in Idaho, I think we're as well-known as Euro-Disney at this point."

"Oh, you're very kind. The way I see it, there aren't many digs going on in Germany at the moment, so, when you don't have much choice, it's any port in a storm, as they say. They've got to find a way to give their students experiential credits, after all. And thank Father B's God that we found his golden cross! And then him. And then all his friends. And then all his other friends. I mean, it's like the gift that keeps on giving, innit"?

"Yeah, it must've been a real party down there. I think Nylah described Pit B as 'a rave of the dead'."

"Up until tonight, I would've said nothing ever gets you down, Everly. You really have that buck-up spirit. My father would love you."

Everly emptied her little shot glass, starting to lose track of how many of these she'd had, but she did find the liquid courage made it easier to ask the uncomfortable questions. "How did you end up at the same university as your father? I mean, that hardly ever happens. And in the same department, too. And, while I haven't met your father, I guess, um… well, I confess I was just a little bit surprised when we first met."

Trevor smiled. "Oh, I get it. You thought I'd have a posh accent. Pronounce all my 't's' very carefully at the end of words. Get all my syllables just exact. Right?"

Everly blushed, looking as awkward as she felt. "Well, I mean, you kinda come from Cambridge royalty and I guess I thought that was synonymous with people who sound like they do on the BBC."

"Cambridge royalty? Are you mad? Well then, Dad really *has* made his dreams come true. You know where he's from? London. Lon-don. Stepney, if you must know. Come up from his roots, my dad did. Bloody genius, but my Grangie owned a florist's and my Grandpop, he was a plumber. They didn't quite know what to do with their brilliant little son, so they put everything they had into his schooling. He even married his girlfriend at sixth form, not that that went too well once he decided to become somebody else."

"Girlfriend at what? Do you mean like a childhood sweetheart?"

"Oh, is that what you call it? Sure, then. Right. I don't think he ever wanted to be from Stepney—that's a part of Tower Hamlets—and his people come right down from Old Kent Road. And I don't think he ever wanted to admit to being the son of a man who crawls around under houses in cobwebby spaces and runs into the occasional rat. Mum worked herself nearly to death to help put him through his doctoral degree, but the way she told it, he needed a wife which would help him fit into that erudite life he wanted to lead. So, he dumped her, and me, and traded her in for a posher model. The way Grangie told me, he went off to school and came home with all these degrees and a posh new accent to boot. She said he was always terrified of those Cambridge folk seeing him as a 'them' and not as an 'us'. He wanted to fit in, most desperately, but not with his parents. Not with his wife. And not with me. My step-mum, Amelia, now she's the real thing. She comes by her snobbishness honestly, 'cause she can't help herself. Born into it. Oh, he's so proud of her."

"So, you were raised by your mom? And your grandparents?"

Trevor nodded. "Mum. Lovely woman she was. Died a few years ago, sadly still resentful of dad, his new wife, and their new life. Yes, I was raised by her and two sets of grandparents, none of whom were too keen on my father's 'life choices.' Proud of him they were. But disappointed, all the same."

"So that's why you sound like, well, um, yeah, like you do."

"I guess I just patterned myself after the people I felt the closest to. And I certainly didn't want to pattern myself after *him*. I hate all that snobbishness. I just can't live that way."

"That explains a lot, actually! But you slip into…" She was suddenly too uncomfortable to actually say it.

Trevor looked at her for a moment. Then he sat up and squared his shoulders. Rather than his usual way of sitting back into himself, he seemed to jut his chin and chest out a bit more, which instantly gave him an air of confidence. Everly took notice. This looked like a man who was the commander and chief of a dig, or well, perhaps of Cambridge itself. "Of course, I can sound just like him. He forced me to attend school there. He lives his life in this pathetic pretend. And I suppose I do the same, when I must. When I'm there, playing our family charade, there is the clear expectation that I am… someone else." Then Trevor seemed to relax, to slide backwards into his frame. His chin withdrew ever so slightly, and his brows furrowed just a bit, making him look like he usually did, like he was questioning himself and not totally sure of the path forward. When he spoke, his voice rose again to the range she'd gotten used to and that East-London dialect was back. "But I could never, ever, sound just like him when I was around the people who really loved me. It would've felt like such a betrayal. Like they'd be expecting me to dump them out of my life, just like he did. So, welcome to the two sides of Trevor Payne. Who I'm most comfortable being and that other person that I have to pretend to be."

"You don't have to pretend with me. Or with Nylah. You must really like it when you can be onsite."

"Right. When I'm at a dig, I can really just be myself and relax, right? At least I know all these dead people aren't judging me, by how I talk or how I think. 'Cause, you know, they're dead. So the only show that's being put on is actually by them. As their story comes out bit by bit, you understand who they were, and what they cared about, and how they lived their lives, and yes, of course, how they died."

Trevor looked at her a moment and she realized that he'd probably lost track of just how many he'd had as well. He blew out through his lips, puffing up his face. She was fascinated by how elastic his face could be at times.

"But as a kid, whenever I visited, my dad had me round the department. I spent much of my time in London with me mum and grandparents, but when I was in Cambridge, I was at Cambridge. After school, I helped out in the labs, odd jobs and the like, but I got to know everybody. Dad made sure I got to know everyone important anyway. And he leaned on me to fit in and apply for university there. I'm sure Dad leaned on the admissions committee because I got in. Oh, he can be a bear if he isn't getting what he wants. And I got through school, no choice but to become an archeologist like him. And then someplace along that line I became a faculty member. I call it one of the greatest acts of nepotism in Cambridge history. I had few papers of my own, although I was credited on plenty of my father's work. And his cronies'. But if I'm being honest, mostly I just swept up the floor, actually."

Everly toyed with her glass. She searched for what to say. Trevor was a nice man. He was key to her getting tenure. And earlier this evening she'd managed to get tears and snot all over his shirt. "That's quite the admission. Or, Trevor, the revision of history. Surely, you're being too modest." It had become clear to her that while he actually had plenty of decent publications out there, he was not the award-winning kind of scientist she had hoped for as a mentor when she thought she was working with *Senior*. Or, to be honest, in a dig partner, as he turned out to be, but here she was. Trevor wasn't meticulous about labeling, measuring, and documenting—despite that being what every archeologist wanted in their lab. But he lacked no imagination in finding meaning. Every object was fascinating to him, not for what it represented, but for what it *might* represent. The more fantastical, the more far-reaching the theory, the more enthralling. His father was led by fact, but Trevor Junior was led by the stories he fantasized about those objects. "You know, it sounds like your dad loves you very much. And certainly, you must have deserved it. No one could make a faculty job happen out of thin air. And certainly not at Cambridge!"

Trevor burst out laughing. "My father is a giant. A king. Above the law. Or the academic law anyway. If they didn't hire me, he threatened to reveal all their secrets."

Everly looked at Trevor who was now pouring both himself and Father B another glass. Thunder started to rumble outside. He topped off hers yet again as well. "All their secrets? What secrets? What kind of skeletons in a closest could Cambridge have?" She realized how awkward that sounded about an archeology department, which had rather a lot of skeletons lying about. "I mean, metaphorical ones. Not the ones they'd already done a ton of research on, that is."

Now Trevor was staring into his glass. "I dunno." He looked up at Everly. "Maybe they re-used their tea leaves all day without telling anyone." He bit off the words sarcastically. "It was a different time. Men weren't shamed at sexually harassing their secretaries back then. These days they're ashamed of being so incapable as to *need* a secretary. But back then, oh no, they thought it was their right. 'Me too' would only have solidified them in the club. Badge of honor. But should you accuse them of violating *propriety*, well, that could get you a bloody fistfight in a back hallway."

Everly tried to digest what she had just heard. As someone who used the same tea bag all day, she couldn't quite understand what Trevor was talking about. While even the threat of harassment would cost you your career these days, she couldn't imagine a time when tea could do the same. She shook her head. "So, they gave you a faculty slot. And then what?"

Trevor sighed again. "And then I proceeded to disappoint the great doctor Payne, Senior, in every way possible. I'm just a knob. I've never published in the Journal of Archaeological Research. Bollocks! I've never even published in the Cambridge Archaeological Journal. Finally eked out a promotion from the lowest ranks, but I can feel it from them all. I'm a 'them' and not actually welcome. So, I took to the field as much as I could. Not because I love it, actually. It's just an escape."

That made a sad kind of sense to Everly. Trevor was obviously a man who was uncomfortable in his own skin. Awkward, even. He was always so nervously chatty. And there was that whole wiggle thing he had going on… but the alcohol seemed to make him slow down. She thought he was probably the only person she had known who might make more sense drunk than sober.

"It sounds like your father wanted you to walk a mile in his shoes."

Trevor was again silent for a while. He emptied the shot glass and winced. "Yup, that's pretty much what my career's felt like."

"Huh?"

"Just burns all the way down." He thumped his chest a couple of times as he gave a small cough. "But, no," he continued, "he didn't want me to walk a mile in his shoes. He wanted me to walk *all* the miles in his shoes. The whole bloody trail." He picked up Father B's glass, closing his eyes as though he was reveling in the familiar sensation. "Everly, do you know any faculty who don't belong? Who're there, but they… shouldn't be there? They've just been there so long that no one can remember when it all started. They're like fixtures 'round the place."

Everly took a tiny sip of the dark liquid in her cup. "Sure, we have a couple of old relics. What would an archeology department be without some old relics, even among the living?"

Trevor snorted a laugh.

She took one more small sip and decided that she definitely liked this stuff. "A couple who made tenure two decades before and haven't published since. Just wanted to teach a tiny little group of willing students their favorite subjects. I call them Professors of the Boutique Classes."

"Well, that's how the whole lot of them see me. It's just that I'm not ancient. I mean why am I there? Yay, privilege?" He waved his hands but disgust and shame tinged his voice.

Everly didn't know how to answer that. She changed the subject. "You had to grow up in your father's shadow. And I had no one to shine bright for me. As you now know, my mother's life was cut short by a little old man who shouldn't have been behind a wheel at all. First, in her mid-thirties, her future was snuffed out, and ten years later, her very life followed suit. It would have been better if she'd just had the luck to go all at once."

"Oh no, Everly. How can you say that?"

"Because it's no way to live, not being yourself. At thirteen, I had to learn terms like *paraphasia* so I could understand when the doctors talked about how her words were all jumbled and her sentences meaningless. Or *confabulation* for when she said things she dead-on believed in, but they weren't true and she couldn't realize it. Like her Grammy being alive still. Or that she needed to go downtown because she was winning some fabulous award. Or that she had a meeting with the prime minister at one-thirty. What was that other one? Oh yes, *neologism*. She would create new words that didn't really exist, which sometimes could be really funny. And then, of course, there was the post-traumatic amnesia, which didn't need a soft explanation for a child to understand. That was exactly what it sounded like. I sure wished I could have gotten some of that. But every second of the accident, of how I called out for her to look out, of how she turned to me to see what I was screaming about instead of looking towards the car, of how that little old man backed right into her and she went flying, of how it was all my fault, every second of it all is burned into my memory. I sat over her on the pavement, screaming, while the blood was coming from the back of her head. And someone called an ambulance. That was the longest night of my life. It seemed like hours before Dad showed up."

"Not your fault!" Trevor gave a heavy sigh. "I'm glad you had your dad to lean on." He lifted his glass and gave it a little twist.

"My dad? Oh yes, I had a guy in my life that took the title of dad." She knocked back the rest of her glass and Trevor refilled it for her. "He was all fun loving and happy. That's how I remember him from my childhood. But after the accident, I saw him for what he was. A loser that my mother did everything for. She took care of everything. He was there for the decoration and the fun times. He crumbled to pieces and expected me to step into the role of taking care of him. So much for being strong for your kid."

Trevor looked uncomfortable. "Ouch." He looked around the tent, at anyplace except Everly, seeming to not know what to say. "It sounds like you were strong for everyone… but you didn't have much family life, at least it doesn't sound like it, after you were thirteen."

Everly took another sip and swallowed hard. "Yup. That's a pretty good read on that. By the time my mother finally passed, ten years later, it was death by a thousand cuts. I spent the first two years praying for her to heal and the last eight praying for her to simply be delivered. Brain injuries are bad. In her case, she did okay for a while, but eventually the damage led to a series of strokes. Every time I'd visit her, she'd have lost what little ability she'd worked so hard to regain. It was like she was stolen from me in bits and pieces. By the time she died, I'd already grieved a hundred times. But not Daddy. Oh no, old Daddy-O sized up that if she wasn't his wife, he could start dating, which he did before the first year was up. He stayed married though, since he needed the benefits. Yup, by fifteen, I fully understood the concept of benefits. He stayed married 'til the end… legally. But after she stopped recognizing him, he didn't go back to see her. He said he couldn't stand to see her like that. Didn't want to remember her like that. So, he just abandoned her."

"So much for 'for better or for worse. In sickness and in health'."

"Yeah. He only signed up for *better*. And, uh, *health*."

They were silent for a while, each sipping their little glasses of Riga. Trevor sat back on the couch, deep in thought. Then he gave her a hard look. "Everly Bergeron," he announced somewhat formally, "you are a self-made woman. And that's impressive. I would've given a lot in my life to be a self-made man. Or any man of me own making." He gave a sarcastic chortle. "Well, apparently that's a lie, 'cause I didn't give enough, did I? I mean, I could've broken away, right? Could've run away and joined the circus, but instead I stayed. I pretended. I hid in my father's shadow, just like he told me to."

Everly looked at him with real empathy. "Trevor, it's all a circus. Your life, my life. Even Nylah's life. We each get our own circus. If you survive, which you have, you've learned to be your own ringmaster. Tame your own lions. Ride your own elephant."

He gave her a quizzical look.

"That's your job. To run your circus. That's your job in life. And Trevor, from my standpoint you *are* a success. You're a great ringmaster. You've got a faculty job at one of the world's most prestigious universities. Who cares if you got in the club via some kinda crazy trap door. You're *in* the club. No one's gonna kick you out. You're master of your own dig here. And you know what? You're good at it!"

"Even with my," he looked a bit ashamed, "horrible note-keeping system?"

"Maybe that's why you've got me and Nylah, to bring organization to your brilliant insights. That's what teams are for."

"We do make a good team." He suddenly looked happy.

"Right! We're making amazing progress here. You're on to something." She tapped the table a couple of times with her fingers. "Something new and different and surprising. You really get this. And your dad…"

"My dad…." He sighed heavily and looked deflated.

"Yes, your dad, and I bet your stepmom too, they love you. I would bet they actually idolize you. Oh sure, don't look at me like that. All your parents and your grandparents too, they poured everything they had into you and loved you the best they could. They're flawed, but at least they're there. They loved you the only way they knew how, and they tried to give you what was most precious to them."

He looked pensive.

"And you are the person you are because you didn't run away. Because you stayed and mastered your own lions and tamed your own elephants."

"You know, that's very philosophical of you, Everly! You're quite the logical type. I can't believe that *you're* practically telling me there's some type of divine plan. It sounds a bit like something I'd write in my novel. While I like that kind of stuff for my imaginary friends, I don't like it when it applies to me. But I get it." He turned to Father B. "I bet you didn't like the divine plan laid out for you either, did you? Surrounded by the Black Plague. Eh. Doesn't sound like fun. Here, have a drink." He slid one of the empty glasses over to the skull.

"Yeah, even I would take my life over his: the lives around him cut so short by the black death." Everly shuddered. "And whatever else it might have been."

Trevor picked up Father B's skull. "But it would be exciting, wouldn't it? Figuring it out. Understanding where it came from. Staying two steps ahead. I don't think this bloke died of the plague. I think he was too smart for that. But something—or someone—else got him. Something he couldn't stay two steps ahead of."

Chapter 22

Father Bernard Trōst
September 1348

There was no denying it: Bernard was worried. There had been no trade wagons from any town this spring. Or at mid-summer. September, more commonly called *wood month* in the highlands, had just started, bringing with it the first visitors since fall of the previous year. The news they brought was dreadful—a sickness was spreading throughout the Holy Roman Empire. It would start as a sniffle and progress to a fever and in short order, turned its victims blue and covered them in buboes. *The Blue Sickness* they called it and they spoke with voices filled with fear. It was a new kind of plague. The previous November, or the month of slaughter, the plague hit Marseille over in Franconia. From there it had spread to everywhere else, even to his home city of Cologne. The drivers told him that in April, ugly uprisings had begun, with mass murders of Jews. His little village was lucky that any drivers were found at all to come with goods to sell and trade. People were afraid and it was doubtful that there would be another caravan this year.

Bernard looked at the wagon, a paltry load by comparison to any other he'd seen arrive in the village. He made a mental note to call a town meeting to plan for a harsh and difficult winter. The people would have perhaps three months still where they could hunt, gather, harvest their animals, and think about how to replace the staples they usually counted on from trade. They would have wool aplenty, but they couldn't make bread or soup from that.

With concern, he noted that the deliveries from Uncle Eberhard were half their usual size. He opened the accompanying note.

My Dearest Nephew Bernard,

I write with blessings and prayers for your safety and well-being. Events do not fare well in the city of Cologne—or any other city in Germania, Franconia, the Holy Roman Empire, England, Aragon or Castille. The Lord does not smile upon our neighbors to the south. A great mortality is visiting the lands. Mostly the people call it the Blue Sickness.

Three days. I hear that is all it takes. Three days. On a Sunday a faithful mother will be in church. On Monday a fever will begin, with pains throughout her limbs and fatigue such that she cannot cook food for her children. Then the lesions start to appear. She is dead by Thursday. And by the next Sunday, her children are with her in Heaven. My dear nephew, plague is upon us.

I do not go out of my apartments. I have sequestered myself in prayer and assigned mass to others to conduct. I do not give last rites nor perform baptisms. I will not meet with the dukes or knight commanders. I would not even meet with the King of Germania, were I to be summoned. I know my superiors, the archbishops in Bonn, are similarly sequestered in prayer and contemplation, assigning the daily functions of the church to their bishops and deacons. I urge you to withdraw from active ministry and sequester yourself in prayer and reflection. Don't go out among your fellow man during this time. The numbers of the dead are staggering. When it started, of ten men, three to four would die within a week. Three would be left untouched. Three would be marked with the scars from the pustules, but at least they lived, even if to tell a grim tale. But now, oh now, my dearest Nephew, the pestilence seems to spread on the wings of the angel of death and at least three quarters of the population falls ill, if not more. Of those, eight of ten are taken by that grim reaper of men's souls. I have been told that as the graveyards fill up, there is no place to put the bodies, so they are simply stacking them in the basements of the larger churches. I wonder if this is the end of days?

I am truly sorry that I can send you so little at present. There is not as much to be had in the city as in previous years.

His uncle went on with the news he could gather, which was practically nothing about family as he was taking no visitors and accepting no letters himself. Uncle Eberhard hoped the countryside was faring better and promised that Bernard was in his prayers daily.

Bernard could feel his heart racing and he was glad his robes were long and bulky, since his knees were shaking in fear. He had never experienced plague, but the stories that the old ones shared were the stuff of nightmares. He crossed himself three times.

Bernard noticed that he also had a scroll from his sister. He set that aside for later. He needed to meet with the town leaders as soon as he could get the goods designated for the church and manse unloaded.

◆ ━━ ◆ ━━ ◆

As he left the town meeting, Adelman, the candlestick maker, caught him by the arm.

"I think you're right to warn us about the hard winter to come. The sickness that's taken the land."

"Yes. Thank you, Adelman," Bernard replied. "The news was most concerning. We will have to all stick together. The church will do all it can."

"I wasn't sure bout ye at first, with your new-fangled ideas and all. But it was the pits that helped me see ye are a right good man for our village, just the one to see us through this. Though your sermons nearly put me to sleep, if I were to be confessing right now."

"Oh! Really? I'm so sorry. I'll have to see what I can do about that." Bernard thought he gave rousing homilies, intellectually challenging topics to help enlighten the local populace. How in the world could they be boring? "The pits, you say?"

"Right. Pits! Who needs trash pits, thought I, but I'm starting to see the benefit now. At first I thought that was just tom foolery. And three of them, well, I thought the other preacher likes to make his parishioners suffer by their lonesome to atone, and you must like us to suffer in community, by digging huge pits out in the hot sun."

"Oh! Suffer? How interesting. And what made you change your mind?" Bernard found Adelman's comments to be most confusing and somewhat concerning. He didn't intend to make anyone suffer.

In his rough highlands accent, Adelman answered, "Well, three years ago we lost one of our sons. He got a deep cut from a broken metal tool. Sharp it was. Abandoned by someone who must've been frustrated with it breakin' and didn't have the means of havin' the blacksmith repair it. But me boy wasn't watchin' where he be going and he tripped on it. Mighty sad."

"I'm so sorry to hear that." When Bernard arrived, he had noticed quite an abundance of abandoned trash in the streets, old tools as well as discarded food and human excrement.

"Aye. The cut he got, it festered." Adelman looked off in the distance and wiped away a tear. "And it was a horrible death. I so miss that boy. Good boy, he was." He took a deep breath and turned back to Bernard. "But now that we's got a place to put trash, me other sons won't need be so worried. Me wife goes about town with a barrow on the wheel and she picks up all she can find that people's discarded. She drags her barrows out to the pit and throws it all in. Says it's safer now. And she sleeps better. Truth be told, so do I."

"Yes. Thank you for sharing your story." Bernard held Adelman's arm compassionately. "I also sleep better knowing that our Valley Village is a safer place for all. I appreciate your wife's service to the people of our town. I'll say a special prayer for her. And, with your permission, I think that's a good story to share with our community to inspire them to do good for one another as well. To bring goodness from tragedy. That's the ultimate redemption: goodness from tragedy."

"Well, well, well!" Adelman said with astonishment. "Margreth will be so pleased. Next time you come to my shop, I'll give you an extra beeswax candle, on the house!"

Bernard smiled at the man as he shuffled off to rejoin his family after the town meeting.

◆━◆━◆

After hours spent with the town's leaders and talking with the town residents, Bernard finally made it back to the manse. He made very weak barley tea with no honey at all, knowing that he would need to make his stores last as long as possible. It would never be enough. He would need to ask the local herb woman about mountain teas. He'd heard her talk of a dandelion tea, which sounded dreadful, but dandelions were plentiful, as was mint and sage. He would need to start picking and drying the plants so he'd have sufficient stores to get through the winter. He decided to speak with her the next day. For now, he picked up his cup and grimaced at the very weak liquid within, and then opened the scroll to Adelaide's first letter. It was a long one.

July, The year of our Lord 1348
Dearest Bernard,

Life in Cologne has nearly come to a standstill. There are no dinner parties. There is no shopping. No new dresses. No ribbons. I think even the food might be starting to be scarce. It hasn't hit us yet, because of course, our household can afford to pay. I might have been married off, traded like a cow, and indeed my husband believes I am a cow! He calls me a cow within my earshot. My only solace is that at least Father had the good sense to sell me into a wealthy family, if one that fails to be truly devout or even of the nobility. Prices have been rising and rising all year. I'm sure even Father would describe it as a pinch, although until now Gerung has always encouraged me to purchase whatever I wish.

But things have changed with the shift of fortunes and the anxiety in the city. Gerung doesn't want me to leave our manor. He says it's not safe. That mobs are attacking in the streets. I don't know why he is worried—the mobs don't attack devout Christian women. I know my cross and my faith will protect me. You are a priest, I have no doubt that you could make him see reason, if only you were here. But you are not. You are many a week's journey away and thus I am stuck here in the

She went on for another page of her complaints about her life with Gerung. She made many references to some type of interloper in their house, but while her complaints were vehement, she was so vague that Bernard couldn't understand what she meant. He was relieved when he saw that her next section was about good news and without complaints.

sins are they, that they remove most of their clothing even though the people on the street are there looking at them. They sing and pray and scourge themselves to suffer for Christ and absolve our city of its sins, so that God may remove this plague and we may worship Him in community once more. Isn't that lovely? I thought it was one of the most beautiful sights I have ever beheld.

These men were so noble in their suffering, their blood spilt, like the blood of holy men, blessing the walls of the buildings and the dirt on the street. I have never felt so uplifted in my life. It was as though I could feel the weight of my sins being taken from my shoulders as I stared at them. Such a sacrifice! It made me start to pray upon how I could help relieve the burden of sin from the world. Maybe I too might help end this terrible plague. With such devotion, I am sure these men will cure this blue sickness in no time at all.

I hope you continue to be well. I was so pleased that in your last letter, there was no mention of any signs of the blue sickness in your town. I can only think that you must be praying very hard and have won God's protection. I must confess, I didn't understand that bit you wrote about the cats, but I can understand that living in the beautiful valley with the mountains about you is good for balancing your humors, which would, of course, help keep you safe from sickness.

"Flagellants? Suffering for all of men's sins? That's very odd." It didn't surprise him that Adelaide approved. After all, she had worn a hair shirt on her wedding day. But he did find it curious that the church would condone or at least stand silent on the mass suffering. "Christ died to redeem mankind because He was holy. He did not redeem man because He suffered. He redeemed man because He was God."

While the suffering of mortal man might replicate the suffering of Christ, it could not *replace* it. "Mark me, there will be no good to come of this."

Chapter 23

Adelaide Trōst Engelhaft
October 1348

Adelaide was heading down to the kitchens to talk with the steward about what was to be served at dinner in the following nights. Even though she wasn't prone to eat much, there simply had not been sufficient choices in the last two evenings. A household like theirs had standards that needed to be upheld and she didn't want to hear any more of his excuses about scarcity in the city. If as many people were dying as she heard, then there would be more food available, not less. He was a wretched steward and she decided that she had never liked him.

On her way she ran into Rivkeh, which surprised her. Despite the fact that they had lived in the same household for the past five months, she rarely saw her guest about the manor.

"Oh, my Lady!" Rivkeh looked startled, put down the two buckets of water she was carrying, and gave Adelaide a respectful curtsy. "How are you, Lady Adelaide?"

"I have been well. I'm surprised to run into you. You hardly ever come out of my rooms."

"Oh." Rivkeh sounded shy and nervous. "We don't wish to intrude on your kindness. We want to honor the sanctity of your house, particularly given your incredible generosity in allowing our household your rooms. I must say, my Lady, that you are one of the most generous women I have ever met. It's very saintly of you. Your reputation is well deserved."

Adelaide felt herself relax at this comment and thought that maybe Rivkeh might not be as annoying as she had previously thought. "Well then... I'm so glad it's working for you. If I might enquire, just where are your four children sleeping?"

"We decided to have one room serve as a chamber where we can play music and read while the other two rooms serve as sleeping spaces. The little ones, Esther and Yosef, sleep in the blue room with my husband and I. The two older children, Adasse and David, sleep in the yellow room with Mishael and Yieltil."

Adelaide paused. "The yellow room? What yellow room? Wait, do you mean my... closet?"

"Oh, yes, I believe that your dresses hung there when we first arrived. But after your servants moved them out, we could see that it is a lovely yellow color, like buttercup flowers."

Adelaide puzzled out sleeping in a closet, thinking it would be a dreadfully small and cramped place, with of course, no windows at all. "And the four of them sleep there?"

Rivkeh nodded. "It is working out well."

"How did you fit four beds?" She thought of the enormous bed she slept in now, big enough for herself and Gerung, when he chose to join her.

"Oh, well certainly..." Rivkeh looked like she was trying to figure out how to explain it. "A regular-sized bed, like yours, my Lady, would not fit. But we found that putting small beds on top of one another did allow for each person to have their own bed and still allow for a little desk and space for two chairs! Our two husbands worked it out. They are very clever indeed." Rivkeh gave a little curtsy again.

"Yes, yes of course. Gerung's cleverness never ceases to amaze me." Adelaide looked down at the buckets of water. "Why aren't your servants fetching water for you? And why are you fetching water in the first place?" For a moment, Adelaide wondered if Gerung had had the audacity to give these intruders her bath.

"I do as much as I can to be helpful. We all do. Mishael and Yieltil can't really be our servants any longer, now can they? So much has… changed." Rivkeh appeared to choke up for a moment but then regained her composure.

Adelaide puzzled on this statement. "Once a servant, always a servant. Some things don't change even when circumstances do."

"Well, we are all servants of God, at any rate. And I find carrying water for our family, Mishael and Yieltil included, helps me be a servant of God."

Adelaide liked that idea. Being a servant of God. That's what those flagellants were, to be sure: servants of God. They were men on their way to becoming martyrs. *Martyr.* That thought struck her and Adelaide was frozen for a moment with the realization that she, too, had been waiting to become a martyr. Her whole life had been about waiting for the moment that God was going to call her, to call her to be a nun, to call her to be a sacrifice, to call her to be a *martyr.* She imagined that it felt like those players from the Guild wagons in the processions before this great mortality was released upon the masses, where the actors waited behind the stage to be called for their turn in the drama. That was like her life: waiting to be called for her moment on the stage. And waiting. And waiting.

"My Lady? Are you all right?" Rivkeh's concerned voice broke into Adelaide's thoughts and her hand was on Adelaide's arm.

Adelaide shook her head and brought her attention back to the woman before her, and the heavy buckets sitting at her feet. "Are you washing the floors?"

"The floors? Um, no. Are you sure you are well, my Lady? Yes? Um, we are practicing *netilat yadayim* and *arvut hadadit.*"

"What? I'm sorry? What did you say?"

Rivkeh took in a little breath and tried to smile. "*Netilat yadahim* is part of our *halacha*. It's the rules that God gave us to live by. We wash our hands before we eat. The water is for washing."

"What a strange rule."

"All communities have rules. I believe that you say your rosary, which is part of your community's rules. Our community lives by *halacha*."

Adelaide nodded. "And what were the other words you said?"

"*Arvut hadadit.* That is why I carry water. We are charged to have a mutual responsibility among our community, to honor the dignity of all life, that God made all equal in His eyes."

"Everyone equal in God's eyes? How fascinating." Adelaide knew exactly what her father would have said about such a belief, that anyone who believed that would never be part of the nobility. "I am curious what your children do all day. I never see them."

"We do not wish to intrude. The children are busy. We brought the few books we owned and their slates and they study to gain skills in reading and numbers. They practice their music, since we brought with us all the small instruments, and Adasse is learning to sing. She has a lovely voice, although she is quite shy. I'm sure she would sing for you, Lady Adelaide, if it would please you."

Adelaide left their conversation wondering if she would ever have to endure a world where she carried water for others and obeyed the law of those unpronounceable words that Rivkeh used. She didn't want to hear a voice lifted in song if it wasn't singing a hymn.

After dinner, the door to their apartment opened and Gerung entered. "My Lady."

"My Lor… husband. I'm rather surprised to see you."

He looked at her, on her knees, with her rosary beads in her hands. "I hope I'm not interrupting you, in your private moment with God."

She rose, her devotional feelings now diminished. "It is fine. I find myself finished."

"Oh well, all right then. I'll just change my clothes." He walked over to the closet he now shared with his wife. His clothes had only ever filled a corner and now they only had a corner allotted to them. He came back into the room, untying his belt and purse and started to unbutton his elaborate cotehardie. "I shall so miss Italian Damask," he said as he held the tunic in front of him and followed the design with his finger. "It's truly lovely."

"Why will you miss it?" Adelaide came over to him and looked at the tunic in his hand, wondering what was wrong with it. "It looks to be in fine condition."

"Trade has nearly halted. Too many of the caravans have lost their drivers. Too many merchants have died in the vain attempt to maintain their shops. Or they are hoarding what little they have left and are trying to hide away, hoping the specter of death doesn't spot them out on the street and decide to strike them down too."

"Surely good Christians have nothing to fear!"

He looked at her. "From the afterlife? Or from the plague itself?"

She felt unsure of the answer, wary that this was one of his logic traps. "Both."

"You are probably right." He slumped. "When there is so much to mourn, grieving for Italian damask does seem a waste of time, doesn't it? And there is so little time we might have left." He started to undo his under blouse to put on the more casual and comfortable garb he had lain over a chair.

"What are you… dressing for?" she asked.

"I am going to listen to music tonight. Aahron and Rivkeh's children will be performing. Would you like to join us?"

"I think… I will decline." She fussed with her ribbons a moment. "Just how long do you think they will be staying with us?"

With a sigh, he said, "I don't know, Adelaide. They can't leave here until it's safe outside. Clement the Sixth has ordered the killing of the Jews to stop, reminding the faithful that Jesus himself was Jewish, so this is like killing Jesus' family! But they are crazed, if not with fear then with jealousy and greed." He started working on the ties that held up his leggings. "It is appalling to hear about, much less see. I wish I could do more, bring more people to hide out here, but it's too late. The madness is upon us now. So, our friends will stay until there is a chance of escape."

She watched her husband undress. She didn't see him this unclothed very often and noticed that he seemed to be losing weight. Of course, he slept naked, but she was usually asleep by the time he came to bed, if he came to bed at all. He had nearly ceded his apartments to her and often slept in a guest quarter, although those were more like what would have been servant quarters in her father's house. "They hardly come out of my rooms. I never see them about. I was surprised to see the wife today."

Gerung gave a heavy sigh. "Rivkeh. She has a name, it's Rivkeh." He turned to her as he started to untie his hose from his breech belt.

"Did you know they have a religious rule to keep their feet inside their house when sickness takes the land?"

"Oh yes, we've talked about that. It's called a *bava kamma*, or something very close to that. Aahron has told me all about it. They had been staying inside their house, only going out at utmost necessity, because of it. I don't know if it protects them or not, but at least their children don't have nightmares about the carts of the dead." Gerung shuddered. "I hate to imagine being taken away on one of those, thrown in a mass grave." He sighed sadly. "But what can be done? There are just too many people dying every day. I hear that the basements of the major cathedrals are just stacked with bodies! They are running out of places to bury them." He shuddered again and stared off at nothing. "Those poor souls may lie there for centuries, their discarded husks slowly mummifying over time."

Adelaide didn't want to dwell on such images of horror and decided to focus him on their houseguests. "She told me they also have a rule about not sharing food!" Adelaide wondered how in the world people ate, if not off a trencher, and those were always shared. "It's a part of breaking bread. It's a part of fellowship."

"I think the rule is more about prohibiting taking a bite and putting your uneaten bit back in with everyone else's food. That's just common manners, Adelaide. My mother taught manners and etiquette like it was a religion. So, if someone else's religion teaches etiquette, then so be it."

"I think their ways are… unChristian." Adelaide sniffed.

"Well, yes. That would be because they're Jewish." He shook his head. "Their company happens to be delightful. Their children are intelligent and talented. Why don't you come and hear their music tonight, Adelaide? I'm sure you'd like it. You don't have to be shut in here all by yourself day after day."

Adelaide stiffened. "I'm not shut up here all by myself."

Gerung looked at her and then looked around the room. "And just who is here with you, my good Lady?"

"The Lord."

"I assume that you mean the divine one, not the one to whom you're married? Oh, not funny? Well, I tell you what. You can have your evening with just you and God, and if the spirit so moves you, please join us for some music and wine down in the entertaining chambers. We should take joy where we can in these dark times and find solace in one another's company."

He walked over to her and gently pulled the collar of her dress down and to the side, revealing her shoulder. "My dear, that discipline

258

is not healthy for you. Your back is scabbed and wounded. A loving God does not require that of you."

She stiffened and pulled her sleeve back up, covering her wounds. "If you take this one from me, I will simply obtain another."

"Yes. I know."

"I suffer for the Lord's pleasure."

"Adelaide, I don't believe that brings pleasure to any lord of any kind." Gerung finished dressing.

"You look like a servant in those casual clothes."

"I am taking an evening's entertainment in my own home with friends. I don't think anyone will care what I look like."

After he left, Adelaide paced for a bit and thought about joining the others, but the idea of community joy made her feel too uncomfortable. Then she thought of the flagellants. Now their noble work was genuinely exciting. Her heart raced as her mind fantasized about walking naked in the street and scourging the sins of others away, as a true martyr would, but then the disappointment crashed down upon her. As a woman, she could never do that, but she would beseech the almighty with her own voice. She decided to stay up the entire night praying for the sins of her countrymen so that God would show mercy and end the plague that was tormenting the populace. However, as she settled down to worship, the thoughts of the flagellants kept intruding onto her mind, distracting her from her prayers. Eventually, she fell asleep, despite her best intentions, slumped over on the floor.

She dreamed of walking in the streets as naked as Adam and Eve before the apple and using the scourge while the people of Cologne cheered her on, calling out blessings and thanking her for her martyrdom and intercession that would spare them the horrors of the plague. She was bloodied, the red lines streaking down her back and running down her legs, a golden crown of thorns sitting gloriously atop her head. In her dream, when she turned around, the footprints of the path were pooling with her blood and the people were anointing themselves with it, in joy and blessing. And they were saved. She felt pure. She felt holy. She felt powerful. But more than that, she felt free.

Chapter 24

Nylah

The sun was shining and the team was taking a rare day off, using the window of time without that circus of volunteers as an opportunity to hike in the wilderness and picnic in the valley. Everyone needed a break from dirt and dead bodies. Getting a respite like this was a rare and precious highlight in Nylah's hectic summer where she'd suddenly emerged as the CEO of what was turning out to be a small excavation company. After faltering at life the last couple of years, she felt the wind beneath her wings. She was an organizer. A translator of complex information for the masses to understand and appreciate. An alchemist of chaos into mere complexity. She finally felt like, well, she felt like herself.

And with the whole package—part enrichment and part distraction—came Hans. Nylah loved walking next to Hans, their fingers clasped together as they walked through the hills. She'd never had a boyfriend like him. Man, that had been hard to explain to her mother, that she was dating a foreign dude. A White foreign dude. But he was kind and sweet. He was a font of arcane knowledge. He was handy and could fix stuff. He loved food as much as she did. He found her fascinating. That last part was a new experience for her. It was one thing to date a guy who found you convenient, but Hans thought she was dope. He called it *geil*. She was his *Hammer geil*. At first she thought he was calling her "his girl". That was all right too, but when he explained that it translated to "beyond awesome" in English, she was more than satisfied. Better yet, Dr. T and Everly seemed to think he was okay enough to let him hang around, so while Nylah didn't have her mother's carefully judging eye, she figured that Dr. T and Everly could pass for the kind of adults who could sift the con man from cute man. Yeah, they both seemed like they'd been trounced by life a time or two and that jaundiced eye could help you spot a wolf in sheep's clothing. So far, they thought he was "cool". And so did she, only she might use the term *dope*. Which of course she had to explain to her bosses because they totally misunderstood at first. Then she just switched to use their post-hip descriptions and called things "cool". Then they understood what she meant. It took a lot of flexibility to work with these pre-old people.

But for now, she was with her *Hammer geil* boyfriend, holding hands on a summer day, walking through a made-for-Hollywood setting. After moving through some thicker brush and startling a slow-moving bird, the sight of which excited Hans greatly, they found a lovely spot in the grassy valley among clusters of purple flowers. As they lay down their picnic blanket, Hans was careful that they didn't crush any of the blooms in the process.

"These are called liverwort, but most people like to call them anemones. They're special flowers and somewhat endangered. We have them in our botanical garden. They used to grow throughout Bavaria, but now they are rare. Only in unspoiled valleys like this one."

Trevor seemed delighted. "So, you're saying that this valley we're in looks to us a lot like it did to the people seven hundred years ago? They might have enjoyed a picnic on a sunny day just like this one, sitting amongst these same flowers?"

"That's dope! I mean, that's so cool," Nylah said. "To think that so much could change and yet then again, not so much."

"Except they didn't really picnic back then," Everly said, falling into teacher mode, as she looked around at the faces of their small troupe, apparently not realizing that she'd just spoiled the magic of the moment. "What?"

Hans shrugged. "Time does change things, yes. For those people, if they came here… with a picnic," he grinned, "they would likely have curious neighbors!"

"Like ants? You mean ants?" Trevor asked, brushing one away. "That never changes."

"Actually, I mean like birds. The bird we startled back in the tall grass was a Black Grouse. Very rare today. Plentiful back a thousand years ago. People at the time of your little village would have thought them a nuisance. And probably a tasty treat with its uniquely gamey taste. Not so popular now," he said in response to Nylah sticking her tongue out. "But because it was so sedentary, it was a relatively easy bird to capture."

Nylah gave a laugh. "You mean that bird that looked like it was wearing Elton John's sunglasses?" Trevor and Everly laughed as well, agreeing. "What was that crazy stuff anyway?"

Hans explained, "You know how a chicken or a rooster has a crown? A headdress? I don't know the English word. Or a turkey has it under its chin."

"A wattle?" Everly asked. "In Canada, we call that a wattle."

"A wattle," Hans sounded the word out. "It is the same thing, only it has the red wattle around its eyes, yes, looking like wild sunglasses. They were prized for their long black tail feathers, the males anyway."

"What else would have come by their picnic?" Nylah asked, loving to hear him expound on all these details that she would never remember.

"Among birds, the most common would be Stonechats, Grasshopper Warblers and one called the Northern Wheatear. Deer, of course. Those have survived the centuries quite well, as have wood mice. And marmots."

"Marmots! Please let's not talk about marmots!" Trevor groaned and was greeted by a round of snickering.

"But the thing they would not have wanted to see would be the wild boar." Hans had a much more serious look on his face.

"Wild Boar, stuff of legends!" Trevor actually wiggled in his excitement, then looking around him as the others shot him looks, he said, "Oh c'mon! Wild boars are in all the great old stories, trampling about. Brave hunters going on quests. Feasting on wild boar."

"You are not wrong. The sighting of a wild boar would bring the local lesser nobility to the hunt in a heartbeat, as you would say." Hans nodded as he explained.

"Lesser nobility?" Nylah asked.

"*Ja vohl.* In Germania, as it was called at that time, the large land holders were in the North, where civilization was more organized. The poor were serfs, bound to their land and their masters. But here in the South it was just many little towns, many minor lords, and a much less connected system."

"Right!" Trevor said. "You really know your history, Hans. That's so true! The people in these hills had more ability to control their lives than anyplace in Germany or France or even England at the time. Down here, the lesser nobility had 'dwarf estates' they were called. They didn't bother the little towns and poor people very much. So, the folk went their own way. It was freer here."

"That is what I studied in university." Hans nodded. "So, while the church was very powerful in the cities and the knights and lords were in charge in the north, in the south, eh." Here he shrugged to finish his sentence. "But a boar would bring the lesser nobility out in force."

"Right!" Trevor interrupted again. "For the thrill of the kill!"

Hans nodded patiently. "And that is when they would start to notice the nothing little towns. And maybe conscript the men into service. Or perhaps take a lovely maiden for a mistress. Therefore, it was not popular for the little villages to bring notice upon themselves.

They wanted to be free and left alone. If they had wild boar, they would try to drive it off…"

"Unlikely," Everly said.

Hans nodded. "Or kill it themselves."

Trevor looked around the group. "Also, unlikely. Those were nasty blighters."

Hans nodded again. "We don't see them these days, but at the time of your little town, they would likely have had some. They would run, leading their herds, and trample everything in their path."

"Very destructive," Everly said, nodding in agreement.

Hans pointed to the pass between two of the taller mountains that surrounded the valley. "There is a *Hochmoor*, back then often called a *hohes venn*, or a high bog, in that direction. It isn't much now, but *Hochmoor* is a botanist's dream."

"What's a high bog? Like a swamp?" Everly asked.

"Well, *ja*, a bit like a swamp. It is drier now. You see, the soil there is clay, which captures the water. And there is little way for the water to make its way out, so it gets trapped there. Not enough for a lake, but enough to make it… um…uh…"

"Boggy?" Nylah asked.

Hans gave her a warm smile. "*Ja*, boggy. Like a marsh. It supports many beautiful flowers, like Elvina and Swamp Heath. And many, many lizards who live around an old stone wall."

"Lizards?" Nylah asked. "Let's not go there then. I can skip the lizards."

"No lizards in New York City?" Hans gave her a wink.

"Not that kind of lizards. Lounge lizards, sure. Creepy, but not wiggly." Nylah shuddered.

"There was a legend that a tree grew there. A very rare tree. I've searched for it several times in what remains of the *Hochmoor*, but there is no trace." Hans looked disappointed.

"What kind of tree?" Trevor asked, intrigued.

"A poison tree. Today we only know of these growing in a place called Florida, but the fruit and sap contain strong toxins." Hans looked at Nylah. "Your Native Americans used the poison on their arrows to fight the Spanish. And they won." He looked back to where the bog lay hidden in the hills. "It would be quite a discovery to find evidence of such a tree here in Bavaria."

"Oh, not expected then? An unusual finding?" Trevor asked.

"It would turn the field upside down."

"Oh!" Everly said. "So, it's the holy grail of botany, is it? We're looking for a holy grail too, in our little village that was ravaged by the Black Plague. Except none of our samples yet have returned a positive hit for the *Yersinia pestis* genomes. It's a tricky bacteria. Maybe our samples had more disintegration than we thought."

"Or," Trevor said, "it's possible that we're barking up the wrong tree. In general, really rural areas like this one were spared the devastation of the plague. Not on the trade routes, you see, so many of them survived. But this little village was wiped clean off the map. Hardly a trace left."

Everly gave a heavy sigh. "It was the Black Plague. There are no other logical culprits. The dates fit. The mass graves fit. People starving up in highland town in winter would be very susceptible, even with barely any exposure from trade. They could be hit particularly hard."

Nylah looked at Hans. "They do this all the time. Honestly, they're like an old married couple. Tedious, isn't it?"

Everly rolled her eyes and Trevor said, "We've made incredible discoveries so far. And if it wasn't Black Plague, well, that *would* turn medieval archeology right on its tail now, wouldn't it?"

Hans nodded. "Nylah keeps me up-to-date on your exciting findings. Your website is very professional."

Nylah smiled and felt her cheeks heat up.

"Yes, Nylah's done a bang-up job! We've got nearly a half a million followers," Trevor said.

"Close to six-hundred thousand," Nylah said, correcting him.

Everly startled. "That many? Whoever would've thought that regular people would be interested in archeology."

"And I thought it was only anoraks who could be interested in archeology!" Trevor said. "I mean, Everly, of course *we* know it's absolutely fascinating."

Nylah was still getting used to them being on a first name basis. It was dope that they were and all, and way beyond time, but still, it had been nearly a whole summer of *Dr. Bergeron* this and *Dr. Payne* that, so it sounded strange to hear them speak to one another like real people and not like some characters in a period drama. Ev hadn't budged on what happened to bring about this new era of familiarity however, which made Nylah all the more curious.

Trevor continued. "I always thought that the only people who would want what we dig up is, well... us." He looked at his companions. "Or maybe a museum. While I love the field, for the average person, you know, I think they might find it boring. Hans, it's like your flowers. Are people interested to see them or know their Latin names? No? What they really want is a picture for their screen saver, right? Or to have them delivered to their front door and then put in a vase on their table. They don't want the actual living flower that they need to tend and worry about. But not the botanists. To the botanist the actual flower in the ground has worth and meaning. Archeology is like that. People want the story behind the artifacts. They like to see the artifacts, like in a museum, sure, on a school field trip, but they'd really rather have the movie about Indiana Jones or something, because they romanticize the adventure of it all. Well, as Nylah and Everly can attest, it's a lot of dirt and very little romance." Trevor looked awkward for a second and quickly took a drink from his bottle of water.

"Ah yes, botany has very little *die Romantik* either. Aphids, *ja*. But we do not dig up golden crosses. That has drawn the eye of many to you. How are you keeping it safe?"

Trevor looked a bit confused. "Keeping it safe? From what?"

Hans gave Trevor a level look. "From being stolen. It is a cross of gold. Even people who do not care about history do care about gold. And gems. And beautiful rings."

Everly waved off the concern. "It's all up at Brandenburg. They've got it on display in their archeology building. It'll be fine. They have a lot of artifacts up there in the vaults and some really beautiful pieces on display."

"But not the gems. They are not with the cross. Or the ring," Hans said.

"Oh. How do you know about the gems?" Everly asked.

Hans said with a shrug, "I was up at the university. I saw the display. There were no gems with the cross. It is like the artifact is blind without its gleaming eyes." And then he casually reached for more of the cheese and bread. "And it was on your website, but just briefly."

Nylah thought about that. She'd updated the website so many times, almost daily in fact, because that's what drove traffic—always an evolving story with new and interesting finds—that she couldn't quite remember what might have been there before. She thought it was very sweet that Hans would check out her work and notice small details. She reached out and held his hand.

"Tell me, if the gems are still here, then do you have other artifacts on the site that might endanger you all?" Hans asked. "I would like to know that my *Hammer geil* girlfriend is safe." He picked up Nylah's hand and kissed it.

Everly answered him first. "Not anything that would interest anyone other than a collector, really."

"But you are finding much jewelry, no?" Hans asked. "There was a gold and diamond ring you found with that first body?"

"Well, yes. But it's all seven-hundred years old," Everly said. "And these weren't the nobility we've been digging up, except for, of course, Father B. Most of the people were the better-off folks of a very small town, yes, but nobility? No. There's the occasional semi-precious stone, mostly because the people of the day had rather magical beliefs about the various protections different gemstones gave them—warding off evil or sickness and the like. But the rings and necklaces are mostly bronze or copper. Again, seven-hundred-year-old bronze and copper. The peasant class weren't allowed to wear anything fine. Shopkeepers and workmen had strict rules of what their jewelry could be made of." She shook her head. "The nobility really wanted to keep people in their place."

Trevor looked away at the mountain tops and nodded, deep in thought. "Maybe you're right though, and we should stop thinking like archeologists. I mean, no one wants to steal manky old bones, now do they? And we've got a lot of those around right now after the last excavation! But you've got a point about a gold cross… or the gems that used to be on it. And a couple of the rings."

Everly said, "To some people, they could be more than history."

"Right," Trevor agreed. "Now, Nylah's done an ace job on the website making everyone think that we're in Idaho. Someplace called Sun Valley that is apparently actually filled with snow. But the news has done less of a good job of keeping our location secret and God only knows what all those students are putting out there on social media."

"Right." Hans nodded in agreement. "That is a big risk."

"We make all the students and volunteers sign NDAs," Nylah said. "I go over with each of them the risk to the site and the artifacts about leaking dig information, including our location. Jesus, it's a circus enough already."

"But, Nylah, you can't stop them from leaking the information," Hans said. "They're kids."

"Oh yeah I can!" Nylah answered confidently. "I explain to each and every one of them that I am monitoring their posts and for the students if they post anything about our location or the findings, they will fail the class. A big old 'F' on their transcripts. Screw their GPAs."

"You don't. Tell me, you don't actually say that to them?" Everly blanched.

"Sure! And the volunteers are told that there are master lists clearing them for archeology sites all over the world. You like Southern Germany? Imagine getting cleared to work our sister dig in Fiji!"

"We don't have a sister dig going on in Fiji!" Trevor objected and then looked downcast. "Oh, now I want to be on that dig in Fiji that doesn't exist."

Nylah shrugged. "They don't know that. And Fiji's a great draw. I'm telling you, they want to be on the nice list! Kind of like getting that TSA pre-check pass in the States for flying. And if they leak anything, then I'm blacklisting them. They'll never be invited anyplace worth going again."

"Nylah, that's just not true." Everly looked like she didn't know what to say.

"Sure it's true. I've made a list. I'm checking it twice. Want the tropics? You gotta be nice."

"Naughty volunteers roll the dice," Trevor said.

"And find they get on the blacklist for life," Nylah replied.

"It's still not right, Nylah. I mean it's not ethical. But it's so clever that I might have to write that into my book." Trevor laughed.

"Grave robbing is not a dead art," Hans said, still serious in the face of Trevor and Nylah's obvious mirth. "They don't care about failing a class or being blacklisted. They're much more efficient today than they were seven hundred years ago."

"Yeah right! Today they show up with guns!" Everly said, not being mirthful at all.

"Oh, c'mon, this isn't New York. It's rural someplace in Europe. Everyone knows they don't allow guns in Europe!" Nylah said dismissively. "And don't worry! I've got this. In addition to the whole Sun Valley thing, I geolocated our dig about a hundred and fifty miles away from here. The website is full of red herrings to make sure our little paradise doesn't turn into more of a circus than it is!"

Everly picked up the last piece of cheese and chewed it thoughtfully. "We've reached the bottom of Pit B. Got all the human remains processed, labeled and boxed up. We'll be going back to just Gunther and his students next week."

"And the ten best volunteers," Nylah added. "What? What are you looking at? I needed to have some incentive package to motivate them. And you have to admit, those people are pretty dope. I don't know what they did before they retired, but they are excellent site volunteers."

Thunder interrupted her, as it rolled and rumbled in the distance. Hans started quickly packing up the remains of their picnic, looking nervous. "You know, there's this ancient German legend called the 'Wild Hunt'. A ghost-team of mounted riders thunder across the sky in search of their victims. In some versions of the tale, the ghostly riders are a portent of doom. In others, the danger's real because the unwary can be swept up in the cavalcade. A bit like the danger coming toward us now." He pointed at the distant clouds gathering over the mountain tops.

"Oooh! I love thunderstorms," Trevor said as he looked at the dark clouds.

"With thunderstorms, the danger is real here in the mountains." Hans continued to pick up napkins and plates.

"Right! There's a great old song about that German legend, you know. It was made famous in the American West." And then Trevor started to sing in a deep voice, without a trace of his British accent, "Yippie-yi-o! Yippie-yi-yay, Ghost riders in the sky. Cowboy change your ways or with us you will ride, trying to catch the devil's herd, across the endless skies. Yippie-yi-o, Yippie-yi-yay." His chorus was broken by a loud rumble of thunder.

"Excuse me, can we get off the picnic blanket please?" Hans asked, some urgency in his voice.

As everyone started to move, Nylah asked, "Excuse me, Dr. T, was that a song?"

"Yes, a great song!" Trevor answered her. "Been recorded by maybe a dozen artists around the world. It's the story Hans was talking about. Couldn't you tell I was doing Johnny Cash?"

Nylah looked a bit confused. "Johnny Cash?"

Everly waved her off. "Don't worry about it. It's another one of those nineteen-fifties things."

"Well, excuse me! That song was a big hit in nineteen seventy-nine!"

Everly laughed. "Trevor! You're almost up to the nineteen eighties! Next we'll hear some Madonna, perhaps? Or, if we're really lucky, we'll go post millennium and enjoy some Taylor Swift."

Hans finished putting away the last of the picnic materials. "Now those are some artists I've heard of. Everyone, please start to walk now." He continued to try to hurry them along as they walked and chatted.

Nylah took Hans' hand, noticing that he felt kind of clammy. She turned to Trevor. "Dr. T, why do you know all these oddball songs anyway?"

Trevor sounded aghast in his response. *"Ghost Riders in the Sky* was not an odd ball song. It spent sixteen weeks at number two on the country music charts!"

"Number two? Really?" Everly said. "Can I request some Beatles? I mean you're always singing something. Do you take requests?'

Trevor pulled a small digital device out of his pocket. "This is the most important piece of equipment for a dig: your music playlist. It's long days out there and you might be in the pit for ten hours. Tunes, they're your friends. Having the right playlist makes a dig go much faster and helps keep everyone in a good mood. And the best part?"

"What?" Everly asked.

"They don't have to actually listen to me sing."

"I don't know. I kind of like your singing." Everly smiled but didn't make eye contact with Trevor.

Trevor blew out his breath and looked anywhere but at Everly.

Nylah was going to say something clever, but a crash of thunder made the whole group jump.

"Quickly now! We are all going to go back to camp as fast as we can. Those ghost riders in the sky are more than legend. Portents of doom are not to be taken lightly. *Schnell* now! *Schnell!* Lightning strikes in the mountains are very deadly."

The foursome scuttled down the hillsides as fast as their legs could carry them, finally understanding that Hans had been trying to alert them to the dangers of mountain thunderstorms. It was a frightening trip for Nylah, who was not used to being outdoors in bad weather. As she glanced over her shoulder, the black clouds roiled and she did a double take, stopping for a moment.

Hans took her hand forcefully and pulled her along. "No time to stop now, *Liebchen*. We must get away from the storm. Very dangerous."

"Sorry! Right. It's just that it looked like, the clouds looked like…"

"Like what?" he asked as he hurried her along.

"Like shrouded, cloaked figures were moving in the clouds. It was freaky. Like those old specters of death from the Middle Ages."

Hans was quiet a moment, then he shouted out to their small party, "No time to waste. Run if you can. Get down the mountain!"

Lightning split the sky behind them and thunder boomed in a deafening roar as the four made their way down the hillsides in a dead heat.

What Nylah didn't tell Hans, what she wasn't sure she would ever tell anyone, was the impression she had of the glowing red eyes of the cloaked figure in the dark gray clouds. She knew she would never forget that sight. She might be in the safety of Hans's arms tonight, but she was sure she wouldn't be able to sleep.

Chapter 25

Aahron
April 1349

Aahron sat in a chair, a tumbler of wine untouched before him. With a small cloth, he dabbed at his eyes and then wiped his nose. He watched a trio of physics silently walk past him as they departed the house. Rather than evoking hopes for health and healing, their plague masks, with the grotesquely exaggerated beaks and wide, empty eyes, made them resemble carrion birds of death. Their cloaks, like dark wings, spread and flapped behind them as they strode down the hall, not speaking a word. After a while, in the distance, he heard the clang of the front door as it closed.

"How could so much misery flood the world?" he murmured aloud and leaned back in his chair, the sadness engulfing him. He thought of his neighbors, friends, and relatives—now all dead. The ghetto where they were forced to live suffered the same plague, but to a lesser extent than the freer sections of the city, where people came and went as they wished, many in defiance of the quarantine laws now in effect. The Jewish laws of his people, their *halacha*, made them stay home during epidemics, instructed them to wash their hands frequently, and to not share food. Maybe that had protected them from the ravages of the

274

plague, but it had not protected them from the ravages of the Christians themselves.

"Bless Clement the Sixth," Aahron said aloud as he touched his hand to his forehead and then his lips, "for he ordered the persecution of the Jews to cease." He shook his head. "And may Charles the Fourth, even though he is the newly elected Holy Roman Emperor, meet his Justice in the eyes of God." Aahron growled. "Making the property of any Jews killed in the riots freely forfeit... no wonder the local authorities turned a blind eye. Dead. All dead. Burned. Ashes." The tears streaked down his face as he thought of all those murdered and of the whole section of the city that had been the home to his people, which was now gone. The ashes no longer smoldered but he was sure the bitter taste in the air would endure in this city, standing testament for a thousand years to the crimes against humanity committed there.

"I'm sorry to disturb you." Adelaide's voice made him jump.

He stood and gave her a small bow. "I am overcome with grief, my Lady."

"Yes. Today looks to be another sad day. I have just come from Gerung's bedside. He has asked to see you. He would part with you."

Aahron wondered how a wife could be so calm at the impending death of her husband? His family shed far more tears than hers did, but he kept those thoughts inside and simply nodded.

"I must write to his family to let them know his condition has made a turn for the worse. I'll send a messenger." She sighed and looked towards the ceiling. "I think if I pay one of the remaining servants enough they will be willing to run a note through the streets to let Gerung's father know."

"His father is in mourning over the death of his own wife, victim of this horrible plague," Aahron said.

"Indeed. Many have died. But for the grace of God go we all."

"My Lady, may I ask how you remain so strong in the face of all this tragedy and grief?"

Adelaide gave him a look that made Aahron feel like an incompetent fool, but, he reasoned, reducing wholly capable people to that perception was one of her talents.

"I commit no sin therefore I have no fear. I have nothing to hide before God, so I am content to live, or die, as God wills."

"My Lady," he answered with a bow. Aahron watched her as she swooped off, her skirts swishing, the ribbons dangling from the braids in her hair dancing on the breeze she made as she strode down the hall to write her missive to her father-in-law.

"No sin. I would think that the inability to love is a sin indeed." He walked quietly to the small room where Gerung had isolated himself just four days ago. He entered, trying to make as little disruption as possible.

Gerung turned his head toward the door. With a weak hand, fingers tinted black, he waved Aahron over. Aahron worked hard to keep a pleasant look on his face; it was a challenge as Gerung's neck was covered with bulging red sores and the tip of his nose looked a dark blue.

"Ah, Aahron, my good friend. I am glad to have a chance for last words with you."

"Last words? You have more words than any man I've ever met!"

"Then you have not met my brother-in-law, Bernard!"

"You're looking better. The potions and pastes must be working."

Gerung gave Aahron a sideways look and shook his head. "No, my friend. They know nothing. They don't think for themselves. Their fumigations simply make it harder for me to breathe. They offered to sacrifice a goat and tie its entrails to our door in order to cure me."

Aahron's brows knitted. "And what would that do beside expand the suffering to a poor goat?"

Gerung nodded. "Precisely." He sat quietly for a few moments, as if to gather his strength. "Aahron, while I feel better just seeing you, I am dying. I will not survive this."

Aahron sat next to the bed in the dim little room. He wished he could hold Gerung's hand, but he was too afraid to touch it and Gerung certainly wasn't reaching out. "Just six days ago we played games and drank. We danced!"

Gerung nodded weakly. "It was so fast once I got the chills. It won't be long now and I will find out first hand if God has any justice."

A tear slid down Aahron's cheek. "The world will be a darker place without you, Gerung."

Gerung gave a weak chuckle. "I don't think my wife will see it as such. She will undoubtedly say this *is* God's judgment of me."

Aahron shook his head emphatically. "This cannot be a judgement of God. You are a righteous man. This is not about punishment, my friend. This is sickness and mankind is simply no match for this devilry."

"Try to find it in your heart to forgive her, Aahron."

"I don't know what you mean," he answered, but Gerung looked at him sideways, calling him out in his lie. "I will do my best."

"Good. Perhaps you will succeed where I have failed, for I find myself a bit at peace with my death knowing that I will be free from my marriage. Isn't that a sin to feel thus?"

"It is hard to live peacefully with a match that works poorly." Aahron silently blessed Rivkeh and their parents, who had brokered his own very happy match.

"I shouldn't blame her. Neither of us had a say. She was told to behave a certain way and I was stupid enough to believe that the woman I met was the woman she was. I had hoped for a life partner. And I suppose she was that, for the few months I had left to live. Who would've known it would be so short?"

Aahron started to weep. He could not help himself.

"Ah! Don't cry for me, my friend. Let our last moments together be spent in constructive thoughts. First, I want to apologize to you and your people."

"Apologize? I don't understand, my friend. There are no apologies to be made. You are a righteous man. And when we played cards last weekend, I was kidding when I accused you of cheating."

Gerung smiled but said, "I'm serious, Aahron. What my people are doing to your people is the very definition of evil. I cannot understand it and yet I cannot stop it. Your people are more vanquished now at the hand of the mob than they would have been at the hands of Satan himself who delivered this plague." He coughed weakly.

"Rest, my friend. Don't get yourself worked up. You have moved beyond these worldly concerns now. The people are angry. They are angry at the evil that has befallen them, and when anger takes a man he cannot see, cannot reason, cannot love. He thirsts only for vengeance."

Gerung nodded sadly but did not speak.

"That mob is taken by the darkness in a way that is more complete than those who the angel of death wraps in his cloak when he delivers them, whether they be plague victims or murdered Jews," Aahron answered.

"They should not have done this."

Aahron nodded. "Agreed." He breathed a heavy sigh and stared away at a wall. "Anger strips a man from his soul. Divorces him from God. Prevents him from seeing the humanity of his fellows, who all become 'the other'. In anger, man becomes a base animal, a wolf foaming at the mouth and cast from its kind." Aahron turned back to Gerung. "It is better to never let such anger enter your heart, for it takes you from the light of God. Never is a man more in the pocket of evil than when he is angry. Be at peace, my friend. Walk in the light of God. May the angels protect you on your journey."

"Before I depart, I have another worldly concern before I… before I… shed my mortal coil. It is my wish that you and yours survive this plague, but you cannot do so in Cologne." His blackened hand waved towards his desk. "I have written out all the particulars. And my will lies there. I have bequeathed to you a carriage and two wagons, loaded with provisions."

Aahron was overcome with emotions at this generosity, and he felt overwhelmed with the directive. "You are so kind, but where will we go? I was born and raised in Cologne. I know no other place. And of no other place where Jews escape the evil fate that awaits them here in the West."

Drawing a breath with effort, Gerung said, "You must go east. I had been making inquiries before I fell ill. King Casimir the Third of the Polish lands has invited Jews. He protects them. You can live there. It is the only place that will be safe for your children. You must go."

Aahron felt a ray of hope. He had started to come to the conclusion that they would all await their death here in Cologne, if not in the ghetto and their own home, then in Gerung's grand manor. If they were not delivered by the pestilence, then at the hands of the rabid Christians who needed a scapegoat for the plague, since the agony of the flagellants apparently produced insufficient suffering to please their cruel God. "If that is what you wish, we will take the wagons and go." Aahron worried about them being murdered on the road, or even before they could leave the city walls.

Gerung gave him a fleeting smile. "Thank you for not fighting me about the idea. I'm afraid my gift comes with a burden, my friend, with my final wish."

"Anything. I will do anything you ask, Gerung."

"Take Adelaide." Gerung looked at the expression on Aahron's face and started to laugh, which caused a weak coughing fit. Aahron helped him to sit up and offered him a sip of water, which Gerung gratefully accepted, grasping the cup in his grotesque fingers. "I know, it will be a distasteful experience. But just to her brother's village in the southern mountains. If she stays here, she will die, or worse, she will be left with no one to take care of her. Or worse still, my father will marry her off, maybe even to himself. He sees only her beauty and does not realize that she is not suited to marriage."

"If you wish it, we will take her—if she will come. She can be… headstrong."

"I will make sure she will go with you. Aahron, I know fully what a burden she will be, the pain she will cause you. And I'm sorry for that. But she will be your cloak of protection through Cologne and on the roads. No one will see you as Jews if you are with her. Let her adorn the wagons with her crosses. If you can stand it, wear them yourselves for the journey until you are safe and then burn them for all I care. Let her think she has converted you and she will use the power of her station and family titles to obtain safe passage. It is your only option."

"It will be like wearing a hair shirt of the Christians." Aahron grimaced.

"Don't mention hairshirts or she'll probably outfit you with those too! And a discipline, to boot."

Aahron could see Gerung shudder and was sure that this time it was not with the chills. He gave his friend a slight smile. It was all he could do in the moment.

"She's not a well woman. Pray for her. Forgive her. She doesn't understand." Gerung coughed again and lay back down. "Perhaps if we'd had a lifetime together, I could've expanded her world, helped her to experience joy. Self-acceptance. Love even. Sometimes I don't think there's enough love in this world for Adelaide to heal." He gave a sad sigh. "But that is no longer my responsibility. It is my hope that she will find what she needs in her brother's care."

"We will take her. We will let her be our cloak and our dagger. And we will live, my friend. My grandchildren will be named for you. They will know the story of the righteous merchant of Germania."

◆——◆——◆

Gerung drew his last breath in the early hours of the morning. Adelaide allowed his body to be loaded on the death cart without any formalities. Aahron and Rivkeh watched in horror as their friend and protector's corpse was pulled away in a pile of other unfortunates, to be laid in a common grave. With him went the bodies of two servants who had died in the household in the last two days.

"Those men are greedy. They asked too much to haul away corpses," Aahron heard Adelaide say as she swooshed past him.

Alone in the courtyard, Rivkeh looked at her husband, tears in her eyes. "That was ill done, my husband, and I don't know how I will live with either Gerung's death or his burial."

Aahron took Rivkeh's hand. "I know. I know."

"At least he was wrapped in a fine sheet. I hope he is buried in it."

"Even if they steal the sheet, I helped him put on his fine Italian damask tunic before I left him. He knew he would be buried in whatever he was wearing, so we dressed him for a grand party in heaven."

"Oh, he would like that," Rivkeh said, a smile crossing her face for the first time in days. "He would like that."

◆ ⎯⎯ ◆ ⎯⎯ ◆

A month later saw their wagon caravan lined up in the courtyard of the manor of Engelhaft the Younger. Adelaide was now the owner, in conjunction with her father-in-law, and the grand house would be managed by the steward until such time as she could return. Aahron looked around, wondering where she was and whether she was going to change her mind at the last minute. It had been quite a scene when Adelaide had heard the reading of the will and found that she could determine her own destiny but in a limited range of options: to marry her father-in-law or to be removed from Cologne to her brother Bernard's care for the duration of the plague. Not only was a match with her husband's father most unChristian, she exclaimed that she detested the man and would not suffer for the saving of his soul in particular. She desired to return to her father's house even though they were struggling with the sickness at the moment.

It had taken hours of patient conversation in which Aahron had to coddle and indulge a hysterical Adelaide, eventually convincing her that the piety she demonstrated had moved his family to convert, but that they only trusted her brother to minister to their souls, given what they had seen in Cologne. Adelaide was so moved that she assented to this plan. And now the journey was about to begin… he hoped.

"Papa, must I wear this?" His daughter, Adasse, came up to him fingering her new wooden cross. She had little Esther on her hip. Esther was playing with a necklace bearing her own little cross made of wood.

"Cross! My cross!" Esther said gleefully, playing with her new toy.

Aahron gave them both a kiss on the tops of their heads. "Yes, my love. That's your necklace. Your very own. A gift of the Lady Adelaide." He turned to his oldest daughter. "Adasse, you must smile and nod in agreement with the things that the Lady says, even if your heart tells you differently. You must be pleasant and keep the Lady happy." He leaned over to whisper in her ear. "Hear me, my child: this is a matter of life and death for us." He leaned back with a sad look on his face. "Too heavy a burden to put on the shoulders of children, but such is the fate of Jews throughout history. Will you do this? Can you do this?"

Adasse nodded, a solemn look on her face. "I am thirteen. Practically a woman. I understand. You can rely on me, Father."

"That is my good girl!" Aahron hugged his daughter. "I will try to keep you in a different wagon than her since your mother will need help with the little ones, but be forewarned: the Lady Adelaide may want the company of a young lady and then there will be nothing I can do. Of course, when we stop to eat and rest for the nights, all nine of us will be gathered around the same fire. Play your part well." He looked about. "Where is your mother?"

"She's helping the Lady Adelaide."

"Ah, there they are." He patted his daughter on the back and she took Esther and climbed into their designated wagon.

Rivkeh walked up to Aahron with a smile, her arm around David and holding Yosef by the hand. Aahron gave a start to see the same wooden cross about their necks as well, and then reminded himself he would simply have to get used to it.

"Papa, how long will this journey be?" Yosef asked. Only five, he was eager to be a big boy like his nine-year-old brother.

Aahron leaned back on his heels. "That is a good question, my son. It will be a long one."

David asked, "I know we can't know for sure, but will it be a year?"

With a good-natured laugh, Aahron said, "No! Not a worry about it taking a year! We measure the distance in landmils. A wagon train can make about a landmil, maybe two, per day. It's about sixty-five of those to get to our destination." Aahron hoped they could pass through the gates of the city. That was the first set of trials, or else their journey would be a very short one indeed.

"Sixty-five landmils!" David breathed out heavily, blinking a couple of times. "I've never been on such a long journey. And, Papa, where is that? Where are we headed?"

"A mountain town called the Valley Village of the Three Mountains. It is a pure place of sun and great beauty. We believe there is no pestilence there and we will be safe. And it should take us a month or two to get there, if we have luck with us. Worry not, for we are well provisioned for the journey."

Rivkeh gave David a hug and picked up Yosef. "It's time for you two to get in the wagon with your sisters. You all will continue your studies as we journey, so you'll be busy. The time will fly by."

David nodded and took Yosef from his mother, helping the five-year-old climb into the back of the designated wagon. Rivkeh turned to her husband. "Do you really think this will work?" She grasped the cross about her neck.

"It has to. We have no other choice."

"At least the little ones don't understand."

"And the big ones understand all too well."

She nodded to his neck. "It's time to put yours on."

He sighed heavily. "You have caught me. I was delaying as long as possible. May I be forgiven?"

"Quickly now, she'll be coming through those doors any minute." Rivkeh had a smile on her face but worry framed her eyes. "Will you be all right driving the carriage?"

"Oh yes. I think it won't be hard. Mishael will have the much more challenging time, what with that cross loaded into the back of the wagon carrying the children. But he's got the oxen. It will be slow, it's a heavy load. Yieltil will drive the supply cart. I'm sure by the end of this journey, we will all be well acquainted with taking care of oxen, draft horses, and carriage horses. Even David will know how to drive a wagon."

"The children will be comfortable enough, I dare say. I put mounds of blankets and rugs and pillows over the cross, so it looks almost like a piece of furniture. The bigger children will be able to lean upon one side of it as if it were a chair or a lounge and the little ones can sleep in the well of softness on the other side." She shook her head. "I've always lived in fear of the cross. Now we're taking refuge in it."

"Gerung intended for us to take two wagons of provisions. He never anticipated that the Lady would demand that the cross go with us."

"It will be fine. The soft household goods are with the children and are light to balance out the load. The other wagon carries the stores. And the carriage…"

"Will carry the Lady. Will you ride with her?"

"When she asks me. Otherwise, I will ride with the children or with Yieltil in the supply wagon."

"Ah! Here she comes." Aahron smiled broadly at Lady Adelaide as she crossed the yard towards them. Out of the corner of his mouth he said to his wife, "Why don't you join Mishael?"

Rivkeh nodded and departed.

"Ah, my Lady Adelaide! You look ready for a journey to a new and happier tomorrow. Let me help you into your carriage."

As she was about to step into the carriage, Adelaide stopped. "Why is my carriage loaded down with so many crates and boxes?"

"Because, my Lady, it is a journey. The oxen of the third wagon have all they can bear. It is a long trip and we must not overtax the poor beasts. That would be an unChristian thing to do."

"Why? What is in the third wagon?"

"The cross, my Lady. It weighs so much that only light items, like blankets and pillows, some clothes are there, along with the children, who are small and light. All the heavier items must be divided between the second wagon and the carriage. Not to worry, my Lady Adelaide. The road is rough between here and the South of Germania, and some places might have no road at all. But the extra weight on your carriage will keep it steadier and help to smooth out the bumps. I will be driving the carriage for the most part. Would you like any company as we start our journey?"

Adelaide looked at the two following wagons with some apprehension. "No, I thank you. I believe I'll spend today's journey in quiet reflection."

He nodded. "Your Bible is on the seat, awaiting you."

She smiled. "Your conversion is the only happy thing to happen to me in the past year, Aahron."

"Let us start this journey to a safer place and happier days ahead for all of us."

She gave him a brilliant smile. "Yes. Let's do just that."

The small caravan pulled out through the gates of the manor and onto the nearly deserted streets. He hoped a watch wasn't out, for the quarantine orders were strictly in place now. But only a few people sullenly looked out their windows as the wagons passed; no one shouted anything or called the alarm. He wondered if anyone had the energy left to shout anymore.

They came to two gates as they passed through the corridors of the city. These had been abandoned and were left shut and barred, but not locked. Aahron, Mishael, Rivkeh, and even little David pushed at them, working together to lift the iron bars until they came free and the gates swung wide. The first set of gates they struggled again to push closed but left them unbarred. The second set of gates they simply left open, feeling the pestilence had already closed everyone in enough.

Before long Aahron could see the city gates themselves. Once through these, they would be in the free countryside, itself fraught with a different constellation of dangers. Aahron peered ahead and then leaned over a bit to shout to his passenger. "My Lady! There are guards at these gates who might need to be persuaded to let us pass."

He slowed his horses, hailing the guards. Somehow, they didn't seem surprised to see the wagon train pull up. In a perfunctory way, the first guard called out,

"Ay! Why do you come to the gates? The city is shut."

Aahron gave a wave and said, "We journey to the countryside to our remaining family, as we have lost nearly all our brethren here in Cologne."

The second guard walked over and stood by his companion. "What's this? More rich folk escaping the hell of the city?"

"Right you are. Off to some country estate no doubt," answered the first guard. "Third time this week alone."

"They'll be no rich folk left. No nobility. It's becoming a city of equals." The second guard nodded his head knowingly.

The first guard snorted and answered, "Equally dead. We're all equally dead."

"They'll be too. They just don't know it yet. The angel of death is equally happy in the city as in a country manor."

Adelaide leaned out the window of the carriage and called softly up to Aahron, "What's happening?"

"I think we will need to convince them of our mission, my Lady."

Adelaide nodded and then leaned out the carriage window towards the guards. "Good day, good sirs. I bid you greeting and bless you."

The second guard looked at his companion. "Oh yes, right you are. More nobility trying to run away."

"Good sirs, please to open the gate as we are on a holy mission and must not be delayed."

The first guard leaned into the second. "Holy mission. That's a new one. Tryin' to save their skins, they are. Let's learn more about this ruse, shall we?"

The second guard nodded in reply.

Aahron climbed down from the jack box of the carriage. "My Lady, I believe your presence will be required for the conversation."

Adelaide gave him a regal, single nod of her head and proceeded to step down from the carriage. "Good sirs, we are on the mission from the bishop himself."

"My good brothers in Christ," Aahron addressed the guards. "Let me show you what we are transporting at the behest of the good bishop." He and Adelaide led them around to the second wagon, Aahron loudly extolling the virtues of the cargo and rapping on the side of the wagon several times. As he reached the behind-end of the wagon, he lowered its back gate to reveal a huge cross filling the bed. Off to each side lay large humps covered by rugs. "You see, this is our blessed mission."

Adelaide gave the guards her brilliant smile. "We are taking this cross to a holy village in the south. It is part of the charge put upon us by the bishop himself, as a move to please God and end the pestilence, protecting both Cologne and the village."

"And just who are you that we should let you out of the gate?" the second guard asked.

"This is the Widow Adelaide Trōst Engelhaft herself. Daughter of the Duke Trōst of Lotharinga. Favorite of the king. Niece of the bishop. Former wife of Engelhaft the Younger. Undoubtedly, you've heard of her generosity?"

"She's the wife of that nice merchant king?"

"Right, isn't his name Grimholt or Gerung or Georg or something like that?"

"Gerung. My husband's name was Gerung."

"Right! Him! Good tipper he is. Always tipped the guards when the caravan of goods come in through the gates." He leaned over conspiratorially and added, "And round about this time last year, he came with a whole barrel of mead for the guards and drank with us. A gift he said, because we was all so efficient at moving his caravans right on through. He said efficiency should be rewarded."

The first guard looked at the second, then at Aahron, and then at Lady Adelaide. "What do you mean *was*? Not him too? Oh, the grim reaper, he only takes the good 'uns, don't he?"

The second guard nodded, also with a sad look on his face. "Only the good die young. We are sorry for your loss, my Lady. Not many like Engelhaft the Younger. Man was an angel."

"I am also the only daughter of your duke."

The men shrugged. "Don't have many dealing with dukes, now do we? Too high and mighty they are, I guess."

"Right you are," the second guard said. "He's never come to have a drink with us or tell us what a good job we do at our stations."

Aahron could feel that this interchange was starting to go sideways. "The Lady Adelaide, poor widow of the esteemed Engelhaft the Younger, is well known in the city in her own right. She is generous to a fault, giving away alms to the poor. Perhaps you've heard of her?"

"I think I have heard of her. Got a good reputation, she does," the first guard said to the second.

"I could use some alms meself," the second guard answered.

Behind Adelaide's back, Aahron pulled a bag of coins out of his tunic, weighing them in one hand. He had the full attention of the guards now. With his free hand he put a finger to his lips, then he pulled out a second bag of coins. "The Lady is most concerned for the feeding of your families, with prices moving up and people afeared to open their shops. She is a generous benefactress, just like her husband." He raised his eyebrows and hefted the bags of coins again.

The guards looked at each other. "She's got a good reputation she does," the first one said and he crossed his arms and looked at his companion.

"Right you are. And now she's on a mission to save that little village, by bringing them this huge metal cross, dragging it across the south with a team of oxen," the second one answered.

"Far be for me to stand in the way of a holy mission. And by the size, and I assume weight, of that cross, her mission is of dire import." He turned to Adelaide. "We will let you pass because it's the right thing to do. May I help you back into your carriage, my Lady?"

"Oh, yes, thank you. And may God in his mercy bless you," she said as she climbed the steps and got settled once again.

The second guard turned to Aahron. "May God in his mercy bless me, but I'll take your blessing too."

Aahron smiled and handed each guard a bag of coins. "We will have another wagon an hour behind us. They will mention the Lady and our party. They are late to the caravan. Please let them through."

The guards looked at one another and shrugged, then nodded at Aahron.

"May the light shine on you and may you be protected in the days to come," Aahron said solemnly.

The second guard looked at the first and chuckled. "Well, that's a right nice blessing. Usually, it's all about Christ and suffering and such. I don't know about you, but I've had enough suffering for one life's time."

"Oh, shut up and help me open this gate."

❖━❖━❖

Aahron breathed a sigh of relief as he saw Cologne disappear into the distance and knew his children had long since emerged from their cocoon of blankets and pillows and were sitting as comfortably as they could, leaning against the huge cross. A wagon full of servants would have made sense. A wagon full of children who answered to obviously Jewish names, would have put them all in grave danger.

"May the light shine on the others and may they be protected in the days to come," he said aloud as he clicked the horses to pick up their pace a bit. All the other surviving Jews Gerung had hidden away in his household and employed as servants would be getting away from the madness of Cologne in the next wagon. Aahron wished them the best. He did not expect to see them again.

◆━◆━◆

Six hard weeks later they pulled into the promised village. Six weeks of Adelaide's sermons. Six weeks of her instructing the children on the Bible. Six weeks of her extolling on the virtues of their suffering as they rationed their food and nursed unending bruises from the rough travel.

When they reached the valley, Aahron found it to be uncommonly beautiful. The village was on the small side with one noticeable stone church, also small as far as churches went. Adelaide exclaimed that she recognized St. Cyprian's from the drawings her brother had sent her and directed Aahron to pull their little caravan up close by. A man in long black robes came out of the church, curiosity and surprise on his face.

"Adelaide? Adelaide! I had no idea you were coming! We've not had a caravan nor a wagon arrive in several months. We've been isolated from the world here in our little valley. Come in! Come in all of you! Hello, hello! My name is Father Bernard Trōst. I'm the priest of St. Cyprian's."

290

Adelaide hugged her brother and then suddenly broke down, overcome by emotion, and started to weep. Bernard put his arms around his sister, helping to hold her up. "Dear sister, let us get you into the manse."

Later, after Adelaide was settled into a room and resting in a proper bed, Bernard joined Aahron and his party in the kitchen.

"Hello, I'm so sorry I didn't get to meet you properly. Again, my name is Bernard. Friends of my sister, you are most welcome here."

Aahron stood and shook hands. "I am Christoph. This is my wife, Elizabeth, our older daughter Eliza, and this is my older son, Christopher. Our little ones are Beatrice there sleeping on her mother's lap, and my little boy is Johannes. Our companions are Dominicus and Reynette." Aahron gave him a little bow. "We are grateful for your hospitality. It has been a long six weeks on the road."

Bernard looked at them, his brows furrowed. "These are your names?"

The four adults nodded, looking at one another in trepidation. The three older children stood as if frozen.

"These are the names you were born with?" Bernard asked again.

Aahron was the first to shake his head. "I was given the name Aahron at my birth."

"Ah! You are Jewish then?"

Aahron nodded and gave a quick, nervous glance towards his wife. "Yes. Is that a problem?"

"Not for me. Jesus was a Jew and so I've always had great respect for the religion of Mother Mary, Joseph, and their family. I mean, it always seemed to me that you can't be wrong if you were part of the holy family, now can you? I'm pleased to host you. My sister said she was traveling with a band of Jews, and so forgive me for being surprised to see you all with crosses around your necks and to hear such Christian names."

"If it please you sir," Yosef interrupted, "these are the names that the Lady Adelaide dubbed us on the trip. 'Good Christian names', she said, and it's how we've called one another for the past month or more, to please the Lady."

Rivkeh ran to her son, putting her one free arm around him and pulling him to her, shushing him while she balanced her sleeping daughter.

"My dear, um, what is your given name?"

"Rivkeh."

"Frau Rivkeh." Bernard inclined his head respectfully. "You have nothing to fear here. You are most welcome, and I thank you for bringing my sister to me. She was rather… well, rambling as I helped her to her rest."

Rivkeh said, "Good Father, she has struggled these past three weeks, insisting on fasting too many days. Our provisions were low and she said she would suffer so that the children could eat. She is a good woman at heart."

"She is. And she always dearly loved to fast. And suffer for others. Her heart is most generous. I was able to get her to take some drink and eat some dried fruit before she lay down. But she was not a clear bearer of the news. What of the outside world? And why are you here with no advance messenger?"

Aahron cleared his throat. "There is much to tell, and none of it good."

"Please, sit down, all of you. Make yourselves at home. I will make us some sage leaf tea and bring out some sustenance and then you can tell me everything."

As they sat, Aahron informed Bernard of the plague and great mortality that was coming from it. Of Bernard's mother, which caused the priest to weep. Of Gerung's demise, which caused him to weep again.

"I knew that devilry was upon the world when trade ceased and from news from my uncle, but I had no idea it was like this." Bernard crossed himself three times and then stroked the cat that leapt into his lap, scratching it three times on each cheek successively. "Any word from my uncle, the bishop?"

"He lives last we knew, but we could not see him. He is secluded in prayer and won't see or communicate with anyone," Aahron said.

Bernard nodded and murmured, "So he remains thus."

"Will we be safe here?" Adasse asked.

"Safe?" Bernard said, wiping another tear from his cheek. "Only God can keep us safe from plague, my child."

"It's not the plague which frightens me. It's the bleeding men!" she answered.

Bernard looked at Aahron in consternation.

"You truly have had no news of the wider world?" Rivkeh asked.

"Children, you go and lie down now. There were some couches in the other room. And chairs. Adasse, David, take the young ones." After the children left the kitchen, Aahron turned to Father Bernard. "Jews are being slaughtered. Burned alive. Thrown down wells. Stabbed to death in the streets. Although Clement the Sixth, may he be blessed and survive these cursed times, has ordered the killings to stop, the Holy Roman Emperor has declared that all property of Jews is fairly forfeit once they are killed. I would be surprised if there are any Jews left in Cologne. Most murdered in their beds or by their front doors. We are only alive because Gerung, your brother-in-law, gave us succor, took us in."

Bernard looked horrified. "And my sister disguised you as Christians on the road…"

Aahron nodded. "Although she does believe that we mean to convert."

"My friends," Bernard looked at them all in turn, "My family… you are welcome to stay here as long as you wish. The manse is quite small, as is the church. Let me ask, I take it from your manner that you don't actually wish to be baptized, as my sister instructed me to do?"

"She told us many times that you would baptize us. Take us to a river and dunk us in the cold water," Yosef said as he came around the corner and ran to his mother's lap. Rivkeh held him and shushed him.

Slowly and without conviction, Aahron shook his head. "Gerung wished us to head east, to the Polish lands, where Jews are welcome."

Bernard nodded thoughtfully.

"We think if we leave within the month, we can be through the mountains before the snows start," Aahron added.

Bernard nodded again, three times. "Then you will be given rest and as much in the way of provisions as I can spare. We will see about hiring a huntsman to give you more meat, which they dry here in a most interesting way. They make it into sausages that will remain edible for some time. It is a most curious way of life here. I don't recommend the sausages made of marmot." Here he made an unpleasant face and little Yosef laughed. "But the cheese here is unlike any I have tasted. We must provision you with many wheels and bricks of cheese."

"We thank you for your kindness," Aahron said.

Chapter 26
Wilhelm
September 1349

Wilhelm was struggling to keep up with his friar. That man could walk fast when he was determined. But then again, Friar Tuck could walk fast when he had nowhere to go. Wilhelm appreciated that his friar felt important enough to walk with purpose, no matter the occasion, or even if there were no occasion. It made Wilhelm feel important, a novel experience only known to him since the good friar had taken pity on him as a child and found him useful as an adult.

"Wilhelm, we need to get more of these people to come to our service. We have empty pews. And, well, their souls need to be saved. And if they aren't in our pews, if they aren't repenting and finding the Holy Spirit, their souls will be unsaved. This is our duty. We need these people to… uh, be saved."

"You never said a truer word, Friar Tuck. Never a truer word. Your new style of preachin' is powerful. The people are a feeling it. Word is gettin' round. We had two more people last week than the week before. And that's what you'd call a pattern, it is! It's like a small wind that's growing into a breeze, it is! It's like the foothills leading to the mountains: it starts small and then it swells up and surrounds you!"

"Yes, that be so. We did." Tuck then snarled and looked away. "There's that Father Bernard again. His pews are full. They are to standing room at his service, I hear."

Wilhelm looked in the opposite direction to where his friar was now facing. "Yes, and he's got a woman with him! A beautiful one. What's she doing here? She's new." Wilhelm elbowed Tuck. "Look at her. Have you ever seen the likes of a woman like her before?"

Tuck turned toward Bernard and his new companion and then back to his acolyte. "Wilhelm, that is what city women look like. They braid their hair with ribbons and have lace-trimmed fine dresses."

"Look at her smile! She's got nice teeth, just like Father Bernard does. How do you think they come by those nice teeth?" Wilhelm gave a little wave and Bernard and his companion started to approach them. "Ooo! Here they come. Well, this be an opportunity, ain't it? She looks like an angel, she does. I've never seen such sunny colored curls like that. Look at how she walks! It be like she's floating on the air."

"Mark me, Wilhelm, she'll be rich, spoiled, and materialistic. If she's got a soul, it will be hard to find. Women are like that." Tuck gave a low growl. "And now Bernard's got a wealthy patroness to boot, in addition to his uncle. Well, it can't be helped now. We must meet. Here they come." Friar Tuck stiffened, looking proud and scowling.

"Father Bernard! Good day to you!" Wilhelm said happily. "And to your lady companion!" He wasn't sure what to do upon crossing paths with a lady like this one, so he gave a low bow, waving his arms about in what he hoped was a gallant gesture. In reality he looked a bit more like a chicken that didn't want to be held and was flapping its wings.

"Ah! Wilhelm, my good fellow. How are you today? Bless you, my son—you are always so pleasant and friendly. Your feet look happy!"

Wilhelm did a happy little jig. "They are! The cobbler said an *angel* stopped by his shop and told him to give me these new boots. I never in my life owned nothin' so fine. But Friar Tuck said I was shriven and the rewards of heaven would shower down upon me. And so they have!"

Bernard gave a hearty laugh. "Then may you wear them well! And I see that you are in the company of the good friar." Bernard turned to the woman with him. "Adelaide, might I introduce you to two of our town's long-term residents: this is Wilhelm, he is the acolyte at the church of St. Drogo."

"Saint Drogo-Erasmus, if you please," Friar Tuckerschade said.

"Oh! Right. Thank you for the reminder. St. Drogo-Erasmus." Bernard gave a respectful nod to Friar Tuckerschade before he continued. "And Wilhelm frequently accompanies the good friar of that holy establishment, Herr Karel Tuckerschade." He gave a smile to his sister. "Friar Tuckerschade, Wilhelm, if I might have the honor of introducing you to my sister, Lady Adelaide Trōst Engelhaft. She is newly widowed and has traveled all the way from Cologne to join me here in the Valley Village of the Three Mountains. I am showing her about the town and introducing her to the folk of our little community." He turned back to his sister. "Most people just call the town the Valley Village."

Wilhelm repeated his exaggerated, chicken-like bow and Karel looked askance at him and then gave a slight but respectful incline of his head.

"My lady! You *are* an *Engel*—an *angel!* I knew it!" Wilhelm had never seen a woman as fine as this apparition in front of him and he didn't quite know what to do. How the breeze lilted her hair, as though the angels were brushing it at this very moment. And how the ribbons in the braids that framed her face shone in the sun. He was impressed that his friar could stay so calm and collected. But of course, he could: he was Friar Tuck! He could do anything.

"Master Wilhelm," she said as she inclined her head.

"Did you hear that! She called me *master!*" Wilhelm giggled and elbowed Friar Tuck in his excitement.

"Good honorable, Friar Tuckerschade," Adelaide said as she inclined her head.

"Please 'tis just Friar Tuck. I'm a humble man and don't need the fullness of my name to prove my worth. Everyone calls me Friar Tuck, as my fair and heroic ancestor of the old stories was called."

"You're a descendent of Friar Tuck? Of Robin of Locksley's band?" Bernard said, the shock ringing clearly in his voice.

"He was a hero, he was," Wilhelm said, proud of his friar. "Saved the little folk, he did! And our friar's just as good. Surely, he'll be sainted one day as well."

"Wilhelm, I, um, don't believe that the friar from the old stories was ever sainted…" Bernard said. Then he turned to Karel. "You are a descendent of Friar Tuck?"

"Aye."

"A friar… with children?" The shock resounded in Bernard's voice.

Wilhelm looked at Friar Tuck, confused at what Bernard was getting at.

The friar nodded. "Nay, but he had a sister and she had many a bairn in her day. I am a direct descendent of her offspring and he was many times my great uncle." Karel sounded calm and unruffled.

"Well, that makes sense, don't it! It be all in the family," Wilhelm said enthusiastically, happy it was all so easily explained.

Adelaide seemed to ignore her brother. "Honorable Friar Tuck, of, excuse me, what was your church's name again?"

"Saint Drogo-Erasmus, my Lady."

"I have heard much from my dear brother about St. Cyprian himself—a magician! A pagan sorcerer. A non-believer."

Wilhelm was surprised to hear this. No one had ever told him this story before. He looked with incredulity to Friar Tuck.

Karel put a reassuring hand on Wilhelm's arm. "Wilhelm, Cyprian is patron saint of the devil himself!"

In a whisper that was meant to be quiet, but which was powered by his own shock, Wilhelm said, "Then why did we ever preach from there? The house of the devil?" He quickly crossed himself.

"Not quite, good Wilhelm," Bernard jumped in. "Before he *converted*, Cyprian used his magical powers to control the minds of the people, who found him most captivating and fascinating."

"Yes, and he tried to turn his powers onto a woman of faith, the Saint Justina," Adelaide said, giving Wilhelm a look that melted his heart. "He saw her walk by and he cast his spell, but it held no power when compared to her devotion to Christ, which acted to shield her from his evil. He followed her, mystified as to why his power failed. She told him that his powers were no match to the power of the Lord!"

"Huzzah… the devil defeated by a woman." Wilhelm was impressed and pondered what fabulous tales could be told about the saints that protected his little church. "Wonders will never cease. But wait a minute… why did they name the church after ole Cyprian and not the woman? She sounds like the hero."

"Christ will always shield and protect a devoted, chaste woman, such as Justina," Adelaide answered rather stiffly. "Christ protected us on our journey here from Cologne, and that was long and arduous, I assure you."

Wilhelm was impressed. This lady from the big city of Cologne had made a long journey that was arguous. He wasn't sure what 'arguous' meant but he decided it could be that they had arguments with people along the way. "I am heartfelt sorry for you, my Lady, and all those people who disagreed with you." She gave him a mystified look but Wilhelm turned to the priest. "Father Bernard? I can't understand how that old Cyprian got a church named after him. And a nice one, too."

Bernard straightened himself up. "As I was saying, he used his charisma, much helped by his fair countenance, to control and manipulate the people, but Saint Justina foiled his attempt to control her by making the sign of the cross. Shocked by his defeat, he decided to investigate this Christianity, which a thousand years ago was a fairly new religion and not broadly accepted."

Adelaide interrupted him again. "And what that old magician learned captivated his heart, saying that the joy and wisdom he discovered was a thousand times better than any of the pleasures of a sinful life! Though the early followers of Christianity were despised and persecuted, they did not care the sufferings they endured, for they were beloved by the Lord and knew a greater reward awaited them."

"My lady," Friar Tuckerschade said, inclining his head, "you inspire me greatly. I can feel my next sermon starting to blossom forth in my heart just listening to your lovely description of this history of such a divine conversion."

She turned to the friar and slowly a brilliant smile grew on her face. Wilhelm wished she would smile at him like that. "Those who are willing to suffer for the glory of the Lord are always redeemed."

"Indeed they are," Friar Tuckerschade replied.

"Friar Tuck. Friar Tuck." Wilhelm tugged on the sleeve of his superior. "That's a great story. What's the great story of our church? We have two saints! Our story must be twice as good! Who did Drogo and Erasmus try to control the minds of?"

It was as though Friar Tuck hadn't heard him.

"Friar Tuck?"

"Oh, uh, what Wilhelm? What did you say?"

"What's the story of our church? What great things did Drogo and Erasmus do?"

Adelaide still had the brilliant smile on her face. "Yes, Good Friar. What are they the patron saints of?"

"Well," Karel started off slowly. "Saint Drogo is the patron saint of those who are humble. Those who are left behind by others. Those who cannot hear or speak. Those in need of the Lord's mercy. Those who are not deemed to be beautiful in the sight of others."

"The patron saint of the… unattractive?" Bernard asked.

Adelaide shot her brother an admonishing look and then smiled again at Friar Tuckerschade. "Amazing isn't it, that a man as fair of face as you would helm a church named for St. Drogo."

Wilhelm was annoyed that although he'd asked the question, everyone seemed to be directing their conversation anywhere but at him. Then he looked at his friar and wondered if he felt well. The man's jaw was tight and looked even more square than it usually did. And he had some color in his cheeks. Wilhelm hoped he wasn't coming down with fever. "And what about St. Erasmus. What was he all about?"

Karel looked only at Adelaide as he answered. "He also goes by Saint Elmo and sees over the souls of those who take to the sea. He is the patron saint of sailors."

Wilhelm scratched his head. "That seems funny, as there ain't no sea here. We've got a lake over yonder, but no sea."

"In the mountains, away from the ocean, Wilhelm, Saint Erasmus is held as the patron saint of abdominal pain." Bernard looked like he was doing his best to keep the line of his lips perfectly straight.

"Patron saints of the unattractive with abdominal pain. Well, then," Wilhelm said in a self-satisfied way, "they need the love of the Lord too, don't they? And I would say a lot more than magicians do!"

Karel ignored Wilhelm. "And what brings you to our humble village, my good Lady?"

She took a deep breath and exhaled. "The death of my husband. It is tragic, this pestilence that stalks the wider world, is it not? I'm so glad it has not yet visited this village, for it is ravaging Cologne."

"What's happening in the big city?" Wilhelm asked, feeling a sense of anxiety rising within him.

"It's plague, Master Wilhelm. It will brush a mother on Monday and by Wednesday it will shake her. On Thursday her children will be orphans and her sins will remain unshriven at Sunday mass. One of three in the city lies dead in mass graves. Perhaps even more. My husband fell from the blue sickness, as they call it now; the great mortality, as some are starting to refer to it. It was his last wish that I join my brother in the hopes that I will be safer here than in Cologne.”

“Plague!” Wilhelm looked at Friar Tuck for reassurance. “Surely, Friar Tuck, a man as right with God as you can prevent the plague from coming to our town!” He noticed that the Lady looked appraisingly at the friar, as if to peer into his special powers with the divine. “If only you knew him as I do, my Lady. He’s a holy man, he is!”

Bernard interrupted his thoughts. “I was hoping that my sister might consent to become a teacher here in our village. She is a woman of letters and books and could be an inspiration to the youth of this town, particularly the little girls, as they learn to read and write and do sums.”

Karel nodded towards the priest. “Your brother has many an idea for the betterment of our little village. He does not approve of the humble ways we’ve been following for generations. He’s built cesspits now. Even put a latrine on the impoverished side of town for the poor folk. Talks of building a free school for the public. He’s even built a bridge over the ford in the narrow river that runs swift and deep outside of town. Says a bridge with a gate will help keep the wild pigs from easily crossing at the narrows, help protect our crops. Your brother has a great many an idea for change.”

“He was ever thus. Just like my late husband. A man of many ideas for improving the lives of others who did not ask to be re-made.”

Karel gave her a slow half smile and a nod. Wilhelm felt confused by their exchange. He liked the cesspits, thought they were a great idea because it kept the shit off his new boots. And the bridge would keep his shoes dry. When he’d had to cross at the ford he’d always slip on a rock and end up with his feet itching for a couple of weeks. He wasn’t sure what a school would do though, or how that would help a man keep his shoes clean and dry.

“I am sorry for your loss. Your grief must be hard to bear,” Karel said to Adelaide.

"I bear it as best I can and carry forth the final wish of my late husband." After a beat she added, "May he rest in peace," but it sounded to Wilhelm like an afterthought.

"Now that my sister is here, at least until the pestilence passes, I thought she would benefit from meeting people. And teaching children to read would be a good way to fill her time. I think it would be a good way for her to deal with her grief."

With a tight-lipped smile, Adelaide replied, "I have a perfectly adequate way to deal with my grief, my brother."

"Father Bernard! Father Bernard!" A young girl came running up to them. "My ma sent me to find ye. The builders are having a struggle with the gate at the bridge. They need your help."

"My help?"

"Yes!" She nodded. "Said it was you who drew up the plans for the construction. But theys done got the paper wet and theys can't reads it now and theys need you to tell them what the picture said. So's theys can build it."

Adelaide turned to her brother. "And that is why you didn't write me back? You used the paper I sent you to draw up construction diagrams for a bridge and a gate? And cesspits? And other 'public improvements'?"

Wilhelm thought Bernard looked like he'd practiced hard at that patient smile.

"I didn't write you back because all trade has been halted with the hard-hit cities, which are all under quarantine, by order of the Holy See. There was no one to carry my message to you. So what else could I do with the paper?" He turned back to the little girl. "I can't abandon my sister."

Wilhelm thought the Priest looked quite perplexed and wondered what he himself might be able to do to help.

"Adelaide, I know you do not enjoy the dirt and mess involved in construction, but might you accompany me?"

"A building site is certainly no place for a woman."

The little girl objected. "No! No! Me ma's a woman and she's one of the bricklayers."

Wilhelm noticed how proud the little girl looked and it brought a smile to his face. But then he looked at the fine lady, who appeared to be trying to say something but was spluttering a bit. He hated to see her in such distress and wondered what he might do to help someone with as nice a smile as hers and halos of blonde curls like that.

Bernard turned toward the little girl. "All right. I will come, but I cannot leave my sister. She is new here and does not yet know her way. I'll need to escort her back to the church before I can join the builders."

"We can take her!" Wilhelm said with enthusiasm. "We knows the way and we can show her all around the town, right Friar Tuck?"

Wilhelm looked at his friar and thought it was funny how both he and Father Bernard shared a tight-looking smile. *Maybe they learn that in schooling to become men of the cloth. I'll have to practice mine, since I've got me aspirations.* And then he thought, *She called me Master Wilhelm. Master…*

Father Bernard jumped in all too quickly, "Oh, I wouldn't want to burden you with my sister."

"Not at all!" Wilhelm insisted. "It would be interesting to get to walk about with a woman of books and letters. I can't read meself, but it would be lovely to have that talent."

"Not books. Just *the* book. I am a woman of *the good book*, Wilhelm. Of the Holy Writ."

Wilhelm looked confused again.

"A virtuous woman of the Bible."

"Oh! Well, that's nice, that is! Friar Tuck, he's a man of the Bible."

The little girl tugged on Father Bernard's robes. "Me ma needs you. I don't want to get into no trouble. She said, 'no dawdling', and I don't mean to dawdle. I needs bring you straight by."

Adelaide turned to her brother. "Oh, go on, Bernard. How could anyone be safer than in the hands of the good friar? A man of the Bible and, according to Wilhelm, destined to be sainted one day."

Under his breath, Bernard muttered, but Wilhelm alone heard it. "It's not his hands I'm worried about…"

"What?" Adelaide asked.

"Oh, nothing." Bernard looked to Friar Tuckerschade. "If you would be so willing, I would be in your debt."

The friar nodded solemnly but didn't say anything. Wilhelm jumped in. "We'll be happy to! We have a little church. Miss Adelaide, I was the doorman I was, but I been raised to the acolyte!"

The lady gave him a small smile and nodded her head as Bernard looked worried but allowed himself to be led off by the little girl.

Wilhelm and Karel escorted Lady Adelaide around the town, with Wilhelm pointing out where shops were and Karel introducing her to people they passed. Karel introduced her as the widow, Lady Adelaide Trōst Engelhaft, but Wilhelm noticed that only rarely did the friar mention Father Bernard or St. Cyprian's at all. Wilhelm observed that people seemed far more interested in speaking to Friar Tuck now that he had an angel on his arm. *Well, angels are interesting, aren't they? It's not every day that you get to meet one,* he told himself. He got momentarily excited when their little trio came upon the cesspit project, but quickly dampened his tone, remembering the sting of his repentance and not wanting any repeat of that reckoning with God, no matter how lovely the rewards of heaven had been afterwards.

Wilhelm noticed that Friar Tuck seemed to be engaging in conversation easily with the lady, and the two were having an animated discussion of certain passages of the Bible. Karel listened much more than he usually did, and the lady seemed excited to recite what she obviously knew quite well. Wilhelm thought she seemed rather pleased to have such an engaged audience. He wondered what it must be like to have an attentive ear listening to you with the intensity that his friar was giving to the lady?

For his part, Wilhelm talked to the chickens and ducks and goats all the time, and they were patient, not as much as the cow of course, but they listened. But not like Friar Tuck though. It was like he was hanging his next breath on her every word, memorizing her statements, as though she was giving a biblical lesson.

As they came upon the poorer end of town, Wilhelm noticed that the lady looked distinctly more nervous.

"My Lady," Karel said as he made a sweeping gesture to the meaner streets. "This is where the true calling of the Lord lies. 'Tis not in the fancy cathedrals of Cologne or Bonn. 'Tis not at the feet of the Holy See. Nay—'tis in the mean streets where the *humble* servant of the Lord is called. 'Tis with the people who need ministering to the most. I believe that humility before God is what we should truly aspire to and so it is here that I hang my cap. 'Tis here that I do the Lord's work. Not for the glory of gold or huge stone buildings but for the glory of God and the restoration of the souls of these poor people. My mission is to help them feel the presence of the Holy Spirit. 'Tis to bring them round and make them right with the Lord."

"Oh, that is wonderful! That is my mission as well!"

He turned to her. "Your mission?"

She blushed. Wilhelm couldn't believe that she could have looked lovelier, but seeing her face with a blush on her cheeks made his heart skip a beat.

"Yes, well, um, my late husband was a man of many ideas. Many radical ideas. I did not share them. I worry that he was taken by the blue pestilence as a retribution and lesson by God that he should have been more devout, and less... far ranging... in his opinions."

Friar Tuckerschade nodded solemnly. "And how does that translate into your mission?"

"Well... well, I suffer to please God, so that it might lessen poor Gerung's time in purgatory, for I am sure that he has not been welcomed through the gates of heaven. I fast three days a week. I am... disciplined... in my practice."

Wilhelm felt like she was speaking in code and looked at his friar, who was studying this apparition before him. Friar Tuckerschade stroked his square chin with his hand. "Not many understand how suffering pleases God and redeems us of our sins."

Her coy look at him was accompanied by a small smile. "He did not approve of it during his life. He was strongly critical of me."

"It sounds as though, forgive me for saying this, that you were not well matched?" Karel asked.

"Indeed!" Lady Adelaide sounded excited, as if she was not used to finding empathetic understanding. "I was committed to the match without my consent, and I found him to be a partner who did not share my devotion or humility."

"Humility is a virtue," Karel said, his eyes looking at her closely. "Are you a woman who embraces humility?"

Adelaide smiled at Friar Tuckerschade and blushed, her perfect teeth bright and lighting up her face. And then she modestly looked down.

"Of course, you are." The friar smiled back at her. "Engel—an angel indeed."

Wilhelm's eyebrows furrowed. He examined the look on the lady's face first and then on his friar's, and then the lady's again. They didn't seem to know he was there. They certainly hadn't acknowledged his presence for quite a while. He wanted the lady to smile at him like that, but he felt invisible. Not invisible like the breeze, because you felt that. Nor like the sun, because its warmth would reflect on your cheeks after a while. He just felt... invisible. Like the mosquito before it bites you.

"Would you show me your church?" Adelaide asked.

"Are you sure? A lady like you, used to the might and earthly glory of the big cathedrals, might be shocked at how the Lord calls to his humble servants. 'Tis a meager space."

"Was Christ not a humble man? Homeless at his birth?" Adelaide said, her chin raised.

"Indeed." Karel offered Adelaide his arm and continued his tour, talking on about the pride of men being their downfall, even those in the clergy, and the beauty and power of the simple and humble, comparing it to flowers of the field. "If you care to come to our service, I'm sure you will see the power of the Holy Spirit work its way through our people in ways that the Almighty does not reveal to those who are arrogant and worship only the gilded halls and glinting crosses."

"Christ didn't pray on a golden cross!" Wilhelm said excitedly.

Adelaide only had eyes for Friar Tuckerschade. "Christ was crucified on a wooden cross. He was a simple and humble man of the Lord."

"Wood is good enough for his true followers, for those who would be close to the Lord," Friar Tuckerschade answered her. "You know, you have to be careful about those with ideas that will pull you away from the Almighty, those who will force you from the path of righteousness. I call them the *warped*, for they are worthless, arrogant, rich, pompous, elitists who are damned. They are like wood left in the rain. It bends and twists. It becomes unusable, unworthy of God."

"They are *warped*! Oh, Friar Tuck! You must be the cleverest man of my acquaintance! That is brilliant. I must write it down when I get back to my room and study it. *Warped*. Oh, so clever! It is as though you know what I suffered in Cologne."

Karel Tuckerschade smiled in a way that Wilhelm had never seen before. *And was Friar Tuck… blushing?* Wilhelm wondered. *I tell him all the time that he's clever. I tell him all the time that he's going to be sainted someday and somehow I think that's much better than being clever. But he never blushes when I say it.* He peered harder at this strange twosome.

Adelaide went on, looking like she was blushing in reflection of the friar's response to her compliment. "I surely want to hear mass at your church. I would imagine that with a mind like yours, and a heart that is so pure, that your homily must be divinely inspired. And not at all boring."

"'Tis the humble role of a clergy to be the gateway to the Holy Spirit, to forgiveness, to redemption of the masses. 'Tis a burden and it can wear on me, but 'tis one I must bear."

"You are not just a friar: you are a spiritual warrior. A hero."

Wilhelm watched as the lady seemed to clutch more tightly to Friar Tuck's arm. He followed them about the tour of the town, which seemed to take far longer than need be. The friar introduced her to people of the village, showing her off as though she was his personal angel, all but forgetting that Wilhelm was there and was the one who invited the lady to join them in the first place. For her part, the lady swooned over Friar Tuck's humble little church, exclaiming that she could feel the Lord's presence in it far more than the church her own brother preached in, comparing it to the glistening temples of the heathens. Friar Tuck seemed to like that even more than hearing he would be sainted someday.

Wilhelm eventually left them to go and find the cesspit on the other side of town and he didn't care if Friar Tuck saw him or not. Part of him wanted his superior to see him being disobedient. But Karel didn't notice. Didn't notice when he left them. Didn't notice that he was gone. Wilhelm needed the services of the cesspit, but more so, he wanted to sit and think and work out why he was feeling these strange emotions that were making a tumult of his usually optimistic mind. It was with dark and angry thoughts that he kicked the dirt on his way across the village.

Chapter 27

Everly

Trevor was once again staring off at the mountains.

"They're beautiful, aren't they?" Everly said. "Only missing the songs of disobedient nuns echoing through the hills."

"What? Huh?" Trevor tore his gaze away and turned to look at her. "Did you say something about… disobedient nuns?"

She waved him off, deciding that she shouldn't even try to be funny. "It's just that they struck me too when I first arrived. So beautiful."

"Oh, it wasn't the beauty I was thinking of." He turned back to the pass between the two tallest mountains. "Hans said there was a bog up there, a *Hochmoor*. We call them fens in England. I've always been fascinated with them and I would really like to see this one."

"You weren't thinking about hiking up there by yourself, were you? Not after those riders in the sky nearly trampled us all? From what I remember, we got back to our tents soaked, freezing cold, and terrified. And you want to go back?" She stared at him. "Oh, look at that face. You want to go back."

"I've just got this gut feeling…"

"Oh no, oh no. Here we go again." She turned and started to walk away.

"I'm sorry! I can't help it! Where are you going?" Trevor called after her.

She spun around, walking backwards as she called out to him. "To arrange for a trip to the mountain pass. I know you, Trevor. You won't be able to let this go."

She really liked how his face transformed from looking like a little boy who was in trouble to a smile growing and then breaking across it with excitement sparkling in his eyes. That alone might have been worth the trip that lay before them.

Nylah turned out to be equally excited, in that the dig hired Hans as a hike guide, a local botanist familiar with the terrain to take them up the hills and tour them around the fen. She would take photos, Everly was sure plenty of them would be selfies of her and Hans in the picturesque mountains. They would go as soon as the weather held absolutely no hint of possible thunderstorms.

◆ ⸺ ◆ ⸺ ◆

When the weather presented itself, Everly wore her good hiking boots and some of the new photoshoot clothes that Nylah had ordered for her that were made just for this type of activity. She threw a tiny packet labeled *rain poncho* into her small backpack just in case, and then went to the food tent to load up on snack bars and fill her canteen with water. Everything was already laid out and labeled. Everly picked up her designated pile of supplies. Although she was alone, she said aloud, "Nylah, you'd better run the world someday. It would be a much more organized place."

"Thanks!"

Everly jumped, having not heard Nylah enter the tent after her.

"You always know what people really think of you when you catch them talking to themselves!" Nylah gave her a big smile.

"I guess that's true. And I meant it. You ready?"

"Sure. As long as two conditions are met: first, there are no ghost riders in the sky," Nylah said and her face darkened.

Everly remembered their rained-out picnic that had kind of freaked out the team's youngest member. "Weatherman guaranteed sunshine today."

"And second, Dr. T doesn't start singing."

"All bets are off on that one." Everly chuckled and thought that his singing was really growing on her. She looked at her watch. "I guess it's time." They heard a car pull up and give a two-beep greeting.

"There he is. It *is* time!" Nylah started to head towards the tent flap and then she turned to look at Everly. "I can't believe that for one day I'm the actual boss of my boyfriend. This is the best summer ever!" She dashed out of the tent, leaving Everly laughing.

"Oh, the joys of being so young and innocent."

They started off as a foursome and left the dig site under the direction of Gunther for the day. "You're sure he doesn't mind?" Everly asked Trevor once they were well on their way.

"Ole Gunther? All the students to himself? Telling all the volunteers what to do? Fielding any press questions all by his lonesome. That is my friend's definition of heaven, let me tell you. The thing Dr. Gunther Heintzelman loves the most is a little bit of the limelight. You see, he started out as a drama student, thought he was going to make it in the theater, but when that didn't pan out, he had to turn to his fallback career."

"Archeology is his fallback career?"

"Yes. It comes with benefits. Very important, benefits. Particularly when you have parents breathing down your neck."

"Sounds like you fellows might have done some boy-bonding?" Everly said. "Well, archeology looks like it's working out for him. So, tell me, does Gunther have any talent? I mean, beyond digging in the dirt?"

"Oh my, you should hear him at karaoke. He wins our battle every time. Too bad the bloke didn't make it as an actor. He's got a great voice."

"And he looks like a movie star too."

They were interrupted by Hans calling out that they were reaching one of the more interesting sights of their journey up to the mountain saddle: a tall rock formation standing sentinel in the middle of a meadow.

"From here you could see the little village, probably like a miniature town on the valley floor. It would be a good vantage point, *nein?* You could see what people were doing, and because of the large rock, you would be very hard to be seen in return." He put his hand on the stone. "And this rock is full of spaces... what would you call them?"

"Nooks and crannies. Those totally fit the definition of nooks and crannies," Trevor said.

"Right then." Hans nodded. "A good hiding spot, *nein?* I always wonder what the people who lived here would have thought of this rock, what they might have hidden in it. Some spaces are big enough for a person to hide in."

"Wow. And it's just out here all by itself," Everly said, thinking it looked like a stone age version of an obelisk.

"This is our first way-point. There are no trails or posted signs. We are navigating by my compass and by natural markers, which I will show you along the way. I hope you have lots of energy remaining. This is just our first half hour of our journey. We have two more hours to hike still," Hans turned and started walking through the low grasses that lined the valley floor, the mountain saddle rising above him.

It was so beautiful that Everly thought the entire summer might have been worth it had she only experienced this. No tourists. No trails even. No one came up these hills but for some wild goats, and they had probably lived on this mountain for generations, maybe since the time of their village even. Hans pointed out various flowers and birds that they saw, and some geological features. They refilled their water bottles at a mountain stream, and it was the freshest water Everly had ever tasted, the perfect accompaniment to the font of information that Hans offered about all the plants and animals they saw along the way.

They hiked on and on and finally came to a little rise.

"I want you all to be careful now and to follow in my footsteps. No fanning out now. We go one-by-one. We are starting to approach the *Hochmoor*, and the botany is delicate. I don't want anyone harming the endangered plants here."

They all lined up with Nylah following Hans, Everly following Nylah and Trevor bringing up the rear. Nylah took pictures of everything that Hans pointed out to her, as he was also excited to document the flowers and fauna they were seeing.

Everly was surprised that the ground wasn't boggy at all. It also wasn't teeming with life like she pictured bogs and marshes would be. It was rather dry actually, and just dotted with purple flowers here and there. She did notice that those plants that had flowers usually also had some vicious looking thorns on them as well.

"Ah! There it is!" Hans called out.

Suddenly there was a little rise before them. He led them over it, carefully picking a path so as to incur as little damage as possible, and they came to a shallow bowl in the saddle of the mountain. "Here is the heart of the fen. And this feature you might find interesting: look at this remnant of a low stone wall. Isn't that curious?"

"Why would there be a stone wall here?" Nylah asked.

Hans shrugged. "That answer is lost to time. Unless, that is, your friends can figure it out. But it is not unheard of to have a way-station along a travel path. Putting one here would help travelers crossing the mountains and probably give them a place to rest and be out of the weather just where they needed it the most."

Nylah looked around her at the relative desolation. "Yeah, but it's really out of the way to build a honeymoon cabin. Hard to Airbnb something way out here. Huh."

Trevor and Everly were already packs off and crawling around the wall, investigating.

"I can't believe this. Look at how solid the stones are," Everly said. "Who would need a three-foot-thick wall atop a mountain?"

"Right. This would be a substantial building. What time period do you make of this, Ev?"

Everly's heart skipped a beat. She wasn't sure if it was the discovery of the remnant of the wall or him calling her 'Ev'. Nylah had naturally slipped into calling her that. Everly had never shared with them that 'Ev' was what her mother had called her. It felt special. It felt close. Like a secret name used only by people who loved her.

"Ev? Hullo, Ev? Are you all right?" Trevor asked her.

"Oh, uh, yeah, sorry. I got lost in a memory there for a moment."

He nodded. "You must've seen some powerfully interesting stone walls then." He gave her a wink. "Can you date it?"

She looked closer at the joining between the rocks and blew out a breath. "It's not typical for Middle Ages construction. You know, this is just weird."

"What are you thinking? I'm wondering if it's what I'm thinking."

"It just looks…"

"Yes?" Trevor looked at her expectantly.

She didn't want to say it. She felt like it would risk all her credibility in his eyes, but it was her best guess. "Ugh. It looks Egyptian."

"That's just what I thought! You're brave to have said it first. Don't know that I would have."

"What looks Egyptian?" Nylah walked over to join them, looking down at the wall.

Everly sat on the remnant of the structure and pointed to two stones, sitting abutted up to one another. "See here? In the Middle

Ages, they used mortar, a kind of cement, to hold buildings together. I mean, sure they used cement too, but not on anything this big."

Nylah looked around at the mountains rising above them. "Mortar here? Like where would they find a Home Depot?"

"Precisely!" Trevor answered. "In the medieval period in Germania, they mixed lime and sand. To get the lime, they burned chalk or limestone. There was a whole guild which took that on. Sand they got from everywhere—river beds, quarries, the sea shore."

"The sea shore. Right. Uh huh." Nylah was still looking at the expanse of sky and the vista that offered no sea shores, quarries, or rivers.

Everly bent down to look closely at the joining. "But there's no mortar here. Now in England at the time, they did dry stack stone walls but those were smaller stones and more roughly put together. This is large, I would even say huge, pieces of stone just put together." Hans and Nylah both came close. "This would have been a real art form at the time: these stones are perfectly cut to nestle next to one another with virtually no gap. Probably why they are still here. You see, normally stone walls allow little seeds to take up residence in their cracks and you see mosses and grasses, sometimes even trees growing out of them, and those little invaders bring down the walls over time."

Nylah inspected it closely. "You know, this looks like modern buildings in New York."

"Uh huh. I know. And that's really, really creepy. Hans, are you sure there hasn't been recent construction, like in the fifties or the sixties, even the nineteen forties? Maybe during the war? Could this have been a strategic point at any time in recent history?"

Hans shrugged. "Bavaria was not much involved in either the first or second World War. The action, it was up north, just like all the other history in Germany. Not much happens down here."

"Well, this is a real conundrum, innit?" Trevor scratched his head. "A hundred years and a bit ago, in World War One, someone could have built a stone bunker up here. That's the most likely explanation."

"I thought they used cement back in the twentieth century. I mean this still isn't where you'd put up a building with a façade like those on Fifth Avenue." Nylah said as she looked around. "Where's the rest of the wall?"

"Good question. Yeah. Lots of good questions," Everly said as she felt her brows furrow. None of this made sense. "From what we know of history, and to be honest there is a lot we don't know, the technology to make walls like this, of this massive size, is either very new or very old. You saw this type of construction in ancient cultures, like Egyptian and Aztec, and you see it starting in the twentieth century, but Middle Ages… not so much. This wall isn't of the same time period as our little town. My guess—it's era World War one or two. So, yes, cool, absolutely, but not relevant to our little town. They never would have set eyes on this bit of stone." She patted the wall a couple of times with confidence.

"Except," Hans said, "I did some research to prepare for our excursion before we came up. This wall was made note of in the sixteen hundreds by a minor nobleman on his hunt for a wild boar. I can show you when we return to base. But there are no records of a castle being here or any other such large structure."

Everyone looked at one another.

"Well, that leaves us with Egypt. What would their builders have been doing up here? In the middle of nowhere?" Trevor asked.

Everly took command of the conversation. "Let's not jump to conclusions. The only evidence we have is of a pretty sophisticated building technique that was in play in multiple cultures around the world… just not here. Let's see if we can figure out the size of the building. Nylah, you and I will follow the line of the wall this way. Trevor and Hans, you follow it that way. We're looking for footing stones or other indications of any abutting walls."

The two teams turned in their different directions and started searching for any clues they could find. Trevor called out to the women:

"If you find any evidence of Noah's Ark, give us a big shout. And Nylah, take pictures!"

Everly chuffed.

"What does he mean by Noah's Ark?" Nylah asked.

"He means that this wall is a unicorn finding. When digs that were highly suspect couldn't explain extremely unusual findings, like when they would find the remnants of a ship up in a high mountain, they wouldn't go for the obvious that a lake had been there at one time. No, they would just jump to 'it must be Noah's Ark'. And instantly gain a ton of press and lose all their credible funding."

They followed the wall for twenty more yards. "Where'd it go?" Nylah asked. "It's like it fizzled."

"Yeah, like it peters out. I don't know, look around on both sides for it turning or for evidence of the rest of the wall. There should be dozens, if not hundreds of more stones here that once were a part of this wall. They should be scattered everywhere. And there should be evidence of earthen ramps to move these huge stones."

"What if this is the top of the wall?"

"Huh?" Everly shook herself in surprise. "Say that again."

"It just struck me that maybe we can't see the rest of the wall, like fallen over, because this is the top of the wall. All the other stones are, well, underneath these."

"No way. That's… impossible. That would make this wall eons old. I mean, really, really old." Every looked around them, knowing they were running out of time. "Older than Egypt. Or Aztec. Hey, there are some stones over there. Let's check that out."

They walked another thirty or so yards towards a pile of rocks stacked atop one another. As they approached, Everly could feel her heart beat faster. "Oh my goodness. Oh my god. I can't believe it."

"What? That these are normal-sized stones?" Nylah was looking about them as if trying to find what was getting Everly so excited.

"Nylah, radio Trevor. This is a cairn."

"A what?"

"This is pile of stones that marks an important site. In this case, it's a burial cairn."

The radio crackled to life and soon Trevor and Hans joined them.

"My, oh, my, what have we here?" Trevor asked.

"Had this been in the meadows outside of the village, it would have been covered by vines." Everly stood with her hands on her hips as they surveyed the cairn.

"Or blackberry bushes."

"Or blackberry bushes." She conceded the point. "But up here where change comes so slowly, we can still see the stones that mark this grave. I wonder how old this is? Nylah, would you please run back and get my backpack? I need something out of it."

"Sure." Nylah and Hans jogged over to where everyone had set down their packs.

"We have to make a decision."

"Right. What decision?" Trevor asked.

"Do we explore this or do we call the police?"

"Police?"

"Yes. This could be a recent burial. Anything in the last fifty years would represent a cold case. A hiker who died and was buried by friends. Or enemies. A murder. Hidden up here for God knows how long?"

"Right, yes. These rocks are very settled. Look at how they are nearly connected to one another. I think we explore. I think it's old. Very old."

"Can we? Does our permitting cover explorations this far from the dig site?" Everly didn't want to get into trouble with the local authorities.

Trevor sat back on his heels. "Let me think. I believe we're in the clear. The permit says the village and surrounding areas so that we could include the suspected pits." He looked around him. "I think this includes the surrounding area, so we're good to go."

"What would your dad say?"

"Oh blimey! Him? He'd have had these rocks off of here already, are you kidding me? Rules were fine when they were his rules. Other people's rules… not so important."

Nylah and Hans returned with her bag. "Thanks!" Everly unzipped her backpack and pulled out and unreeled wires with orange flags on them.

"You brought flags?" Nylah said, surprise in her voice.

"I'm an archeologist! Of course I brought flags."

"Oh my God, I love you, Everly!" Trevor said as she started to stake out the burial site and he started removing the stones.

Everly startled for just a moment. She hadn't heard those words in decades. Her mother used to say that, before the accident. Then her father would say it, but only when he needed his daughter to do something for him. It was strange to hear it from Trevor now, so casually, so comfortably. He said it and it felt like her most favorite, comfortable old sweater. She took a deep breath so as to not betray any emotion. "Take pictures, Nylah, every step."

"Right, boss!"

They worked in earnest for a while and then Everly stopped and froze. "Trevor…"

"Anything good?"

"Oh yeah. Bones. Hardly any. Really old ones."

"Find in poor condition. That's wonderful!"

"Why is that wonderful?" Nylah asked.

"Because that means we don't have to call the police!"

Nylah stared at him and then at Hans, who just shrugged at her. But then Hans shook his head and said, "I'm afraid I have to rain on your party, but we have to start back down in the next fifteen minutes in order to be safe with the light. Don't forget, we still have more than a two hour walk ahead of us."

It was with great reluctance that Everly left the find. They still didn't know anything other than the remains were old and in poor shape. Who was this person? What was their story? What heinous sin could they have committed that would have consigned them to a lonely, shallow mountain grave? She was committed to return and find out more, but for now, they had to leave.

As they hoisted their packs she turned to take one last look at the grave. It was surrounded by orange flags, but they had replaced all the stones to protect the find from any weather or wandering animals. "We'll come back. You won't be alone for much longer."

Chapter 28

Adelaide Trōst Engelhaft
November 1349

After all she had heard about St. Drogo-Erasmus, Adelaide was eager to attend the church service led by Karel Tuckerschade. She had to admit that initially she was taken aback by the small and dingy visage of the structure itself, but her views had been transformed by his passionate discussion of what it meant to be humble before the Lord. She found Karel himself to be so engaging that no matter if he were preaching in a field under a tree, it would be to her as though he spoke in a grand cathedral. He was mesmerizing in his passion. She felt she could stare into that face, look into those eyes all day as he spoke of redemption and faith and salvation. She walked down the street, intent on finding her way back to his humble little church, but unwilling to ask anyone for directions.

For her first months in the Valley Village, she had, of course, attended her brother's masses, but poor Bernard was so dull as to put one to sleep. Indeed, she saw a few of the parishioners succumbing to the drowsy pull she also fought to stave off. His singing voice was fine enough for the chants, but his divine transfiguration failed to move her. The services were neither transformative nor transfigurative. It wasn't the body and blood of Christ—it was just dry crackers and wine. His service was perfunctory and no matter how she tried, she just couldn't feel the Holy Spirit. She didn't know what was wrong. Perhaps it wasn't Bernard? Perhaps it was all she had been through? The unsuitable marriage. The plague. The loss of her mother and then her mother-in-law. Gerung following his own mother into death, and while Gerung's absence had been somewhat welcome, it did lead to her rather narrow escape of being wed to her father-in-law. Or it could be that the arduous journey deadened something inside of her. Or this tiny town up in the mountains. *Or living with Bernard and his maddening need to do everything thrice over*, she thought. She longed for more. She longed for meaning. She longed to feel something. But with no city, no cathedrals, no markets, no ribbons, no masses calling her name— no one calling her name, actually—in all the quiet here she felt nothing at all.

God bless, Christoph, she thought as she crossed herself and remembered that man who had brought her here with his family, helping her escape that blasphemous marriage bed. She credited herself for their conversion, all eight of them, and felt an inner satisfaction that her intervention would be noted in heaven. Adelaide thought of Elizabeth, the woman who previously held that unpronounceable Jewish name, as she looked down at the ring on her finger. It was strange but lovely. A gold ring with a red and green enameled dome on it, supported by a multitude of intricate arched columns and etched with a strange writing that she couldn't make heads or tails of. Adelaide had never seen anything like it. She had been riding in the carriage with Elizabeth when their little caravan was stopped by a roving band of self-proclaimed guards of the roads. Elizabeth seemed terrified and with a shaking hand, asked Adelaide to hold onto the ring for safe- keeping, explaining it had been the wedding band of her mother-in- law and had served as hers as well. Elizabeth had made the astonishing claim that these guards were not sanctioned but rather were "volunteers", searching for goods to steal, for mischief, for murder. And she had trembled with fear.

Adelaide watched Christoph's tense negotiations with them until, impatient, she stepped out of the carriage and gave the band a good talking to, a lecture in Christianity, and a promise that her father, her father-in-law, her third cousin, and her uncle would hunt endlessly for anyone who slowed her progress to save the Valley Village in the southern mountains. They would be excommunicated—condemned to an eternity in hell. Christoph had jumped onto her line of persuasion and then explained the Lady Adelaide's connections in great length: daughter of their duke. Wife and daughter-in-law of the most powerful merchants in Eastern Germania. Third cousin and favorite of the king. Niece of the Bishop of Cologne. As Christoph extolled Adelaide's power and authority, she saw the bandits lose their resolve. And then she began to wonder why she was given so little respect wherever she went? Why did people, particularly men, never seem to listen to her? Never find her words inspiring? So often treat her as though she were invisible. But that Friar Tuckerschade had listened. *Karel Tuckershade. Karel.* She turned the sound of it over in her mind, thinking it a respectable name. Most men dismissed her—her father, her brother, her husband. But Karel said she was inspiring. That he was going to compose a sermon based on her ideas. What could be a higher compliment than that?

After he had given her that extended tour of the village, they had crossed paths a couple of times, leaving her to think that she would see him often. But she hadn't seen him in over a month now and found that she was looking for him around every corner. His face filled her dreams. She imagined how his deep, resonant voice would paint such powerful imagery that it would save the souls of those in attendance of his sermons. Sermons that she inspired. She sighed as she walked the streets and toyed with the two wedding bands on her hand: the one that Gerung had given her and Elizabeth's. Now that she thought about it, she hadn't seen the newly converted family in some months.

She expected Elizabeth to return to retrieve her ring and she planned to admonish the woman for owning gold. Everyone knew commoners were not allowed to wear gold. Maybe that was why she hadn't come back? In her conversion, she recognized her station in life and accepted the limitations that came with it. Adelaide resolved to ask her brother their whereabouts.

She looked down the street and realized she was here. There was the little church in front of her. Unassuming in its footprint or visage, but she was sure that what it held was inspiring. She entered St. Drogo-Erasmus quietly and took her seat beside another woman. Looking around, she observed that there were rather a lot of women making up the faithful today. Wilhelm was there, of course. Clearly, the people who came to this church were in need of spiritual renewal, and, she thought, financial renewal as well. She couldn't suppress a shudder when it crossed her mind that these people might ask her for alms; they so reminded her of the bedraggled in Cologne who would pull on her fine clothes, try to touch her braids and grasp at her ribbons.

She was glad that today she was discreet in her attire, making a break from her life of finery—a break inspired by her thoughts and fantasies of Friar Tuckerschade. "I am embracing my humility," she told herself as she dressed earlier that morning. She had fasted, of course. She practiced her discipline as her back could tolerate. But until today she had not yet given up her ribbons. "A nun wouldn't have ribbons. He said as much." She'd lain her beautiful blue ribbon down in a drawer. "A nun would be humble and choose to be decorated by the Holy Spirit coursing through her." She thought that sounded lovely but had no idea of what it actually meant. She starved and suffered and still no joy flooded through her. Perhaps today she would be given the grace to finally understand.

She noticed the vase of dried flowers on a small table by the altar. Simple. Humble. *An altar should be humble as the flowers of the fields*, he had said. And there they were. He lived what he spoke. Even though it was November, there were flowers.

She sat quietly in the pew and tried to avoid making eye contact with the woman sitting next to her, as she was giving Adelaide a knowing kind of smile, but then the service started. It began similarly enough, with the Friar following much of the same routine as her own brother over in St. Cyprian's. Then Friar Tuck stood behind his little lectern on a small box to raise himself up. She understood that this was St. Drogo-Erasmus' version of the pulpit from which clergy were known to bestow a sermon or words of wisdom upon their flock. She could feel her pulse quicken in anticipation of his words. His resonant voice spoke of their suffering, and the small party in the pews made grunts of agreement and acknowledgment. He told them of their longing for a better life, for the hereafter, where all their sins they had confessed to him would be forgiven.

"They are wrong to tell you that you were made for self-reflection! You were made to reflect the Lord himself! You will find the Lord through fasting and prayer and listening and trusting in me. I am your guide, not those *warped* of the town who would use and abuse you. Some say, 'How can you fast three days a week when you have to work in the fields?' Well, I say you can fast and 'tis God who will support you. 'Tis Christ himself who will give you strength!"

Adelaide felt her heart skip a beat. In the weakness of her fasting, she felt dizzy and lightheaded, but she attributed the sensations to the power of his words. *Perhaps it is God who is with me now, humbling me before him and filling me with the Holy Spirit?* She listened to Friar Tuck's words and felt both opened and understood in a way she had never experienced before. For the first time, here was a man of the cloth, someone safe and protective, who spoke of God in the way that she saw the Lord.

As he preached, his energy rose and the churchgoers became more engrossed in his sermon, as did Adelaide. Before long, he was nearly shouting from his tiny pulpit.

"I promise you, your suffering will be rewarded. It will be rewarded when you give in to the Lord! I can see the rewards of heaven hanging just above your heads. Who will join and open themselves, accepting the bounty of heaven? Do you feel it? Let me hear you! Do you feel it! The Holy Spirit is waiting to enter you! To fill you with joy. I see it. I feel it! Do you feel it? Will you let it enter?"

"I feel it!" Wilhelm jumped up to his feet. "I feel it!"

"Look at him! Look at Brother Wilhelm! Saved by the Lord. Christ smiles on him! Who will join him in opening himself to the Holy Spirit?"

A woman said from her seat, "I feel it! I feel it!" And then she, too, started to rise.

Adelaide watched Wilhelm as he moved out of his pew and into the aisle, eyes closed, and he started to sway and move and undulate his arms about. The woman joined him, and then another woman in the small crowd.

"Do you feel it? Do you feel it? Show it!" came Friar Tuck's commanding voice.

One of the parishioners started to say something, but Adelaide couldn't make it out.

The friar shouted, "Join in when the spirit touches you! If you don't feel it, then I ask why you are here? To be in this place, in this space you must be right for this church! And if you aren't right for this church, you aren't right in the eyes of Heaven."

Adelaide watched the parishioners get up out of their seats, one by one, moving as if on puppet strings. Wilhelm started to speak strange words that were unintelligible to her ears. She wanted to be filled with the Holy Spirit. She wanted to be moved by the Lord.

"So, my friends, you can see that the Holy Spirit is among us! Those who are worthy can feel the spirit fill them! It moves them! It speaks to them and through them! Look at the joy on their faces as God frees their souls." He rose up to his full height behind the pulpit. "Can you feel it?" he shouted.

A few more voices called out "Aye!"

Even louder he shouted, "Can you feel it?"

More voices responded, "Aye! Aye!"

"If you can't feel it, it may be that you're not a friend of this fellowship. You may be a *warped*, like all those other unbeloveds out there in our town. Why haven't you opened your heart and your mind to God and to my words? God may be wondering what you are doing here—are you an apostate?"

She didn't want to be warped. She didn't want to be an unbeloved. She had felt unbeloved all her life and now she prayed fervently for the Holy Spirit to fill her. Hearing the babble about her, Adelaide understood that this was what Karel had told her about speaking in tongues: that when the Holy Spirit came upon them, they would speak the Lord's words, which, being mere mortals, they could not understand. She looked around her at all those who were touched by the divine and wondered why she was not.

Friar Tuck thundered from his pulpit: "If you are worthy, if you are touched by the divine, then you too will be chosen to move with the Lord and speak His words."

Adelaide saw him smile at the women dancing and swaying throughout the church, seemingly proud of how they channeled the presence of God. She saw him give her a disappointed look. She felt her heart start to race. She was not an apostate! Not one of the warped, like those who attended her brother's masses. Gerung was an apostate and look what had happened to him. A deserved fate, she was sure. With a look of fear painted on her face, she glanced at the woman sitting next to her. The woman's head shaking ever so slightly and her lips mouthing, "No, no, no", as if she was speaking what Adelaide was feeling. Suddenly her eyes rolled back in their sockets and her head fell backwards. She drew in a breath that sounded choked and strained and her body shook. She flopped forward and then, after a moment, started to rise. Adelaide watched her as one hypnotized, unable to look away from this grotesque yet fascinating display. The woman stood up, her eyes closed, and started to undulate, her arms waving, and her hips moving, gyrating. She called out a few times, "Oh, my Lord! Oh, my

Lord!" and then she started to say words and sounds with no meaning at all.

Adelaide watched her, fascinated, unable to move. Then she saw Karel looking at her again, looking disappointed. Perhaps angry even. She couldn't bear that look so she closed her eyes and started moving her arms in subtle waving motions. She opened her eye just the tiniest sliver to study the woman next to her and started to emulate what she was doing. Moving her arms in larger circles, she started to sway. She moved her body, knowing no one would judge her, as nearly everyone was lost in a trance of their own. Suddenly she felt more freedom than she'd ever experienced. No one was watching her and no one was expecting her to be invisible. She didn't have to stand erect and perfect at the side of the room, merely being an object to decorate a space. She could move under her own volition, and since it was God's will that she was moving this way, which it had to be because she would never let her body move like this otherwise, no one could criticize her. Peeking, she saw how Karel looked at her as she moved about, with an absolute babble now coming out of her mouth, and it put a smile on her face. She wanted this holy man to smile upon her for any reason at all. She wanted his approval like she had never desired the approval of any man she had ever met. She wanted him to have eyes only for her. He was the closest thing to the divine she had ever known, and it stirred up feelings in her that were novel and confusing, but she felt no confusion when she danced to the music in her head, danced to the words of his sermon, and spoke in a tongue which was foreign to her but inspired by God. She was in the moment and wrapped in a light-headed delirium and joy coursed through her. She had been waiting all her life for this feeling: she felt free.

Chapter 29

Father Bernard Trōst
March 1350

Bernard rose out of bed, tired of the dark and cold. He thought longingly of the days of spring that felt as though they would take all too long to arrive, although in reality they were just around the corner.

"Do not let dark days fill your mind with dark thoughts," he said aloud, trying to embrace the presence of the Lord and of his calling, but he knew that would do little to keep him warm as he did his errands about the town today. His faith couldn't even keep him warm in his own house. He stirred up the coals and added more wood, then put on a kettle to heat up water for a morning cup of mint tea. He had never liked mint, but the flavor was growing on him through scarcity—it grew plentiful as any unwelcome weed, and all the usual barley and sage teas were increasingly hard to come by. He'd long since used his stores of dried dandelion leaves. Mint was easily harvested and dried for the dark days of winter, so he had worked in earnest last fall to put by as much as he could, and now he was reliant upon those quickly diminishing stores. He was nurturing little pots of the plant, putting them in the windows for sun, and sprinkling them with water. It was an herb of hardy spirit, even if of unwelcome taste. For Bernard, spring could not come soon enough.

He heard Adelaide starting to rouse upstairs in the manse. He hoped her mood would be better today. She'd been quite short with him lately. He thought that might have something to do with her excessive fasting. He'd never been a good faster himself, and once he lived alone, he found that he ate a breakfast every day, even on Fridays. Meals were a highlight of his solitary life, even if he now had to get very creative and make a little stretch a long way. By the time Adelaide came downstairs, he had laid out slices of dark rye bread and some cheese. Today was not a fasting day for her so she might just partake of sustenance, even if it was before she took communion. Happily, she was pleasant enough and they sat down together.

As they ate and talked about the household tasks that needed attending to, he noticed a glint on her finger. By way of making conversation, he asked, "What is that ring you wear, my sister? The one in addition to your marriage band? Might I examine it more closely?"

She handed it to him and he turned it over, studying the unusual piece of jewelry.

"Where could this have come from? Most extraordinary."

Adelaide nodded. "Yes. I liked it as well. Came upon it by chance. Asked to hold it for safekeeping and then never have had the opportunity to return it."

"Return it? Return it to whom?"

"Oh, that Elizabeth woman."

"What Elizabeth woman?" Bernard was confused. He knew of several Elizabeth's in the town, it was a common name. But none that would possess such an unusual ring—and a ring made of gold to boot. Copper and bronze were allowable jewelry for the common folk, but the sumptuous laws prevented anyone of this village, apart from him or his sister, to possess gold.

"Yes! Elizabeth. You know her. You baptized her. She asked me to hold it for safekeeping. I've had it for so long now I don't know if she's ever coming back to collect it. I'm starting to grow attached to it. I think she's abandoned it, so I wear it from time to time when I think of her. I wonder if I might run into her in the village?" Adelaide looked thoughtful for a moment. "Although, I must say, she's very good at hiding in a corner and not being seen."

"Oh? Are you going out today?" Bernard noticed that she didn't answer his question. He examined the ring much more closely. "I've never seen a ring like this. It makes sense that it's not yours as every ring I've seen you wear is adorned with precious stones, like the beautiful, inverted diamond of your marriage band." He looked briefly at his own gold ring set with a diamond that his mother gave him when he came of age. For some reason, it always made him think of his dear uncle. In reality, when one was the son of a duke, such things were not uncommon. Given the rings his uncle wore as a bishop, the man had encouraged Bernard to keep his family ring, saying: *Never know when that will come in handy. You might be a son of God, but don't ever let anyone forget that you're also the son of a duke!*

"There's something odd about this ring. I can't think of who it was that gave it to you. I baptized her, you said?"

"Yes, Elizabeth. That woman who arrived with me when we came last summer from Cologne."

"You mean Rivkeh? Her name is Rivkeh, Adelaide. Not Elizabeth."

"No. I gave her a new name. A Christian one. And you sound just like Gerung now. You really do."

"He was a good man."

"He was a Jew-lover. I converted those people! I did! Don't you remember them? They asked you to baptize them when we arrived." She looked puzzled for a moment. "I meant to ask you—where are they living now? I know this house is too small for all eight of them, but where did you settle them in the town?"

"They could not stay, Adelaide. They were Jews. I did not baptize them."

"Bernard! That was so unChristian of you!" Adelaide said in a chastising voice. "I did not think you to be so prejudiced! Surely a convert is even more beloved by the Lord for how they have found their way to the truth."

"What? No, I didn't refuse to baptize them. They just didn't deeply want to become Christians. They were Jewish, from a long tradition of faith in their own community. I didn't baptize them because they didn't ask it of me and I didn't demand it of them."

"But they were *my* Christians! *I* converted them! You mean… my conversion didn't hold?" Adelaide looked incredulous. "All those hours of educating them on the journey."

"I don't believe they ever truly converted. But you did help them to escape alive, which I think was more important than any conversion. They went east not a fortnight after you arrived, to where the Jews are welcome. They haven't moved across the village. They moved over the mountains to the Polish lands. They had to leave quickly so they wouldn't become trapped in the winter snows as they crossed over."

"The Polish lands? Why would anyone do that?"

"So they can live. In peace. And not be murdered in their beds or as they walked down the street. So they can practice their religion and worship God as they have been taught."

"But why would they want to do that once they had discovered Christianity?"

Bernard shook his head and decided that Adelaide would never be able to understand a diverse society. She had one view of the world and struggled to see that God loved diversity in all things. Had made all men. Of course, she was like most of the populace that way, and so very unlike her former husband. "Why would Rivkeh give you her wedding band?"

"We ran into bandits on the road. Thieves. I told you. Christoph and I warned them off. Elizabeth was so scared she could hardly breathe. Asked me to keep the ring, to hold onto it. I guess I put it in my bag and never thought about it again until I discovered it a few months ago." Adelaide looked thoughtful. "Said it had been her mother's wedding band."

"Oh, that's tragic. She was so afraid of being murdered for being Jewish, that she gave up her own wedding band. Adelaide, this is a Jewish wedding ring. And it certainly shows the wealth and station within her Jewish community to have a ring made of gold. This dome and these little columns are so interesting. I wish I understood more about it and what it meant."

"What do you mean by understood more?" Adelaide took the ring back from him and examined it.

"I'm sure it's full of symbolism. And look there—that's writing in the Hebrew tongue. I don't know what it says, but I'm sure it's some kind of blessing."

"I'm wearing a ring with Jewish symbolism and Hebrew writing?" She put the ring down on the table and looked at it suspiciously. "If she has left the village, left Germania itself, I'm sure I don't know what to do with it. I thought that once she felt safe she would come back by and ask for it. I've been so busy with my church duties that I hadn't realized how time had passed."

Bernard reminded himself to soften his expression. "Yes, I wanted to talk with you about that. You seem to be very involved at St. Drogo's. Adelaide, there's a position for you at St. Cyprian's."

"A magician's church? A sorcerer's church?"

"No. A saint's church. My church."

"I have found a church. A church where I feel the Holy Ghost and the presence of the Lord."

"You could feel that in St. Cyprian's." He looked at her but she didn't answer him. "What is it about St. Drogo-Erasmus that draws you so? It's that friar, isn't it?"

It was a very slow nod of her head that showed agreement. "He is quite engaging from the pulpit. It's like standing in the presence of Jesus himself under the fig tree, teaching the people."

"What?" Bernard was incredulous. "That friar is like Jesus himself?" He started nervously tapping his teacup in three beat sets.

Adelaide noticed and then stiffened a bit more. "Yes. He starts talking and you can feel the Holy Spirit enter the room and move the people. I've never experienced anything like it. It's captivating."

"And when I preach," Bernard asked, "what do you feel then?"

She looked away from him and after a beat answered, "Sleepy."

"Are you saying I'm boring? Boring? Me?"

"Well, Bernard, you could put a little more energy into your sermons. You are so calm. You talk about being, well, calm. You speak of self-reflection and yes, it's soothing. So soothing that I can, at times, find my head becoming drowsy."

Bernard chewed hard on his crust of bread, trying to find the sense of calm he often preached about.

Boring indeed!

"You know, Adelaide, something confuses me about that Friar Tuckerschade. The bishops have assigned priests sermonizing, hearing confession, and giving mass. Friars have been assigned, well, mathematics. They regulate and enforce the modesty of clothing, prescribing the rules for the guilds."

Adelaide snorted. "Trust me, they're losing that battle."

He had no idea what she was referring to but he decided to stick to his point. "It just doesn't seem to me that this Friar Tuckerschade is staying in his hierarchy. He's giving mass. He's hearing confession."

Adelaide gave her brother a sharp look. "Friars are authorized to do all of that."

"When they are traveling, yes. They are supposed to travel from town to town, to fill in the gaps of where their betters, the priests, can't get to or haven't been stationed yet. But he seems to have been here all his life."

She shrugged. "No one can travel now. The whole world's under strict quarantine by order of the Holy See himself. Of course, he has to stay with his church. His people, his faithful, are here."

"And he thinks he's a descendant of that Friar Tuck character."

"And he is. That wonderful holy man is his ancestor." Adelaide's voice was full of confidence.

"Adelaide, not only was Friar Tuck *not* a holy man, he might never have existed! It's a bit of fairy tale."

"I don't want to hear you say such things." She started to rise.

"Can he do math? Friars do math. That's their role. Their place. Something is not right here, my sister."

"Of course, he can do math. I'm returning to my room to say my rosary."

"Sit down, sit down, sit down. Finish your tea, my sister."

Adelaide resumed her seat, but she looked daggers at her brother.

◆━◆━◆

Bernard went out into the cold, dissatisfied with the outcome of his conversation with his sister. She had stormed away from the table, unwilling to enlighten him as to what she did over at St. Drogo-Erasmus, only describing it as "good works to help save the town from that pestilence!" She retreated to her room and then shortly thereafter, left. He couldn't understand what was happening to her. She'd never been easy and lighthearted, to be sure, but since she came to the Valley Village she had been even more extreme. For the first weeks she'd been exhausted and weak from the journey and then after that, was distracted for some weeks. Bored he would say, were it anyone but his sister. And then, last November, she started attending that little bedraggled church on the other side of the village. She went from distracted and bored to absent, attending as many masses as she could, and she was thinner than ever. He didn't even want to think about their disastrous conversation about her hair shirt and her discipline. He knew that Gerung had burned the hair shirt she had re-made from Bernard's own cast off one, but somehow, she had gotten hold of a replacement.

"The Lord does not ask us to wound ourselves, my sister. He does not require your blood for His glory. He wants you to be happy, He wants to fill you with the Holy Spirit, which you will find in peace and quiet reflection and contemplation. My dear sister, in the stillness you will find the loveliness, the holiness and the peace that we all seek."

"Perhaps you are mistaken, my brother. Perhaps your comfortable life here, eating breakfast—even on Friday, a fasting day—is leading *you* astray. Perhaps the Lord does fill me with the Holy Spirit—in spite of your apparently poor opinion of the state of my soul. Perhaps I walk and move and talk as the Holy Ghost wills it. How dare you tell me what the Lord requires of *me!*"

It was like he didn't even know who his sister was anymore.

◆—◆—◆

He wore his sealskin cloak when he went out into the bitter air, wondering where she could be, and then figuring he already knew. He was able to purchase bread and cheese, but prices were high and options were scarce. With no supplies coming from Uncle Eberhard, he had been glad for the infusion of coins, gems, and household goods with Adelaide's arrival. Not to mention, a whole barrel full of books that Aahron brought with him as a gift for Bernard.

Aahron had well understood the grave situation in Cologne and shared with Bernard how Gerung had carefully planned out all the details of their escape. He knew that few would be left in the manor in Cologne, if anyone remained at all, and he had divided the riches of the household between the wagons so that each group might have the resources to start a life over in a more welcoming and hospitable place. Much was available for Adelaide, but a considerable wealth had been bestowed upon Bernard and Aahron's family as well.

Bernard's main concern was affording bread and soup to feed the hungry of the town who didn't have the resources to withstand the continued halting of trade or travel, particularly as the cold months dragged on. Everyone was having to get creative. He wondered how mint soup would taste?

A sob caught his attention and he turned his head. He ventured to follow the sound, entering the space between the little buildings until he went around the corner to a small alley. There was a young man crumpled in a heap and sobbing heavily. Bernard ran to his side.

"My good fellow! What is wrong? Why do you carry on so?" Bernard worried that the pestilence was now upon them at last. That this man had seen the horror and lost a loved one: a harbinger for what was to come for them all. Bernard had never experienced plague himself, but Adelaide's stories were the stuff of nightmares.

The young man was cold as ice. "I been abandoned."

"Who abandoned you, my son?" Bernard asked, stroking the man's hair, and trying to comfort him. He could not have been much beyond twenty winters by the look of him. It would certainly feel like abandonment to have one's family members perish.

The man looked up at Father Bernard and caught his breath between sobs, finally calming down enough to speak. "Me Pa. Me Ma. Me sisters."

"Oh, that's terrible! All of them? Not all of them."

The man nodded. "Aye. Said 'Don't come back'. Said I'm forsaken." He curled back up into a ball and, after a moment or two, started to sob again. "It's over. Me life is over."

Bernard blinked a couple of times. "At least they're still alive. Buck up, man! Your life isn't over just because you had an argument with your parents! I've had big arguments with mine and I'm still here. I'm happier even so. What's your name, son?"

"Jo… Jo… Johannes." The man was blubbering.

"How old are you, Johannes?"

"I be twenty-two."

"Tell me about yourself. Are you trained in a profession?"

Johannes shrugged. "I was pouring ale at the tavern. In summer I helped work the fields. Harvested a lot of grapes. No special skills. Can't work iron. Can't make shoes. Nothing to redeem me in their eyes. Me life is worthless. I should just go up into the hills and let the great boar trample me and eat me!"

"Come now, man! If you cry like that, those tears will freeze on your cheeks. Here, get yourself up. Help me carry my goods back to the manse. There you go, that's a good man."

Bernard helped the young man to his feet and gave him the parcels to hold. "There, see? You're of service already. You're not worthless. Come on back to St. Cyprian's and the manse. We'll have a cup of tea. Mint is all I have left."

Johannes stood still. "A man like you, a priest, would be seen with a man like me? A priest would be seen talking with a man like me? Sheltering a man like me?"

"Well, let's see now. You are a human being, correct?"

Johannes looked up with puzzlement, his mouth half open.

"You are a man and not a tree?" Bernard clarified. "You're a man and not a goat."

"Oh right, yes. A man."

"Good. Humanity is my business, so with you being a human you fit right in. Come along!" He set off at a brisk pace and kept Johannes engaged in light conversation until they reached the manse. Once they got inside, Bernard brewed up pot of what served as tea these days, intoning a prayer over the steeping mixture as he dropped three precious mint leaves in it. Turning to the young man he said, "So no more of this talk of the great boar trampling anyone. Besides, the cold would get to you first."

"That would be all right. Me Pa said as much. Or that maybe a wolf should have me, given what I am. You're very kind, mister priest, but I be worthless. Me life is worthless."

Bernard found some bread and cheese and nuts, and he made Johannes eat. He couldn't get the man to confess what had angered his parents so. Johannes would only keep saying that his life was worthless and talk of ways that he could end it before he brought more shame to his family.

Bernard kept the young man at the manse with a watchful eye on him all the time for the next two days, much to Adelaide's surprise. Bernard kept him busy with small jobs, but none that involved any knives or rope. "No need to tempt fate," he said to himself. Distraction was a useful tonic when one's thoughts were so dark and heavy. Little tasks could distract the mind and a heavy heart.

Johannes did everything that Father Bernard bade him to, without showing much emotion beyond his maudlin countenance. He ate with little gusto, as though every bite was a last meal. The only thing in the manse he reacted to was the hanging in Bernard's receiving room.

"Father Bernard! What is this wonderful bit that's a hanging on the wall? It's cloth. I never seen anything like it!"

"Oh that—it's a tapestry."

"A tapestry." He sounded out the syllables of the new word.

"Yes. It's like a painting." The confusion on the man's face informed Bernard that this fellow had never seen a painting either. "It came from my mother, God rest her soul. Tapestries help decorate a room and they help to keep it warm. All the stone walls can be so cold and they can make echoes, even in a small house such as this one. But tapestries help soften the sound even as they add great beauty to the space. Don't you think so?"

Johannes was entranced. "Look at him. He's so beautiful. How could someone not love a face like that?"

"Yes. He's the archangel Gabriel. Of course, I don't believe that angels look like men at all, but how else can the artist conceive of them and weave them in, but to depict them as men? And in Gabriel's case, a perfect man."

"He is perfect."

Bernard often found Johannes standing in front of the tapestry, staring in wonder. Well, it was a wonderous thing. A piece of art. An object of beauty.

After a week, the March sun shone brightly and Bernard took the opportunity of a nice day to take Johannes out for a walk.

"So, my good son, has your heart lightened any during the last few days? You've had food. Rest. Tasks to complete. A tapestry to stare at. Has that brought you any greater peace?"

"Father Bernard, I can't thank you enough for your kindness. I'm afraid it's all wasted on me though, for there is no salvation for one such as me."

"And are you still of a mind to end it all? End your life? Climb up into the mountains and offer yourself up to the first wild animal you see as soon as you're out from under my wing?"

"Aye. It's for the best."

Thinking, Bernard nodded once for the Father, once for the Son, and once for the Holy Ghost. He sought the wisdom of the Holy Trinity and prayed for help in saying the right thing. Johannes had been immutable that his existence was meaningless and that he bore a shame that was crushing him. "You know, that first animal you run into might be a marmot. Lots of those in the hills. And you're mighty big for them to munch on. It would take a very long time to die."

Johannes gave a chuckle. "Leastways, I probably don't taste as bad as a marmot does," he said as his face wrinkled.

"What is it that makes you feel your life is worthless?" Bernard must have asked this question ten times already, but he got the same answer.

"I cannot say. I daren't say. Especially not to you. You're a man of the cloth! You'd be madder than even me father was."

"I doubt that. And remember that I'm a man who specializes in forgiveness. Comes with the territory. It's a part of the job," Bernard assured him. He led Johannes out to the grape field, cut into the side of a steep hill. "Johannes, look at that hill and tell me what you see."

"I see the grape vines. All scraggly-like since they're still dormant and haven't grown their runners yet or even thought about leafing out. I've helped harvest grapes every year since I was ten summers old. But there's no point in coming out to the terraces now."

"And you can still harvest the grapes when you are twenty-three summers old, and thirty summers old and fifty summers, if you're lucky enough to live that long."

Johannes blanched. "I don't want to think of that many years of shame and pain. It would be better to be dead as a young man. There's no reason for a person like me to be alive." He sighed deeply. "No reason."

"I think there's a reason. And I think it's right there, etched into the side of that hill."

Johannes' eyes searched the dormant terraces as if to find what Father Bernard spoke of.

"I'll tell you what I personally believe: it's about realizing God's vision. The lives we have now, those that we're living, might not feel like it's God's vision for us, but I believe they are a part of the great tapestry God is weaving. We are a miracle of a work in progress, but we're unfinished, you and me. If we leave before our thread comes to its natural end, then we leave a hole in God's work, and that wouldn't be a good thing, now would it?"

Johannes shrugged. "No, I suppose not. But I'm already letting God down, so leaving a hole wouldn't be much worse."

Bernard sighed, realizing that Johannes was a tough nut to crack. He'd never run into anyone who wanted to commit suicide before and he didn't quite know what to do or what to say to the young man. The fact that suicide was a sin was indeed a part of his training. How to prevent someone from committing the act had not been. He was finding that he'd been taught a rather lot of judgement but not a lot of remedy in his education to become a priest. "We are here to finish God's work, though we are imperfect. Though we cannot see His ends. We are part of a grand design because no matter how meager we may feel, every thread is a part of the weave. Every thread is required for that magnificent tapestry. You are important, Johannes. You just can't see it now. You have some role to play in God's grand artwork that is Earth."

"I do?"

Bernard put his hand on Johannes' shoulder. "You do. Trust me. You do."

Johannes looked down and then wiped a tear from his eye. "But why do we have to suffer so? Particularly when we're made all wrong."

Bernard shook his head. "There is nothing about you that is made wrong, Johannes. Really. I mean really. You are as God made you, and if God made you then you must be all right. And as for the suffering you feel… even I do not know. Yes, you're surprised? It's the truth—I don't know everything. I believe we should live our truth. I'm God's disciple, at least I try to be, but I'm not God. I do my very best to understand Him and His purpose, but I have to pray just like you do, just like we all do, for His grace and for Him to shine the light on me." Bernard looked at the man and then looked around for a way to explain. "Come. Walk with me." They walked a short distance over to the edge of the vineyard, close enough to touch the dormant vines. "Here, look over here. You see the vine stalks growing out of the ground?"

"Aye."

"And the soil? It's not the thick, dark dirt where we plant our oats and wheat and vegetables, is it?"

Johannes nodded.

"No, it's a rocky soil here. Not the rich mountain loam that we seek out for gardens."

Johannes looked from the vineyard over to the valley where the grasses were starting to come green in patches and early crocuses dotted the fields here and there.

"Our parents and grandparents have taught us that some plants grow better in different dirt. For some reason, the grapes grow better in this rocky soil. And look at how tortured those naked vines look. See here, this twisted and bent vine reaching up from the ground, grabbing for the sun. Soon it will stretch its arms as far as it can. We support them on the strings here. See how the growers use the sinew and the braided reeds, and as the vines grow, you've seen how they gently wrap them round and round. Then they grow, captured, growing along the strings, outstretched in their forever. A season to us—a forever to them."

"Aye, I've seen that. A forever to them. A season to us," Johannes repeated.

"Our French brothers call it 'espalier', but to me it always reminds me of Christ nailed to the cross, stretched out and tortured, baking in the sun. Such a horrible sacrifice he chose to make, but what a beautiful outcome, no? That you and I, and all our brethren, will live in the glory of His name for eternity? Our sins washed away in His blood. And this vine produces grapes that we have learned to make into wine. Wine, like the blood of Christ himself, is a gift. It's a sacrament."

"Wine is a gift indeed." And then Johannes added. "And ale. And beer."

Bernard decided to give those last additions a skip and go on with what he hoped was a useful lesson for the young man. "The vine appears tortured in its life. Christ was tortured in His life. And sometimes our lives can feel torturous as well. But we are being fashioned into something beautiful. We just can't see its beauty and its holiness from where we stand. When you look at your life, you see the vine, but what is to come is the wine. When you are the wine, you will have lived God's purpose."

Johannes stared at Bernard. "I will become the wine?"

"Yes, my son. You will become the wine. It will take time. God gave you life. Can you give Him a little bit of time so that your grapes can grow and mature? Can you trust Him and have faith?" He put his hand on Johannes' shoulder, pouring every bit of prayer into the hurting soul in front of him.

Johannes took a deep breath and held it in for a moment. "I will try, Father Bernard. I will try."

◆━◆━◆

Two days later there was a knock on the door of the manse. A woman Bernard had never formally met, but who he thought he might have seen at mass once or twice stood there. She had black hair, which was unbound, and she might have seen thirty-five summers in her time. Though the years were starting to catch up to her, it was clear that she'd been quite good looking at one point. "Good evening," Bernard said as he inclined his head. "And how might I be of assistance?"

"Hullo. I understand one Johannes is staying here with ye?"

"He is. Are you… family perhaps?"

She smiled in a knowing way. "Not by birth, I'm not. Rather, I am of that kind of family that just seems to flow together through the courses of life."

Bernard wasn't quite sure what she meant, but the image that came to mind was of many years ago now, spending time with Gerung and his brother Wolfgang. Friends. They had been friends. Perhaps that's what this woman was to Johannes? "Of course, won't you come in? My name is Father Bernard."

"Mine be Jezzie. Just Jezzie."

He brought her to the kitchen and put on the kettle for some mint tea. "So, Jezzie… is that short for…?"

"Jezebel."

Bernard blinked a couple of times and reminded himself to not betray his surprise with the look on his face. "What an interesting name. Um, tell me, how do you know Johannes?"

"I don't. Not yet." She was absolutely matter of fact.

"Oh." Father Bernard felt taken aback. "Then, why are you here?"

"His Ma asked me to come and collect him."

Bernard nodded. "Oh, so his family is ready to mend their rift? I told Johannes that he should just hold on. Things would come right."

Jezzie bit her lip. "Well, that was very optimistic of ye, wasn't it? I bet you're the kind of priest that babbles on about love and kindness, aren't ye?" She shook her head.

"I should hope so." He wondered at the townsfolk here who felt so free to speak their minds. Growing up in his world, people said the right thing. The polite thing. The thing that would not cause disagreement or ruffles.

"Not all the world is loving and kind." She looked beyond him to where Johannes was coming through the door. "Johannes, is it? Me name is Jezzie. Do ye know me?"

"Me parents have spoken of you. Not kindly."

She nodded. "I would imagine not. But I've come to offer ye to go with me."

"And just why should he do that?" Bernard asked.

She answered straightaway, "Because I won't judge him. I won't ask him to change. I won't expect more than he can give."

"Will you keep him alive?"

"I won't do anything. It's up to Johannes to stay alive, if that's what he chooses. All the choices will be his." She turned to the young man. "Ye know what I am. And ye can surmise what I offer. I offer ye the choice to be who ye are and live as ye wish. Or not. I'll help ye as I can but I'm not here to be your mother or your girlfriend or your benefactress. I'm just a few steps on the path ahead of ye. The choice is yours."

Johannes looked nervously at Father Bernard. "What… what am I supposed to do?"

"You are welcome to stay here with me. I can involve you more in the church. We can find you a profession. I will do all I can to help you deal with your suffering so that you remain here on earth with us. And some day, you'll find your peace." Bernard gave the young man a small smile. Who could want more?

"I thank you for your kindness. You are a most gentle man, Father Bernard." Johannes looked at Jezzie. "And madam Jezzie, if'n I go with you, well, I… I…."

"You'll be whoever ye are. You'll have no one to please. You'll eat if ye earn money to buy your food. You'll sleep if ye choose to, when ye choose to, where ye choose to. You'll live or die if ye choose to. But ye won't have to pretend to be anything you're not, not while you're around me. You'll have no minder."

Bernard looked at this woman in shock, not knowing what to think. "Johannes, if you stay with me, if you get lost, I'll do everything I can to find you."

Johannes looked at Father Bernard with an expression that the priest could not read. Then he looked at Jezzie.

"Don't look at me. If you get lost, I'll not come to find ye. Your choices are up to ye. If ye get lost, I would assume that's what ye wanted."

Silence held the room for several moments. Then Johannes said, "I'll go up and get me things." He departed the room, leaving Father Bernard and Jezzie to look at one another.

"If you are not a part of his family and you don't care whether he lives or dies, what interest *do* you have in the boy?"

"He's a grown man from what I can tell. And I don't have a particular interest in him. But I know his type. And I know that the path he walks is one I've been forced down. His parents throwing him out, wishing he was dead. Told him that, they did. Cruel of them, wasn't it? But it be a cruel world."

"And your parents, they threw you out?"

"The lad's path and mine be the same, but we come to it different ways."

"I'm sorry, I don't understand."

She gave him a knowing look. "Oh, Father Bernard, I come from no family. He comes from a holier-than-thou family. And by the look of that diamond ring on your finger, I'd say ye come from a highborn family. Third or fourth son, are ye? Educated but no place to go? Got dumped into the church. Tell me, just who'd ye offend to get stuck way out here?"

Bernard startled. "I hope I offended no one, Madam Jezzie. I asked for a post like this. And if you must know, I am the first-born son. And I chose this life."

"First born of who?"

Bernard felt suddenly shy, like he should feel ashamed of his family and privilege, but that was silly. It was disrespectful. It was likely blasphemous. "Of Duke Trōst of Lotharinga."

"Oooo! Ye are quite high born, aren't ye? In another life, ye could have been elected king." She shook her head, and made a *tut, tut, tut* sound. "Must've been quite a blow to your father, the duke."

Bernard realized that this woman was a skilled negotiator, and it would be best to not focus the conversation upon himself. She was shrewd. Sharp. Better to keep the topic focused on her. He wanted to know what kind of person came and called for a stranger to take them away and then not care for them. "Why do you say you come from no family? Surely, you had a father and a mother?"

The woman named Jezzie nodded. "I had a mother. Dear woman. Bit dull witted, mind ye. But me father could be one of many a soldier. Me mother didn't even know him. Not really. So many men want to pluck a rose, it can be hard to remember them after a while."

"Ooohhh!" Bernard thought he understood now. Gerung and some of their friends had once swooped up Bernard on their way to a tolerance house to experience "some of the lesser evils". They ended up in a peculiar part of town that Bernard had never visited before. Oh, his father had been happy to see him go, encouraged him even. Hoped it would make him "normal". But Bernard had spent his time in the tiny house simply talking to the woman, paying her handsomely when someone banged on the door to signal that his time was up. "So, your line of work, is a family profession?" Now the name she had chosen for herself started to make more sense.

Jezzie had a mysterious small smile on her face. "Not one that me poor mother chose. But ye see, when the soldiers come through, they take what they want. They eat our food, they conscript our young men, they take our animals, and they have their way with any women they can find. Given that they're bearing arms, there's no one to say them nay. Me mother was herding the sheep when a couple of scouts came by. They stopped for some fun, which was, of course, no fun for her."

He remembered several lectures on this very topic as a part of his seminary training. The clergy at the seminary seemed to be very interested in sex and conception. And the profession of prostitution, now that he thought about it. "But it must have been, uh, pleasurable, if she conceived you. Everyone knows that a woman cannot conceive unless she experiences, as the French say, 'the little death'. That is science!"

Jezzie took a sip of her tea and gave him a sideways look. "Father Bernard, your 'science' is made by men who have never known a woman's pleasure. Rape is not a pleasure. Not for a woman. It is a beating. It is a sacrifice. It is war on a woman. And only a man could demand 'the little death' must have happened in order for an unwanted child that he planted there to take root in a woman's womb."

Bernard contemplated this. The only prostitute he had ever met had been a shy young thing. She had been nice. A very good listener. "You speak against the teachings of the church. And you are a… a prostitute."

"Yes, well, tell ye what, Father, I'm already bound for hell, aren't I? Saying the truth can't add much to the toll of me sins, now can it?" She looked thoughtfully at Father Bernard. "Ye really didn't think the church fathers would ever get anything wrong? They'd be perfect in their understanding of God? Well, if that ain't pride, I don't know what is." She laughed heartily at the confusion on Father Bernard's face. "Ah, the angels in heaven are laughing at the hypocrisy and conceit of man. Particularly the church-man. Oh, don't worry there, Father, they laugh at women too. I'm sure the angels are laughing at me all the time! Just laugh with them, that's my advice for ye."

Bernard sat back in his chair, turning her words over in his mind. Then he looked at her curiously. "Might I ask, how did you become a prostitute? And not at a tolerance house sanctioned by the city leaders?"

"I'm just going to tell ye the truth: there was nothing else for me to do. I had no family. My mother scraped by and some nice farmer let us live in his barn with the animals. But no apprenticeships would have me. No trades would take me in. And what's a woman to do when every door is shut in her face? So, I became a woman of business, you might say. Made me own fortune. And while the highborn likes of ye look down on the gutter-snipe likes of me, it's your kind makes my kind every day."

Bernard looked perplexed. "The church lays your path? Is that what you're saying?"

Jezzie nodded. "My path. Johannes' path. Every day. Every day you clergy rant on about judging the unworthy and how righteous it is to shun the sinners, ye turn the populace against their own. Ye leave helpless children to be raised with the pigs and cows and chickens and ye leave them no way to make a life. Well, there be other ways to make a life. And since I'm no longer a part of society, then that makes me free, don't ye think? And it will make Johannes free too."

Bernard nodded slowly. "I do understand the desire for freedom." He looked pensive. He couldn't process what Jezzie was saying about Johannes. "But the soldiers—they just do to you what they did to your mother."

Jezzie shrugged. "Soldiers be a funny lot, ye know. When they be taking what they want, they're a brutal bunch. Like stallions round mares in season. But when they be paying for their pleasure, they're rather a different animal. Quite shy actually. Looking for direction or lessons, I'd call it. And they talk. Tell ye about their families, their troubles, their fears. Father, ye might be surprised but there's as much talking as anything else. I find meself feeling almost like they come to confess to me that what they cannot bear to speak to their priest! Perhaps because they know I will actually forgive them, and if they go to the likes of Friar Tuck, they'll get due penance for their transgressions!"

Bernard ground his teeth and under the table clenched his fist three times at the thought of Friar Tuck. Priests and friars did hear confessions and giving out atonements and penance was a part of the training. However, the thought that men would want to talk with a prostitute rather than a clergyman shocked him… but then again, he had talked with the girl in her little hut, hadn't he?

"I never liked the tolerance houses. Evil they can be to a woman. Charge her rent for the inadequate hut they make her live in. Force her to dress according to their laws. Tell her how much and what kind of business she must do each day. And then one day I discovered that armies often bring in free-lances for hire! Did you know that? These men fight for you, for a price, and a day, and then they move on. I thought I could be like those mercenaries and become a sort of a free-lance myself! Turned out to be the far better option. When you're in my line of work and independent-like, ye travel with the army. Learn a lot of useful information, I assure you! It has its benefits because you visit cities and you see the world more than a man like ye would know. You're surprised, aren't ye? It's freedom. And I've got me favorites in each of the cities I travel to. They're excited when I come back to town, I tell you."

Bernard was puzzled. "Then why are you here? There is no tolerance house in the Valley Village. What made you come to this tiny town? I can't imagine there is much business for you here."

She laughed out loud. "There's business in any and every town. Size doesn't matter, let me assure ye as one who knows. There's always those who seek out the talents of a woman like me. But I'm here because of the pestilence. Tell me: what do the nobility and the rich do whenever sickness comes round? They leave. They go to their country estates, don't they?"

Bernard nodded.

"Well, that's what this is for me. My country estate. Away from the big cities and the disease. And while plague battles mankind—and wins—ye know the armies give it up for a while. Can't really fight while you're too weak to hold a weapon, can ye? And I wound up here as the last of the battles played out and the sickness scared them all into going back to their farms. Their liege lords couldn't make them fight, couldn't rouse them to hold up a pike towards the angel of death. And so here I was and here I stay. At least until all this passes."

Bernard nodded slowly, feeling like he was getting an entirely new kind of schooling from this woman. "And you'll take Johannes… and…"

She nodded. "Best ye not ask what ye don't want to know."

Johannes came into the room with a little bundle of clothes that Bernard had given him. Bernard got up and walked over to him. "Johannes, is this what you choose? To go with Jezzie?"

While the man looked unsure, he nodded. Then he nodded more vigorously.

Bernard went over to a little wooden box on a table and opened it. "I would like for you to take this, if you'll have it. It's a wooden cross. Know that God loves you. Know that you are welcome back at St. Cyprian's any time you choose."

Johannes nodded and let Bernard put the leather thong around his neck and he grabbed the little cross and smiled. "Thank you." But he almost seemed eager as he turned his gaze to Jezzie.

"I'm not sure I totally understand what's happening here tonight," Bernard said. "Or that I agree with it."

Jezzie put her hand on his elbow. "'Tis a powerful thing to be free. To live as one is called. To live under one's own direction. Here in the south, we have only minor nobility. They barely have control of the lands and no one gives a damn who is king of Germania. In your north, the nobles bind the serfs to their land. Mark me, Father, the people will fight back against the oppression of the knights and the church. Ye can't deny men the right to make a living and to feed their families. Nor women either. Ye can't deny them the freedom to be who they are." She looked at Johannes. "Men will always take the risks of flying free over any gilded cage that could imprison them in comfort and slavery."

Bernard looked at her, amazed to hear such thoughts from a woman of the night. And yet, almost uncomfortably he recognized her for the wisdom that fell from her lips. *The people of these small towns will never cease to amaze me,* he thought. *No education and yet wise as Solomon.*

She looked sharply at Johannes. "Are ye ready? Still coming?"

Johannes nodded but he didn't speak. He gave a long and grateful look at the priest and Bernard saw a glint of hope reflecting a meaning and purpose in life. The knot in Bernard's stomach relaxed for the first time since he'd met Johannes. He started to think that this young man's vine was not going to wither and die in the dirt. He might not have the life his parents wanted for him, but he would live.

After they left, Bernard sat long at his kitchen table with a cup of untouched cold tea. "Your garden grows in mysterious ways, Lord. Mysterious ways. But it grows." He crossed himself three times and bowed his head to pray.

Chapter 30

Trevor

Trevor couldn't help but walk with a little bounce in his step. Everything about this dig was exciting. Today he and Everly would be working on a new discovery site over on the poorer "Tower Hamlets" side of town. Of course, for Trevor, he could be digging a trench in the backyard with Everly and that would be almost as exciting. Or maybe digging in the sand at the beach. "Constructing sandcastles! Ahh, that would be nice…." His mind filled with images of them on holiday… together.

"What about sandcastles?"

Trevor nearly jumped out of his skin. "Huh?" Everly had popped up beside him, seemingly from out of nowhere. Again. She did that all the time and he never got used to it.

"Sandcastles. You said something about sandcastles."

"I don't know what you're talking about." Trevor knew he sounded nervous. He wondered what else he'd said aloud. *Oh my God, if I talk in my sleep, I'm a dead man.*

Everly laughed. "Yeah, yeah, you did! I mean it just seems funny. Archeology is all about finding the permanence in what has proven to be impermanent. Sandcastles are about as impermanent as you can get."

"Right. It's like anti-archeology. Oh my gosh, now I love them even more."

"I always enjoyed them as a little kid. We'd make a pilgrimage to Woodbine or Bluffer's Beach." She smiled as they walked. "I know, it's weird to think of a beach in Canada, or people in bathing suits in Canada. But yes, we have both beaches and bathing suits. Yes, they're nice."

"We English are very proud of our beaches too, although the world seems to think of us as just a cold, rainy island. And, well, rather the opposite of a tropical destination."

"I loved to build sandcastles with my parents. But I was such a geek even then."

"Were you?" Trevor could tell his voice sounded as weak as his knees felt. *She was an anorak as a little girl!*

"Oh yeah. I would correct the castles they were building. All the parts had to be right, you know, if it was a medieval castle of Europe that's just way different than a Ming Dynasty Chinese palace. Of course, none of them ever looked like anything but lumps of sand, except in my imagination—but to me, they were magical places."

"They were?"

"Oh, I'm boring you. Sorry."

"No, it's all right. Really. I'd love to hear about your sandcastles."

Everly looked like she didn't register the comment. "Today should be truly exciting! Did you see the report from Gunther about the readings on the metal detector two days ago?"

Trevor nodded. "Right. I was there. It went bonkers. The follow up testing is promising. Something's down there and it's big, whatever it is."

"Nylah's theory, wait for it, is that it's a cannon."

"A cannon? In Tower Hamlets? Facing the mountains? Lord, that girl's got to get some regular college history under her belt. Just what would they be shooting at? A wild boar? Not like you're gonna hit that with cannon shot."

Everly chuckled. "She does have an imagination. One created from watching movies and playing adventure video games. Not quite a historically accurate orientation to her summer job."

"Between that and the dancing skull of poor Father B on the website, honestly, I don't know what my father would do about her if he were here. But she's bloody brilliant. Do you know that another foundation contacted me yesterday and wants to help with funding for our dig? I mean, they're throwing money at us!"

"That's incredible."

"Right. And Nylah's got such a good eye for photography, I bet we could publish a book documenting the whole thing."

"Nah, hold out for the movie rights." Everly gave him a wink. She looked about them as they walked through the streets. "Amazing, isn't it? We've got so much staked out here, and there, and over there that you can nearly see the village. It's almost like walking the streets seven-hundred years ago."

"Well, it is if you've got the imagination of Nylah!" Trevor chuckled. But he thought Everly was right: the dig was starting to shape the little town. A house stood here. Something larger, like a business stood there. A well, a tower, a church. "The footprint of the little town is starting to emerge from seven hundred years of slumber. As she wakes from her long dream, her secrets are starting to reveal themselves."

Everly stared at Trevor.

"What? What did I say now?"

She shook her head. "I might have to take back all those nasty comments I made about your book and actually read it, Trevor. You're quite the poet."

Trevor could feel he was blushing. "Well, um, oh, here we are. The students have started to gather. And Gunther's here, back from his trip." He called out, "Hello, mate!"

The two men shook hands. "*Guten morgan!* I am glad to be back here with my students and you for the dig this week. And I heard through the grapevine that you had a very exciting trip up to the saddle? I've never been there myself, but it sounds like you made quite a discovery."

"It could be. We'll have to go back and check it out. I'll be sure to keep you posted." Trevor wondered how Gunther could know so much. He clapped his hands and rubbed them together. "Let's get started, shall we? We all look entirely too clean!" The students responded with a collective, knowing chuckle.

The crew spent a good two hours making progress before they uncovered the tip of the huge metal object that the radar had indicated was down in the earth. As they removed the dirt from around it, documenting its emergence from the hard clay that encased it, Everly suddenly said, "I know what this is."

Gunther looked at her. "There is only eight inches of a metal tip. What do you think?"

"It's a cross! It's one of those crosses that medieval churches put on their spires."

Trevor looked at the metal. "It could be a lot of things. A statue. A sculpture. A cross is a possibility. It's certainly not a cannon."

"A cannon? Who would think it was a cannon?" Gunther asked, surprised.

Everly waved away his comment. "A student. Don't worry, not one of yours. No one with a degree in archeology thought it was a cannon or a merry-go-round or an airplane. No worries! But I really think it's a church spire cross."

With a look of excitement on his face, Trevor said, "Well, let's dig it out and find out. If you're right, I'm treating for a dinner out in town for the three of us."

Gunther smiled and nodded appreciatively as he called his students in to double their efforts. In another two hours, they had the object unearthed, photographed, measured, and documented. *"Verdammt!"* was all Gunther could say.

"So, you win, Everly, and dinner's on me." Trevor scratched his head. "But blimey! Why would this massive cross be here?"

One of the students looked at Dr. Payne. "Be here? In this section of the village?"

"Well, actually, I mean in this village at all. Gather round you all. Take a look at this cross. It's nearly as big as any of us. Where have you seen a cross this size before?"

Most of the students just shook their heads.

"On top of a church in Bonn, maybe?" one of them guessed.

"That's right. On a big cathedral with a footprint like nothing we've found evidence for in this village. Nobody would be daft enough to drag the kind of stone up here that you'd need for the foundation to be able to support a structure which could hold this massive cross." He looked around him, imagining the kind of building the cross was made for and thinking of the massive stones in the wall up in the saddle of the mountain. He reminded himself to focus on this moment and the here and now with the students. "The one church that we've found in town was too small to support this monster. And this cross is all the way over here in Tower Hamlets. So why was that?"

"There must have been a church standing here!" an excited student said.

"Maybe someone was into crosses?" another one suggested. "Like, really, really into crosses."

"Okay. Hmmm. Agreed that people in the poorest end of town wouldn't just go about collecting massive crosses, now would they? It's not quite like a porcelain figurine your grandma might have."

Several of the students sniggered.

"I see you know exactly what I'm talking about." He gave them a wink and a chuckle. "But we've no evidence of a church either."

Everly looked thoughtful. "What about a little church? One that couldn't put it up high, so they just used it however they could. Like next to the door to call the faithful."

Gunther nodded and looked thoughtful at Everly's suggestion.

"Right," Trevor said. "Possibly. A good hypothesis. But how might such a cross even come to be in a nothing little village like this?"

"Cesspits!" Hannah called out.

Everyone looked at her.

Trevor said, "'Fraid I'm not following you, mate. Say more?'"

Hannah looked distinctly nervous. "Well, it's just that you also said, why would a little nothing village like this have cesspits? It's not the technology of rural towns of the time. We have uncovered evidence of what major cities had in terms of infrastructure, which was a surprise. So maybe someone came here. And they brought their big city knowledge with them. And their cross."

Everly nodded. "Hannah, just say when and you can be my doctoral student!" Hannah blushed furiously, and Everly continued, "That's a really neat hypothesis. We do have evidence that something unusual was happening in this town. During the Black Plague, and just about any plague for that matter, the nobility would quickly retreat to their country estates. We don't have any evidence in either the historical record nor from anything we've uncovered in our excavation to suggest that a country manor existed here or that this was a noblemen's retreat. But that doesn't mean that an isolated few didn't take refuge here during the dangerous times. And they could have brought their understanding of the technology of the day with them."

"And their religious beliefs too," Trevor said. "If they were bloody scared, they could just possibly have dragged this behemoth with them as a talisman to ward off evil. In this case, the plague. But why it would be here… hmmmm."

"Why wouldn't it be here?" Matthias asked.

Trevor pointed and started to walk toward the faint marks they had uncovered about fifteen feet away that could possibly suggest the footings of a small building. "Look here. If you use a lot of imagination you could possibly see this structure that may have been here as a church. But look at it with today's lens. What would it look like?"

Everly looked thoughtful and then rubbed her chin with her hand. "You know, I hate to say it this, but it reminds me of this dinky, dying little strip mall we have in Toronto. It was really run down, even the vape shop didn't make it. It had a little hole-in-the-wall church there." Everly looked around at the faces staring at her. "I know, it sounds weird, but that's what I see."

Matthias gave a grunt. "I am going to cross Toronto off my bucket list." All the students snickered.

"Well, vacation travel hot-spots aside," Trevor said, "back to where in the world would they have gotten such a massive cross?" He scratched his head. "It would be worth a fortune to the right buyer, but out here in a mountain village in the poorest part of town? No way to know. But if there was a church and it did come into possession, what could they do with it?"

Otto looked puzzled. "Maybe we just haven't found the footings of the church. We haven't dug down far enough."

"If a big building collapsed here, big enough to hold this cross, where are the stones now?" Gunther said.

Trevor touched his index finger to the tip of his nose and then pointed it at Gunther. "Right you are, Gunther. Let's go with that idea. Stones fall down, then they should be scattered everyplace right? But the village was abandoned. And huge stones don't just migrate on their own."

"But in history, didn't the people use the stone again, in other buildings? Maybe that is why we don't see it?" asked another student.

"Alright, mate," Trevor answered, having no idea what this kid's name was. "That's a theory, but what's the problem that still remains?"

The students all looked at one another and then back at Trevor.

Everly answered the group: "It's a good thought, Karsten, but then all the footing stones for the other buildings of significance that we find would all be very similar in type and cut. But so far, we haven't found that, have we?"

The students shook their heads.

Trevor nodded. "So, no scattered stones, no repurposed stones, and all that means: no big church ever stood here." Trevor pointed across the short edge of the cross. "Look at this beauty: not a mark on her. But let's pretend there was such a church. Think about a church in this abandoned town, over the centuries, with this beautiful cross pointing up to the sky. And one day, the roof, with all the weather and never a repair, and it just can't hold out any longer and it caves in. What do you think would've happened to her if she'd fallen from the height of a church rooftop? Even one that was smallish and not a huge cathedral like those in Cologne or Bonn?"

"It would be broken," Heidi answered.

"Right, mate! At the least we'd see marring, denting, scraping, breaking. But this cross is as intact now as the day it was cast. It's never fallen from any kind of a height. It almost looks like it was wrapped in silk just to get it up here to the mountains!"

"Dr. Payne, could it have been made here?" Otto asked.

"I'll ask Dr. Heintzelman to answer that. Gunther, you're the expert in Middle-Ages iron works."

Gunther shook his head. "No evidence in this town for anything but a small smithy. Blacksmith. Housewares. Nothing that we can find that would support the creation of such a magnificent cross as this."

Everly said, "So, it's most likely that this cross was imported. Here we might have a little make-shift church that came into possession of this wonderful cross. They'd have no choice but to mount it outside, on a pole maybe. So here it would be, perhaps standing up, almost where it sits now, to call the faithful. But why would they do that when there's a perfectly good church on the other side of town?"

Trevor shrugged. "People are weird, aren't they? I mean, not getting along with one another seems to be the lesson of history, doesn't it? Maybe some of the villagers wanted their own church. Wanted to worship in their own way. It's a mystery that we may never solve, but that's the fun of archeology, innit? Learning so much about these people's lives, their stories. They've left us all kinds of clues and we do the best we can to fit the puzzle together. Oh! Nylah! There you are! Look what we've discovered!"

Nylah walked up to the group and looked down at the huge cross.

"Yeah. Dope. I mean Cool. Um, I hate to drag you from your cross on steroids, but you gotta come and look at something."

Trevor gave a whistle of surprise. "You'd think this town had blackberry bushes growing all over it! Really, Nylah? There's been another find? That's amazing." He saw the stern look she was giving him. He lowered his voice considerably and said, "Not amazing?"

Through a frozen smile Nylah answered, "Not amazing. Dr. T, you and Everly need to come to Command Central. Like now." She looked at the crowd of students all around them, chatting and talking in German. "And don't get the locals riled up."

When they arrived at the main tent, Nylah dropped the entrance flap as soon as the three of them were inside.

"What's the mystery, Nylah? What's going on?" Everly asked. Then she jumped as she looked at the table. "And where did that hideous tablecloth come from?"

"It was my grandmother's, thank you very much. She was quite the fan of garden gnomes." Trevor crossed his arms.

"Is that what those are?" Everly asked, a stricken look on her face.

"You're really going to love the one with the giant troll face on it, I can tell."

"Also your grandmother's?"

"I picked that one out, actually. C'mon, it's funny! Humor? You've heard of humor?"

Nylah sighed loudly. "You little nesting lovebirds might want to forget about tablecloths and sit down. It's about the cross."

"We just came from the cross," Trevor said.

"Not that cross. Father B's cross. The golden cross."

"What about it? It's up at Brandenburg University." Trevor gave a shrug and sat down.

"It *was* up at Brandenburg. Seems it's not just marmots after that thing. There was a break in. Professionals. Went for the cross."

"Bloody hell!" Trevor shouted and jumped up again.

"No!" Everly said heavily as she sat down.

Trevor looked from her to Nylah. "I've never been on a stranger dig in my life. Usually, it's old bits of bone and pottery shards, and no one in their right mind would steal that. But we've been scared nearly to death that the cross would be stolen from here, so we put it in the safest place that would take it, and still, it gets stolen!" He sat down heavily once again. "And I never got to show it to my father."

"Well, I've got good news and bad news. The good news: they didn't get the cross. Other artifacts were taken, but the cross slipped through their fingers."

Trevor jumped up yet again. "That's wonderful! Blimey, they must be real bunglers. I mean the cross was on display in a glass case. It was hard to miss."

"Yeah, it seems that security isn't quite what you might've thought. Story goes, after the cross had been on display all day, one of the faculty took it home to show some friends at a dinner party."

"Bollocks!" Trevor gave a gasp. "That's the kind of shenanigans you'd expect from the tenured professors at Cambridge!"

"The cross was only saved because someone illegally snuck it out as some type of weird dinner party conversation piece?" Everly was wide-eyed in her disbelief. "A trophy to brag about?"

"Yup. So, Dr. T, bad news is that you've got to drive to Brandenburg tonight. It seems the president of the university feels the need to make a personal apology to you. Of course, he feels he needs to make it to Daddy-O, but since you're in Germany and the eminent Dr. Trevor Payne, Senior, is back in England, I think he's perfectly happy to deal with you instead. In fact, given your mild-mannered nature, I think he's far happier to be dealing with you."

"Oh, bugger!"

Chapter 31

Friar Karel Tuckerschade
April 1350

Friar Tuckerschade stood by the cross now mounted to a pole outside his church. It was taller than he with arms stretching wider than his own arms could reach. "A man could almost be crucified on this cross," he murmured as he stroked the metal lovingly. "This is a cross worthy of St. Drogo-Erasmus." Then he thought about it. "Nay, this is worthy of a church ten times the means of St. Cyprians itself! This be a cathedral cross." In his breast he felt a flutter: an unrecognized emotion—pride. There'd been so little to ever feel proud about in his life, having been stepped upon and denied opportunities for being too poor, too rural, too uneducated, too wholly devoid of social connections.

But now he was the friar of a church with a huge, iron cathedral cross, standing right here where every man could measure himself against it. He would have put the cross atop the church, admittedly a more traditional move, but he wasn't sure the rooftop could support it. And there wasn't the money nor the craftsmanship in this little village for such a grand gesture anyway. Nevertheless, he liked the cross affixed to a large pole right outside the little *kirche*, his church. It made the cross more available to the people, made the whole concept of the crucifixion and suffering more palpable to the people. And it brought the people in.

And she was there now, one of the people. She came regularly, twice a week at least. Said she wanted to be a nun, but that had been denied her because of her station in life and because of her social connections. He'd wanted to be a priest, or, were he being truthful, an archbishop or perhaps a cardinal, and in a similar shared destiny with Adelaide, also because of his station in life, a meager friar was all he could actually pretend to. She was a woman of wealth and gave generously to St. Drogo-Erasmus—an influx of coins and goods the like of which he had never seen. He now had a sumptuous rug on the floor of his tiny manse—also a gift from her. At times he would just lie on it, feeling its plush softness and wonder at how the nobility actually lived. She was an angel; he was sure of it. That face haloed in those masses of blonde curls was surely an emblem of heaven itself. Her name even meant angelic: *Engelhaft*. Of course, that had been her husband's name and that man had been anything but, from her description. She'd given that man this cross as a wedding gift so that it could be boldly displayed within their manor—and the apostate had the audacity to stick it in a barn for "safekeeping" until the masons could figure out how to attach it to stone without damaging the structure of the walls themselves. "But the fool didn't hire them before the masons all died, now did he?" Karel growled. "Idiot."

Inside he fumed that someone like Adelaide would be given to a man like that. A woman like Adelaide deserved someone with an equally devout heart. With a soul that was given to the passion of the Lord. A passion they could share together. A woman like Adelaide deserved a man like him. Priests could not marry nor fraternize closely with women. Friars had similar restrictions. He had long ago declared himself as such, and since records of training were not well kept, he had been grandfathered in by the church, accepted as though he were an ecclesiastically-made man rather than the self-made prophet he actually was. And so, the rules didn't really apply to him. They weren't *his* rules. He had sworn no such vows and thus could make his own rules. He ran his own church. He managed his own flock. If Adelaide wanted to be a nun, he would make her one. It was the thing she wished for more than any other on the face of earth or in heaven, and it was a wish that was within his power to grant.

He had a notion to look for her. She often liked to stroll down by the bend in the skinny river. It was a hot summer day and that was a cool place to rest and be alone. There was a copse of trees near a bend that gave one shelter from the sun. It was a wonderful place for prayer. Very private. He had known her to take her Bible there. Perhaps that was where she was? "I should say my most heartfelt gratitude for the gift of the cross. After all," he said, giving the iron another tender stroke, "she didn't give it to Bernard, and that surely is a clear declaration."

With a nod he turned around and started to walk. It would take him nearly three-quarters of an hour to reach the bend at his fast pace.

As he came to the copse, he heard sobbing and he started to run. He found her alone, underneath a small tree, tears streaking down her face. "Lady Adelaide! Are you hurt?"

She shook her head but her bodice was undone and her arm was outside her sleeve. She had blood running down her shoulder. "I am not hurt when I suffer for Christ and atone for the sins of man to end this dreaded plague."

He took her right hand in his and removed the discipline from it, examining it. "I see." He looked at her in awe. While his discipline was a dear instrument to his devotional practice, he had only suspected that her leanings were so similar. He took a cloth from his pocket, wet it in the dancing water of the river as it eddied under the overhanging tree, and then coaxed her to lay down across his lap so that he could start to clean the blood on her back.

She made little sounds of pain as he worked.

"There, there, my child. Your suffering is great and you are beloved in the eyes of the Lord. What sin have you committed that you should suffer so?"

"Bernard says I suffer from vanity. We had an argument."

"Vanity? I remember you wearing ribbons in your hair when you first came to the Valley Village, but they don't adorn your hair these days."

Adelaide sighed deeply and lay her cheek on his knee, looking at the eddy of water before her. "He called my devotion a vanity. Bernard says that I am overly devotional and that you encourage that. He reminds me that my destiny is not my own. But I have faithfully observed my year of mourning for Gerung…"

"May he rest in peace," Karel said, filling in the space that Adelaide had simply left hanging.

"Oh yes, may he rest in peace." She rolled her eyes and waved off the comment, "and then, he says, I am to be remarried. That it is not right for a woman like me to have no one to protect her. And, he reminds me, that the family title might pass through me to my sons, should my other brothers succumb to the plague. It is my family duty." She sat up, seemingly unaware of the dangerous droop her dress made off her shoulder. With brimming eyes she looked at Karel. "He says that I am too beautiful to wither away in a drab little church like yours. He says I am called to higher things." She burst into tears again and fell against his chest. "But by higher he means social connections. Remarrying for my family obligations. All I am to him is a cow to be traded. My love and devotion mean nothing. Oh, Karel, what am I to do?"

Karel awkwardly put his arms around Adelaide as she cried and he patted her back, attempting to avoid any fresh wounds. He didn't know what to say. He'd never been in a situation like this. His hand had brushed against her bare shoulder and the sensation of her skin against his lingered. He started to stroke her head, with those lovely golden curls. He had longed to touch them, and now he ran his hand tenderly down their length.

"I want to be loved for the state of my soul, appreciated for my devotion, and not for the beauty of my face or the value of my family lineage. It's so unfair that I am solely judged for things that I cannot control."

He searched for something to say, anything that might help in this moment. "Women are not judged for their beauty alone." He thought about that. He certainly didn't ever think of the looks of any of the women attending his church. Well, perhaps with the exception of Lady Adelaide, but those other women had no such graces to recommend them. And social connections and lineage played no role in his life whatsoever.

She pulled away and looked straight at him. "Are we not? It seems to me that a woman in today's world has so little she can draw upon to make her worthy in the eyes of others. Piety should matter. Her stitching or embroidery should matter. For those of ignoble birth, their ability to prepare food or scrub the boards should matter, but all a woman seems ever to be judged upon is her countenance. That is the truth of a woman's life." She slumped forward and faced the water dancing before her, hugging her knees. "Or her pedigree."

Karel sat forward alongside her. "I admit that I find myself most confused at the moment." He used his cloth to dab at the little beads of blood that were reforming on her back and shoulder.

"Well, I can understand that. For you are pure of heart and absolute in your devotion, and that is how people judge you." She looked back at him and raised a finger to touch his face. "Not for your square jaw line or the handsomeness of your eyes. A man like you should have been born into the nobility, and then letters and books would have been your province, but still, even without those privileges, you are a master of the people, the caretaker of their souls, their portal to the Holy Spirit. No one is thinking about how handsome you are as you lead the sermon." As she spoke, her finger traced his face and then tapped his heart. "Except maybe me."

"Indeed," he said, but sounded very unsure of himself. He felt waves of emotion at hearing her words, being described in a way he had never heard before. He felt she was echoing his most inner thoughts. He felt seen. He felt understood. He wondered if this was what it felt like to be loved?

"You are judged for who you are. But *me*...." She snorted. "Tell me honestly: do you count vanity as a sin?"

"Yes. Aye, of course." He was amazed at how his own voice held so little conviction.

"Women are admonished for their vanity, but beauty is all a woman is valued for. Her fairness of face, her ample bosom, and I would add her fertility, but since men seem to be happy to have bastards with any woman at all, clearly it is beauty that counts. A woman blessed with a fine smile and bounteous hair is a woman blessed indeed, for she can overcome an ignoble birth and live comfortably as the wife of a merchant. Or, more likely, become the mistress of a noble lord first and then, when he's done with her, become the wife of a baker or craftsman."

"Is that what happens to women in the cities?" Karel was indeed surprised. He had never thought of what a woman's life was like. Women were there to produce things. Like food. Or clothing. Hearing her words created new stirrings inside him that he was unaccustomed to.

"Even here, in the countryside, you prize your cows for being excellent milkers, don't you?"

"Well, aye. Aye, we do. Of course."

"To blame a woman for vanity seems a bit like telling your most prized cow every day what a fine milker she is, bragging to your neighbors for the quality of her milk, and then when the cow is proud of her milk... to admonish the poor beast for being vain! What else has she ever heard? What else does she have?"

Karel thought about that. It made sense to him. While he'd certainly always thought of women and cows in the same way, Adelaide was no cow. She should never be a beast of burden. Her soul had rare and precious worth. He knew it from the length of her lashes, from the blueness of her eyes, from the flaxen curls that always managed to escape her headscarf. Only those beloved of the Lord Himself could be gifted with such a smile and skin so fair. When he sat with her, he felt like he was sitting in the presence of an angel. "And yet vanity is a sin."

"Agreed." She sighed heavily. "Bernard says it is a vanity that I want to make my own choices for my life. Vanity. Humph! We are born to sin, are we not? No man walks without sin on this earth."

"Nay. And no woman either."

Adelaide nodded. "And no woman either. Since we cannot escape sin, since it is our destiny, then what must matter is our devotion. It is in how we atone for our sins." She looked down at her shoulder.

Karel reached up and touched the shoulder that bore the evidence of her love of the discipline. "Atonement is the path to holiness."

She smiled slightly and reached around to touch his back. "You are a man who understands sin and the need to share the suffering of Christ in atonement."

Karel trembled and nodded. He had never been touched by a woman in that way.

She withdrew and stared at both her hands on her lap. "My husband…" She followed with a perfunctory and hollow, "may he rest in peace. He admonished me for my discipline. He burned my hairshirt and took my discipline from me, refused to allow me to abase myself before the Lord. Said he didn't want to see the marks on his wife and that if I were so determined to suffer, I should just suffer to be his loyal wife. *That* would suffice to absolve me of my sins!"

"He did not!"

"Yes! He was not like you, Karel. He did not appreciate how suffering is the path to heaven. He would not humiliate his body and prevented me from doing so to mine. But you, I think you have a special relationship to the suffering of Christ."

He looked at her as she blinked with those long lashes. "You are a woman most pure in the eyes of the Lord, Adelaide. I think you could do no wrong in the eyes of God, even though your husband prevented you from showing your devotion. If you choosing your own path is a vanity, then I am sure the Lord would forgive you. I would forgive you." He put his palm to her forehead and said in a commanding voice: "I, Friar Karel Tuckerschade, do hereby raise you up! I name you a holy sister of my church. I declare it to be so. You are now a part of my church and a part of me."

Tears leaked from her eyes again and she took his hand and kissed it, as though he were a bishop wearing a ring. "I only ever wanted to be a nun. To suffer for the glory of the Lord." She gently touched his shoulder again. "You have seen my devotion." She looked at him shyly. "I have never seen the devotion of a man of the cloth." She looked despondent and stared off into the distance. "I don't know how to judge my own devotion or whether I am truly worthy of any of God's forgiveness."

Karel faltered. Surely this woman who had suffered so much for the love of Christ would know, should know, that her devotion was admirable. She had a good point though: coming from a family so far from God, so absent of the practice of devotion, that she would have no way to gauge her own practices. "I could, I could, um, well, so that you can understand your own practices, I could show you the fruit of my own labor."

Adelaide's eyes flew open and she turned her face back toward his. "You... you are the kindest, most admirable man. To imagine that you would make such a sacrifice... a sacrifice to educate me to further my own practices." She was nearly breathless. "You are the most generous man our Lord has ever created, I'm sure of it."

Karel felt nervous. But every fiber of his being wanted to show her. He'd flagellated himself just the night before, so his wounds were fresh and aching. He felt holy. This felt like a holy moment between two people—and she was now a holy sister of his church. She was now a part of him. He slowly started to remove his clothes while Adelaide watched him. With the reveal of every wound, every scratch, every scab, she called out exclamations of delight and praise.

At last, he sat down next to her in their shady patch with nothing but his short cloth over his loins. The fresh breeze felt like a divine touch on his skin and assured him that this moment was a good and blessed one between them. She touched each of his injuries with a slow and gentle tracing of her finger. He felt she was blessing his holy orders with the simple touch of her delicate hand.

"I have much to be impressed with in you, Karel. Mine own devotions serve only to humiliate me now that I see how you fulfill your holy orders."

Karel shuddered at her words and wondered how they could move as one like this. It was as though their souls were connected.

Adelaide pulled back. "Do I upset you, in my ignorance?" She looked down, blushing with shame. "I might have been a highborn lady at one point in time, but I am now just a simple… unworthy…" She choked up and could not finish her sentence.

Karel gently put two fingers under her chin and raised her face to look at him. More than anything he wanted to look into those beautiful eyes, the windows to her soul, her beautiful soul that was so intertwined with his. "I'm sure you have nothing to be ashamed of, my Adelaide."

"I have had no idea whether my suffering is adequate with no stick to measure by, so I persisted in the dark, consumed with worry at my unworthiness." Slowly, she started to pull the blouse off, freeing her other arm. Then her skirt, adding them to the pile of her already removed clothes until she sat next to him with nothing on at all. "You see, I have much to strive for. Just look at me. I have not suffered as you have."

Slowly, with a gentle touch he examined the wounds on her back, and the little scars on her breasts and legs. He had never seen a woman like this and was amazed that women weren't anything like cows or bitches with pups. They were marvelous creations of God. He felt as though every touch was worshipping creation itself. He could not help what it was doing to his body and knew that Adelaide noticed. The simple loin cloth had long since fallen off.

She reached for him and stroked him, a feeling he had never known with any hand save his own. "There is another way to suffer."

He groaned. "I don't know this way of suffering." His breath was gasping.

"As a married woman, my fate was to learn this kind of suffering. My husband quickly eschewed taking me as a husband does a wife, and assured me that this alternate was suffering in the extreme, and he would groan in his pains. I will make you suffer, if you ask it of me. I could teach you a new way of suffering."

"A new way of suffering… yes, I submit to suffer…" he managed to choke out, not at all understanding what she was talking about but being grateful for a new lesson in suffering.

"You may groan, so that I know I am causing you unendurable suffering and bringing you closer to God."

As her head dipped down and she commenced her conception of torture for a man, he did indeed oblige her with more groans than his lips had ever uttered in his life.

After she was through with him, they lay in the grass, he shaking almost uncontrollably as she continued to draw on him with her finger, tracing lines of past scars all over his naked body. "How do you feel?"

"Like I have been touched by the divine," he said, his eyes fixated on heaven. "It was excruciating and yet there was something of beauty in it at the same time. It was so wonderful that had my spirit not been so uplifted, I would be sure it was a sin. I would be sure that we had just sinned."

She lay there quietly for a while, staring up at the sky. "I do not wish to sin. I live every moment of my life trying to avoid sin. Perhaps it is the destiny of man to commit sin. Maybe we cannot help ourselves." She sighed heavily. "If that is so, at least we both know what to do with sin and how to bear the atonement."

He nodded. His shaking was starting to subside. "If you want, I will pray on how I might bring you similar suffering, my Adelaide."

"Oh, I do suffer when I am around you. I ache badly. And I know this to be a holy thing between us, because I never did ache like this for my husband."

Their voices joined in an automatic, "May he rest in peace."

"Tell me about your ache."

"It is not a pleasure, for then I would know this to be sin. It is like hunger. Like when I fast for three days in God's name. It is like the unsatisfied longing I feel when I smell the aromas of the feast, but am vowed to starve."

"You are so strong."

"I know not how strong I am. That feels like a vanity."

Karel thought for a moment. He pinched her nipple and she jumped with a quick *ouch!* "We could test you. We could test how strong you are."

She blushed furiously. "You would do that for me?"

"Oh Adelaide, I would do anything for you. I mean, for the state of your soul."

Chapter 32
Adelaide Trōst Engelhaft
August 1350

The day was sunny and the air laced with the evasive scent of late summer's mountain flowers as Karel and Adelaide walked up the highland path.

"Are you sure we will be safe, Karel? I've heard rumor there is a wild boar that roams the foothills of the mountain on the other side of the skinny river." Adelaide looked about them nervously.

"I don't think we have anything to worry about, my dear holy sister."

She loved it when he called her *holy sister*. From the power of his ministry, with his own hand, he had bestowed upon her the thing she wanted the most in this world, and now she was a nun. His nun. A holy sister in the church of St. Drogo-Erasmus. It was her destiny fulfilled.

Karel shook his head and looked about him, exuding a sense of calm. "The boar you fear lies dead at my own hands. We are safe."

Adelaide felt her heart race at the thought that there was no miracle this man couldn't perform. She found that her heart often beat wildly in his presence. Together they had discovered so many ways to help one another atone and she found the suffering exquisite in a way that her solitary practice had never yielded. Had it only been the pleasure without the suffering that was mixed in, she would have felt guilty. But he assured her that as long as they were suffering, their atonement was genuine and complete.

Surely, she reasoned, *those flagellants in Cologne must have been experiencing some pleasure as well, or they would not have whipped themselves so industriously.* Her wounds were nearly healed from her last disciplinary practice. He had helped her through the hardest parts, as she had helped him in turn. She loved how he could make himself vulnerable to her and give over his power to her, to help him achieve such abasement for the glory of their Lord. She was sure that together they were responsible for saving the entire village. The plague had not entered the town and the only reason that could be was that their suffering pleased God and redeemed all the poor souls of their valley. It was their suffering that kept the angel of death at bay.

While she felt safe in his presence, there was that other rumor from the townspeople that gave her pause. "The villagers talk of a devil that roams these hills. Cloaked in gray and taller than any living man. Grotesque, they say, with a huge head. Red, glowing eyes! They say that he leaves a trail of poisoned green blood that will burn you, should you step in it."

Karel gave a slow smile.

"You smile! You make fun of me!"

He became suddenly serious. "Oh nay, Adelaide. I would never make fun of you. I laugh inside at the stupidity of the villagers, but perhaps they're right. Maybe they do have much to fear. But you and I—we have nothing to fear. We are right with God. The Holy Spirit fills us. We are protected."

Adelaide felt the knot in her stomach relax a bit. He was her protector. As long as she was with Karel, she was sure she would be safe. "When I'm with you, I know I'm right with God." She reached for his hand, and he took it as they walked along. "What is it that you want to show me?"

His face glowed with happiness. "I have discovered a secret: a secret up in the hills that the Almighty has entrusted me with. Aye, I am its guardian. There is a low stone wall, or what is left of one, from eons past, from the very start of the world. And beyond that, a most holy place that I would share with you. A place that will be our secret alone."

"A place of the Lord? Up in the *Hohes Venn?*" She was surprised. Stunned even. A high fen was a bog, a rather dangerous place. A sparse space of scant growth and little to recommend it as lovely and inviting. What would the most holy Lord put in a bog?

"Aye. The world began in such a place! And you'll see it. The roots of it all. Holy ground."

"Holy ground," she repeated and then said to herself, *perhaps the ruins of an ancient cathedral?* She could not imagine how, but that was the point of miracles, wasn't it? To bring into being that which the simple, humble mind of man could not imagine. The Southern ranges of Germania sprouted a few small towns but certainly there had never been sufficient population this far into the wilds to sustain a cathedral! Even St. Cyprian's was small by any standard, and it was the largest building in the village.

She trusted Karel. He was her friar. He was her spiritual adviser. He was the guardian of her soul. No doubt that she would go to holy war for him. Of course, she would! She was now as good as any nun in any order ...*but my order is that of St. Drogo-Erasmus*, she thought proudly. It may be different than how nunneries worked in Cologne, but that didn't matter anymore. *The rest of the world could be dead from the plague, as far as we know. What does it matter what the rest of the world thinks? We are saving our village.* She immediately blushed at the rebellious thoughts that were crossing her mind. She had been raised to be quiet and demure, lessons which her parents had, at times, beaten into her:

Don't talk out of turn.
Young women don't have opinions.
Ladies are to be agreeable.

"Holy sister, you are flushed. Need I slow down? I'm sorry, I always forget that I set such a pace." Karel's voice was so kind.

"Yes, if we could stroll a bit more slowly, I think that would help."

"Of course, my dearest."

She was relieved that he didn't pursue her thoughts, for she was afraid he would find them blasphemous. More than anything, she wanted to be worthy in his eyes. Worthy of his miracles. Worthy of his protection. Worthy of his admiration.

Adelaide knew the day was beautiful. The hills were magnificent, framed by the mountains behind them. The tinge of fall was teasing the air. Her brother Bernard wholeheartedly enjoyed days such as these as a gift from God, but such gifts were not meant for women to enjoy. For Adelaide, enjoyment must be balanced with atonement, lest she stray into sin.

She walked alongside Karel in silence, contemplating how different he was from her own brother. The church had not seen fit to elevate this man to the priesthood, which puzzled her. While her brother defied their parents, defied convention, he even seemed to defy the orders of the church itself; to Adelaide, this quiet man beside her seemed to be full of the Holy Spirit. He followed the holy orders exactingly. Exultation was in his every step. She could feel the energy emanating from him as they made their way in silence. Why could Bernard not be more like this Karel Tuckerschade walking alongside her? Bernard was so quarrelsome, so critical since he had come to this little town. And so uninspired at the pulpit.

At last Karel's pace became very slow. "Soon, we will find the remnants of the blessed wall. Come, follow me. You must step in my footprints, for the ground can become dangerous here in the bog."

Adelaide felt a blush of fear, but then reminded herself that Friar Tuckerschade was purely good and would let no harm come to her. "This has been quite the walk!" She breathed heavily. "Tell me, why does God keep this treasure in a bog?"

He stopped and turned to look at her. "Ah! It is in the high fen to keep it safe. Only the worthy may approach, and God does not make the way easy, does He?" He smiled knowingly at her.

She blushed. "No. He does not."

"Not for His chosen ones. They must prove their worth." He turned back to the path. "We have come the long way around so that I can show you this. The approach from the near side of the village is… well, 'tis far more dangerous. Frightening, you would call it. Unnerving. But from this side, with me, you'll be safe. And here, step carefully, holy sister, here, when we crest this little rise, you will see the wall."

She clambered behind him, cursing her skirts. And suddenly the land slowly fell away revealing the high fen, his *Hohes Venn*, with sparse, short trees and bushes here and there; the land dotted with flowers, but mostly rock and dusty earth.

"Isn't it beautiful?" He had a broad smile on his face.

She looked around trying to spot the beautiful thing he was pointing out to her. "Um, where is the wall?"

"Oh, let me show you." He took her hand again and helped her along the path until they came to a low, wide, remnant of an ancient wall. It might have been thirty feet long and it made no corner. It was just a straight collection of huge blocks of stone. It looked out of sync here, and to Adelaide's view like there was no human hand that could have crafted it. The stones were larger than any she knew of in the cathedrals of Cologne and where they met, it was as though they had been cut with the thinnest, sharpest blade imaginable. It was an impossibility. She stared.

Karel interrupted her thoughts. "You see here, fair Adelaide, the lovely liverwort that grows by the wall?"

She pulled her attention away from the stone to the delicate flower. "Liverwort? What a horrible name for such a beautiful and delicate flower! In Cologne we call such flowers anemones, but they don't grow as heartily as they do here."

"They are the same. Different varieties bloom at different times. 'Tis August and this variety blooms up here in the hills for one last time before the snows come."

Adelaide looked over the wild field behind the low scrap of wall, searching for something complimentary to say. "It's like the angels have dropped purple dye, splattering it across the hillside. It's so lovely."

Karel seemed suddenly nervous, looking as though he couldn't quite form his words. She looked at him curiously.

Then, as though he could not contain himself, he blurted out, "The anemone, as you call it, my Lady Adelaide, holy sister, is like unto you." The moment was suddenly awkward between them, then he said, "For it modestly bends in the wind, yielding to the breezes sent by the angels."

Adelaide exhaled deeply and bowed her head. "I thank you for such a generous compliment, as I strive for modesty in all things. But if this flower were like me, it would indeed be called the liverwort, for I am unworthy. Until I came to you, in this whole world I had no place. Not like the flower at all, but rather like that spider there. You see it, hiding in the crack between the stones, peering out, afraid to be seen in the sunshine, lurking in the shadows." She bit her lip.

Karel bent down on a knee and examined the spider, which backed up out of the sunlight to hide in the darkness of the crack in the wall. "I find spiders to be fascinating creatures," he pondered as he rubbed his chin. "They are industrious, hardworking, self-reliant, and," Karel shouted as he slapped his neck to kill a biting insect, "they help clear out the devil's own dratted mischief!" He pulled his hand away and looked at the small spot of blood smeared there, a mixture of the insect's and his own. "Pesky servants of the dark these biters are." He turned back to Adelaide. "So, Lady Adelaide, the spider is a most noble creature of God's creation, and if you resemble that humble servant, then you are also worthy in His eyes. You certainly are worthy in mine."

Adelaide could not stop the smile on her face. Gerung's final wish, his final words to her were: *Be happy, Adelaide. I wish that you might find a way to be happy*. Well then, he would be smiling down on her from his perch in purgatory now, because she had never felt so happy in her life.

Karel picked a flower for her and handed it to her. "You could put it in your hair, then you and the flower would be like sisters."

Adelaide felt her heart skip a beat. "I would be afraid to break it, it's so fragile."

"Here, let me help you then," he said as he gently wove the stem of the flower through her hair. He then picked another and another, weaving them into a crown. "There. Now you look like God's creation indeed."

She slid her hand into his again. If it were sin to feel thus, she would do any amount of atonement to feel this way.

"Now I want to show you the most glorious mystery remaining on earth. Here you must tread carefully, for no regular man has been allowed to see this. Only me, for I am the guardian. But you must touch nothing, do you understand? Nothing, for 'tis a peril to do so."

She nodded her head solemnly.

He led her on a path that was tricky to navigate and eventually they came to stand in the sight of a few scrawly trees, twisted and stunted, bearing small ugly green fruit.

"It's… it's an apple tree?"

He smiled broadly. "'Tis *the* apple tree!"

"*The* apple tree," she repeated but had no idea what he was talking about.

"Oh, don't you see it, Adelaide! Don't you know where you are?" He took both her hands in his and looked deeply into her eyes. "I have brought you to the last remnant of the Garden of Eden. This is all that stands after the flood of Noah destroyed the world. The great wall now reduced to the bitter pieces that you saw. The garden, hidden away and now disguised as a high fen, a bog, because of the downfall of man. And those trees… they are descended from the tree of knowledge! Adelaide, you are standing on holy ground."

Adelaide looked around her in amazement. "How do you know this to be true?"

"Because to touch the tree is to touch death. Because with the rainbow, the Lord promised to never send another flood to destroy mankind. But he did not promise to allow the wickedness of humanity to reign unchecked. And so, he has sent his plague to punish the sinners. But you and I stand here by the tree of knowledge, untouched by the sickness, we stand here as did Adam and Eve, for the Almighty does forgive! And like the cherubim, he has assigned a new guardian: me. And as my Eve, a holy sister of my church, you are now made guardian with me. The Lord has revealed this to me." He gestured with his arm to the Garden.

Adelaide's heart was beating wildly. "Of course, the Blessed Garden would endure, but given the sin of Eve, it would diminish over the eons since time began."

"But it would endure nevertheless, because all that is made by the Holy Hand endures in some fashion." Karel looked as though light was emanating from him, his face filled with excitement and conviction.

"And God has chosen us? Are we to be the new Adam and Eve?"

"Aye, that is what I believe. But we will be wiser, for we will not eat of the forbidden fruit. We will remain ignorant of the knowledge destined for the angels. And we will remain guardians, with one another, here, in our Eden."

She fell to her knees at his feet and kissed his hand. Her heart was racing now.

He smiled at her. "The Almighty chose me some time ago to find this treasure. He entrusted me with His secret garden. And then, He brought me you. Like He made Eve from Adam's rib, you have been made into a holy sister of my church. And now you, like I am, are a guardian. It is your destiny, my dearest Adelaide."

Through several breaths, she tried to calm her spirit, which felt like it was soaring with the clouds racing across the sky. "I have never felt worthy."

"You have never been so worthy, my Eve." He bent his lips to meet hers.

Adelaide felt elated. All of her suffering, her fasting, her flagellation, and now she had been taken to the Garden of Eden. Earthly rewards that were beyond anything she ever could have imagined. She had been the daughter of a duke. Third cousin to the king. Niece of a bishop. Widow of the wealthiest merchant in Cologne. But none of that could ever hold any meaning now. Now she was to be the mother of a new mankind. A post-plague mankind. It was her destiny to help rebuild humanity.

Karel led her to a small shelter he had constructed so that he could gaze at the wonder of the tree of knowledge and its forbidden fruit. They sat for a while but soon they sought one another out in their excitement at being anointed guardians. Adelaide tasted the flesh of passion, only lightly punctuated by her healing wounds. She quickly ceased to think of right or wrong, for nothing they did now could be anything but blessed. They had been chosen.

Later, as they lay in one another's arms and Adelaide felt more happiness than she had ever known, the little ring of that Elizabeth woman crossed her mind. Surely, as the mother of a new Christian race she should not be the holder of a Jewish ring. She resolved to give it to the first woman she met on the morrow.

Chapter 33

Nylah

Nylah walked into their Command Central tent and got herself a cup of coffee. While the food might be stored and prepared in the facilities tent, they always seemed to gravitate to Command Central to eat, drink, talk, and plan. The coffee pot lived here, as did the tea kettle. Trevor and Everly were already there, hot mugs in hand, but each drinking something different.

"Hey Dr. T, how was the groveling from Brandenburg? Must've been nice to have a president kneel to you." Nylah laughed and pictured having that kind of experience. She'd never met a president of anything, including the student body at her former high school.

Trevor pulled a face. "Brief. Not that exciting. I think once he realized old 'Silver Hair' wasn't there, then he thought he could just give me a punch in the arm and say the German equivalent of 'Bollocks, old boy!' and go about his merry business."

"So, what did you do?" Nylah asked. "That doesn't sound like any kind of powerful apology to me."

Everly stopped what she was doing, listening in.

Trevor looked at them and shrugged. "I asked to see the cross and where it was displayed. And I learned that the thieves did make off with one of our treasures—that beautiful Jewish wedding band. Isn't that tragic?"

"No!" Everly's face went pale. "Oh no."

Nylah asked, "And the gems?"

"And did they get Father B's ring?" Everly still looked stricken.

"No and no. All safe. I would never let the priest's ring be far from his remains anyway. I told the president that I decided to improve upon their security measures."

Everly snorted. "I bet they took that well."

"They actually didn't much appreciate me amending their 'enhanced safety protocol' that he assured me was secure, but the damage is done, innit? I mean, they've got no standing to argue with me after such a colossal bungle, now do they? Not only was there a successful theft of their museum pieces," then he corrected himself, "*our* museum pieces, but the only reason our cross wasn't pinched as well was because a faculty member'd already nicked it! I mean, he *twoced an artifact*."

"Twoced? What's that?" Nylah asked, confused.

"Taken Without Owner's Consent."

"Oh right, yeah, dinner party entertainment. Right." Nylah said.

"Anyway, it's safe now. No more worries. Enough said."

Everly looked at Trevor. "And… where is it?"

"Enough said."

Everly raised her eyebrows and looked at Nylah. "Right then. Moving along on our agenda for today, we have the excavations of what we're calling 'Pit C' on the schedule." Everly pointed to the area on their site map.

Nylah giggled. "Yeah, Heidi and Hannah were bussin' yesterday with that tiny bulldozer thing you have."

"They do seem to like driving the Bobcat," Everly answered with a smile. "And with them behind the controls, no thorned berry bushes stand a chance! I'm sure those shrubs were quaking in their roots!"

Nylah snickered and wondered what they would find in that third pit. She was about tapped out from dealing with legions of the dead. Some days she was numb to all the bodies and others she found it bothered her. A lot, if she were being honest with herself. She felt a hot patch on her pants instantly burn and then quickly start to turn cool. "Oh damnit!" she said, realizing that she'd just spilled her coffee on her lap.

"Just one of many dirt stains from today, I'm sure, Nylah," Trevor said.

"It's not the stain. It's the loss of coffee. This is precious stuff!" She held up her cup dramatically and accidentally sent another tide of hot coffee over the edge. "Oh, shit!"

"Language, Nylah," Everly said.

Nylah tried to wipe the spilled coffee off her pants with a tissue. "What did all these dead people do when they spilled their coffee? How did they curse back then? Oh, they probably didn't have coffee."

"That alone would be enough to curse about in my book!" Everly gave her a wink and gestured with her cup without spilling a drop. "They drank this rather disgusting thing called barley tea. And some of the poorer folk might stew local herbs, but tea as we know it was not a thing for the folk of this village. Nor were potatoes actually. Potatoes weren't brought to Europe until the sixteenth century."

"Wow! Life without coffee or potatoes. Fuck that!" Nylah said.

"Language!" Everly repeated, but she laughed as she said it. "You know, that reminds me… I have a book that discusses cursing and blasphemy in the Middle Ages."

"Of course, she has a book on that. She's got a book on everything!" Trevor said, clearly impressed.

"Wait a sec and let me look it up." Everly tapped away on her tablet, hunting through her digital library. "It's here… someplace." She briefly looked up at Nylah, who was still wiping her pantleg. "You okay? That didn't burn you, did it?"

Nylah shrugged. "No one to sue way out here anyway."

"Good, because first aid is not my strong suit."

"Neither is empathy," Trevor whispered.

Everly laughed at him. "Good one!" She turned to Nylah. "Archeology is an entire profession of discomfort. Probably why we think it's so cool to dig up evidence of things like young women being buried with their favorite disciplines in hand and hair shirts on their backs!" She searched in her tablet and then announced, "Got it! These examples are a bit later than our dig, as they come from about fifteen-hundred, and it's obviously history from Spain, but here's an entry about one Diego Mexias, a cleric nonetheless, who said, and I quote, 'that there is nothing except being born and dying, and having a nice girlfriend, and plenty to eat'."

"Man of faith!" Trevor called out.

"Clerics had girlfriends?" Nylah pulled a face at this news. "And how is that a curse?"

"Oh, back then, speaking against the common doctrine was equivalent to cursing, but yes, this section is more about blasphemy."

Trevor came over with the coffee pot and topped off Nylah's prematurely emptied mug and then poured more for Everly. "Don't know how you drink this stuff!" he said as he made a face. "Truth is, these people were probably a lot like people today. You see all that crap in the news about who's shagging who, how to know if your lover's cheating on you. I bet they did all that back then, too. And I bet it was easier without all the cameras and people constantly taking videos on their phones, drones buzzing overhead watching your every move. Just look at the wilderness around us. Back then, you could sneak off. I bet they got away with a lot, even those who were pledged to the church."

Everly nodded. "There's a lot of evidence of materialism, even way back then. Here's another random guy, Pedro Gomez el Chamorro, vowed to God there was no soul." Everly read from her tablet. "And the cause of his metaphysical despondency? The weather. He was tired of the cold."

Nylah wrinkled her nose. "He'd probably love global warming then."

Trevor nodded. "I bet they would, actually, I mean it was awfully cold back then. No central heating." He chuckled at his joke. "It's important to remember there's a difference between religion of the elites and the everyday people. The elites had reputations to uphold. They filled the upper echelons of the church you know: it wasn't just anybody in the ranks of bishops and cardinals. Oh no! They were latter born, educated, extra sons that the nobility didn't know quite what to do with. So, they threw 'em into the church." After taking a sip of his own cup of tea, he added, "And that's probably why they thought that having a nice girlfriend was one of the more important things in life. It wasn't like they got to choose their profession. So, my guess is that they rebelled, mostly in little ways, but for some, undoubtedly, in big ways too."

Everly peered at Trevor. "I once knew a really intelligent, very creative soul who was forced into his profession by his parents. Nice guy. So that happens, Nylah. Even today."

Nylah wondered why in the world Trevor looked a little bit pink-cheeked in response?

Trevor raised his mug and in a quiet voice said, "Cheers," and nodded, giving Everly a little smile. Then turning to Nylah, he added, "The peasants actually had more freedom in what they believed, mostly because no one paid them any attention or ever listened to them. And there's evidence of cursing during gambling or playing at games, things like bowls or pelota, and people would say all kinds of blasphemous things in jest."

Nylah chuffed. "Then that hasn't changed much. Now it's at video games, sporting events, teachers behind their backs…"

"Traffic!" Everly added.

"One's parents… behind their backs," Trevor added. "And, if I were being fair, I would guess also at one's children, also behind their backs. Although that's not from any kind of firsthand experience."

"Oh yeah, I'm sure my mom sounds like a sailor when she's frustrated with me!" Nylah said. "In fact, I've heard her when she's thought she's hung up the phone, but hasn't." They all laughed and then sat quietly for a few moments, each lost in thought.

Trevor broke the silence. "So often we think that agnosticism is a modern invention, but really if you look at the evidence, back in the day, a fair number of people were agnostic, or at least skeptical. But they had to play along, or they'd be persecuted by the church. There wasn't any kind of option to be atheist, but people were doubtful, that much is clear."

"Well, yeah. I'd be instantly skeptical if I was told to use that crazy-ass discipline thing!" Nylah couldn't believe what they had told her about some of the more unique religious practices of the day.

Trevor laughed. "Me too, Nylah. Me too." He sipped his tea. "I remember reading that a man, his name is on the tip of my tongue… let's see, oh yes! It was Anton! A Jewish shoemaker by trade, Anton… Anton… oh yes, Tapiazo. He was forced to convert or he'd be tortured and murdered."

"Christian values," Nylah said with disgust.

"Yes, actually, back then, those were Christian values. It's not a time that Christianity has much to brag about itself, does it? Our poor Anton complained that in the synagogue they used to sit on benches and wear their hoods, but in the church they knelt on their knees and then stood, lots of times, over and over again. He referred to worshipping as a Christian as playing at 'bobbing up and down'."

Everly reached for a bottle of flavored coffee sweetener. "Yes, I remember studying the Inquisition at Soria. The converted Jews were comparing their new religion to the old one and finding the new one to pale a bit by comparison."

"You studied the Inquisition at Soria?" Trevor looked impressed.

Everly blushed slightly.

Nylah thought that the geekiness of these two was unparalleled in the entire universe.

"Yeah. It was an essential part of mastering medieval culture." Everly smiled at Trevor for a moment and then turned back to Nylah. "I also remember a woman, just a peasant farmer, but her name was Juana Perez. She lived in the late fourteen hundreds. I was always touched that even that early, even in that dim era, here was this really enlightened woman. She said the good Jew would be saved, as well as the good Moor, in his law, for why else had God made them? Amazing, isn't it? Even the simple people had wisdom, and sometimes much more so than those with power in the church. I wouldn't be surprised if it was a common belief at the time, among those who were more educated and enlightened."

"Just curious, Everly… why did ole' Juana stick with you so?" Trevor asked.

Everly looked uncomfortable. "Oh, um, well." She stammered a bit and then admitted, "I wrote a song about her."

"No kidding. You a musician? On top of all your other talents?"

Everly was dismissive. "I played a little guitar at the time. You know, a very limited five-note range with my voice, but I was young and inspired by the philosophical wisdom of simple people who had no education at all—and yet they saw something that rings with me as a truth even today, half a millennium later."

Nylah noticed that Dr. T had a smile on his face.

"You're just full of surprises. We'd like to hear you sing sometime. No? Well, we'll see then, won't we?" He smiled and nodded. "So, just like today, Nylah, the people of these times were complex. We can't paint them into a corner. A very select group had a massive amount of power over daily life and they controlled much of what the masses thought and believed. Remember, there was no social media. There was no news. The elite could write letters but the peasants, the poor, and even much of the merchant class just had Sunday gossip. And if the priests at the church decided to say a few words, what we would call a sermon today, then that was about all the information the people had."

Everly nodded. "Yeah, Nylah, these people, the amount of information they consumed in a lifetime was about the same as you would read in a Sunday edition of the New York Times."

Nylah's eyes widened. "Whoa, such narrow lives."

Trevor chuckled. "I dunno if *they* felt they were narrow. I mean, you don't know what you don't know, right? So, if you think you're busy or if you think your life is full, then it is. And I would guess that most of their time was filled with finding enough food to eat and staying alive. For men, not getting conscripted into someone else's holy war could take up some time and energy. So, probably most of them didn't have the chance for, let's call it 'personal reflection'."

"Poor Friar B!" Nylah said, feeling sympathy for their resident dead team member.

"Don't let Trevor hear you demote the skull!"

"For sure and certain," Trevor said, picking up Father B with what Nylah could only assume was admiration and respect. "While today priests, preachers, fathers, friars—in the Catholic church, well, they're all the same thing basically; that was not true in the Middle Ages. There was a much stiffer hierarchy back then and clergy swore an oath to obey their superiors, but not everyone's superiors: the superiors of your own order. It could get really complicated. And clergy were strongly tied to their monastic community, like the Benedictines, or to a religious order, like the Dominicans. Those were the folks who vowed to be poor and gave all they had to their Order or abbot or prior. You've heard of St. Francis of Assisi?"

"Yeah, the dude who loved animals. He was like the founder of the green party, right?" Nylah said.

"Not quite, but, sure, close enough. Let's go with erstwhile patron saint," Trevor said. "And who knows? Maybe you're right, in a mystical sense. St. Francis is credited with the idea that men of the cloth needed to go out among the people, to preach and to pray. They educated the people, in a manner of speaking, and they served the sick. They were traveling preachers."

"Oh, so like we talked about how Friar Tuck traveled around with Robin Hood."

"Who might never have existed. That was kinda 'around the fireside' story-time stuff," Everly said.

"But these people, these people in Pit C did exist. And in the next day or two we'll release another legion of the dead." Nylah shuddered. "It's a wonder I can sleep at all."

◆━◆━◆

Two evenings later, the dig in Pit C had started to reveal its secrets. A veritable mountain of archeological finds, and much to Nylah's relief, not a bone among them. Wearing gloves and working carefully with a soft cloth, Nylah worked in the specimen tent alongside Everly, Trevor, and Gunther, who was staying late with them this evening after the students had been bussed back to their local accommodations.

"Careful with that," Everly advised her. "I know it's seven hundred years old but it could still have a sharp spot."

Nylah looked up. "Ev, why would they have the Grim Reaper's big old badass blade?"

"It's a scythe. They would have used it for harvesting."

"And in war, if they got involved in such," Trevor added. He looked up thoughtfully, "But what we know from the history of the day is that little mountain towns like this were so far away from the action, it's unlikely that blade ever saw human blood. They rarely got conscripted by the local nobles, who were poorly organized at the time. So, follow Everly's advice and don't make your blood the first human blood to stain that old blade." He gave her a nod.

"Yes, Dr. T. I've gotten just about all the muck off this one anyway." Since it didn't fit in any kind of specimen box, she set it aside for the mass photography session that would be held the next day when the light was better and picked up another tool covered in dirt and clay from the bins. "Damn, this one's heavy." She sat down and started working carefully with the soft brush, just like Everly had shown her. "I mean I'm glad to be working on this and not be surrounded by a sea of bodies."

"Right! No bodies in Pit C, whatsoever!" Trevor said.

"What is this thing anyway?" Nylah asked.

Trevor put down his artifact and came over to examine what she was working on. "Nylah, I believe you are holding a swage. They were used to head bolts or swage large items."

She looked at Dr. T. "I have no idea what you just said."

Everly sighed. "It's a blacksmith's tool. That's how they would make their mark or set the template for other tools they were making. Like for making a bolt or a screw."

Nylah chewed her lip for a moment in thought and then asked, "Why's all this stuff look like it could be in a garage sale?"

Resuming his seat, Trevor asked, "A what? Do people in America sell their garages? I mean, how would you disconnect a garage from your house?"

"*Ga-ridj*?" Nylah asked. "Even when you aren't talking in tech terms, man, Dr. T, you can be hard to understand."

Everly laughed. "But don't stop, it's cute."

Nylah noticed that Trevor blushed and looked away, bending down over the object he was cleaning.

Everly said, "Trevor, people have yard sales, sometimes called tag sales or garage sales, where they sell their old used junk to other people, who probably don't really need it, but do like to feel as though they're getting a deal. It's kind of a big thing in both the US and Canada."

"Oh! We call those 'car boot sales'. People load up the boots of their vehicles with possibly sellable junk and go out to a rented field with their hopes high. You'll have a hundred cars all set up like little Gypsy tents, boots to the wind. All independent little shops, as temporary as a dandelion seed blowing in the breeze."

Everly stared at Trevor and then shook her head and refocused on her task. "I don't think anyone expected to find such a trove of grave goods. And in such amazing condition. The whole pit. The whole pit is full of tools and furniture and household goods. It's an amazing archeological discovery."

"Right, being packed in clay for seven hundred years hasn't done nearly the damage I would have expected. Some of these tools, particularly the blacksmith tools, you might use today," Trevor said. "Chisels. Hammers. Grinders. That wheeled barrow! But my favorite," Trevor said with some excitement, "is the clay pot with the lid! Can you believe it? So many of them, shattered in the pit. But one, just one, made it through all time intact. Other than you, Father B," he nodded towards the skull that was always with them, as though he were a consulting teammate, "that's the most important thing we've found."

Nylah looked up in surprise. "Not the cross? The golden cross? The clay pot is more important than the gems?"

Trevor shrugged. "There're a lot of artifacts like those already in museums. We know they had such treasures, particularly in the cities and where there were concentrations of wealth. But for a small village like this one to have had lids on pots? Certainly, that was for food storage. What we know of the time is that most people used baskets, not that they'd be very good when it came to keeping mice out."

"Yeah, right, but we know these people had marmots, and they would need a hell of a lot more than a basket when it came to warding off a marmot!" Nylah said. "They've got big, nasty teeth!" She put up two fingers to mimic the large incisors.

Trevor shuddered. "I don't want to talk about marmots. Beastly things. Like giant, fuzzy rats. Mad, they are, for chomping down on your hat! But it's a new discovery for this era and this kind of a town to have had sealed jars. So many of them too, from the numbers of the shards. Unusually advanced."

Nylah sighed deeply. "It's almost Egyptian, you know."

Gunther, who had been quiet up until now listening to their banter as he worked, engrossed in cleaning his artifacts, looked up at Nylah. "What do you mean?"

Nylah looked at her three companions, all so much older than herself. Sometimes she felt stupid when she made her observations, but the three of them weren't like old teachers. Ev was very much like an older sister and Trevor and Gunther really felt like friends, too. Sure, they laughed at some of her ideas, like the chariot parking lot or the cannon, but it was in a teasing way, a lot like the kids at school. You knew they liked you when they gently teased you. You knew you were "in". She took a deep breath and plunged ahead. "Well, everyone knows that in the Egyptian tombs, they gave you everything you needed for the afterlife, right? I mean, that's like in how many movies? It wasn't just gold; it was everyday stuff. Super nice everyday stuff, to be sure, but I saw a special with my mom where they had chariots and pots with lids and tools and plates and just everything you'd need to set up house. For, like, you know, eternity. And this stuff we're cleaning up? This ain't trash."

"Oh my god." Everly looked pale and turned her head towards Trevor.

"So right!" Trevor answered her. He turned to Gunther. "We need to do a comparative assessment of all the tools we found beneath the bodies in Pit A against all the tools found in Pit C."

Gunther, who also looked very serious at the moment, said, "I have a colleague in Switzerland who wrote me two days ago about wanting to get her doctoral students involved. I will write her back tomorrow. Once we get these tools photographed and documented, the comparisons should be easy." He turned to Nylah. "Good job, Nylah!"

"Thaaaanks," Nylah said, drawing out the word. "But can somebody explain to me what the heck we're talking about? Go ahead, Dr. T. I can see that you're turning into a chipmunk again, you're getting so excited."

"Right. I guess I do that, don't I?" Trevor said as he scratched his head and wiggled with energy. "Nylah, in a typical dig you find only broken tools, because people have thrown them away. Nobody throws away perfectly good tools. I mean, why would they?"

"Why would they indeed?" Gunther asked, putting his index finger to his nose and pointing at Trevor, mimicking what Trevor himself did all the time.

Everly picked up the thought. "Yeah, in the pit where we found good old Father B, below those bodies was what honestly looked like trash. Even by their standards. Everything we found made sense. The shape it was in didn't surprise us—we were just stunned and happy to find their trash pit which would give us an indication of the kinds of tools and everyday things they had. But finding intact goods, everything intact, in Pit C just turns the whole dig on its head."

"What do you mean?" Nylah asked. "How so?"

Everly answered, "So there's trash and there's grave goods. Trash is the broken stuff people dispose of. From what we can tell, Pit A was a trash dump until the plague and the need to put the bodies someplace. I suppose their graveyard couldn't accommodate the influx, so they put their dead in the pit already dug and already in use. Not glamorous, but expedient. Bodies on trash: we can reason that out. But grave goods are perfectly good and useable things meant to honor the dead and help them in the afterlife. But there were no bodies there at all."

"Right," Trevor said, "it was just a jumbled-up car boot sale, but with no cars."

Gunther grunted and said, "Other than religious icons, people of the Middle Ages did not bury their dead with grave goods."

Trevor added, "And they only buried their dead higgledy-piggledy style in plague times. Otherwise, even in mass graves, like after a war, people were carefully laid out, usually in coffins, all in tightly packed rows."

Nylah went back to the tool currently in her hand and started carefully removing the ages of caked-on dirt. "This haul reminds me of

Pirates of the Caribbean." She noticed the three adults all stopping and staring at her once again. She sighed. "Surely, you've seen those movies? No?" She crossed her arms and leaned back in her chair. "I bet you've all seen every Indiana Jones movie ever made. I bet you all own copies." She could tell from their guilty expressions that she was right. "So, in the Pirates movie, they have to lighten their ship, and in a panic, they dump everything overboard, including the rum." She added with a laugh, "Now that I've *had* German rum, I get what a tragedy it was to throw the rum overboard!"

"Say more…" Trevor's voice came across as breathy.

Nylah looked up at the top of the tent. "Well, I mean, it's like people were panicking and they just threw everything overboard they could find."

"But they were on land," Gunther said.

"Right. So, in a panic they hauled everything they could get their hands on in town and threw it in a pit, even the good stuff, like the rum." Nylah shrugged, a smile on her face as she imagined the mass dumping happening on dry land. "And we did find the barrel too! People were just as crazy back then as they are today."

"But why would they do that? What would make them throw away a whole town's worth of perfectly good… well, everything?" Everly asked.

Trevor bit his lip. "People believed in curses back then, didn't they?"

"They wanted to get rid of it. That is certain." Gunther nodded. "They must be very frightened to 'throw everything overboard', as Nylah said."

"Why didn't they just burn it?" Nylah asked. "That's what they do in the old movies. They burn everything they want to make disappear."

Trevor nodded. "Well, that's partly because the movies need to have a good visual, right? Something exciting for the audience! But starting a fire took serious resources back in the fourteenth century. I would guess they were exhausted after pitching that huge haul into the pit, as that would be nearly the Herculean task as it has been for us to pull it all back out again!"

"You know what I like best about this dig?" Nylah asked as they all became quiet and looked at her. "It's all a big mystery. Something weird happened here. And bad. I mean weirder and worse than the plague."

"What could be weirder and worse than the plague?" Everly asked.

"I don't know, team," Trevor said, "but we're going to figure it out." He nodded at Father B. "Get ready for a long night!"

Chapter 34

Father Bernard Trōst
February 1351

Jezzie knocked on the door of the manse of St. Cyprian's, calling out, "Father Bernard! Father Bernard? Are ye here?"

Bernard came around the side of the building, wrapped up tightly in his cloak to fend off the extremely cold weather of the day. "Hello? Can I help you? Oh, Jezzie, it's you." He looked at her curiously. "Services are Wednesday, Saturday and Sunday. Have you come to confess your sins?" The joking tone in his voice made it clear that he had no such expectations. Having been friends for the past year, he knew her too well for that.

Jezzie gave a hearty laugh. "Ye folk of the priesthood, you're all the same! Nah! I haven't sinned in two weeks. No one around here I'd want to sin with!" She shivered. "It's too cold for sin, anyway. Nah, but the butcher's given me work—honest work." She gave him an exaggerated wink. "So's I'm making deliveries for her, and that makes for bread in me basket too. I've brought ye your order, so unless these are the wrong cuts of meat, then I've got nothing to atone for."

Bernard laughed and took the delivery from Jezzie. "I thank you kindly and I'm happy to hear that you have honest work. Does this mean you'll be changing your profession now that the butcher and baker both hire you?" He gave her a friendly smile. "It is written that Mary Magdalene left the profession and became a favorite of Jesus."

"Oh, don't get your hopes up too high, now there, Father! There's good money to be made, I can travel if I want, once the spring comes and if this dratted plague goes away." Then she added, "Please Lord!" as she looked at the heavens. "Particularly if there's an army about, the work is easy and mostly 'tis not too unpleasant." She looked up at the sky again, adding, "Please Lord!" With a chortle, she continued, "…unlike handling slabs of raw meat that will get smelly if you don't cook them up. And there's no Jesus to tempt me to change my ways." She gave him a laugh and a little twirl. She cackled and looked him up and down. "What is you wearing? I never seen a cloak quite like that!"

"Oh this. It's a gift from my uncle in Bonn from when I first moved here. It is quite unique. It's called a *Seehundfell* cloak. It comes from the Sea Dog, what the English call a seal."

Jezzie touched it, oohing and ahh-ing over how unusual it was. "Seal skin? As a cloak?"

"My uncle is sure I'm going to die by freezing, up here in the mountains. Seals live in ice water, and cloaks made from their skin are nearly indestructible. It's very special to me."

"And is it warm, like he thought it would be? So, you won't die of freezing?"

"Yes, indeed!" Bernard laughed. Giving her a wink, he added, "It is so warm that I think I wish to be wrapped in it when I'm laid to rest so that I'll be cozy for eternity!" He looked at her, bundled in many layers of well-worn clothes. "But you look cold and you're not wrapped in seal skin. Would you like to come into the manse? Would you like something to drink? I have some pressed apple juice or some hot tea perhaps?"

Jezzie looked suspicious. "Ye wouldn't be trying to save me soul, now, would ye?"

"My job is to save souls!" He pretended to be affronted. "But today, I'm just serving tea and not salvation. I was just about to have some and the water'll come hot before long." Bernard had no idea of how to turn Jezzie into a good Christian. Maybe that was hopeless. But bringing people into the light took time and gentle encouragement. And generally speaking, many pots of tea.

"I'll have some tea then. Thank ye, Father Bernard," she said, sounding most genteel and proper, even with her low Southlands accent. "Ye know, by all standards, ye are a very good man."

They settled at the kitchen table and Bernard put the kettle over the flames to heat the water. He brought out his pot and two cups. He blessed their mint tea, making the sign of the cross over it three times. Bernard was worried that she was about to point out how he ritually did things in threes. He didn't want to explain it. He couldn't help it. It lowered that feeling of anxiety that would arise in him. Completing things in threes helped keep the worry at bay. He had enough worry, so he would take any salve that he could. But she surprised him by not bringing that up at all. She seemed to take everyone's peculiarities in stride with no judgment whatsoever.

As he poured the tea from the pot, he said, "You have a kind spirit and…" he sighed, "well, you are who you are, Jezzie, with no apologies. I'll give you that. If you ever *do* want to come to Sunday service, you could confess and I could help absolve you of your sins, should you decide to commit them again, that is." He gave her a smile.

She leaned back, giving him a wry look. "Ye wouldn't be extracting free cheese and bread and the like from me, in order to forgive me, now, would ye? I don't work for the cheesemaker. Not yet."

Bernard blinked in astonishment. "Cheese and bread to pay for your sins?"

"It's the atonement. The atonement that keeps the likes of ye fed."

"Jezzie, when I give people atonements it is to bring them at one with God. At-one-ment. That's the meaning. Not to feed my belly. Atonements usually involve redressing the harm done to another or taking actions to better the community in order to repair the damage one might have done to others. Where does cheese come into that?" Bernard was baffled at her suggestion, feeling a bit horrified that it might be what she thought of him, particularly after saying he was a good man. There had been an undercurrent of suspicion against him from the moment he arrived, and while most of the villagers now came to St. Cyprian's, there was a group that would give him dirty looks in the street and he couldn't fathom why. Sometimes they would mutter as he passed them. He thought he heard one of them say 'warped' once, but that made no sense at all.

"Oh! Well, that's different then, isn't it? Although it would be easier to just pay a loaf of bread than to help ye in building yer latrines or digging your trash pits outside the city. That's hard work, it is!" She nodded emphatically as she took a sip of her tea.

"It is hard work. Work that all can be proud of." He raised his mug in toast. "And look at how it's impacted our community! Our streets are cleaner, smell better and although I know this isn't related, fewer people have had the stomach illness that gives them the runs! With the trash pits, we'll have fewer vermin in the village as well." He gave an involuntary shudder. Mice and rats greatly increased his anxieties.

"I've been attending St. Drogo's of late, and if you've sinned, everyone knows to come with foods the friar likes the most, and then they's can avoid being punished for their sinning. Of course," she added conspiratorially, "there be some that like it. I'm not one of that ilk but knowing that avoiding punishment is as easy as bringing along a basket of edibles makes it worth the risk to attend such an entertaining service." She chuckled. "Do you have any *kekse*, you know cookies, to go with this tea?"

"Uh, let me see." Bernard was confused. Unsettled. As he bustled about and found an odd version of rosemary shortbread biscuits, what the locals called *heidesand kekse,* that one of the parishioners had brought him, he asked, "What about the service at St. Drogo's is entertaining?" He put three of the little biscuits on a plate and set them down on the table, making the sign of the cross over them three times. "I always believed church was supposed to be inspiring. Instructive. Enlightening. Definitely not entertaining. Or are you just pulling my liripipe, as they say?" Having known known Jezzie for the past year, he understood that she was a woman who believed she possessed a dazzling sense of humor. *Stunning is probably closer to the right word*, he reasoned.

"I would say that nearly everything at old Drogo's is entertaining. You should go sometime, see what the old friar's up to. It's a little loud mays-be, but well worth the time spent." She let out a big sigh. "I'd open a mint tea shop of me own, if I had the chance. Probably wouldn't be a success though, because I'd drink all me wares!" She cackled again.

Bernard laughed with her. Jezzie might be a wanton woman, but she was also an excellent information source if you could get her talking. He made a mental note to list *heidesand kekse* and mint tea in his arsenal of information extraction tools. Undoubtedly, he would never have accomplished so many of his current civic improvement projects had he been without her counsel about who to speak to, who were the townspeople everyone listened to, who to seek out for the actual work. When he'd arrived in town, he'd had to bribe the people with wine, but after he got to know her, she made his job so much easier. And if she had insight into St. Drogo's, he was interested to know. His own sister attended there regularly but never spoke about it. If he were being truthful with himself, he rarely saw Adelaide anymore. She slept at the manse but she was off "doing the work of the church" most of the days. Much to his disappointment, she was still not interested in teaching the town's children.

He wondered what drew Adelaide so effectively to such a small, rustic kind of church? The sister he had always known would've found St. Cyprian's to be far too unimpressive for her willing attendance, much less St. Drogo-Erasmus, as its poor friar insisted it be called. But now she was different. She dressed more plainly. She'd even stopped wearing ribbons in her hair. That was unlike the Adelaide he'd always known. Ribbons had been her calling card. Her currency. The one material thing that she loved. But now she seemed to be in love with St. Drogo's itself. He had laughed at her prank that she was a nun of that church. She had not laughed and he suddenly wondered if she had been joking?

"Good Father," Jezzie said as she helped herself to a biscuit, "your problem is that you're *too* good. You're boring!"

Bernard slumped in his chair. "You aren't the first person to tell me that. I'm doing the Lord's work." He looked at Jezzie. "How can that be boring?"

She smiled at him indulgently. "You're too serious. Ye speak in this nice little voice and ye say such nice little things. And that's good and all, but it's not very entertaining. Now you take Friar Tuck: he thunders from the pulpit! He picks some phrases from the Bible, but then he'll find something in the town that's all a buggerin' him and he'll sermonize and rail on that. He sets the people straight. And as he preaches, the spirit of the Holy Lord do come to some and they move about and speak in His spirit. They be filled with the Holy Spirit. Those that move the most seem to get less of ole' Tuck's punishment."

"I don't understand. Everyone is filled with the Holy Spirit at mass."

She gave a chuckle. "Now there's the holy spirt and there's the Holy Spirit, you might say. As ole' Tuck calls to them to open themselves to the Lord, the people start to move and dance. They start speaking in tongues that no man can understand. It's all a big babble and they're all gyrating and writhing." She smiled. "An you know, if it's a slow day, I'm more than happy to get them started! Although it's actually more fun to hold back and just watch."

"What do you mean, get them started?" He looked at her, confusion all over his face.

"Oh, I'll start to roll me eyes up in the back of me head and then I'll start to sway and moan." She demonstrated for him as she spoke. "And then I'll get up and start moving about. I like to gyrate me hips and do a little wiggle. And I might throw in some growls and howls for fun."

"And what do the people think when you act thus?" Bernard could not picture the services at St. Drogo and knew he would have to erase what he was seeing right now from his mind, as it was most unseemly. He reached for his tea to calm himself.

Jezzie stopped her gyrations and turned towards Bernard, standing tall with pride and defiance. "Don't you know, they all follow me! Jobst, Wolf, and Heinrich. And Bechte, oh isn't she just holier-than-thou? But once she starts dancin' for the Holy Spirit, you'd think she was retired from me line of work! Else and Fye just the same. Those prudes by day who think they sit in judgement of everyone else in this town. But they follow me, and they wiggle and shimmy something fierce." She gave a full-throated laugh. "It be just like me ole' days dancing in a brothel in Franconia, 'cept now we all be wearing all our clothes. An that gets hot, let me tell you!"

Bernard's hand stopped a few inches before it would have reached his mouth. He looked at Jezzie over his cup. He recognized some of those names as belonging to the townspeople who shot him dirty looks and muttered at him in the street, but who, in reality, he hardly knew. "Please sit down. That is not seemly behavior in a house of worship. Or even in the manse."

"Oh, it be welcome over at ole' Drogo's. They'll be writhing on the floor, gyrating their hips in ways that rival any house of pleasure I've worked in. And they babble on in words that make no sense, and the good preacher insists it's the *Lord speaking through them*! Ha!" She slapped her knee.

"The Lord is speaking through them? While they speak in babble?"

She gave him a wink. "Now you're gettin' the picture! Nearly as enjoyable as confession." She nodded sagely. "Oh, I have a good old time with ole' Tuck over that!"

Bernard drew in a breath to speak, stopped for a moment, and then, pulling himself together, started again. "Confession is a holy sacrament. I have never thought of it as a 'good old time'. Through confession you are taking the first steps to atonement. Confession of all serious sins after baptism is necessary so that you can come into the light of the Lord. It is necessary so that you can be shriven of your sins."

"Like I said, Father Bernard, you're boring. The ole' friar, he hears your confession and if it ain't good enough, he pushes you for more."

"For more?"

"Right you are! Ole' Friar Tuck seems most keen to hear all about me adventures. Oh yes, he likes every word about every sin I engaged in in the Tolerance Houses I worked in from time to time, from the most mundane kiss to the seductive dances, to pleasin' the masters as they peak through the peepholes to watch others at the game who don't even know they're a part of a show!" She laughed again and took another biscuit. "An' it be funny to be telling him, 'cause sometime he don't know what I mean, and I has to explain it to him. He's right gripped by it. His imagination's as engaged as any man I seen, but the poor bloke done got no outlet, do he? Nah! All he can do is beat his frustrations out on his flock." She nodded sagely. "He likes his punishment, he does."

"His punishments?"

"Oh, aye. He promises to relieve you of your sin himself. He's your gateway to salvation, he says. And many of his group take him up on it, what with the welts and scars to attest to the kind of atonement he offers. At least it's fast. It's not like the atonement you offer, with your patience, reflection, and harmony. Service to the community. Nah, that's too much work for them. A good whipping and they're all set to go. Much faster that way."

Bernard winced, thinking of Adelaide. "This is the sacrament he offers them?"

"If ye are going to try to bring the Drogo faithful over to good ole' St. Cyprian's, ye'll need a cat-o-nine tails to beat the seven-deadly-sins disciplines he gives to his poor folk. Makes them himself he does. Before you came to town, a few people liked to follow him, whichever church he was in, here or there. Mostly they was those with no family. Those who seemed to feel lost and ole' Tuck, he seemed to give them a place. Like that young Wilhelm who dogs his feet. He's got nowhere to go, no one to love him, and so he gets something from Tuck. Maybe 'tis not a good something, but even a bad something's better in the eyes of some people than to have nothing at all."

Bernard started. He had come from a world of privilege and promise. The idea that a preacher would give out disciplines and encourage their use, he had heard of. But that the preacher would administer such punishments himself was not a part of the church as he knew it. "There are those who feel closer to God through suffering." *Those like Adelaide.* "But I would think it would be better to have nothing at all than to have the taste of such bitterness be what you know of the Lord's love and mercy."

"That would be because ye preach peace, patience, reflection, and harmony. The kind of atonement that brings ye and your soul together, or so that's what I've heard ye say. But that just not be Friar Tuck's style. He's an energetic man. He believes in energetic sin. And of course, energetic punishment that brings your body under his control." She leaned back and looked at Bernard more seriously now. "And Drogo's be growin'. It be growin' like I've never seen it. Suddenly, nearly a quarter of the town wants his style of sermons, an they're flooding his little church. He's giving sermons four times a week now. He's got crowds. Some of them are there for the entertainment, like me, but some's there for the serious worship."

"Why would anyone go if they are only going to be whipped when they confess?"

"Oh, that's an easy one! At St. Drogo's, ye don't have to change. Ye just has to pay. Whether that's bring some edibles as your indulgence or taking Tuck's lashes on yer back. It's so much easier to have the bill paid in full, and then ye can go out and sin again if ye want."

Bernard stared at Jezzie and could not speak.

"Take old Cuonrat, for example."

Bernard tried hard to picture the man but he could not. "I do not know him."

"I'm not surprised. He's devoted to Friar Tuck, he is. But mostly because Cuonrat's got a problem. He doesn't like his own wife and what he really wants is a piece of his brother's. A lot of pieces, if I'm being honest. But his brother doesn't like to share. The brother's wife has a similar problem in that she likes Cuonrat more than the brother she got stuck with, so the two of them, you know." Jezzie winked and made rude hand gestures to illustrate what Cuonrat and his sister-in-law were up to. "So Cuonrat doesn't want to change anything but to trade out his wife for another. He doesn't want to give up the sin: No! He wants more of it! If he came to confession with ye, he'd have to forsake the woman he wants and who wants him back. But by attending St. Drogo's, all it costs him is a brick of cheese now and then and maybe sometimes, a lashing." She shook her head and said conspiratorially, "Sometimes he takes the lashing because then he feels better for the suffering. He can forgive himself if he's suffered a little bit."

Bernard tried to speak a couple of times and finally managed to say, "And does he, does this friar beat you, Jezzie?"

"Oh, he's got better uses for me! Most of my sins, the ones he wants to hear about anyway, have already been forgiven long ago. After all, there's no Tolerance House in a village this size. But occasionally, to absolve meself of a more recent sin, I'm sometimes asked to help, well, you might say, *comfort* someone who might have had a bit too much punishment. Sometimes the friar gets carried away on poor Wilhelm. At those times, my atonement has been to pleasure the man while he's still in all the pain from his lashing."

Bernard blinked and thought of poor Wilhelm, so devoted to his friar. "Oh my! And when he is so beaten?"

She smiled at him. "I generally find the most important parts of him are still quite functional. He can move a little and I can do most of the work. And he finds it quite pleasurable. I believe he can tolerate the pleasure because of the pain. There are those folk who are into the pain first, and then the pleasure afterwards. An there are folk who can only allow themselves the pleasure because they've taken a dose of the pain. So, for them, it equals out, don't it? If they suffer, it gives them a little bit of room to sin. It's logical."

"It's not logical." Bernard felt frozen. He had never heard of this in any of his seminary schooling. He'd never seen dancing and babbling in a church service. He had no idea what to say. "People go to St. Drogo's for all of that rather than come to hear a message of love from St. Cyprian's?"

"Father Bernard, you're a good man. A righteous one. But ye aren't mesmerizing like the old Tuck. People in St. Cyprian's don't fall under your spell. But at Drogo's they tell him he's their master. Preaches about doomsday, he does, and how he'll protect them all. Not many paid him much mind 'til ye came to town. But with your preaching about learning and sharing and loving one another, I guess people just felt like they needed to choose a side. So, while more of the town now comes to St. Cyprian, there are also more making their way through the doors of St. Drogo's all the time. It's the entertainment factor. I'm sure of it." She looked at the plate. "Say, ye wouldn't happen to have any more of those little biscuits now, would ye?"

Chapter 35

Wilhelm
March 1351

Wilhelm picked up the eggs in the nest. "Oh! Friar Tuck will be happy about this! Even the duck laid an egg and that's a rare day, that is! The good friar does love his duck eggs." Wilhelm wondered what to do. Friar Tuck had said he was not to be disturbed and that confused Wilhelm. His master had never given him instructions like that before. At least not before *she* came along. The only time the friar didn't want to be disturbed was when he was speaking to God, and then he would walk high up in the mountains. "But now he's got a nun in his church and they seem to talk to God together." He walked over to the door and looked at the little house where Friar Karel Tuckerschade lived. "Why wouldn't God talk to an acolyte? It's not like I be still a doorman. I got raised up, I did."

He looked down at the eggs in his little basket and wondered if nuns outranked acolytes. "I suppose they must," he said dejectedly. He remembered the times he'd cooked up the eggs in different ways to please his master, and they'd enjoyed the eggs together. "I suppose I could cook them up for the three of us. There's five eggs here, there is, and she's a bitty little thing. Fasts three days a week." Then he got a brighter idea: "Maybe today's a fasting day and all the eggs'll be for Friar Tuck and me!" Even though he'd been told to not bother the friar, he decided the occasion of the eggs warranted interruption. "At least I could take a peek and make sure he's not talking to God right at the moment."

That idea lightened Wilhelm's spirits greatly. And if the nun did want to eat an egg, well, that still left two each for him and his friar. He made his way to the little manse and very quietly slipped in the back door so as not to disturb God if He was visiting. He set the egg basket down on a little table in the tiny room off the kitchen area, where he sometimes slept, and crept over to the door. *What good fortune!* he thought. *It's open a crack.* He put his eye to the crack, expecting to see the good friar on his knees in prayer, surrounded by light. *Maybe I'll see an angel.* The thought gave him a greater thrill than the five eggs had.

Wilhelm did not see what he had anticipated. There was the friar and he was there with that Lady Adelaide, now Holy Sister Adelaide. Wilhelm peered more closely. As Adelaide came around into his view he took in a sharp breath. "She's naked as the day she was born," he said, but so quietly even he didn't hear his voice. Her hair was unbound and her curls made a wild riot of her golden locks. Then she knelt before the friar and kissed his feet. She gathered her wild hair and pulled it over one shoulder. Wilhelm saw the friar raise his hand with the lash in it.

"Oh, he's going to deliver her of her sins." *I suppose even a nun can sin and repent.* He thought he should leave but he was suddenly curious. He cried out a good deal when his master saved his immortal soul from the perils of hell by whipping the sin out of him. He wondered what the lady would do. He put his eye back to the crack.

Friar Tuck raised the lash and brought it down on her back. She breathed in sharply but she didn't cry out. *That's funny. When he gives me the lash I'm facing away from him, but she's before him. I wonder if that's how ladies get their sins removed or if that's just special for her?* He had to admit, he was impressed at the stamina Adelaide showed. With each strike, she never let out a cry. A little moan perhaps but not a cry. *She's a lot tougher than I would have thought for such a little thing.*

Then a stranger thing happened. Friar Tuck threw off his robe and as Wilhelm watched he found himself staring hard. Now Friar Tuck was equally as bare as his supplicant. *Why that's... that's... that's the thing that Jezzie did to me. I liked that,* he remembered, as he looked down at his own crotch. He'd never figured out how to get Jezzie to do it again and when he'd asked her, she'd just laughed at him. He put his eye back to the crack. *It looks like the master likes it too.* Wilhelm noticed that Friar Tuck tried to lash Adelaide once or twice but it was half-hearted. He was moaning too much to focus on delivering atonement. *They look like they could use some help,* he thought but he wasn't about to go in and offer to lash them both. He found this most curious as it was not the same as his experience of being relieved of his sins. He'd secretly peeked in at other's lashings, which always looked a lot like his. This was new and different. He began to wonder if the lady had committed a much worse sin and thus her particular punishment was different. After all, Jezzie had told him that her act on him was part of her atonement ordered by the friar. So far in his mind, what he was seeing made a kind of a sense to him.

After several minutes the lady stood up. She had a big smile her on face and it looked like Friar Tuck was shaking and trembling as he stood there in front of her. She put her hands on the friar's shoulders and he just crumbled to the floor, kneeling before her. To Wilhelm's amazement, now Adelaide had the lash in her hands and Friar Tuck was kissing her feet as she delivered blow after blow to his back. Wilhelm wondered how strong she could be because the friar wasn't making a sound. But he was moving up her legs and then Wilhelm peered, intensely curious. *Why, that's what Jezzie did, but it's like it's in reverse.* He'd never seen anything like this. Clearly the lady was suffering something terrible because she was moaning and she'd dropped the lash. She was clinging on to Friar Tuck's shoulders with her back all arched and her breasts pointed up in the air. He'd never realized how ample her bosom was until this moment and realized that he was enjoying the sight. *She's got a lot more to offer than Jezzie does.*

The lady seemed to cry out and start to falter, seemingly unable to stand. Suddenly, she was scooped up in Friar Tuck's arms and laid out on the rug on the floor and then Wilhelm knew exactly what they were doing. That was just sex. They rolled a lot. *Ugh, they're going to leave so much blood all over and don't you know just who he'll ask to mop it all up?* He didn't stay for the end. He knew how it ended. But what he'd seen bothered him: there was tenderness there. There was desire. There was lust. There may have been love. But none of that was redemption for sin. He went back out to the barn where he usually slept. He took the eggs with him.

A bit more than an hour later, Friar Tuckerschade came outside his little manse. "Oh, Wilhelm! There you are. I thought I told you to stay away this afternoon. I wanted to be alone here… to pray."

Wilhelm nodded slowly. "So's ya did. But I didn't think that meant that you'd pray or talk to God in the barn. And the animals still need tending to, whether God's visiting you or not." He picked up the basket. "And look—we got five eggs. A duck egg too!"

Karel Tuckerschade eagerly took the basket. "Will you look at those? Hmm. I think I'll ask the Holy Sister Adelaide over for an omelet. I've a bit of that cheese left. Say, did the sage winter over this year? No matter, I can use the dried herbs." He looked back up at Wilhelm. "Thank you, Wilhelm. We will enjoy these!" Then he turned and headed back into the manse. Suddenly he stopped and turned back around. "Oh Wilhelm, I was cutting up a chicken and somehow I spattered blood all over the main floor and I got some on the rug. Clean that up by the time I get back."

Wilhelm watched Friar Tuck walk until he was out of sight. Then he sat down on a milking stool and stared at nothing for a long time. In his slow mind he started to put together what he knew. Then he started to cry.

The next day found Wilhelm exiting the cesspit just as Father Bernard passed by.

"Oh, Wilhelm! I'm surprised to see you here. I thought the people from St. Drogo's eschewed the cesspits and latrines?"

Wilhelm looked curiously at the priest. "I don't know what 'a shoe' means, when you say it like that, but I do have great love of the boots you had the cobbler make for me, a long time ago now." He looked shyly at the priest. "You know, just yesterday, I pressed old Adelman about what an angel really looks like and he said he looks like you. So, I thank you, sir."

"You are most welcome for the boots, Wilhelm. Truly, it gave me joy to see you wearing them every time we passed. And by 'eschew', I meant only that it is unusual to see people from your congregation use the cesspits."

"Oh, I like the cesspits! I think they be a great thing that you brought to the town."

"Really? Well, thank you, sir!"

"And I like the bridge too. That gate you had made does a right good job in keeping the wild pigs on the other side of the skinny river. They always used to come across the ford, they did, and they would ravage the gardens something fierce. But they don't seem to like to swim so much, now do they? Or maybe they don't like taking a bath?"

"What the skinny river lacks in breadth, it makes up for in it's current. I would imagine the wild swine would be shy around it if they can't use the ford." Father Bernard nodded sagely.

"Well, that was a right smart idea you had. You've had a lot of right smart ideas."

"Wilhelm, would you care to take a walk with me? Perhaps we could stop by the manse. I believe I have some rosemary shortbread biscuits, you might know them as *heidesand kekse*, I call them cookies. Elizabeth, one of my parishioners likes to bring them by. They aren't

414

quite the same as they were before all the shortages, but she makes a very good try at it. And I could brew us up a pot of mint tea."

"You would have tea with me? From St. Drogo? I mean, St. Drogo-Erasmus? I thought our churches were at war?"

"There is no such thing as a war between churches. We are all brothers in Christ and children of Mother Mary. Come, my friend, there is no quarrel between us."

Wilhelm was stunned. This priest spoke to him like an equal, which Friar Tuck certainly never did. He offered him little shortbread cookies, although the priest didn't eat any of them himself, saying "I'm afraid that I always eat three, and three cookies will make me too fat for my frock! You help yourself, Wilhelm. You look as though a few cookies wouldn't make you grow out of your clothes.

Wilhelm consumed eight. The whole batch. And Father Bernard just laughed. "It's not a sin to enjoy good food. It's a blessing, Wilhelm. It's a blessing."

"Is there a way I could be blessed a bit more?"

Bernard laughed again. "I'm afraid that is all there were! But I'm sure Frau Elizabeth will bring me more before too long, and if you'd like I'll be sure to save you some."

"You would do that for me?" Wilhelm was astonished.

"Why not? For someone who was so kind about my civic improvements, I would happily share my biscuits."

They sat and talked a while and then Bernard invited Wilhelm out for a walk. Wilhelm happily went and felt relieved that walking with the good father wasn't a scramble to keep up, as it was with Friar Tuck. It was an easy pace. Father Bernard was so easy to talk to.

"Tell me, Wilhelm, who are your people? The families out here in the Valley Village of the Three Mountains seem so close and yet I don't know to which you belong."

"I don't belong to any of them."

"None? I didn't think anyone here was unattached."

Wilhelm shook his head. "A fever came and it took me parents. And I was alone. Friar Tuck, he found me a sleeping in his barn. I needed to keep warm and he had a cow, so I snuck in there. Aye, cows are powerful warm." Wilhelm shuddered. He'd heard himself sound a bit like Friar Tuckerschade and he never wanted to speak like him again. "I never had no one or nothing. Old Friar Tuck took me in from when before I was a man."

"It sounds like a kindness that he took you in." Bernard nodded.

"It was *like* a kindness. I'm not sure though, now. I'm not sure of anything now. I took care of his animals. I cleaned the little church. And as I grew up, I became his man." He smiled suddenly. "I was the doorkeeper and he moved me to an acolyte."

"An acolyte! Now that *is* a promotion!"

Wilhelm nodded, but felt conflicted and confused. "Right you are, but somehow, I can't tell you what changed. I still took care of the animals. I still cleaned the church. I still cooked for Friar Tuck. And I still served as the doorman, because we didn't have no one else. And then one day, he all of a sudden wanted field flowers on his altar. Said God wanted it. So, I got those when they was in season. And dried them for the winter months."

Bernard nodded again as they walked, both of them enjoying the sunshine on the cool day. "Yes, I see. Hmmm. you've certainly been his man. His right hand man. I don't know how he would make it without you."

Wilhelm didn't speak for a long time and appreciated that Father Bernard allowed him the silence to muddle through his thoughts. Suddenly he burst out, "I don't want to go back."

"What?"

"I don't want to go back to St. Drogo-Erasmus. I don't… I don't… I don't think there's a place for me now. Not anymore." He felt sorry for the animals, not knowing who would take care of them now, but with every passing moment his resolve firmed that he never wanted to go back there again. Not after what he'd seen. Not after what he'd realized. He looked at Father Bernard. "Can I come and be your right-hand man?"

"Oh…" Father Bernard sounded honestly surprised.

"I mean, I've got a way with animals, good at them, you might say. And I can make an omelet that Friar Tuck always said tasted like sin. I always thought I was a bad cook, but I think he meant that it was not that bad actually."

Bernard burst out laughing. "I cannot pretend to know what Friar Karel Tuckerschade intended by his comment, but back in Cologne if someone said a food tasted like sin, they meant that it was utterly delicious. So good that you'd want to eat as much of it as you could, and thus fall into gluttony. But no one ever did that. It was just a saying. A compliment."

"A compliment?"

"A compliment. Like the rosemary biscuits. It's easy for me to eat too many of them, they're so delicious, but that doesn't make those little cookies a sin. The cookies are a blessing. A gift. An act of kindness. It is how we receive them that extends that blessing or can fall off the path into sin."

"Did I fall off the path when I's had all eight of them?"

"No, my son. You delighted in something wonderful, and I'm sure the angels in heaven itself took delight at your joy. You have an ability to find rapture in food that is inspiring."

"I would be happy to cook for you, if you'd have me. And take care of your animals. And clean St. Cyprian's, although it's so big I don't know how long it would take me. And I can sleep in your barn with the cows.

Bernard stopped walking. "Are you so unhappy?"

Wilhelm nodded and felt his eyes staring to well up. The tears spilled down his face and much to his surprise, Bernard didn't chastise him. He wrapped his arms around him and held him. And Wilhelm cried and cried, sobbing like a child. He felt the pain and grief of fifteen years of his life rise up, emotions that had been beaten down with the lashings that were supposed to relieve him of his sins. When he could finally speak again, he said, "I'm drowning in me heartache, I am. It's been here all this time, but kept at bay by the pain of paying for me sins. The pain of me skin keeping me from knowing the pain of me heart."

Bernard patted his back. "One pain does not substitute for another. It only covers it for a while, but in the end the truth will come out. In the end, the light always wins."

Wilhelm nodded but he wasn't quite sure what the priest meant. "The light always wins." He nodded again. "Can I please come and live in your barn? I can't go back. I need to come to the light."

Bernard nodded. "Yes, Wilhelm. I cannot say no to a man in so much need. But you cannot sleep in the barn."

Wilhelm nodded. "I understand. I can sleep in a corner of the church's anteroom if you'll let me."

Bernard opened and closed his mouth a couple of times. "I mean that you'll have your own room in the manse, Wilhelm. If you are to be an acolyte at St. Cyprian's, you will live in the manse. As an acolyte, you will assist in setting up and cleaning up the alter. You'll carry the processional cross. Light candles. Hold the Good Book at service. When trade opens up again and we have incense once more, you'll swing the censer to purify the air. You'll wear robes. And you'll only cook for me because you feel like cooking and sharing in the bounty of what you cook. That will not be your duty. You will not be a servant. You will be an acolyte."

Wilhelm started to cry again and he got down on his knees and started to kiss Bernard's feet, but the priest took him by the shoulders and brought him up to sit straight.

"Wilhelm, I am a man. I am not a God. I am only a man who seeks to bring light to this world and to heal those I meet. My feet are not worthy of being kissed."

"Are you not the gateway to the saving of me soul, then?"

Bernard shook his head. "No. I am a priest. I am here to teach you to come closer to God, but your relationship with the divine is yours, Wilhelm. I hope to be a teacher but I am not a gateway. No one needs my permission to seek God. I am merely one of His signposts on the path to finding Him."

"Oh, that's beautiful, that is. That's what I want to be."

"Let me ask you, if you leave St. Drogo's, what will the friar say?"

"I've been replaced. I don't think he'll even notice, except when he wants an omelet. And he'll get someone else to take care of the animals in a jiffy, if'n it gets them out of a lashing in recompense for their sins."

Wilhelm felt a sense of something he didn't even know how to name. A lightness to his heart. A sense that tomorrow might not hold the same pain and horror that yesterday offered. It was a sensation as distant to his being as the taste that rosemary shortbread biscuits had been: it was hope.

Chapter 36
Friar Karel Tuckerschade
April 1351

Karel Tuckerschade finished sweeping the floor of his little kitchen area in the tiny manse that came with St. Drogo-Erasmus. While the task usually surfaced a cold anger that the beautiful rooms at the manse of St. Cyprian's had been his for a time, today was different. He felt on top of the world. Everything was starting to be laid at his feet. His church had four times the parishioners who had ever crossed his door for a service. There must be more than thirty people come to hear him now, and people had to stand in the back. His heart filled with joy at the thought of Adelaide in his life. They surely were anointed by God to be the new father and mother of generations of man. God was wiping out the populace of Germania and Franconia, the Papal States, the Holy Roman Empire, Genoa and England—rather than water, the flood was rising tides of plague and sickness this time—but the high ground of their village had been spared. Spared by their suffering. He was leading a holy cause, he was sure of it. And given that the Valley Village had been cut off from the outside world for a year or more now, the plague must be very severe indeed. No one dared come. Or, more likely, no one could come.

"There won't even be a 'Holy Mother Church' left after God's done wiping the earth clean this time. It won't matter at all that they would never sanctify me as one of their priests. Them and their rules about literacy."

Education was hideously expensive and reserved for the sons of nobility. As a boy, Karel Tuckerschade had been an acolyte for the priest of this village. A mean old spite, Father Beschädigt was, but he made sure little Karel learned his Biblical passages, whipping the lad for every mistake. He made sure Karel could recite the passages just fine, and in some parts of the world, that was all it took to be made a man of the cloth. It was all that had been required of that mean old Father Spite in his time, anyway. That man didn't need to tie suffering to redemption. He just enjoyed it. Oh yes, Friar Tuck was a great improvement over Father Spite.

Karel stopped and leaned on his little broom, daydreaming for a moment. "Maybe there won't be any church when the plague ends. Or any Germania. Just our little congregation in our little village." He nodded a few times and went back to sweeping, imagining wearing vestments and an orphrey. "Have to start over, we will. Create the world and the church anew. And I'll have the authority of a bishop. Nay, the authority of a pope!" Yes, God was smiling down on his most faithful servant.

A timid knock sounded at his door. "I bet that's Wilhelm come crawling back. I don't think I'll take him, the gutless snake. Walk out on me, will he? Well, we'll see!" He enjoyed a moment of briefly imagining Wilhelm's fruitless groveling.

He walked over to the door and opened it.

It was not Wilhelm.

Adelaide stood there, her disheveled hair escaping her cap and haloing her head. It brought a smile to Karel's face: she usually only looked like that after they had been rolling around in the newfound sensual suffering they had been sharing for the past few months. It was a painful delight that brought joy to his life. But her face didn't look welcoming or enraptured, as it usually did during those times. She looked distraught.

"My dearest, my beautiful anemone, what is wrong? Come in." He took her hand and pulled her inside. After looking up and down the lane to make sure that no one had seen her enter, he closed the door and then put his arms around her. She clung to him. Stroking her curls, he tried to soothe her. "You look like you're suffering already, even before you come to me."

She didn't pull away, but she nodded.

"Come. Sit down. Talk to me." He led her to a chair at his little table and poured them some wine. She didn't speak the whole time he fetched the bottle and cups, but rather sat and wrung her hands.

As he stood next to her and poured out their servings, he said, "I would have been worried that something dreadful happened, but since you've been quiet this whole time, I now say you look like someone who feels the need to confess, but 'tis afraid to do so."

She looked up at him, her eyes big and rimming with tears.

He stood over her, with a hand rubbing her shoulder. "I cannot imagine any sin that you could commit. Your suffering is the salvation of others and the forgiveness for any possible trespass. Your suffering and mine has saved the village." He got down on one knee before her and raised her chin on his two fingers. "Someday you'll be sainted, my dear." He imagined them both sainted, living in an eternal paradise.

"No one will ever saint a noble woman, pregnant out of wedlock."

Karel faltered. "What?"

She nodded slowly.

"Pregnant? Pregnant?"

She nodded again.

Karel sat down, running his hand through his hair. Seeing the two of them as the progenitors of future generations was one thing when it was an idea. It was quite another for it to become a reality—and to become a reality before Saint Cyprian's was once again his. "How could this happen?"

"I don't know. We didn't do it for pleasure or debauchery. We made sure we were suffering even so. If there was suffering, there could not be sin! The clergy in Cologne teach that a woman cannot get pregnant unless she experiences pleasure, as my husband so oft reminded me." She breathed out and looked off into the distance before Karel joined her in saying, "May he rest in peace."

"When did this happen?"

"I don't know precisely." She fidgeted with her hands. "I think about four months ago."

"Four months! You are nearly half-way through your pregnancy?"

She nodded. "At first I wasn't sure. I thought it could not be. And then, I have been hiding it, but I cannot hide it much longer." She got up and started pacing. "Soon the world will know and I will be cast out. Even the Church of St. Drogo-Erasmus won't have me. A pregnant nun. I will be a shunned woman." She took her chair again for a moment but was soon back on her feet. "How can I tell my brother? I will bring shame on his church. I'm sure he would send me back to Cologne with a false cover that I remarried, and my husband died in the plague. But he cannot. There is no travel. The whole world is dying out there. I have no place but here."

Karel jumped up and walked over to her. "St. Drogo-Erasmus won't abandon you, even when the church of St. Cyprian's does. Your pregnancy is… is… a miracle, a miracle! I will proclaim it as such to the congregation."

She nodded slowly, but somehow didn't look convinced. "Karel, I think they'll know. They're gullible but not completely stupid."

"They will believe anything I tell them!" He started to pace, thinking his way through this. "We could tell them that you were taken in the night by a stranger. The dangers of being unaccompanied in the dark."

"I don't know. Some innocent could be hung over that. I don't think I would ever sleep again, being haunted by his ghost."

"Have you talked to the herb woman?"

Adelaide nodded. "Through Jezzie."

"Through the Jezebel? The prostitute?"

She nodded again. "She was the only person I could think of who might understand the predicament. She told me what the process is like. Says 'my friend' is late in the game for it. It's dangerous. 'My friend' might not make it. And it might not work." She sat down briefly and then started to pace once again. "I can see no path but to bear this child. And then live the rest of my life in unbearable shame."

Karel was quiet for a few moments. "There is another way."

"What way?"

"We could marry. You, my Eve, I your Adam, and our son, Cain. We could marry and live as a family."

She looked around her at the little manse. "Karel, it's one thing to dream of being the mother to a new mankind. It's quite another to be noble woman, pregnant, and unmarried. And you are a friar. Sworn to celibacy, just like your namesake, your uncle many times removed. You know no profession other than the ministry. What would we do? You will be defrocked, and that shame will follow you for the rest of your life. Cain will be not a boy but a blight, given his parents." She burst into tears and sat down heavily in the chair. "It would be better to be dead," she said as she sobbed.

"Don't ever say that, my dear." Karel put his arms around her. "If it helps, I would not be forsworn. I made no vow to be celibate. I made no vow to anyone but God. It is from Him that I take my Holy Orders."

Adelaide stopped crying. "What do you mean? I don't understand."

"I apprenticed under a priest in this village when I was a boy. I became his acolyte. He taught and trained me. But there was no bishop to promote me. No ecclesiastical system watching over us. This village has been forgotten. So, when he died, I took my orders from the Lord, to be shepherd to these people and to bring them to salvation. I became the friar. Friar Tuck."

She looked confused. "You are not a friar of a Franciscan order?"

"Not a Franciscan one."

"Nor a Dominican order?"

He shook his head.

"Are you telling me that you are free to marry because you are not a sworn clergy at all?"

"I am free to marry because I have taken no vow of celibacy, poverty, or obedience to any man. I am obedient only to the highest authority."

"The pope?"

Karel shook his head. "No. God. I mean God."

She sat back in her chair and slumped, blinking slowly. "I have been the daughter of a duke. Third cousin to the king. Niece of the bishop. Widow of the most powerful merchant in Cologne. And I gave it all up to be a nun for you. A Holy Sister. The guardian of the garden of Eden. With you. My destiny. But you are not a man of the cloth. You are not an emissary of the Lord. You are a fake. It was a lie. My destiny was a lie. The truth is… it is I who am the apostate. Not Gerung. It is I."

"How can you say such a thing?" He picked up her hand and kissed it. "Our love is ordained by God. Our son, Cain, is the child of a new world, remade anew by God."

Her eyes narrowed as she looked at him and she sharply withdrew her hand. "Our love which I thought was a precious gift was… it was…" she struggled to get the words out, "a most unholy thing. If you are not a sworn man of the cloth then what we did was not done solely to suffer. You said you were a man of the cloth, but you're only a man of rags with a rag tag clergy too stupid to see you for what you are."

Karel stiffened. "I'll try to forgive that, given your hysterical state. Maybe it would be better to end this pregnancy after all."

She looked around her like a caged animal. "I have to leave. I can't breathe here. It's like there's no air." She got up and went to the door. Before she left she turned to look at him, tears streaking down her cheeks. "You aren't the holy man I thought you were. You're just… a man. And I have… I have sinned."

And then she was gone.

Karel stood there, immobilized for several moments. "Pregnant?" He started pacing. "I will have a son." He stood up straight and squared his shoulders. "Cain. My son." He could feel his heart beating faster. *A family.* He started to feel something growing deep inside. A realization. A new want. A need unrecognized and unfulfilled. *But how to get the congregation to accept?*

"She is the most blessed of women. Long have we been promised a second coming. A savior, born of a woman who committed no sin but instead suffered in the service of mankind. Long have we awaited a miracle, in the darkness of the plague. In the depths of the despair of mankind, with the Lord washing the world clean with sickness. And at last, here in our humble company has the Lord decided to reveal his miracle. He works in mysterious ways, my friends. And He has blessed our Holy Sister Adelaide to carry His seed to start the world anew. Conceived in prayer and suffering for the saving of mankind. Look in wonder upon her face, for she is blessed among all women. Our new Mother Mary: our Holy Sister Adelaide. Rejoice! For the day we have long awaited has come!" His voice rose to a crescendo as he finished his rehearsal for his sermon.

It was times like these that Karel sorely wished he could read and write. Committing all his thoughts to memory was difficult. He was much better at working himself up and then spontaneously weaving his thoughts into a sermon, but not quite as good at remembering all the details for a repeat performance.

He stood up straight and with a different cadence and emphasis said, "Holy Sister Adelaide! All rejoice! For the day we have long awaited has come—our new Mother Mary. All hail, the Holy Sister Adelaide!" He gestured as he would when he gave the sermon and looked to where he imagined her standing, looking shy and humble, but glowing with happiness to be carrying the good news within her. But the space was empty. She was gone.

He looked at the door. She had left calling herself names. Apostate. Sinner. She had said he wasn't a man of the cloth. He was, though. Just not their cloth. Their rules didn't apply to him and now they didn't apply to her.

"You are being tested by despair, my love. We are all tested in one way or another." But no answer came. He was alone.

"She'll be back," he told himself reassuringly. "Pregnancy makes women act upset. Anxious. Worried. Of course, she's worried. She's emotional. She'll calm down. She'll be back. Tomorrow. She'll be back."

He started to pace and rehearse his sermon announcing the miracle to the congregation of St. Drogo-Erasmus. He worked late into the night.

He dreamed of Adelaide standing next to him by the altar. He gave his sermon to a church packed to standing and the people cheered. They insisted that every new babe needed a father to watch over him, in addition to a mother. He told them, "I'm only a friar, but I will willingly step in to serve as a parent with our Holy Sister Adelaide." And he held her hands at the altar and married her, and then she was his nun and his wife, the mother of his child and the mother of the Lord's child who would make the world anew. But then, just as he was about to kiss his bride, the church doors trembled with a *Bang! Bang! Bang!*

He and Adelaide turned to look at the doors. *Bang! Bang! Bang!*

"What is it, my love?" she asked him.

"I don't know."

Bang! Bang! Bang!

He woke with a start.

Bang! Bang! Bang!

Karel opened his eyes at the bright daylight and once again heard the pounding at the door.

"I'm coming, drat it! I'm coming!" He went to open the door to his little manse and found Father Bernard standing there. "Father

Bernard?" He blinked at the surprisingly bright morning. "To what do I owe…"

Without waiting for an invitation, the man stormed into the small receiving room. "I have come to lay your sin before your feet, Friar Tuckerschade." The man sneered when he said the word *Friar.* "This is not to be borne! I must warn you: I have learned of what you preach. I have learned that you ply your tiny flock with lies and manipulation. Telling them that *you* are the sole gateway to salvation. That *you* are the pathway to redemption, while you take their meager food from their mouths and whip them into submission for their supposed sins."

Karel was taken aback but would not allow himself to be challenged by this worthless, arrogant, rich, pompous, elitist who was damned. Bernard was what was wrong with this village. Everything had been all right before that puppet of the church had come to town and stolen St. Cyprian's from him. Karel stood up tall. "I am the gateway and the reliever of their sins."

"You do nothing to bring them closer to God!" Bernard thundered back at him. "Why are you, as a friar, here? You should be traveling and preaching, not tying yourself to a congregation. Friars are to go out among the people. Heal the sick. Educate. Had you gone all the way to the priesthood in your training, then, and only then, should you be tied to a congregation! I'm not even sure there is a St. Drogo-Erasmus on the ecclesiastical roster."

Karel stiffened. "I am in a remote village. This is where the people are. This is where I'm called to be."

"Called to be!" Bernard snorted. "Friars are travelers. You were born here. You are no man of the cloth!"

While Karel was relieved that Bernard clearly had no idea of the situation with Adelaide, these accusations made him start to fume. "Who are you but a usurper to make such accusations of me? And by what authority do you question me? Only a bishop has the position of authority over either of us." Karel mirrored the emotion Bernard brought to the conversation. What he said was true: priests and friars were too close to oversee one another. "We each swear an oath to our own orders."

"Your order? Your order? You are an order unto yourself!" Bernard was red in the face now. "Know this, Tuck: I will be sending letters of inquiry to your order. I will be sending letters to the bishop in Cologne, the archbishop in Bonn, and the pope himself in Avignon! Your unorthodox teaching reflects more of you than of any order in the holy mother church. I'll bet you are neither a Franciscan nor a Dominican. I'll have you defrocked, if you ever were a friar in the first place." He leaned into Karel Tuckerschade, pushing a single finger into his chest. "And if I find that you are not ordained and there is no defrocking necessary, I will have you hauled in front of the archbishop to stand trial."

Karel took two steps backwards. Bernard wasn't threatening just ruination of his church in the Valley Village; he wasn't just threatening humiliation and poverty: he was threatening imprisonment and torture. A sure death that would be slow and painful at the hands of a clergy that weren't known for their mercy.

Karel tried to sound strong and sure of himself, but his voice faltered as he said, "I am doing as the Lord calls me, the same as you."

"The truth will out. There is no way to stop it, Tuckerschade. God always reveals the truth, in His own time, and any lies you've told will be examined in the light of a new day. You can't hide, Tuckerschade. There is no hole deep and dark enough for you. You are a false prophet and you will be exposed."

Karel took a deep breath and nodded grimly, mustering his dignity. "I assure you, you will find me to be ordained. I think you should leave now."

Bernard grunted and turned to head towards the door. Before he went through it, he turned around once more and shouted, "And stay away from my sister!" Then he spun around and disappeared into the bright sunlight.

Karel had to admit that the encounter shook him. Bernard writing to find documentation of his ordainment. To discern his order. To report him to a higher authority. He might tell himself that there was only one higher authority he needed, but even he had to admit that Bernard's promised actions carried real threat. Karel fretted the rest of the day, cancelled his service at St. Drogo-Erasmus, saying that he felt poorly and was fighting off an illness. He was restless that night, with dreams of thumbscrews and being drawn and quartered. He woke up several times, drenched in sweat.

◆━◆━◆

The next day he was in the barn taking care of the animals. For the first time, he was missing Wilhelm. "Good old Wilhelm would have supported me," he muttered as he scooped straw and filth out of a stall. He gave a deep sigh, finding the animals a burden. Wilhelm had managed them since he was a boy, even sleeping out in the barn most nights. But since Wilhelm had left, cleaning the barn, feeding and watering the beasts, milking those that needed it and pasturing the cluster of goats were all just extra tasks that Karel needed to attend to. He had been able to find a couple of parishioners with just the right level of sin to assign their atonement as mucking the barn and feeding and watering the animals for a week, but their infractions could only be stretched so far. He had to wait for another repentant sinner to cross his path to get out of the drudgery that faced him now.

Behind him he heard someone clear their throat. He turned. It was Wilhelm.

"Wilhelm? Wilhelm, my boy! You're back! About time, I tell you. The chores are starting to stack up around here." Karel approached Wilhelm with pitchfork in his hand.

He was surprised when Wilhelm took a couple of protective steps back and gave Karel a distrustful look.

430

"Excuse me, but I'm not here to come back. I'm here to say me piece, as it were, because I can only gain peace of mind by settling out my heart, which is heavy."

Karel froze. These were not the words of the Wilhelm he had known for the last fifteen years. These sounded like the babblings of that dratted Father Bernard. He decided a very different approach was going to be needed here. He set the pitchfork aside. "I'm sorry to hear that your heart is heavy, my son."

"I'm not your son."

"True." Karel nodded and invited Wilhelm to sit down on a hay bale. Karel took a seat on another bale and the two men looked at one another. "You are a man grown from the boy who I found sleeping with the cow in my barn. A boy with no family. A boy who I fed and raised."

"Yes, you did." Wilhelm looked less sure of himself. "And... and… and I did the chores. And cooked for you. And cleaned the house and the church." He gave Karel a harder look. "I was more like your servant." He looked like he was trying to remember something. "An unpaid one." He nodded a couple of times, as though satisfied that he had remembered his lines.

"You were more like my son, helping me in all the responsibilities of our little family. And I involved you at the church. You were a doorman while you were still too young for the role, but you wanted it so. And then I made you an acolyte, just like I had been when I was a boy and a young man."

Wilhelm bit his lip. "You *named* me an acolyte, but now I am one in truth. I carry the cross. I hold the Bible. When there's incense to be had again, I'll swing it in the censer and walk down the aisle of the church. The only duty of an acolyte I did at Drogo's was to set and clean the altar."

"St. Drogo-Erasmus," Karel corrected, amazed at how quickly and how thoroughly Bernard's poison had altered Wilhelm's mind. "The name of your church is St. Drogo-Erasmus." Before Wilhelm could jump in, Karel said, "It's true that you've moved up in life. You're at a fancy church now. We are humble folk at St. Drogo-Erasmus. We don't burn incense. We bring in God's own flowers from the fields when the Lord's willing." He noticed the gold cross hanging around Wilhelm's neck. "We don't have crosses made of gold, either around our necks nor on our altars. Wood was good enough for Jesus. He was crucified on a wooden cross and in honor of His sacrifice for mankind, wooden crosses are all we will ever use. Yes, we are simple men of a simple faith here."

"It's not about the cross being gold. I'm not too good for wood." Wilhelm held the cross hanging at his sternum as though he was hiding it. He sounded like he was puzzling out what he was trying to say. "You beat me something fierce. Me back's got scars on it."

Karel leaned back against the wall and picked up a piece of straw, putting one end into his mouth. "As does mine. Ahh, Wilhelm! The Lord blesses those who suffer. And we suffer to save the world. Our world, our village, has been saved, Wilhelm, because we have pleased God. In the big cities, in Cologne, men walk the streets. Flagellants they are called. They strip themselves naked and beat themselves as they parade their misery and suffering for the masses. They re-enact their sins. Each one lies in the street until all of his brethren have walked on him and struck him with their spiked disciplines. And yet, God continues to strike down the people of Cologne. And Bonn. And every other big city. He has not forgiven those people."

Wilhelm was staring at Tuckerschade, much like he used to when Karel was preaching.

"But he has forgiven the people of this village because of our suffering. Because of your suffering. The scars you wear on your back, like the scars on mine, are the salvation of this village. It's why we haven't had to watch our friends and neighbors turn blue and die in pain and agony. You, Wilhelm, a man of a poor and simple little church, an acolyte of St. Drogo-Erasmus, are part of a miracle of the Lord. You have achieved what the bishops and archbishops and even the pope himself has been unable to do: you have kept the plague away. The Lord favors you, Wilhelm, because of your suffering."

Wilhelm was quiet for a while. "Father Bernard says the Lord is a loving God. He doesn't want us to suffer. We've suffered enough. I know I have. He wants us to be happy."

"God? Or Bernard?" Karel thought, *Bernard certainly doesn't want me to be happy.*

"Well, um, both I guess." Wilhelm scratched his head and looked unsure of himself for a moment. "Father Bernard has shown me that there is another way. That the Holy Spirit is a being of love and kindness. He sent His son, he did, to suffer for us, so that we need not suffer as much."

"Bernard may say a lot of things, but he and his congregation benefit from the sacrifice you made for them. Suffering is a holy thing, as Jesus did it himself to save others, so do we. We are not fully shriven without penance. How else will you *know* you've been shriven?"

"I think a part of you likes the suffering. Life is hard enough. I want to worship a loving God. One who makes me feel like I'm worth something more than pain and blood. I'm worth the living of life."

Before Karel could answer, Wilhelm went on. "And I wanted to come and say some important words. I wanted to close the circle with you, so that I can move on. I need to say thank you for saving me as a boy. And no thank you for how you treated me as a man. I understand now, that for all the hurt I've felt, there can never be enough of 'sorry' from you to heal that pain. My well runs so deep that there will never be enough words from you to fill it. And I suppose I'll live with that. I'll have to anyway. But I'm going to move forward with me life. And maybe someday I'll leave that behind. I'm moving on to a new well, one I be filling up with happiness and peace. But I needed to say both thank you and no thank you, so that I can move on. I need to leave." Wilhelm stood up.

Karel stood up as well. "You have been like a son to me. Like the son I have never had. Could never have, as a man of the cloth. Like the son that God sent to me, to find in a barn. I admit, I am imperfect, but I did the best I knew how to do. And I loved you every day, Wilhelm, my son."

"I'm not really like a son. You don't treat a son like you treated me. Father Bernard says that's not right. That's not the Lord's love."

Karel channeled all the emotion he could manage at the moment into a sincere portrayal of contrition. Yet inside he was furious to learn how deeply Bernard had penetrated and poisoned Wilhelm's mind and heart. How thoroughly Wilhelm had been lured by Bernard's version of a soft, pliable, comfortable religion, just like the soft, pliable, and comfortable upbringing Bernard had enjoyed as the son of a noble. Wilhelm now wanted a featherdown religion in which God never tested you and you could never be found worthy, for there was no measure of worth to be had in *soft, pliable,* and *comfortable.* If this is what Wilhelm wanted, then he wasn't Karel's man at all. He was quickly becoming one of the *warped.* "I hear you, my Wilhelm. It does sound like you've chosen another path."

"I'm starting to learn to read, I am. And do numbers. The good Father is teaching me."

Karel needed a few deep breaths to bring his emotions back under control. For the first time he noticed Wilhelm's clothes. They were… nice. Not the humble garb of a man who worked for a living, but well-made clothes, plain, yes, but with an understated style. They went with his well-made boots. *Warped.* Karel's mind felt like it was being whipped by a winter wind. Then he saw again the cross hanging around Wilhelm's neck: a small cross glinting with a golden shine. *Warped.*

He's been bought. Fool. He's certainly lost to me. "I see. I understand. Well, Wilhelm, you must tread the path to where you're called. As one who was, at one time, a father to you, I hope that you will always walk in the light of the Lord and that your soul will be given eternal salvation." He raised his hand to make the sign of the cross over Wilhelm.

"Are you sure you should be doing that?" Wilhelm looked very nervous now. "I mean, until you've been shriven of your sins, that is?"

"My sins? What are my sins?"

Wilhelm looked anyplace but at Karel. "I saw you and the Lady Adelaide. I saw you lash her."

Karel stiffened and tried to keep his voice calm. "Our Holy Sister's suffering has also protected this village from the plague. She is as holy a woman as I've ever known."

Wilhelm nodded. "That mays be. Mays be. But I also saw what come after. And that was not the actions of a nun and a friar. I told Father Bernard what I saw after he came back from his visit with you. He's powerful mad. He says you're an imposter. And he said that meant that you were a fake. Not a friar and not a man of the cloth at all. And that he would prove it." Wilhelm bit his lip. "I thought you should know."

"Do you think I'm a fake, my son?"

"I don't know what to think that you are. I'm so confused. But I can't ever come back to you now I know what it is to be loved by God. And my mission is to help others be loved by God and not suffer no more."

Karel nodded slowly. He could see only one way out of this predicament. Wilhelm, the stupid fool, yearning for a soft life, had a purpose still. And when he dealt with Wilhelm and Bernard, then Adelaide would come back to him. Was probably already trying to come back to him, but was imprisoned by her maniacal brother.

"Wilhelm, the closest thing to a son I will ever know." Karel got down on his knees before the man. "I humbly beseech your forgiveness for my shortcomings as a father. I beg your mercy, as a man who only wanted to save his friends and neighbors from certain death from the plague. Who sincerely believes in his heart that he hears the calling of the Lord and follows His will. My success will never be enough in the eyes of the Lord, and yet I lay all that I am before Him and His judgement. Let me say how truly sorry I am that I was not enough." Karel's voice broke.

Wilhelm reached down and brought Karel to his feet. "You don't need to get on your knees before me." A tear was running down his cheek. "I know you did what was right by you. And I do forgive you, Friar Tuck. And I thank you, that you didn't turn me out or let me die as a child. But I'm a man now and I'm never coming back."

"I know. Wilhelm, may I give you a parting gift? One that shows my love, even though I didn't express it well while you were my son. I would like to gift you with a barrel of wine—my very best! I'll have it delivered over to the manse tomorrow. And as you and Father Bernard, and the deacons, yes, the deacons, drink it, maybe you'll think of me. And maybe, just maybe, you'll be able to remember me with kindness and think on some of the moments we had when we were blessed."

"You would... you would give me one of *those* barrels? The one we could never tap? The one you said was so special that I could never even touch the barrel?" He blew a whistle out of his lips. "That be a right generous gift."

Karel nodded and held Wilhelm's hand in his own. "After all we have been through, after all we have meant to one another, after the future path that lies before us now, I cannot imagine giving you anything less."

◆━◆━◆

The next day Karel carefully picked out the barrel of wine. It was a special vintage. He found the barrel with the identifying mark on it, indicating that it was only to be parted with at utmost need. He stroked the wood as the four men worked to load it up on a wagon and deliver it over to St. Cyprian's. "Don't let it drop! Don't break the cask. 'Tis a very special vintage! It's a gift for Father Bernard. And, oh yes, the acolyte Wilhelm. A gift for St. Cyprian's itself."

He watched as the barrel and the wagon disappeared down the lane. It was quite a loss, that barrel, but he assured himself that it would be well worth it in the end.

He sighed and knew he needed to get to work. He had a sermon to prepare. He needed to talk to his flock about the end of days, the second coming, a new miraculous birth and immaculate conception, and God's justice. "Sodom and Gomorrah. That's a good topic for my sermons for the next season or so, until a new day dawns."

Chapter 37

Everly

Everly couldn't sleep. She knew she should get some rest but her mind was spinning. So many possibilities. So much discovery. And on top of that, they were scheduled to head back up to the high bog to excavate that lonely grave site on the mountain. And that wall! That crazy wall that shouldn't be there. She couldn't wait to get back. With all of this swirling in her mind, her thoughts kept coming back to Trevor. She got up and went to the tent that housed their showers, not so much because she needed one but more because she just couldn't sleep. As she tried to make her way quietly back through the camp, she jumped at a terrible squeaking sound, like grating metal. She heard a little bit of soft cursing from Trevor and decided to not check it out. Maybe she'd bring it up with him tomorrow that something was in serious need of oil. She crept into the women's tent as quietly as she could and slid into her cot.

"Everly… are you awake?" Nylah's voice was a quiet whisper.

"Oh, sorry. Am I tossing and turning? Keeping you awake?"

"What are you thinking about?" Nylah asked.

Everly wasn't going to admit what she was thinking about. Nylah might be her tentmate. No, more like a little sister, if Everly were really being honest with herself. She thought about that: *Nylah as a little sister.*

They came from such different worlds and yet this summer had brought them so close. But not close enough to confess what had been playing across her mind.

"I was thinking about the tombstones."

"The tombstones that we uncovered last week?" Nylah asked.

"Yeah. When the team found them sunk down under the churchyard and brought them up."

"What about them?"

"Well, there are no dates after April 1351. That means that we can effectively call the month and the year of the great tragedy, of when plague finally hit this town. Ironic, isn't it? Given the plague petered out at the end of that year. They almost made it. Almost. All the dates before then were scattered, people passing like you'd expect in a small town. Here and there. You know the last date we found was April fifth. For a baby. That was so sad. I wonder if it was the first death of the plague or the last death before the plague. And there's no one in the graveyard after that."

"A little baby?" Nylah's voice came softly. And then she sniffed.

"Nylah? Are you… okay?"

"Yeah. I'm okay."

Everly could hear that she was not okay. Anything but okay. She got up and went over to Nylah's cot, sitting down on the edge of it. "What's wrong?"

"Oh Ev," Nylah started but then she couldn't say anything. The tears came and she just needed to cry in Everly's arms.

Everly held Nylah and rocked her and patted her back, waiting for the girl to be ready to talk about whatever it was. She wondered if she and Hans had broken up. Nylah had been quiet about him for at least a week, and it was strange to not see him about the dig site. "I'm here. I'm here," Everly said over and over again. She thought about what she'd want said to her and it struck her that Trevor was actually much better at this than she was. *Empathy not in my skill set,* she thought grimly as she tried harder to be there for Nylah.

"I promise you, Nylah, whatever is breaking your heart will pass. You'll see this to the other side." Everly had had her heart broken by a boy… *maybe*, she thought. She was sure it must have happened to her. Women survived these things. That's what women did. They survived.

"Oh, Ev. I don't know how."

"Is it about Hans?"

"Yeah." Nylah sniffed. "He doesn't want it. I don't know if I want it."

"Well, if you both don't want it, then it should be pretty easy, right?" Everly asked, wondering why it was hard to break up if neither of them wanted the relationship?

"What did women in the Middle Ages do when they found themselves pregnant and didn't want the baby?"

Everly felt her head go for such a spin that she thought for a moment that she'd fallen over. So that's what they were talking about. "Wow. Okay. Um. Yeah. They had both contraception and abortion in the Middle Ages. Drug-based approaches and surgical. When it came to saving a woman's life, Christian physicians didn't hesitate."

"Back then it was legal?"

"They didn't have the same concept of legal. Basically, a woman got exiled for up to ten years from the church. But not if she were truly repentant. Or if she and her husband had divorced and she didn't want to give her ex an heir: the church was pretty clear that you didn't have to carry the baby for a hateful former husband. And sex workers were allowed so they could keep working. In those cases, it was the man's fault for the termination, not the sex worker's." Everly thought that Nylah probably didn't really want a history lesson right now, but she wasn't quite sure of what to say or do. She had never been in this position before, so she just recited what she knew. "They even had what we would call late-term abortions, some even performed by saints, if you can believe it. Saving the life of the mother was paramount to them and there was no judgement. Well, particularly no judgement if you were of the nobility or wealthy. Then you could have medical care and privacy both."

"Oh, so pretty much like the way it is now."

"Yeah. I suppose so."

"Do they scream at you here in Germany like they do in the US?"

"No. They respect holding different beliefs here. No one would try to impose anything on you. But if you need me, I'll be with you whatever." The breathlessness in Everly's voice betrayed her own sense of emotion. "Do you really think you're pregnant?"

"I do. I've never been pregnant, but I do." Nylah wiped her nose. "He doesn't want it. He doesn't want me. I don't know what to do. And it hurts so much. And the worst thing: I feel like a damn statistic!"

"Huh? A statistic?"

Nylah sniffed. "Yeah, you know: Black woman, pregnant. Not married."

Everly put her arms even more tightly around Nylah. "You are not a statistic! You are a brilliant and, might I add, an extremely organized and creative young woman! This could happen to anyone."

Nylah wiped away a tear.

Everly stroked Nylah's hair and held her. "It will be okay. I promise you, it will be okay. I'm not going to leave you to be alone."

Nylah pulled away. "What do you mean?" Tears were running down her cheeks and she looked like a frightened little girl as she looked up into Everly's eyes.

"If he won't support you, then I will. I'll be an auntie to that little baby, if having it is what you want to do. If you want me to take you to a clinic, then okay. We'll do that."

"Oh, Everly!" Nylah broke down in sobs. "You're like the sister I always wanted!" She clung to Everly and Everly continued to stroke her back.

"Same here, Nylah. Same here. I've got your back. It's going to be okay. Complicated, but okay."

As Everly finally fell asleep that night she wondered what, if anything, she should have done, could have done, to prevent the situation that Nylah was now in? Nylah was a woman. A young woman, but not a child. An adult. Free to make her own choices. And complicated things happened to good people. Complicated things happened to people who behaved in responsible ways.

A baby. She thought about what it would be like to have a baby. *I'd like to have a baby.* Then she sat up bolt upright, wondering where *that* thought had come from. She'd never wanted a child in her life. She felt her heart race for a moment. *I'm losing my mind. I'm projecting… I'm starting to feel my biological clock.* She lay back down with the firm realization that this was Nylah's story. She didn't know what twists and turns it would take, but she'd meant what she said: she would be there for Nylah come what may.

Chapter 38

Father Bernard Trōst
May 1351

Bernard sighed as he put the vestments over his black robe. They were lovely. He was grateful to have them, but he craved a simple worship between a man and his maker, one without the trappings of finery. It just felt too close to worshipping the fine cloth, the gold cross, and pomp and circumstance rather than the idea of the divine that was supposed to be behind it all. But the parishioners were drawn by the finery like the moth to the flame. Just look at the paltry little following that Friar Tuck had in his bedraggled little church. It surely was a simple place to worship. A simple place for an uncomplicated faith. But Tuckerschade didn't make faith uncomplicated, did he? Bernard shook his head and sighed heavily again. And now Wilhelm had asked to be shriven of his sins before participating in their blessings, the ceremony, and the subsequent celebration. Three knocks on the door alerted Bernard that the time had come, with Wilhelm happily acquiescing to his new priest's request to engage in actions that mirrored the holy trinity.

"Enter." Bernard turned to the door and was astonished to find Wilhelm walking into the room completely naked, carrying his robes in a bundle in front of him. The priest was speechless.

"I am here, good Father, to be shriven of me sins so that I may be worthy of completing me holy tasks of the church today. I willingly submit." Without making eye contact, he gave a clumsy bow and then lay his little bundle on the floor. Silently he knelt down on the folded robes with his back turned towards Bernard. He took a deep breath, as if to prepare himself for what was to come.

"My son! Why are you naked?"

"I have sinned, Father. You heard me confession. I need you to remove the sin from me shoulders." Wilhelm didn't move, kneeling on the floor. "I willingly submit."

Bernard's hand went over his mouth and his eyes flew open as he looked at Wilhelm's back. He had to take a couple of steadying breaths before he could find any words at all. He couldn't help himself when his hand reached out to touch the scars he saw engraved onto the skin of this poor man. "My son… what has happened to you?" He traced a few of the lines and Wilhelm trembled under the gentle touch of Bernard's fingers. "You look like you might have been attacked by a wild boar."

Wilhelm shook his head. "No. I never seen the wild boar. Me back is marked from the stripping of me sins. I know it's got a couple of scars on it." He turned to look over his shoulder at Father Bernard. "Aren't you going to discipline me, strike the evil from me heart with the lash? Absolve me of me sin? We need to be wholly shriven because we could meet our maker at any moment."

Bernard withdrew his hand and shook his head. It was one thing to hear the tales from Jezzie about what was happening over at St. Drogo's, or even Wilhelm's remarks of "having his sins stripped from him", but seeing it was an entirely different matter. Bernard had envisioned the quick rapping he'd gotten across his knuckles as a boy from an impatient tutor, or a fast strap across the buttocks his father had given on numerous occasions to Adolfus in his futile attempts bring his son's behavior into alignment, but Bernard had never imagined anything like this. "Your back, Wilhelm… so many scars. The scars are from you being beaten?"

"Lashed. Not beaten. No fists. Just a lash or a strap… or a whip or a discipline—whatever Friar Tuck had on hand. And he didn't have the barbed disciplines that those street men in Cologne had, those people that the lady liked to talk about so much. Oh, he was mighty excited to fashion those, but after one spiked him in the back of the head on his backswing, he seemed to lose his interest, calling it a 'new-fangled idea'."

Bernard turned away, wishing he could un-see the image that was now seared onto his mind. "Please stand up, Wilhelm."

"What?"

"Please, be so kind as to stand up and don your robes, man!" Bernard could feel his body shaking. As Wilhelm, obviously confused, regained his feet and started to pull on his robes, Bernard tried to think of how to handle this situation. When he was once again robed, Wilhelm turned to Father Bernard, a look of distress on his face. "I understand that the practice at your, er, previous house of worship included lashing you for your sins, but I do not endorse such actions. That is not the Lord's love or forgiveness, Wilhelm. When I said it before, I meant it—and now I mean it even more!"

Wilhelm was wringing his hands. "But then how do you *know* that you've been forgiven? How do you *know* that you're worthy to serve the church? You might still have all those sins in your head?"

Bernard grasped Wilhelm's arms and held him tightly, looking him in the eye across the arm's distance between them. "You know it in your heart, my boy. You feel it, in here," he said as he lay one hand over Wilhelm's heart and one hand over his own.

"But what if you don't know what you feel?" Wilhelm's confusion was written all over his face. "I mean, there's no denying what I feel on me back, but when it's left all up to me, inside me own heart, what if I'm still not worthy?"

Bernard bit his lip, suddenly understanding his own sister more now in this moment than he'd ever been able to previously. He nodded and with great compassion said, "It is the paradox of the human condition, Wilhelm, that we strive to be worthy of God's love, that we hold doubt in our hearts, that we can never be absolutely sure of our purity or worthiness, but that our Heavenly Father loves us none the less. In fact, the less confident we are of the state of our souls, the humbler and more contrite we come to Him, the more open our hearts are and the more He pours His love into us. For while God does not love arrogance or false pride, he forgives us for being the imperfect human beings He created us to be."

Wilhelm blinked a couple of times. "I'm not sure I understand what you just said."

"I said that your doubt is good for you. The Lord loves you all the more for the doubt you hold in your heart. You don't need to feel the pain in your body to know that you've been forgiven."

Wilhelm nodded, as if trying to work out this new way of living with his imperfections rather than having them erased, washed away in his own blood and pain.

Bernard perked up as an idea crossed his mind. "Wilhelm, I will give you Holy Communion, just for you, before we start on our way. Would that help you to find peace in your heart that you are indeed worthy of serving the Lord today?"

"Communion just for me?" His eyes were wide.

"Just you and the Lord himself."

"Will you not be there, then? How will I know what's happened?"

Bernard blanched and then nodded. "I'll be there as the Lord's emissary, His voice. Just like always."

Bernard surmised that the friar might just possibly have been delivering himself from some of his own frustrations with simple Wilhelm when he sought to lash the sins from his acolyte.

Bernard intoned the prayers and performed the holy communion for his acolyte, which did seem to help the man calm down a bit. Then it was time to get ready for the major events of the day. Today was a big day—a day of blessings and celebrations.

"You seem rather sad today, Father Bernard. Is there something I can do for you?" Wilhelm asked.

"I'm sorry, Wilhelm. I'm just distracted, but I'm not sad. No, not really. I'm just accepting things the way they are. I'll don the orphrey and soon it will be time to put the cross on the pole and hoist it for the crowds to see."

"Oh, that orphrey *is* mighty lovely," Wilhelm said as he bobbed his head and up and down, looking shy and awkward. "I've never seen nothing like it in me life. And now that I'm shriven in heart instead of me skin, I can appreciate it from a much different view."

"Oh? How so?"

"Well, the pain after a lashing makes it hard to concentrate on much of anything else but just breathing, but now that me mind's not pulled away by the discomfort, I can see that the orphrey is the most beautiful thing to ever have been created."

Bernard smiled and stopped for a moment, the orphrey in his hand. "Yes. It is. I have rarely beheld anything like it either." He looked at Wilhelm. "Could you come here and help me for a moment, Wilhelm?"

The man scurried over.

"Right, just stand there, yes, straight and tall. Close your eyes."

Wilhelm did as Bernard bade him, but he winced.

"I won't hurt you. I promise. I swear on the Holy Bible itself, that no harm will come to you, Wilhelm." He could see the man slowly start to relax, his eyelids still fluttering slightly in his nervousness. Bernard gently raised the orphrey up over his head and intoned a prayer of blessing and comfort in Latin, and gently laid the orphrey around the neck of Wilhelm. "You may open your eyes, my son."

Slowly, shyly, Wilhelm followed Bernard's directive and looked down at the embroidered cloth hanging about his neck. His eyes widened.

Bernard smiled. "Just enjoy the feel of it, Wilhelm. Enjoy the blessing I laid upon you just now. Know that you are close to the divine in this moment."

Wilhelm's lips began to tremble and a tear streaked down his cheek. "I… I… never thought to ever touch anything truly holy in me life."

Bernard put a hand on Wilhelm's shoulder. "My son, when you have walked in the fields and touched the flowers that grow there, when you have looked to the sky and felt the summer's rain on your cheeks, when you have known true friendship with your fellow man, you have already touched something holy. This cloth symbolizes charity covering a multitude of sins."

"Forgiveness? Forgiveness for what I've done?" Wilhelm looked hopeful, but the tears still coursed down his cheeks.

Bernard thought for a minute. Wilhelm had confessed his sins, and while they loomed large to Wilhelm himself, to Bernard they were trifling things. He wondered at the scars on Wilhelm's back and the punishments imposed by that Tuckerschade character. How many of that sheepish flock who so blindly followed their friar and his hard ways hid similar scars beneath their wooly coverings? "Forgiveness, Wilhelm. As you wear this now, know that you are absolved of your sins."

Wilhelm choked out a breath.

"And before your tears add to the beautiful decorations on this cloth, I will take it back so that I will be ready for the parade. But remember this day and this moment, and hold your head high, my son, for the sins you bore no longer bear down upon your shoulders."

As Bernard put the orphrey back around his own neck, Wilhelm fell to his knees, took Bernard's hand and kissed it.

"When you rise, if you would be so kind as to fetch the golden cross from above the altar, I would be most appreciative."

"What? Me?" Wilhelm looked as though he struggled to comprehend Bernard's instructions.

"Yes. It's right through those doors. Use the little ladder to be able to reach it. Be careful with it."

"You would allow *me* to touch the golden cross?"

Bernard gave him a gentle smile. "That is, if you wouldn't mind."

Wilhelm nearly jumped in his excitement. "Yes, sir! Yes, sir! Right away, your grace!"

Bernard chuckled and decided it was better to not correct Wilhelm that *your grace* was reserved for those of bishop and above. If he were truly lucky, his uncle Eberhard would fail to wrangle that kind of an ecclesiastical career for his unambitious nephew and Bernard would never require such an address. Of course, there was also the issue that Wilhelm would engage in such self-punishment for his error. The man might not eat for two days. Or worse, beat himself with a lash again. At least Bernard had gotten Wilhelm to hand over his discipline. Bernard was making real headway in helping Wilhelm to see that God was love, not some type of angry, punishing parent—and still, old habits died hard.

In short order, Wilhelm returned reverently holding the golden cross in his hands. "You know, Father Bernard, I wondered if I might be too weak to bear the cross, but it's lighter than I thought it would be! I dunno, I mean I've never actually touched such gold before but I always thought it was a heavy thing, like lead or iron. But this is light like it's borne upon angel's wings!"

Bernard enjoyed the simplicity of his new acolyte and thought to himself, *Wilhelm, simple as he is, might be the closest thing to a holy man that I will ever meet.* "Actually, Wilhelm, you happen to be right! It's light because it's made of wood. Ironwood to be precise." Bernard gave a little chuckle. "While my uncle favors me beyond what I deserve, I'm afraid even as a bishop, he doesn't have the ability to gift our little church with solid gold crosses." He raised up the golden cross that hung on a long chain around his neck. "Now this cross is made of gold, but it was a gift from my mother when I became a priest. It was her blessing of my calling. I wear this daily and it is precious to me because of what it symbolizes."

"The richness of heaven?"

"A mother's love of her child, like the love that the Lord has for all His children as we find our paths in life."

"Oh, that be beautiful."

Bernard gently touched the cross around Wilhelm's neck. "And that is what your gold cross symbolizes as well, my son: a parent's love for their child."

Bernard then stroked the large processional cross held protectively in Wilhelm's arms. "Though made of wood, this cross is certainly ornate and beautiful by any standard. Now ironwood takes great mastery to carve. I've heard craftsmen refer to it as devil wood." He laughed. "But it is strong almost like metal itself. This cross will last until Judgement Day and yet it will be light to carry and shine like pure gold. But it's only wood that is covered in gold and decorated with gems."

"Not solid gold?"

Bernard shook his head. "A princely gift indeed, but not one that would possibly draw the ire of Clement the Sixth." Bernard gave his companion a wink. "Which is always an important thing to consider. And you know, Jesus was a simple man. He was a carpenter. I think he would appreciate wood more than gold."

"Wood is good enough for Jesus," Wilhelm said in awe.

Bernard nodded. "Now, shall we mount this on its pole and go out and call the faithful?"

They paraded through the streets with Bernard relieved that his hands were free and not carrying the pole and the cross. Wilhelm seemed to be walking on air, he was so thrilled with his task. If he got tired, he never showed it. That made Bernard smile, as did the fact that he got to spend most of the parade greeting and blessing people, inviting everyone in the town to the celebration to follow. By the time they made the full circle through the village and back to the church, they had a huge band in tow. Word spread quickly of the blessing and celebration of the new improvements. They stopped at the bridge and blessed both the bridge and the gate, with Bernard speaking of how this would help to keep the wild pigs out and prevent hunger in the winter from the devastation the swine brought with them. They stopped at the latrine and the cesspits, blessing the convenience for all in this town, that no man, woman, or child need be without the comforts that modern science of the fourteenth century had to offer. Bernard just ignored Wilhelm when he asked how it could be the fourteenth century when it was only thirteen fifty-one.

They stopped by the potters, who now sold jars with heavy lids to keep the vermin out of people's food stores. Each family had been given one as well, as a gift from the church. Bernard's generous spending to support all these good works had created a new wealth that was starting to course its way through the pockets of the villagers, and everyone's business was booming. The candlemakers, the smithy, and every place Bernard had led a civic improvement, was graced with a stop for a short blessing and a few words about how this new approach would make their village stronger, more productive, safer, healthier, and a better place for their children to grow up. With every stop the mood grew more jubilant with hopes rising for a better future. Bernard felt both peace and joy. The town now boasted many of the same innovations Cologne prided itself upon. He found he really enjoyed what he jokingly referred to as "town building".

At the final stop Bernard announced, "And now my acolyte, Wilhelm Notheisen and I invite you all back to St. Cyprian's, where we will open a keg of our finest wine to celebrate the accomplishments and the future hope for this village. We will raise a cup for all that we are grateful for, including the fact that the blue sickness, the plague that has cut us off from every other village and city, has not visited us. For reasons unknown, the blessed Lord has stretched His hand and shielded our faithful town. Today we rejoice!"

The crowd cheered and it was a gay parade that followed Wilhelm and Father Bernard back to St. Cyprian's. When they arrived, Bernard told Wilhelm, "Why don't you hand me the pole and I'll return the cross to the altar. If you would be so good as to fetch a barrel of wine, and choose the very best we have for the celebration, that would be most appreciated, my good man." He could hear Wilhelm saying over and over again *my good man* as he headed toward the cellar in the manse.

As Bernard made his way through the crowd, suddenly there was Adelaide before him.

"Sister! You are here. That makes me so very happy."

She had obviously been crying. "I am here." She sounded young and scared and vulnerable.

Of course, she was vulnerable. That was why Tuckerschade had been so interested in her, Bernard thought with a rage. He quickly calmed his emotions. This was a time for tenderness and reconciliation, not recriminations. He noticed that she had one hand resting on her stomach in a most protective way. He looked down at her belly and then up at her. He gave her a small nod, his eyebrows raised with his unspoken question.

She bit her lip and gave a slight nod in return.

He was not surprised after what Wilhelm had told him. He took her free hand. "It is a blessing. Today is a day of blessings and *all* are welcome. *All* are gifts of the Lord Almighty. All, Adelaide, my sister: mother to new generations. Let your heart be lightened, for you bear the hope of the world after the dark times we have walked through."

"But my sin…" her voice cracked.

"Is forgiven," Bernard said with joy and a wave of his hand. He kissed his sister on her forehead. "You walk in the light now, Adelaide. Let God shine His light on you and through you. Today we celebrate His love."

She nodded with a fleeting smile as a tear streaked down her cheek. She gave his hand a squeeze.

He made his way to the front of the church where he then blessed the barrel of wine that Wilhelm and four men had trudged over in a small wheelbarrow. Today was a good day. He always felt close to the Lord when he was giving a blessing, and today was full of them.

It was with another widely shared cheer that Father Bernard tapped the wine barrel and started to pour out pitchers of wine. The Deacons of St. Cyprian's came forward and took the pitchers around to the waiting crowd. Most people brought their own cup or tumbler. Some couples shared. An occasional family had a community mug, but everyone got a healthy share of the wine. After all were served, Bernard raised his cup just like he did at every mass, and sang out loud and clear:

"Through Him, with Him, in Him, in the unity of the Holy Spirit, all glory and honor is yours, Almighty Father, forever and ever."

The people responded with "Amen. Amen. Amen."

Bernard continued to call out, "We praise the Lord for His almighty grace, for holding the plague back from this village. We pray that we may fulfill the Lord's wishes and live in His light, until our dying day. We thank you, Lord, for this day and for every day hereafter. Amen."

"Amen" once again resounded from the assembled masses.

Bernard lowered the cup to his lips and drank. As one, the people followed suit. He thought the wine tasted good. Interesting. It had a slight kick to it, like the more potent wines from Castile, Aragon, and Portugal, and unlike the sweet and sugary wines usually produced in Germania. It had a bit of a fruity taste to it as well, perhaps reminiscent of apple, he thought. He drank deeply for today was a day of celebration after all! He had a second cup and invited the populace to do the same. People were crammed inside the church and spilled outside of it as well, filling the garden and the street. It was a festival unlike the town had ever seen and most of the townsfolk had turned out in their finery to mark the occasion.

About fifteen minutes later into the joyous celebration, he suddenly felt a cramp in his stomach and had to catch himself on a little table. Wilhelm was dogging his heels, just like always.

"Are you all right, my master?"

Bernard grabbed his side, feeling a burning. "I'm not your master, Wilhelm. We are both men of God. I should have eaten something for lunch before I drank the wine, that is all. Oh!" He felt another pang of burning and started to lose his balance again. "Maybe I'll go back to the altar."

"I'll help you, Father Bernard," Wilhelm put Bernard's arm over his shoulder and assisted him to the altar.

Bernard made the sign of the cross, three times as always, and then noticed the look on Wilhelm's face. "My friend, your forehead is beaded in sweat."

Wilhelm nodded. "Me stomach hurts something fierce." His knees buckled and he went down. "Me body seems to be weak." Wilhelm looked at Bernard with clear fear in his eyes, which then rolled up in his head and he fell to the floor, foam starting to fleck at his mouth.

Bernard reached for Wilhelm. "My son!"

A woman screamed and fell to the floor. Bernard would have run to her but he could not have moved had Jesus himself appeared on the other side of the room, beckoning the priest to him. Then a man screamed in a sound of torturous pain and crashed to the ground, writhing and twisting in hideous motions, knocking both people and pews about as he did so.

"What is happening?" Bernard said as another twist of burning pain tore at his innards. Then he too screamed and fell to the floor. There was hardly a person left standing now. The floor was a mass of bodies, some immobile and others twisting in grotesque gyrations. The screams of pain were deafening.

Quickly he grabbed the golden cross that hung long about his neck and with a strength that he knew not from whence it came, he pulled himself up to stand at the altar. He didn't know how he mastered the pain that was tearing through him. He couldn't see clearly anymore: everything was becoming blurry. But he knew that one thing was more important than anything he felt, than any fear that might be gripping his mind. In the loudest voice he could muster he said, "Through this holy anointing may the Lord in His love and mercy help you with the grace of the Holy Spirit. May the Lord who frees you from sin save you and raise you up."

He tried to put his fingers in the chalice of holy water on the altar and flick it at the people who were dying en masse in front of him, but with the spasms in his body all he could do was to violently knock it off the table towards them. It had its intended effect, as several were symbolically anointed with the spray of the last rites.

Then, with a mighty struggle, he said, mostly gasping, "Our Father, who art in heaven, hallowed be thy name; thy kingdom come; thy will be done; on earth as it is in heaven."

He coughed painfully and decided to skip the part about the bread. That was a substance that wasn't going to pass any of their lips ever again. *What could have been in that wine. Yes, it must have been the wine.*

"Forgive us our trespasses, as we forgive those who trespass against us."

Fleetingly he wondered, *Why had he done this? What could he possibly hope to achieve through this devilry?*

"And lead us not into temptation; but deliver us from evil."

Surely, this was the greatest evil imaginable—and he knew precisely from whence it came. He looked over to where his sister had been standing. She was now immobile in a fetal position in front of the image of Mary Magdalene. *At least she is here, blessed and forgiven. She is no longer under the devil's spell and for that I am grateful.* He surveyed the devastation and death that surrounded him. *Please Lord, share your kingdom with these innocents.* He took a painful breath, and sputtered out the final prayer—a prayer for protection, which his flock surely needed now more than ever:

"This is the Lamb of God who takes away the sins of the world. Happy are those who are called to His supper."

He didn't know how he did it, but with his last breath, he said "Amen" for all the people now dying or dead in his church, in the yard, and in the garden who would never be able to say it again. Then he fell forward, prone on the floor, still clutching the cross. While all the other villagers were twisting up into hideous shapes, Bernard felt his own body stiffen, pulling him straight and tall and stretching his arms long in front of him. He put all his thought into grasping his hands tightly to the holy cross that hung about his neck on the long chain. With the last wisp of consciousness granted him, he thanked God profusely for the strength that had allowed him to perform the last rites for the people of his village. Then all was mercifully dark and the pain that had been so overwhelming evaporated into the nothingness that surrounded him, and he knew no more.

Chapter 39

Nylah

Nylah wasn't sure how they made it through the next couple of days. She was quieter than usual because she felt terrible. She was sure that everyone knew it. She didn't dare tell Dr. T what was going on, although Everly thought he would be equally as supportive of her as Everly was herself. They had become like a little family on this dig. Nylah had never experienced anything like it and she was sure she didn't want to let it go. She knew it meant a lot to Ev, too. Nylah would guess that it was something Everly had been looking for her whole life.

Nylah was trying to go about her tasks; first among them was to plan for the trip up to the fen that Hans would guide for and that she didn't want to go on at all if he was going to be there. He was the last person she wanted to be around. At any rate, she knew that in her present condition she couldn't even hike as far as that tall pinnacle of rock full of nooks and crannies. But her mind felt overwhelmed by the thought of a pregnancy and the decision that she was facing. A sudden pain doubled her over and her knees buckled, leaving her in the dirt. In a moment, Everly was at her side.

"Nylah, I think we need to go to the hospital. You're in so much pain and from what I know of pregnancy, it makes you tired but not tortured. It's childbirth that's supposed to be the torturing part. I'm gonna go tell Trevor."

"No! I don't… I don't want him to know." Nylah wasn't sure what would kill her first: the pain in her belly or her humiliation. She felt like a statistic. "And the bog trip…"

"Screw the bog trip. Who cares?" Everly put her arms around Nylah. "Hey, you have nothing to be ashamed of, and you might have a medical emergency. He needs to know."

Reluctantly, Nylah nodded her assent and Everly went to Command Central where Trevor was staring intently at Father B.

"Hey. Uh, whatcha' doing?"

"Praying," he said and then he turned around. "How is she?" After a pause he added, "I'm worried, Everly. I'm really scared for her."

"Yeah. I think it's time to head to the hospital."

Trevor nodded and went to the printer. "I was about to come to you. I looked up the closest one. It's got good ratings. It's about forty-five minutes away. I can call them and tell them we're coming in." He picked up his car keys.

"*We're* coming in?"

"I don't want to leave her. I mean, I know this is going to sound so bonkers but it's like, well, it's like she's our sick child and I'm worried to death about her. If this is what fatherhood is like, blimey, it's torture."

Everly reached out and put her hand on Trevor's arm. "I'll take her. Someone has to stay here. Someone has to run the dig and you've got about eighteen people showing up tomorrow at nine A.M. sharp and they all need to be told what to do for the day. I'll text you with updates. Constantly."

Trevor looked concerned. "You know I'll only get those when the stars align in some weird way. Cell service out here is unreliable at best. Nylah seems to be the only one who can get any consistent signal at all."

"Yeah, she mentions some special international package she bought. Whatever. I'll email you, text you, leave you voicemail. I'll do everything I can. Eventually it connects. You'll know."

He handed her his keys and the printed-out map to the hospital. "You sure? You don't need back up?"

"If I do, I know you'll be there. And, uh, this is awkward but Hans is coming out… but not for Nylah."

Trevor nodded. "Oh right, right. The bog trip. The lonely grave. I'll ask Gunther to helm that. I'm not leaving the site in case you need me. Oh, and I'll be able to twoc Hans' car while he's up on the hike, so I'll be able to get to you!"

"That sounds like it would serve him right." Everly gave a sarcastic snicker. "She really doesn't want to see Hans right now."

"Understandable. Neither do I at the moment."

Trevor and Everly were so tender as they helped Nylah into Trevor's car. The two women followed his directions to the nearest hospital, which wasn't near at all. As they zoomed down the road, Everly mumbled, "I think I can remember how to drive a stick shift in the mountains. Wish this was the beach! It's much flatter."

"No problem. Ease off more slowly on the clutch. There you go. Ow! Okay, okay. That was a painful one. You've got it now, Ev." Nylah tried to find a more comfortable position in her seat.

◆━◆━◆

In the end, Nylah was in the hospital for two days after emergency surgery. Everly brought her "home" to their shared tent for the rest of her recovery. Trevor was there with flowers and chocolate that had arrived, along with two new super soft, enormous pillows.

Through the wall of the tent, Nylah overheard Everly ask Trevor, "How in the world did you get chocolates, roses, and pillows out here? I thought we stranded you when we took the car."

"I'm resourceful." And then he shook his head and said, "Hans came by for the fen excursion. Gunther let it slip that she went to the hospital and now Hans is worried sick. I don't think Nylah told him what was going on—so I did. The flowers and chocolate are from him. He wants to see her as soon as she'll let him."

"Drama, drama, drama, drama, drama. Oh my." Everly sighed. "And the pillows?"

"Oh, those are from me!"

Everly nodded. "That was thoughtful of you, Trevor." As they came back into the tent, she said, "Hi! Just checking to see if we can get you anything?"

Nylah leaned into the pillows which were so soft they felt heavenly. "Thank you both, for being here for me."

"Wouldn't have it any other way," Trevor assured her.

Nylah gave them a weak smile. "That's all I really need. And maybe that painkiller I'm due for."

Trevor jumped to get her a water bottle and the pills.

"So, tell me how the bog trip went? Did they check out the grave?" Nylah asked.

Trevor came over and sat down beside her cot. "Gunther stopped by when they came back, but just for a moment. He said he and his team found the site and recovered the artifacts. Nylah, here's something that you'll be excited about—they found both a golden cross, a small one, like on a necklace, and get this—a ring!"

"A ring? Really?" she asked quietly.

"Right, yeah, 'cause you know, these people were just dropping their jewelry everywhere. He thinks it looks like an important one. He's going to match it against the historical record."

"There's a historical record for rings?" She thought that sounded like the stupidest thing she'd ever heard. "Very Big Brother of them, huh?"

"Well, rings marked important occasions, so with a wedding, who got married and what kind of a ring was given to the bride would be noted in the records. And get this, the both of you: Gunther thinks this lady was of the era of our village. He says the ring fits the Middle Ages. Pretty it was, even though it was still dirty and needed to be attended to with a professional hand at restoration. He'll bring it back once he cleans it up and checks it out." Then Trevor gave them a funny look. "Unless, that is, that one of the professors twocs it to show it off at a dinner party!"

"I'm sure it will make a great story for our web page," Nylah said, her eyes feeling heavy as her painkiller started to work.

They made sure she was comfortable and covered with a blanket that she didn't want and she fell asleep, dreaming of people recording her rings and earrings and necklaces, documenting what she wore like a celebrity.

Chapter 40

Jezzie
May 1351

"Come along, ye!" Jezzie laughed as she called up to the window. "Johannes!" She liked Johannes. He understood her. Walked her path, as it were. In a town this size, there wasn't much call for their line of work. No Tolerance House to be had in a village this small, but there were enough odd jobs to pick up that the both of them could scrape by, waiting out the plague here until he could join her in a more lucrative line of work in the bigger cities. And most unexpectedly she'd found a friend. Mentored him. Shown him that a life on the fringes could be well worth living, despite what his parents thought. "We don't want to be late—it's free wine!"

His face appeared at the window above. "Just finishing up! Won't be a moment."

She rolled her eyes, crossed her arms and leaned back against the wall of the house. "Hurry up or we'll miss the free wine," she mumbled to herself. When you sheltered in a village and did daily work, you lived on a meager income. These weren't the bonus times. No. Bonus times happened when an army was on the march—opportunity abounded when an army was around. The drudgery of honest daily work didn't give you chance for a good tip either, like when a customer might ask for something out of the ordinary. No, with honest work you just put in your day's hours and you got your day's wages. Same day, every day. She kicked the ground. "Stupid blue sickness. I bet it's killed all me best customers."

It made her sad to think of the people she knew back in the cities that she visited. She always toured the cities in seasons to build up the expectation of her clientele, because even a sweetmeat over-indulged lost its allure over time. Scarcity made the heart grow fonder, particularly with the slightly older men who were her mainstay.

She had bolted at the first rumor of plague, before it took hold. She'd seen the like before and thanked the Lord above that He'd spared her once. She wasn't taking chances a second time. "Drop dead like flies, they do." Her voice was heavy and sad and her thoughts were on her most generous benefactors, who surely wouldn't live through the ravages of the plague years. "I'll have to establish all new clients." She sighed. "That'll be a piece of work."

"Right you were! A piece of work, he was. Sorry to keep you waiting. Had to get paid for a not-so-honest morning's labor." Johannes jingled a little coin bag. "But I'm well off now. Maybe I'll buy you a tankard!" He looked more thoughtful. "I do owe you for all you've done for me."

"No need! There's a celebration today. A blessing at the church. Ye missed the parade, ye did. They said little prayers over all town and blessed bridges and holes in the ground and such. And they announced *free wine*, tumblers full, just bring your own cup to the church. It should be quite a celebration."

Johannes smiled and then the expression melted off his face. "On second thought, maybe not. A cup of wine ain't worth the lashing for the sin." He jerked his head over his shoulder at the house they were now walking away from. "You shoulda' seen that one's back. Covered with scars, it was. Said it was his penance. Spooky. But he believes he can sin as much as he likes, as long as he can take the punishment. But I think he gets a little pent up in between.”

“There’s some that are like that.” Jezzie nodded knowingly.

“I told him that if he wanted to pay me double, that would cover the sin, and he didn’t need no lashing to beat it out of him. ‘It’s an indulgence’, said I. ‘And I will make sure it makes it to the church, so you don’t need to go. I’ll have the conversation with God for you’. And you know what he did?”

Jezzie shook her head.

“He paid me double!” Johannes laughed and laughed.

Jezzie sniggered. “Well, aren’t ye lucky then that we’re headed to a house of the Lord!”

Johannes stopped walking. “I’m not going there. I’m not giving up the extra money and I’m not being whipped for me sins. It’s not right. It’s not justice.”

Jezzie pulled on his arm. “Not *that* church! I only goes *there* for the entertainment, not for the punishment. We’re headed to St. Cyprian’s. That’s the nice Father Bernard who ye stayed with. If ye ever did confess there, your atonement would be to help improve the village for all, and not through your fine arts,” she gave him a wink, “but through real labor that would ‘benefit all the citizenry of the Valley Village for years to come’.” She said it like she’d heard it many times. “Ole’ Father Bernard’s as good as they be. And today he’s celebrating everyone’s hard labor to make the village better with a free barrel of wine! I heard him say so! And if we don’t get there, there won’t be none left for us. So, pick up your feet and leave your fretting behind.”

“Oh, that nice Father Bernard! And free wine. You’ve got my ears now! He is a kind man, that priest. Saved my life, he did, when I thought I was broken beyond repair.”

“Different ain’t broken, my boy. It’s just different. You’re not the only one. There’s plenty like ye. It’s a cruel world that sets us apart, but like I told ye, when the pestilence is over, you’ll find your place in the big cities. I’ll take ye. I’ll show ye. I’ve got old friends there who’ve shared many a story of rich patrons that like a little variety. Once the world rights itself, they'll emerge again. And when the minor lords start their little skirmishes and wars again and the armies are marching about, they'll be looking for someone like ye, I'm sure of it. Plenty of business to be done at the back end of an army!"

Johannes smiled. "Rich patrons. I like the sound of that in a city anywhere but here. And I really like the sound of free wine today. But I'm not giving him any of my bonus money, no matter how nice a priest he is. I need to be a good businessman and stretch my resources."

Jezzie laughed. Johannes was a bright lad and learned quickly. He was one of the chattiest fellows she'd ever met, which turned out to be nice. All too often, townspeople didn't want to stop and talk with her. "Far be it for me to get between you and God, do what you want. But, if you're of a mind, I'd like to ask you some questions I have about, well, let's call it technique, with your particulars." They walked on with Jezzie alternately looking surprised and then bursting out in peals of laughter.

As St. Cyprian's came into sight, Jezzie pointed to the church. "Let's pick up the pace, my friend, before the wine's all gone."

But as they got closer, Johannes' brows furrowed. "It's awfully quiet for a festival to be going on. Don't sound like no celebration to me. Where're all the people?"

"Maybe they're still doing prayers or something. Means we haven't missed it. Let's creep in quiet like, so no one will notice."

They went up to the front door, happy that there was no doorman to greet them with a stern look for their tardiness. Given who they were, the doorman would surely have his suspicions as to the reason. Father Bernard might be full of love and acceptance, but there were plenty of those in this town who wanted to be the first in line to throw a proverbial stone. Johannes opened the door quietly and gave her a bow. Jezzie smiled and gave him a curtsy in return before she went through it.

They both stopped short upon entering the church. The entranceway was filled with people, some slowly twisting and groaning, but most immobile and laid out in grotesque positions of pain.

Jezzie grabbed Johannes' arm for support. "What happened here?" Jezzie sounded breathless. She felt breathless. Her heart was pounding in her ears and her legs felt wobbly.

"I don't know." Johannes' voice came out in a whisper. "I helped with the November slaughter plenty of times, but I never saw nothin' like this." With his toe, he gave a nudge to a body near him, and it responded by contracting for a moment, but there was no breath or sound. Then it was still. "They're dead. Or they soon will be." Johannes swallowed hard. "Let's leave."

"Leave? We can't leave! Something terrible's happened here. We need to find Father Bernard."

"Great. Let's go find him. I'm sure he's at the ale house this side of town. That's where I need to be about now."

She gave him a dirty look and held tightly to his arm. "He'd be here with his people."

"You want to walk further into the church of death? This is worse than the church of lashings! I didn't know they did this in church? Why is anyone a member? I'm so glad I didn't stay with him."

Jezzie shook her head and bent down to examine one of the poor unfortunates close to her. "They don't do this in church, don't be a fool. Something's happened."

"It's plague! It's plague! It's here. We're not safe!" Johannes started to back up, looking to escape out the front door but Jezzie stood up and grabbed his arm again and held it fast.

"I've seen plague and this ain't it. Plague takes you slow. Days. You get fevers and chills. Big bumps appear on your neck and in your arm and leg joints. They turn blue. Your hands turn blue. Even your nose turns blue. The plague can take eight out of ten healthy men and ten out of ten of the weak, old, or sick. But this took everyone." She looked around. "It's an eerie dance of death they do, now ain't it?"

No one was alive now. The faint moans had all faded away.

"Is it the rapture? At the one service I went to in the lashing church, he said the rapture would come and lift people up to heaven, and only the sinners would be left behind. I know I'm a sinner, but I'll happily stay so if this is what it means to be raptured!"

Jezzie dragged him through the church, picking their way over the bodies, moving toward the head of the nave. "No. I heard that sermon a hundred times if I've heard it once. The rapture takes you in body and only leaves your clothes here on earth. That's how you know they've been uplifted. Their body and their immortal soul taken by God, but their old rags left behind."

"Oh right. I suppose you don't need your clothes in heaven. Do they give you new clothes then?" Johannes asked, looking worriedly at the bodies he was crossing over and carefully not stepping upon. "Or do you suppose you have to look at everyone's nakedness for an eternity? Even if they're old? Or fat," he said as he passed an extremely plump older couple with their arms clasped and looking at one another in death with hideous expressions frozen on their tormented faces. "That doesn't sound like an eternal reward to me." He stepped faster to keep up with Jezzie.

They came to the altar. Jezzie felt like her breath was taken from her. Wilhelm. Poor foolish idiot, his body a mangled, tortured shape, foam drying at the corners of his mouth. And then she cried out, "Oh no! It's him! Father Bernard! Father Bernard!" Jezzie got down on her knees and rolled the priest's still form over. "Oh, will you look at him?"

"Only if I must," Johannes answered. "Oh, he looks better than the others. He looks like he's… he's… well, at peace. Isn't that odd?" He gave a heavy sigh. "Such a nice man."

A tear slid down Jezzie's cheek and she nodded. "He does. But he's as stiff as a board, like the rest of them. My Lord, and he's standing straight and tall, just like the statues of the saints in the big churches. And he's grasping his golden cross on the chain." She sat back and clasped her hands together, staring at the corpse. Over her shoulder, she said, "He told me his mother gave him that cross. Blessed him and told him she'd always known that the church was his path. Advised him to follow his heart to his own destiny. He always wore that cross. Loved his mother, he did." She wiped away more tears. "This breaks my heart, Johannes. Johannes? Where are you?"

"I'm getting a glass of wine. I need some sustenance about now. All this gruesomeness shakes a man to his core, especially a man like me." Johannes picked up a mug from the floor and went to a side table where half-full pitchers of wine stood for the taking. "Jezzie, my parents might be here among the folk. I'm afraid to look to anymore. Don't want to see what I don't want to see." He poured himself a large draft.

Jezzie gave him a slow, level look. "I wouldn't drink that, my friend."

Johannes froze with the cup nearly to his lips and he looked over at Jezzie.

"Look at them. It was the very last thing they all did. Cursed, it must be."

His hand was visibly shaking as he set the cup down next to the pitcher and he nodded slowly. "So, what do we do now?"

"I think we need to find Friar Tuck. He's the only man of God left in town. He'll know what to do."

"Will he lash us?"

"What? We didn't kill them. We just discovered them. C'mon. Let's get the friar."

They went out the side door and through the garden.

"My God! The garden is full of dead people too! How many do you think are here?"

Jezzie shook her head and with a trembling hand that was hard to control, she wiped away more tears. She knew these people. There was the baker for whom she'd delivered bread. There was the butcher for whom she'd delivered meat. There was Elizabeth, the woman who loved to bring her rosemary shortbread biscuits to the priest and never knew that he fed most of those cookies to her and Wilhelm. "Take me hand, Johannes." She reached out and took his outstretched hand. "I need to feel the living right now."

Chapter 41

Everly

As Everly eased Nylah down onto the cot to rest, Nylah said, "Can you stay with me for a bit?"

"Of course," Everly said gently. "I won't leave your side. As long as you want. How about I send Trevor to make us a pot of tea?"

"I thought you said he was dead asleep on the couch in Command Central?"

Everly smiled. Poor Trevor had hardly slept in the past two days, he'd been consumed with anxiety for Nylah and unable to do anything to help them. "I think he's been exhausted with worry and now it's catching up to him. But a cup of tea would do him good, too."

"Send him to boil water? Even though there's no baby." Nylah seemed agitated beyond the residual pain from her surgery. "There might never be a baby." She reached over and stroked one of the beautiful roses in the bunch.

Everly nodded. "It got pretty scary there for a while. Ectopic pregnancies are frightening things. We were both worried for you. And he says Hans was really worried, too. But you're out of the woods now. The least we can do is let poor Trevor make tea."

Nylah nodded. "I lost a fallopian tube." She looked up at Everly, her eyes full of tears.

"Just one. Good news is: you've got a spare!" Everly tried to sound chipper.

"That'll make it hard for me to ever have a baby."

"True." Everly nodded. "But it won't be impossible. And you're young. You're going to heal quickly. You have so much life in front of you, Nylah. And time. You have time."

Nylah nodded slowly. "I'm sooo sad. I know I wasn't ready for a baby, but with all this drama, I'm actually pretty depressed about it. It's been like the summer of death. All this death all around us. Skeletons and old death and then... and then the little embryo had to die."

"The little embryo felt zero pain. I guarantee you. And there was no hope for it, Nylah. It was lodged in the wrong place. It wasn't a little person. It was a little impossibility. What's important is that we didn't lose you." Everly picked up her walkie talkie and put in the order for a pot of tea with a groggy sounding Trevor. "I told you he needed something to do. It'll be good for him to feel useful."

Nylah gave her a small smile.

"How do you feel, honey?" Everly asked her tenderly. "How's your pain level?"

Nylah shrugged and then asked, "What do you think happens after you die?"

"Uh, Nylah, I don't know."

"I didn't ask what *does* happen. I asked what you *think* happens. That's different. You know, there's no pressure in being cosmically wrong or anything. About me. Or my... little impossibility."

Everly blew out a breath. "Okay, so I'll give it a shot. I think you go on. I don't know what 'on' really means, but I think some part of you goes... on. Maybe you go back from whence you came? Like the little bugger inside you, it wasn't its time. Not yet. But maybe someday. Maybe it went back to wait it out until the time's right for it to... become."

"So, a beforelife. And an afterlife. So maybe all these people we're digging up still are... something? Someplace?"

"Yeah, could be," Everly replied with a shrug. At one time she'd been consumed with the existential questions of life, but since then she'd filled most of her years with trying to complete the stories of the dead. Her own mother's story had been taken from her way too soon, much like all of those archeological relics Everly tried to recover now.

"But that's not what you think. I mean, you sound really tentative there."

Everly brought her thoughts back to the present moment. "Well, like I said, I don't know. But I think they aren't who they were seven hundred years ago."

"Huh?"

"Let me put it this way: when I die, I think a part of me will go on. Soul, if you will. But I don't think I'll be exactly Everly anymore. Everly existed, she will *have* been, but for the part of me that endures, I think 'Everly' will be like a chapter. And that chapter will have closed. It'll be like reading a book, in the case of my life a good book. I'm happy. I'm content with who I am and what I do. But I won't be able to read that chapter again."

"Book, yeah. Not DVR," Nylah said thoughtfully. "So, no instant replay?"

Everly chuckled. "No. One and done in that sense. But maybe we learn from it? Maybe the learning is what survives, instead of the instant replay."

Nylah was quiet for a while. "All these people." She stopped and gently ran her fingers across her belly. "It's like they just dropped dead all at once. You know, like space aliens came from the sky and rained justice down on them or something. Man, it's creepy to think about that now that I've experienced a death too. This is the closest I've ever been to something dying."

"What did you say?" Everly asked. "About space aliens?"

"Space… aliens… raining… justice? You know, don't mind me, Ev. I probably still have some of the after-effects of all those drugs they gave me. And that pain killer. I'm a little loopy, to be honest."

"No, I mean before that. Before the space aliens part."

"Um, what did I say? It's like they dropped dead all at once."

Everly jumped up. "Where is Trevor when we need him! Trevor!" she yelled. She fumbled for her walkie talkie and yelled into it far louder than she meant to, "Trevor! Where are you? Come to the tent now!"

Chapter 42
Friar Karel Tuckerschade
May 1351

The candles were burning in St. Drogo-Erasmus and Friar Karel Tuckerschade was in high form with his sermon. Spittle flew from his lips as he shouted at the packed pews, "You'll see God's justice! Just like Sodom and Gomorrah were destroyed for their wickedness, so too will men be laid low by the justice of God. You'll know it when you see it. Their whole cities were wiped out. Even Lot's wife, disobedient and unforgiven, turned to look back at the city and was turned into a pillar of salt! Don't let yourselves be turned into a pillar of salt—let me warn you away from the sins of envy and greed, of gluttony and coveting thy neighbors' goods. Let me warn you away from debauchery. Let me warn you away from pride. Let me warn you away from sinning without repentance, for all can be made whole again through suffering and atonement. Together our suffering will save the world from this plague, has saved our village already! Only those without the Lord's favor will be turned to salt. They will fall dead as He rips their lives from them. But through me you will find the Lord. I am the doorway to your salvation. I am your protection." He lifted his arms high and spread them wide. He could feel the power flowing through him.

The people were enraptured, shouting "Amen!" and "Save us! Save us!" and "I repent! I do! I repent!"

Suddenly the doors burst open, throwing daylight into the dim, candle-lit church. Karel shielded his eyes from the light with his arm and tried to peer into the blinding beam to discern what was interrupting his service.

"They're dead! They're all dead!" a woman's voice shouted.

It sounded like Jezebel, that washed-up prostitute who sheltered in the village because no city's Tolerance House wanted her anymore.

"Who's all dead?" someone from the congregation asked.

Jezzie walked into the center of the church with her companion, a man Karel didn't quite recognize but thought he might have lashed once before. It was the man who answered. "Everybody. Everybody who's not here."

Jezzie was crying. "We went to St. Cyprian's and everyone's perished. They's all lying all over the place, tortured and grotesque. Twisted."

"Gruesome it is," her companion added. Both were visibly shaken.

Tuck felt an overwhelming sense of fate flow through him. This was his moment. The moment he'd waited for all his life. They were gone. Bernard was gone. Now the town would be his. His new Eden where he would start a new world for the glory of his Lord. These were his Holy Orders coming down from a higher authority than any pope. He could feel it.

"My friends," he began with his voice low and quiet. He noticed how the whole congregation turned to him. "Lucky you are, fortunate you are, blessed you are to be here in St. Drogo-Erasmus today, for your devotion has saved you!" His voice rose in its power as he worked his way through his new inspiration. "This is the justice I have been foretelling! Those who are warped have met with God's wrath and their souls sent to where they belong. Only those who are humble before the Lord, willing to suffer for His glory, will be saved."

He raised his hands in benediction. "It is our suffering that has saved this village from the plague and now the Almighty has seen fit to reward us with life! We are grateful, o merciful Father!"

"Amen!" rang out from several voices.

Karel stood in the silence that was filling the church. St. Cyprian's would once again be his, a church that could hold ten times the number of people as rustic little St. Drogo-Erasmus. In his mind, he could see himself wearing the vestments and orphrey, standing at the altar bearing the golden cross, and preaching his sermons to a crowd filled to standing. His heart felt light.

"Excuse me? Shouldn't we do something about all those poor people over at St. Cyprian's?" Jezzie's voice cut into his vision.

Karel shook himself. "Yes, let us away to St. Cyprian's and see the judgment of the Lord." He felt an excitement in his step, as though he was a king reclaiming his lost lands.

The group followed their friar across the town to the bigger church. Jezzie and Johannes walked with him, telling him everything they had seen.

"We got there late for the blessing and the celebration, not to mention the free wine they promised to all who came, and by the time we walked in, the last of them was dying on the floor."

"They's all twisted up something horrible," Johannes added.

When the group arrived, no one spoke. Some choked out a few sobs, seeing friends and neighbors. They walked around, in shock at what they observed.

Jezzie elbowed Friar Tuckerschade in the ribs. "I think some of these folk need some direction, Friar. It looks to me like a few o' them be pocketing the valuables of the dead. That don't seem right, somehow."

"Right. Right. No pillaging of the dead." Karel felt a mix of emotions. He knew death was going to happen at some point. They would tap the wine. But he didn't think it would be quite so soon or that it would be at a festival. He had imagined it happening in the dark and quiet of a winter's night, perhaps during a storm, and afterward the way would be clear. He thought all these people would be his. This was supposed to be his flock. It was only supposed to be that dratted Bernard and his deacons who were conveniently moved out of the way. Maybe Wilhelm. Yes, definitely Wilhelm. Then a shepherd-less flock would be searching for a shepherd, and good old Friar Tuck would be so gracious in taking them on. But everyone? There must be one and a half hundred. Maybe more. There would be no one to run the smithy. No bakers. No brewers. No butchers. No shearers or spinners or weavers. No tailors or seamstresses. No one to till the fields or gather in the crops. He surveyed the devastation, not sure if his own heart was still beating. As though from a far away place, he heard Jezzie shout out,

"Like the friar just said, no pillaging of the dead!" Jezzie started shouting orders and used Johannes as her lieutenant to bring some structure to the chaos that surrounded them. "Do not eat or drink anything that ye find."

"Right, everything's…" Johannes turned to Friar Tuck, "what did you say back at St. Drogo's?"

"It's Drogo-Erasmus. And I said it's a judgment of the Lord." Karel's voice was barely audible. It was not the Lord judging all these people that he was thinking about.

"Right!" Johannes called out as he walked away. "Friar says this is the judgement of the Lord. Don't take anything from them, for like Sodom and Gomorrah, these people have been judged. And from the looks of it, found to be wanting." Johannes looked at the members of St. Drogo-Erasmus who were gathering around him, in search of any direction at all. "You don't want to be turned into a pillar of salt, do you?"

There was a general murmuring of the people.

Jezzie went back up to Friar Tuck, who was still not able to focus on what was happening around him. "Friar. We can't leave them just lying about. What do we do with the bodies? So few of us can't dig this many graves. We're outnumbered vastly by the dead."

Karel heard her voice distantly ringing in his ears. Something about what to do with being out-numbered. His dreams were crumbling around him, turning his ambitions into a trash heap of broken hopes and dreams. "Trash heap."

Jezzie looked at Friar Tuck, confusion on her face. "Ye want us to put their bodies in the new trash pits?" She looked at Johannes, who shrugged at her and then turned back to the assembled gathering and said,

"You heard what he said! The bodies are to go to the trash pits."

Jezzie grabbed Johannes by the arm. "What are ye saying? That's not consecrated ground!"

Johannes leaned toward her and said softy, "Do you know of any consecrated ground that's got holes in it big enough for this lot? I'm not sure we can fit them in, in any case. Who's gonna' dig the graves otherwise? Besides, it was the priest who had them built and you said yourself they did blessings today of all the improvements. So, it's been blessed and it'll have to do. Oi! You there, get a wagon and a team. We've got to move all these bodies."

A man looked at him suspiciously. "And why can't we have their rings and such?"

Without missing a beat, Johannes said, "It's all damned. They been judged, ain't they, and now they lie dead. So's unless you want to see the same fate that came upon them, don't be taking what's theirs." He leaned into the man and said, "It goes to the grave with them, just like their secrets and the reason this judgement was settled upon them. Poor blighters. Amen."

The man nodded and started shouting orders to the others, with the remaining folks scurrying about to do his bidding.

Johannes turned to Jezzie. "Looks like everybody wants to be a lieutenant." He looked around. "Oi! Where'd the friar go?"

Karel was walking in a nightmare. Like Elvina the goat, the vast majority of the townspeople lay about, twisted and turned by the poison that had wrought its promise. He didn't mean for this. He heard the dull sounds of shouts of orders being given for disposal of the dead, but he didn't care to listen to them. There was something he had to know. Had to understand. He made his way through the entryway and into the nave. He found Father Bernard in the middle of the Chancel. The words of victory that on any other day he would've said to the corpse of his nemesis were silenced by what he saw: in death Bernard looked for the world like a saint already, straight like a stone statue and grasping that gold cross on the long chain he always wore about his neck. He was in repose. At peace. At one with the Lord. Karel tried to wrest the golden cross from him, but Barnard's death grasp was firm and clenched around it. He doubted that any hand would ever pry it away until Judgment Day. Maybe not even then.

Karel knelt down and put his face in his hands, breathing hard. At last he put his hands down without realizing they were clenched into fists. "You will not win this way. You'll not best me." He stood up, throwing his shoulders back and standing up tall to get a grip on himself. He slowly turned around and saw Wilhelm. That looked painful. "You shouldn't have left me," he snarled to the twisted body. "You were mine. Like my own son. To do my bidding." He heard people of his own congregation yammering about him, but he didn't pay them much attention.

Jezzie made her way over to Father Bernard's body, accompanied by another woman. "This man is not to be moved with the others. Not yet."

"What do you want done with him, missus?" the woman asked her.

"I don't know yet. I'll only put him in the mass grave as a last resort." Jezzie bit her lip. "He's the father of this flock and he should be treated with respect." She chewed on her lip and looked thoughtful for a moment. "He's got a sealskin cloak his uncle sent him for the cold storms of winter. I'll find that and we'll wrap him in that first. I'll check the church graveyard and see if there's a reasonable spot to bury him." Jezzie looked up from the peaceful visage of Father Bernard. "He was a good man."

Karel Tuckerschade ignored this trivial conversation. They could overcome all this death. In time, it would all fade into legend and myth and he could make St. Cyprian's his. He threw his head sharply to the side to crack his neck and relieve the tension, and in doing so his gaze fell upon the north transept. A mass of blonde hair froze him for a moment. Then he whispered, "No! No! No!" He started to leap to the transept, not caring if he stepped on a dead body or not. There she was, curled up and holding herself. Wrapped around their baby. Her hair had come loose from her cap in the gyrations of her demise and was now in a wild riot about her head and shoulders, almost blanketing her. He fell to the floor and tried to pry her arms free, to hold her, but she was stiff as though carved of stone. Even in death she would not hold him again.

"No! This was not supposed to happen." The words dragged out of him, barely able to escape his lips for his tears. He was tearing at his hair and beating his chest, but neither the dead nor the living paid him any mind. People were shouting around him and he vaguely heard commands to:

load them into the wagons.

and

throw them into the trash pits.

"You, my love, will not rest in a potter's field. You, my beloved Eve, will rest in Eden." He picked up her body, amazed at how slight she was even halfway through her pregnancy. "You and Cain will be the guardians of Eden forever." Slowly, with heavy heart he carried her out of the church. He no longer cared what happened at the church or what happened tomorrow. Would there be a tomorrow without his beloved Adelaide? He had been sure she would come back to him. What else could a pregnant woman do? It wasn't like they had choices. He kissed the top of her head as he carried her body down the street, away from the scene of corpses being loaded up en masse, piled one on top of another, on a wagon, destined for the newly-dug trash pits just outside of the town. He carried her until he came to a small wheelbarrow. Not likely now that anyone would care if he took it or not, so he gently laid her down in it. He went into an open door of a house whose owners now surely lay dead in the churchyard. Spying a beautiful blanket, likely a family heirloom, he took it and carefully wrapped Adelaide's body in it.

Leaving the disaster of St. Cyprian's in the hands of two well-known prostitutes, he wheeled the barrow up the path, up into the hills, and through the field. He took her by the most direct route. A couple of hours later, when he arrived at the tree, he retrieved a shovel from his little ramshackle work shed and started to dig. He could only dig a couple of feet in the hard clay, so he ended up burying her as best he could and then bringing as many stones as he could find to cover her the rest of the way. That would keep her safe. She would lie close to the tree of knowledge, and unlike the betrayal of Eve, her hand would never pluck an apple nor her mouth take a bite of its fruit.

◆━◆━◆

Hours later when Tuck returned to the town, the sun was setting. He felt broken. He first went to St. Drogo-Erasmus, but no one was there. Like a man in a trance, he wandered through the eerily quiet town and eventually ended up at the garden of St. Cyprian's. Jezzie was there, saying goodbye to those who remained at the church, thanking them for their service. Johannes was at her side.

"Where have you been?" Johannes barked out the question rather rudely. "Left us to all the work, did you?"

Jezzie rolled her eyes at her companion and looked more empathetically at the friar. "Ye do look something awful. You're covered in dirt and bracken, like you've been at a burial of your own. Where have ye been?"

"To Eden. To the birthplace of mankind. And now, the place of eternal rest."

Jezzie and Johannes looked at one another. Jezzie shrugged but Johannes signaled that Tuck had gone crazy. She gave him a slow nod. "Today could be a day to tax any man's sensibilities. Right God-awful day."

"Day of the damned," Johannes said.

Karel looked around him. "There are no bodies."

"We got them all taken care of."

He was confused. "How?"

It was Johannes who answered. "Like you said, put 'em in the trash pits. Worked for a mass grave and there we dumped all the bodies. It was a good idea. We got the majority of them in there, but I wouldn't put it past Jobst, Wolf and Heinrich to have just dumped their wagon over in a field. They seemed eager to loot the bodies and best to do that where no one could see them, now, wasn't it? But I can't keep watch over everyone all at once."

Jezzie wiped her brow. "Leave them to the justice of the Lord, I say. What else can we do?"

"Where's Bernard?" Karel asked.

Jezzie nodded a couple of times. Through tears streaking down her cheeks, she said, "I did my best. I couldn't bury him in the churchyard. There was no grave dug and the ground is just too hard. So, after we got all the bodies that made it into the mass graves covered, we had no choice but to drag him there as well. He's a couple of feet of clay soil on top of them. He's looking over his flock, he is, tall and saintly. He was a good man."

Karel looked at them like they were out of their minds. Then he started to head towards the church.

"And where are ye going?"

"I'm going to get the cross."

"Is the cross still there?" Johannes asked Jezzie. Tuck turned around and looked at them sharply.

She nodded. "It's about the only thing that's left! The people went crazy, terrified about being turned into pillars of salt. They threw the bodies in the first two pits and in the third, they tossed every possession they could find of the people. Jars and food and books and anything of finery that existed, it was dumped because it was cursed." She turned to Johannes. "Didn't ye hear old Ulrich saying that if the Lord smote these people down, then all they owned must also be grievous to the Lord's eye! He was in a right rage, he was. People was throwing tools and candlesticks and anything they could get they hands on, pitching them down the cesspits and latrines when they was just too tired to make the trip out to the big pit."

"Everything is gone? The riches of the town are gone?" Karel was astonished. Today was more than he could wrap his mind around. First the flock that was destined to be his was gone. All wiped away by that stupid priest. Then the woman who was destined to be his lay in a shallow grave up in the *Hohes Venn*. Now all the riches of the town, all the riches destined to be his, had been thrown in a pit? "Why would anyone do that?"

"Don't you know?" Jezzie asked. "Righteous anger! They believe it excuses them from all sinning, don't they now? Believe they do, that they can do no wrong when they have this much hate in their hearts. Can't imagine where it came from now, can you? Just who might've stoked the fires of their righteousness and hatred, hmmm?"

"We'll have to dig it up!" Karel said, a wild look in his eye and rage filling his voice again. He didn't know he could experience emotions at this point and their ferocity took him by surprise. If everything else was lost, the prosperity of the town would be his.

Jezzie gave him a level look. "I had them throw the rest of the barrel in that third pit with all those worldly possessions. And the pitchers of wine. And all the mugs. Are ye sure ye want to dig it up? None of us do."

They stared at one another for a hard moment until the sound of horse's hooves drew their attention.

"All hail! All hail!" the rider called.

Jezzie had taken control of the situation all day and didn't seem ready to stop now. "And who be ye? What's your business in the Valley Village?"

"All hail!" The man shouted again as though a large crowd were gathered around him.

Johannes put his hands on his hips and with a low whistle said, "Why! He's a herald! Me old dad said they had them in Bonn for big news. What say you, Herald?"

"Hear ye! Hear ye! I have come from the city of Bonn to proclaim that the plague has ended and that quarantine has been lifted. You may now gather and congregate. You may travel to other cities and towns. Commerce between regions may start up again, by the order of Louis the Fifth The Brandenburger, Duke of Bavaria and rightful King of all of Germania and Bohemia. Hear ye! Hear ye! The plague has been declared ended. May all praise the Lord most high and His mercy!"

There was silence. Eventually the herald dismounted and walked his horse over to the group. "Usually there are cheers when I say that bit, even for those who don't recognize Louis the Fifth's claim to the throne." He looked about him and shook his head. "Not many left here, are there? Same everyplace I go. Empty houses. Empty stores. Empty squares. But this is quieter than most. Is there a place I can stay the night before I leave tomorrow to find the next town?"

Jezzie and Johannes looked at one another and then back at the herald. Johannes said, "You can pick just about any house in town and make yourself at home."

Karel Tuckerschade watched Jezzie and Johannes lead the herald away to find accommodations. *Pick just about any house in town.* He stared about him as the sun set on a silent, empty village.

Chapter 43

Trevor

Trevor hurried along with the tray of hot tea, trying to balance the teacups, a milk jug, a bear of honey, a sugar pot, the water, and stirrers all on the tray. His walkie talkie was crackling now with Everly's voice, sharply calling for him. He felt a sense of panic that something had gone very wrong. "Oh my God, what am I doing bringing bloody tea when we probably need an ambulance!" But the *keep calm and carry on* part of his upbringing won out over his panic, and he carried the tea to the women's tent first and put off his panic attack until later.

"There you are! Great. Here, let me take that." Everly spoke in a commanding tone as she relieved him of the tray. Empathy was not her strong suit.

"Should I go call an ambulance or just drive the car up to the tent?"

"What?" Everly asked. "Oh, no. Nylah's recovering just fine. It's not that kind of emergency."

"Bloody hell! Then why all the barking through the walkie talkie? I thought... I thought..."

"We have something else for you to think about." Everly took him by the arm and pulled him over to a little stool. She started to pour out three cups of tea.

He did as she indicated and sat down.

"Here. Tea." Everly turned to Nylah and gently handed her a cup. "Sip on this. It's hot. British tea made by an authentically British person always makes you feel better. I put a ton of honey in it. And an ice cube."

"That's not British tea anymore, is it?" Trevor objected. He looked from Nylah to Everly and back again. "So, this really was just a tea emergency. I swear, I thought you were going to give me a heart attack. I was dead asleep on the couch."

"Nylah has something important to tell you. Way more important than sleep." Everly looked at Nylah. "Go ahead."

Nylah looked a bit unsure and Trevor wondered what kind of mystery about womanhood she was about to let him in on. He was absolutely sure he wasn't ready. Everly had walked him through the ectopic pregnancy, the surgery, the expected stages of recovery, future projections for fertility—so much more than he ever wanted to know. He swallowed hard and tried to prepare himself.

"Yeah, so um, we were talking about death and all the dead people out here. And, uh yeah. It looks like they just dropped dead all at once."

Trevor sat on his stool, perched over the teacup in his hand. He looked at Nylah and then at Everly. He was confused but relieved that this didn't have anything to do with woman parts or babies or unintended pregnancies or that Hans fellow. "All at once. Right. They all died at once. You said that. The whole mosh-pit theory. People go to the rave and some of them get crushed. I, I do listen to what you say, you know. We did look again at all the bones and none of them were broken like that. No one had been… trampled."

"Yeah." Everly put a hand on his arm. "But we didn't really listen to what she said. Listen: it's so different from the population dying day-by-day, or week-by-week, or month-by-month as the plague winds its crafty way through the community. Even septicemic plague, which moves fast, doesn't move *that* fast."

Trevor turned to stare at Everly. "Right… right… no plague kills everyone all at *once*." Trevor's unfocused eyes stared off at the tent walls. "A mosh pit doesn't kill everyone. What kills everyone all at once?"

"Bombs," Nylah said as she moved to try to find a more comfortable position.

Trevor gave Nylah a quick stare and turned to look at Everly. "It's the drugs, right? Still on some strong medications?"

Everly nodded.

"And machine guns." Nylah blew out a breath and then took a sip of tea. "Yeah, that too. All dead. Machine guns do it every time. Not cannons, though. They miss some people."

Trevor looked at Everly and thought that maybe there was a good reason she'd wanted him here fast. Clearly Nylah was having some kind of bonkers reaction to the drugs they'd given her at the hospital.

"Space aliens with rainbow fentanyl candy pouring down from the sky! Gets everybody in their Sunday best." Nylah yawned and said, "I'm so tired."

Trevor reached out and grabbed Everly's arm. "Jim Jones!"

"Is he a space alien?" Nylah asked, looking confused.

"Oh my! We've got work to do!" Trevor announced.

Soon, Nylah insisted that she just wanted to sleep. Trevor left the tent, hands full of the tea service, and he tried to not think of how awkward it was that he'd been dead asleep on the couch and dreaming of Everly, and then her voice came barking across the walkie talkie, nearly making him jump out of his skin. He'd brought in the tray of tea and when she took it from him and set it down, she turned around and grabbed his arm—certainly not in the way he'd been dreaming about, but still, that was as close as they'd gotten since the night he'd held her as she cried long suppressed tears of grief and anger and frustration. He'd thought about her a lot since that night.

He was amazed at what it was like to work with Everly. She was his opposite in most ways, a little bit annoyingly detailed, but it was like he was the yin to her yang. "And what would a yin be without a yang?" he said aloud as he headed back to Command Central. The discoveries they'd made together. The insights they'd shared. It made him want to never be on a dig without her. And tonight, there was someone else he didn't want to be without.

He rushed into the lab tent, holding the skull of Father B. Everly was already there.

"She's sleeping. Really sleeping." Everly gave a heavy sigh. "I'm exhausted."

Trevor walked over to her and she crumpled against him. He wrapped his arms around her, Father B's skull still in his grasp.

"Can you please tell me why you have that damn skull in your hand again?"

He pulled back and looked into her eyes. They looked tired. "I think Father B is telling us that there's more important things than research or discovery or science. Like family and taking care of one another and taking care of ourselves. Let's call it a night. All this can wait until tomorrow." With his arm over her shoulder, he escorted her out of the tent and killed the lights and zipped down the flap. "After all, they aren't going to get any deader, now are they? No. Tonight we all rest. Tomorrow we save the world."

Chapter 44

Friar Karel Tuckerschade July 1351

Friar Karel Tuckerschade closed the doors to St. Cyprian's. As the new prior of the church, he felt a wave of relief and satisfaction. Of course, he was very busy, since he also served as doorman, acolyte, and priest. But this was his church now. He had no rival. He thought about the huge cross standing outside the now empty St. Drogo-Erasmus. *I should have that brought over to St. Cyprian's,* he thought, then brushed the idea away as he concentrated on performing the mass before him.

As he walked up the aisle, he led the entrance song, stroking his hands down the white vestments he now wore over his old black robes. They weren't pristine and new, but he still felt regal wearing them. He wished he had an orphrey to beautifully decorate and offset the white, but he brushed that thought away too, lest it anger or distract him from the work at hand. Bowing to the altar, he then turned and started the mass.

His voice rang out clearly as he said:

"Lord, have mercy. Lord, have mercy. Lord, show us your mercy and love. And grant us your salvation."

The Gloria was followed by the Collect, the opening prayer to give his parishioners context for the mass and the homily. He had searched his memory for an appropriate story from the Bible for the Liturgy. He ended up with one that he thought was right, but with literacy not being one of his gifts, he had to settle for a story that fit his mood and sounded biblical enough. He sang both parts of the responsorial psalm since the parishioners' voices were no match for the grand size of this cathedral of St. Cyprian's. At least, he couldn't hear them.

At last it was time for the Homily, the part he loved the most. He didn't need to struggle to remember the bits and pieces of the Bible that old Father Spite had beaten into him when he was a young acolyte: he could just speak freely. Karel knew just what he would lecture about today. Times were hard. It was a Great Mortality that had devastated this little village, along with so many others. They needed forgiveness. No one needed to suffer any longer. This was a new day. They were the people of God and this was their Eden, given them, the worthy, the surviving, the worshipping, the blessed. They would build a new world, post-plague and it would be centered right here in the Valley Village of the Three Mountains. All their sins had been forgiven because they were among the survivors; it was living proof of their worth. He had a long lecture in mind, one that would uplift the spirits of the citizenry of this blessed town.

In the very last pew, Jezzie and Johannes sat together.

"You're right, Jez, this is very weird. Very entertaining though. Do you think he knows there's no one here?"

Jezzie looked at her companion. "No one? Just who're we? And there might be ten other people scattered about."

"I don't think the sleeping ones count for much though, do you?"

She nodded in acquiescence. "I'm surprised to see anyone at all. I only came last week because I saw him parading that golden cross about on a pole through the streets, calling the faithful to mass. I couldn't believe it, to tell you the truth, and I had to see it for meself. I 'spose it worked, I mean, he's got about three people who are at least watching his mass, and that's better than none. I 'spose, anyway."

"I think the rest are here for the show, like me. Wonder if it's sending shivers up their spines like it is mine? Ghostly like. Never thought I'd set foot in here again." Johannes looked around at where death had befallen so many just a few months before. "Tell me, Jez, do you think the spirits of the dead are comin' to see old Tuck butcher this mass like he butchered them?"

She gave him a level look. "I've got no proof of that. I don't *know* that he did it."

"But you believe it." Johannes looked right back at her.

She nodded and stared at Friar Tuck, now deep into his lecture about forgiveness for any sin, and God's love and redemption. "Funny, I think this is the same as the last homily when I came before? Maybe that's the only homily he gives now."

Johannes looked at Friar Tuck. "That would make sense. Tryin' to convince himself that he could possibly be forgiven for his crimes!"

"Shhh! Maybe he did. Maybe he didn't." She shrugged. "Probably did."

Standing in the area in front of the altar, Karel heard none of this whispering. His ears were for his voice alone, filling the air with promises of forgiveness for all of one's sins. At some point, man had simply suffered enough. And they must have, because the messenger had come to tell them that the plague was over and quarantine was now lifted. He ended with the words he remembered his old priest always saying:

"Today this scripture has been fulfilled in your hearing. Amen."

There was no response.

Karel went on to prepare for the Eucharist as he always did, following his best memory of old Father Beschädigt, or Father Spite, as he usually thought of him, and opened the Tabernacle containing the bread and wine. While there was plenty of wine in town, there was, unfortunately, no bread to be had. The baker and her apprentices lay in the mass grave with the others who had suffered her fate and met their day of reckoning. Not knowing how to bake his own bread and not being able to find anyone else to make it, Karel had collected some plants that he thought were herbs, at least they looked like herbs, and he had fashioned them into little eucharist pats. They would have to do. He reasoned that fresh herbs were closer to God's creation anyway, since they had never been re-made into anything else by man.

He picked up the packet of weeds and said:

"Blessed are ye, Lord, God of all creation. Through your goodness we have this… this, uh, bread to offer, which earth has given, and, and it will become for us the bread of life."

He then picked up the wine and poured some into the ceremonial cup and said:

"By the mystery of this water and wine may we come to share in the divinity of Christ, who humbled himself to share in our humanity."

He mumbled some prayers and then said loudly, "Blessed be God forever."

There was no response.

He said quietly, "Lord God, we ask you to receive us and be pleased with the sacrifice we offer you with humble and contrite hearts."

He washed his hands with water and then said, "Lord, wash away my sin; cleanse me from my sin."

His voice called out, "Pray, brethren, that our sacrifice may be acceptable to God, the almighty Father. We ask this in the name of Jesus the Lord. Amen."

Karel looked about his beautiful church of St. Cyprian's. Surely, he had been forgiven of all of his sins. After all the sacrifices he had made, surely his scales were balanced. His standing at this altar was proof positive. It must be. Else why would he be here, offering the body and blood of Christ to the masses?

He held up his little mess of weed packets.

"Take this, all of you and eat it: this is my body, which will be given up for you."

He brought the weed packet to his lips and nibbled it, wincing in its bitterness. He set it back down.

Then he held up the wine and said, "Take this, all of you, and drink from it: this is the cup of my blood, the blood of the new and everlasting covenant. It will be shed for you and for all so that sins may be forgiven. Do this in memory of me."

He took a long draft of the wine, feeling it course through him. It certainly was a feeling of forgiveness and with enough of the holy liquid, blessed forgetfulness would soon follow. He was mildly annoyed that no one came forth to accept the body and blood of Christ. Most were staring at the ritual and at him.

They are traumatized by their losses and in fear that their sins might exact the same price their fellow citizens paid. I'll show them it's safe.

He ministered the eucharist to the unseen, serving the invisible spirts the weed packets and the sips of wine. Between each imagined parishioner, he took a sip of wine himself and reverently kissed the gold cross that was now his.

In the back row of pews, Johannes leaned over to Jezzie. "Are you goin' up for the body and blood of Christ? He looks to be drinkin' a whole tankard full of wine today."

"I wouldn't touch that wine if all eternity depended upon it." She shook her head, staring. "Truth be told, I'm even afraid to watch, lest he get all twisted up like those poor folk, but I can't turn away nonetheless."

Johannes nodded slowly, also staring ahead. "Me neither."

Ten weeks later Karel Tuckerschade had offered mass four times a week, replete with his excess of wine and inedible weed packets. In his sermons he initially promised forgiveness for the totality of one's sins. He had called the faithful to mass, parading in all the streets of the village with the golden cross perched high above his head, but the only ones who followed him back to St. Cyprian's were the unseen spirts of the dead. He was sure Adelaide was among them. If he could drink enough wine, he could almost see her there.

Along the way, his sermons had morphed away from the uplifting message of forgiveness and his liturgy now focused on the devil creeping amongst the living, secretly corrupting hearts, disguising itself as something venerable and holy but in reality simply out to destroy everyone's hopes. His sermons were inspired by his dreams, which were filled with the slithering of the serpent, come to ruin his Eden. He knew he had to protect his domain, whatever the cost. He set out on a mission to determine what and where this Satan-in-disguise could be and after much meditation and prayer, he finally deciphered the devil's secret lair, the object it possessed and used as a vehicle to infiltrate the once-innocent and pristine village. As a warrior of God, Karel Tuckerschade would destroy the vessel the devil used to penetrate the town and pervert its people.

Alone in the shell of the abandoned St. Drogo-Erasmus, Karel was a haggard and thin version of his former self, now aged before his time. With reverence, he put on his old wooden crown; it sat high and tall on his head, adding more than a foot of height to his frame. He carefully pulled out his gray cloak. It wasn't to hide his identity from anyone. There was hardly anyone left in the town anyway. Those who hadn't been at St. Cyprian's on that fatal day, whether they were congregants of St. Drogo-Erasmus or just didn't attend the festival, had been steadily leaking out of the town since May. In wagons, on horseback, or even just walking. A family, a small gathering, or sometimes a duo would set off for better fortunes elsewhere, all wanting to get away from the curse that lay on the Valley Village. But today he was going to remove the curse. He was going to heal the village.

Cleanse it. But to do so, he needed the protection of the specter of the *Hohes Venn*, the demon of the mountain-pass bog.

Karel breathed out deeply as he let the cloak fall about his shoulders. He knew he would look like the specter of death himself as he walked through the empty streets. It felt right to him that the ghost of the high bog would be the messenger on this particular errand. If anyone saw him as he made his way through the streets, he was unaware. Didn't care. The devil saw him coming and that was all that concerned him. In his mind, he was followed by an army of the faithful: all of those who had died in St. Cyprian's, having been punished for their sins, mostly the sin of being in the wrong place at the wrong time.

He threw open the doors of St. Cyprian's and, as the Specter, he strode down the aisle to the altar.

"It's you! It's been you the whole time, hasn't it? Very clever indeed."

He picked up the golden cross, holding it in his hands and staring at it through the slit the cloak made over his face. It gleamed and glinted, the precious stones catching the light from the large church windows. It would pain him to do this, but that was how he knew it was the right thing to do. God called on us to do the most painful acts in His service. Didn't the scars all across Karel's own body attest as such?

He carried the cross on the pole out to the edge of town and came to the pits.

"Father Bernard's trash pits. Thrown away like trash. All of them. Potters' graves for the whole town." He observed the three pits. He could hardly look at the third one, piled high with dirt. The prostitute had informed him that one held the goods of the town, the fine possessions of the folk that should have been his. They were needed as the building blocks for creating a new village, a new village he was going to name Karelsbad. Their family heirlooms, even furniture, but most importantly tools and household goods had been poured over with the celebratory wine and then buried under several feet of dirt. It was too much for him to attempt to rescue and he didn't dare risk exposing himself to the liquid that bathed the goods as they were laid to rest.

What he missed the most were the tools, yet the knowledge of how to use those tools had died with their owners, who themselves were mostly buried in the first two pits in the row. Of course, some of the folk had been scattered across the meadows after their impromptu undertakers pillaged their poor bodies and left them there as carrion, too lazy to drag them back to the potter's field or too cowed at the thought of being discovered for their crimes.

Standing in his great gray robe, Karel observed the pits, noticing how their dirt was now starting to settle. Back in May, the villagers tapped as the porters of the dead, the erstwhile impromptu undertakers, had covered the third pit with a heaping mound of dirt. The second pit, a mass grave of the dead simply tossed inside with no ceremony at all, as though they had been merely goods and tools themselves, had been covered over with a smaller mound of dirt.

"Apparently, they were more scared of the wine than they were of the dead bodies. Maybe they aren't as stupid as I thought?" he said aloud to the empty air as he surveyed the ground. "But they faltered here, didn't they? On your grave, Bernard. They faltered on your grave." He spoke as if the spirit of the man were there with him, standing next to the large but shallow pit at his feet.

It was almost as if he could hear Father Bernard's voice say: "They left it to welcome the bodies of others who might join the townsfolk, through plague or other such scourges, since no one knew when the horror would end. A place to be met by friends for one's journey to eternity."

Karel raised himself up and shouted back at this ghost, "The horror ends now. You brought this upon us, Bernard. This is all your fault. You brought a golden idol to corrupt our people and now I, like Moses, have come down from the mountain and struck the idolaters down. But what I didn't know is that the soul of the serpent resided in the devilwood you brought into our midst! A cross made of devilwood. Very clever indeed. And layered with gold! That should have screamed out its true nature. But I figured it out at last. And now, Bernard, your Lucifer's cross will rest with you for an eternity."

As Karel was about to throw the cross into the shallow pit, the glint of the gems caught his eye. While a cross made of devilwood was surely contaminated with evil, the gems were hard and pure and could ward off the penetration of wickedness. *And they might come in handy,* he reasoned. He pulled a knife from his belt and pried off the gems, gouging the cross in the process and giving himself a rather deep cut to his hand. He observed the scarring on the cross, amazed at the depth of the gold layering over the wood, which was still not exposed. "Serves you right, you minion of the damned." He pulled a rag out of a pocket of his clothes and tied up his hand tightly. He couldn't figure out what to do with the gems in his hand. His pockets all had holes in them and while the compartments worked fine for bulky items such as a soft rag to wipe his nose, they would not do at all for small gemstones that would fall through and be lost forever. Without another idea that he could come up with, he popped the bloodied gems in his mouth, tucking them into his cheek, like a squirrel with his nuts.

As he was about to throw the cross into the shallow pit, he looked at it one last time. The sun was shining brightly and the gold was glinting where it wasn't covered with blood. His blood. The bloodied cross seemed to stare blankly back at him, it's once gleaming gem-eyes now blinded sockets, but it stared at him nonetheless. Shivering, he threw the cross into the pit. "You're damned! You're all damned! And your devil's cross goes with you!"

He retrieved one of the shovels abandoned at the side of the pit. "No doubt to bury more dead. Today we're going to bury Lucifer himself!" Enraged and maniacal, he shouted at Bernard, the dead villagers, the devil, the shovel, and the dirt as he worked to cover the bloody cross with the heavy clay soil that still stood in a small pile next to the pit. After more than an hour of endless, frenetic work he was nearly ready to collapse, but the task was done. The cross now lay under more than a foot of dirt and surely would never be seen by the eyes of mankind again. Additional dirt remained in the excavation pile from the work that Bernard had led, but Karel was too tired to move any more of it.

"Eventually you all will make your way to your master! And take your demon-possessed cross with you!" he sneered at the pit, which was now much shallower than it had been. Suddenly he poked his tongue into one cheek pocket and then the other. There were no gems. He looked about him madly, searching in the grass and the dirt. He looked at the shallow pit and wondered if he should excavate there. His stomach felt upset, which he attributed to his exhaustion. And then it struck him that he could have swallowed the gems as he furiously buried the cross. His stomach clenched and he felt the need for sustenance.

He decided to go and look for food. It was the last week of September, or *Witu-mānod* the wood-month, and soon the weather would turn cold. *Aran-mānod,* their name for August up in these mountains, was the harvest month, but it had slid by with no one to harvest any of the produce from the fields, which now lay rotting. *Herbist-mānod,* or slaughter month, as they called November, was the traditional time to kill animals and prepare meat for the long cold winter. But most of the animals people kept had disappeared one by one, had been rounded up and taken by the departing groups, or had been turned loose and abandoned. With no one to feed or care for them in the village, they had eventually stopped coming back around and lived feral or had just vanished, absorbed into that cruel circle of life that was mother nature.

Karel had ransacked most of the wares at the cheesemaker's but someone else had gotten to the butcher's stores before he'd been able to. Now he was going house to house, breaking in and finding the occasional abandoned bit of grain or basket with an apple or two to eat. If he couldn't find food, he knew where there was plenty of perfectly good wine, which was the sustenance he practically lived on now. And with something in his belly, the gems would be his again before too long. All he had to do was wait.

Chapter 45

Trevor

Nylah was still moving carefully and feeling sore, but she joined them for breakfast in Command Central. Trevor had gotten up early and had pulled together an impressive array of offerings in celebration of their dark cloud of fear passing. "It's a brand-new day! And I called Gunther and asked him to not bring out the crew until after ten-thirty. We can have a relaxed morning."

Taking a bite of her omelet, Nylah said, "I'm a little fuzzy on last night. You all got so worked up when I made a drug-induced comment about space aliens. You both freaked out aaaaand… I fell asleep. Can someone please tell me where the space aliens come in?"

"Nylah, your interest in forensics is bang on helpful here," Trevor said as he picked up Father B once again. He gestured with the skull as he spoke. "The space alien, what did you say, 'poured down rainbow-colored fentanyl candy'? Fantastical image of horror, you really have a knack for description—and *don't* put that on the website. We're talking about Jim Jones."

"Who is Jim Jones?" Nylah asked.

"Blimey, mate, for someone who knows so much about pop culture and trivia, you know actually very little about recent history."

Nylah shook her head. "Nah, you're forgetting that today's pop culture is tomorrow's history. I'm just ahead of my time."

"And you don't lack confidence!" Everly said with a laugh. "Jim Jones was an American preacher who had a long run manipulating people—like from the nineteen-fifties to the late seventies. He ran one of those churches where everybody gives over their houses and money. In the mid-nineteen-seventies there started to be claims that he was abusing his church members and not letting them leave if they wanted to."

"Oh!" Nylah said. "Cult."

Trevor touched his nose with his index finger and then pointed it at Nylah.

Everly continued. "The investigations and news stories heated up and not surprisingly he skipped town, you might say: he took his people to Guyana in South America and set up a commune he called 'Jonestown'."

"Wow, not like he was arrogant or anything!" Nylah said.

"Right. A whole eponymous town," Trevor said. Seeing Nylah's confused look, he added, "Named the town after himself, he did. Arrogance would be a job requirement for a preacher such as him. He said he was constructing a socialist paradise free from the oppression of the United States government. He was a modern populist movement, all by himself! Terrorist by any other name. And government people came to investigate and free the religious captives—and then the government people were shot dead. He knew the game was up at that point, didn't he?"

"And what did they do?" Nylah asked. "Although I'm not sure I want to know. Yeah, this is the summer of death. We're surrounded by dead bodies… and you've got one in your hand."

Trevor looked in confusion at Father B and said with all seriousness, "Actually, this is only part of a dead body."

Everly shook her head. "Before the American Feds came and arrested him, dragging his sorry ass back to face trial, he made everyone drink this Kool-Aid-like punch laced with cyanide. Brainwashed parents gave it to their children. If I remember the details, and believe me, I don't like to remember the details on this one, by the time the police got to their camp, all nine-hundred or so were dead. Him too. They basically died… all… at… once."

Trevor nodded enthusiastically. "Right, he'd rather kill everyone then face justice or have his worshippers turn on him. Children too, about a third of the group. He was into killing children, if you can believe that."

"Talk about your false prophets," Everly said.

"Whoa! That is so evil!" Nylah sipped her coffee and shook her head in disbelief.

"Right!" Trevor turned back to Everly. "And now we know we've been barking up the wrong tree."

"Uh huh. I've been sending out sample after sample requesting they run tests for *Yersinia pestis*, but that's not what we need to look for."

Nylah looked from Trevor to Everly. "Then what is?"

"These people didn't die of plague. They died of poison. We're looking for poison. You said it: 'rainbow colored candy fentanyl pouring down from the sky.' Something that kills everyone fast, indiscriminately. What would be their delivery mechanism?" Trevor looked from Everly to Nylah and back again.

"Did they have Kool-Aid in the thirteen hundreds?" Nylah shook her head. "No, of course not. What did they drink all the time? Well water? River water?"

"Possibility." Everly nodded. "Algae blooms can happen in rivers, and from what we know there was a small river that ran through this valley at one point in time, but it's long since dried up. I don't think there'll be a way to test that theory. Algae blooms smell awful. Hard to imagine anyone would willingly drink that. You know, Trevor, we'll need to excavate the well as best we can, but we'll need a different crew. That's not student work. Wells are dangerous." Everly looked at Nylah. "The sides can cave in and bury you alive while you're excavating.

Seriously hazardous. But in history, wells were sometimes poisoned and sometimes people were thrown in them. Dead bodies spread disease, but that's a slow burn through a city. It's not like poison."

"Wine," Trevor said with confidence. "They drank wine. Even children drank watered-down wine because water was often contaminated, gave you giardia and the like. But once you turn it into beer or ale or wine, the fermentation process kills off the microbes. Beer made civilization possible because it purified water. We know these people made wine, but we can't assume they brewed beer just because they lived in what we now call Germany. So, if it was poison, it was probably delivered in something like wine, probably at a festival or a feast."

"Or a church?" Everly said. "Communion? I mean, they all would have been Catholic. There was no other religion practiced openly here. Despite the Jewish wedding ring, we've never found a hint of evidence that there was a Jewish community here."

"Catholics drink that much wine at Sunday service? I never knew. Sign me up!" Nylah said.

"No, it's just a sip. That would be a really potent poison—and if it was, the last people in line would figure out what was going on, because the people in front of them would be dropping dead," Everly said.

Trevor could feel his mind racing. It was like Father B was talking to him. "Or they could have had a celebration, right, Father B? You could have been leading your flock in a toast. Something special and that would mean that everyone would be given a real glass of wine and they would all drink it at once, wouldn't they? As if on cue. Probably your cue, wasn't it?" Trevor turned back to Everly and Nylah. "Oh no…" Trevor felt a sense of horror and sadness overwhelm him. "Do you think he *meant* to kill them all, Jim Jones style, or do you think he was the victim. Him and his flock?"

Trevor had to admit to himself that he didn't want Father B to be a murderer. He'd developed a kind of a relationship with the long-dead priest. He'd come to trust him. Feel he was the patron saint of the dig.

To think that all this time he could've been talking to and drinking with a mass murderer was a most uncomfortable thought. He thought of Father B as a kind of a friend from across the centuries. He set the skull down on the table.

"Whoa. If he's the Jim Jones of the fourteenth century, then I'd better change the website. I've kind of made him, uh, the hero of the story," Nylah said.

Everly waved off their concerns. "Don't jump to any conclusions. Everything's a theory at a dig site. First, we need to send out more samples to look for a poison. Then we can try to figure out who might have poisoned whom." She began to pace. "Poisoning over weeks or months could allow for uptake into the bones. But a sudden event wouldn't leave a trace in the bones."

"No, but it would be all over the surface, wouldn't it?" Trevor said, chin in hand, thinking. "As the bodies decayed, the poison from their soft tissues would leak out all into their clothing and settle in the dirt and on top of the bones. We might find traces not by extraction but by surface scraping."

Everly put her hands over eyes. "Shit, shit, shit! I was so stupid. I had those kids screen the dirt with the power washers. That will have destroyed the evidence."

Nylah looked horrified. "Not to mention what it could have exposed all of us to!"

Everly put her hand on Nylah's shoulder. "Good thinking. That's the kind of concern that you need when you run a dig. However, unless we're talking nuclear waste here, which we're not, I don't think seven hundred years of disintegration is going to leave much potency. It's a good thought, but not one you need to lose any sleep over."

Trevor sat down and looked at Father B in his empty eye sockets. "You might be a mass murderer. At mass. And still, it's possible that you're innocent. And whoever murdered you and your flock wouldn't show evidence of the poison, now would they? Because they would have been gloating from afar. It wouldn't be on their bones, but it could be around them. I wonder..."

"Nylah, he looks like a man with a theory. Let me get the clipboard out. I think it's going to be an exciting day at the dig!"

"Oh, no, no," Nylah said. "An exciting day at the scene of the crime."

Chapter 46

Friar Karel Tuckerschade
October 1351

Friar Karel Tuckerschade followed the parade route holding the pole erect, his shoulders thrown back, the golden cross floating above the amazed heads of the villagers. He had never felt so proud. His vestments were clean and new and crisp. About his neck hung an embroidered orphrey, its golden threads glinting in the sun. It was all he ever wanted. A church of his own. A flock of souls to tend and lead. The love and respect of his fellow man. A sign from God that he was beloved and important. It had seemed so elusive for so long, and now here he was, holding the gold cross that was his at last. He smiled and nodded solemnly to the villagers, his benevolence equal even to those who had been late to join his flock. He would make the parade route and return to his church, place the golden cross on the altar, and in the pews would be his Adelaide, her angelic face shining as she only had eyes for him. Together they would pray. Together they would eat. Together they would suffer for the glory of it. Early in his life, suffering might have given him structure and purpose, but finding someone to suffer with had transformed him, giving him exaltation. He had found his Eve.

He knew he was the most blessed of all men. It was because of how he had shown his devotion, his guardianship of the Garden of Eden. He had been rewarded because there was nothing he had been unwilling to do for the service and glory of his Lord. He could feel himself falling, each moment of his movement as if slowly suspended, as though he had been granted angel's wings and was learning to float in the air. His thoughts held all his attention captive, preventing him from seeing the debris in the road, his tattered shoe caught on the edge of a branch that littered the dusty street at the side of a hole that no one had bothered to fill. He felt himself falling but did not register the reason until he hit the ground hard, his head slamming on the dirt, the barren, gnarled stick in his hand cutting his cheek as he landed on it. The flimsy string that secured a little pouch around his neck now lay broken.

Slowly he opened his eyes and looked about him. Gone were the villagers, who had only a moment ago been smiling at him, their faces full of the rapture to realize the cross-bearing angel in their presence. Gone was the fine pole in his hands, cruelly replaced with a rough old stick. Gone were the golden cross and his fine vestments. He looked down and picked up the pouch, confusion written across his face. "You cannot leave me, eyes of the angels," he said to the little pouch, "for I am the guardian."

"Eh, there he goes again, look at him now!" Jezzie's voice cackled, cutting through his confused consciousness. "Makin' yer pilgrimage about the village once again, are ye, Bishop Tuck? Or are ye the pope himself today?"

"At least he's got his dreams to keep him alive!" A voice called out from a window where a shutter was broken and dangling from its frame. The occupant's face appeared. "All we got is rotted food and not much of that."

"Oh, Johannes! I was wondering where you'd got to. Didn't Markus tell ye? There's an army marching not three miles away. I'm gonna follow them! There's always business to be had at the back end of an army."

Peals of laughter came from the man standing in the window. "You might not prefer working in a house of tolerance, Miss Jezzie, but at least it always has customers. There's certainly no one left for us here. Well, 'cept for you and me."

Jezzie stood erect and laughed at him. "Are ye propositioning me because you're bored, Johannes? Tell ye what: if you've any cheese left that's not moldy, I'd be tempted to give ye a taste of the wares I can provide!" She turned to and fro to highlight her figure.

"Ah, Miss Jezzie, you know your craft well and will benefit plenty at the tail of an army." Johannes leaned onto the sill, looking up and down the empty street. "I'll join you if you're sure that army men don't always prefer the flesh of women. Mays be that there would be business as well for someone like me."

Karel Tuckerschade heard distant voices and laughter, but wondered where the crowds had gone. Unsteadily, he gained his feet. Reaching into his pocket, he pulled out a small bottle and clumsily uncorked it, given the pouch gripped tightly in his hand. He took a swig.

Jezzie approached him swiftly. "Ah, yer holiness. I think you've had enough of that!" She deftly took the bottle from him as he grasped at the air, trying to reclaim the prize that had disappeared from his view. She walked over to the window, waving the bottle in her hand at the man. "Looks like it just be ye and me and a bottle of wine! What say ye we make it an evening? Bring the food ye can find and I'll bring the last of the wine in this village of ghosts and demons."

Suddenly a snuffing and a grunting broke into their laughter. Jezzie screamed and Johannes reached out through the window and pulled her through it. The two disappeared into the darkness of the uninhabited house.

Karel turned around as the grunting sounds turned to angry squeals. He squinted at the beasts who were furiously pawing the ground. "My flock! You have returned!" He shouted to the heavens; his voice raised in triumph as his delusions took hold of him again.

The wild boar made a screaming sound and chuffed and puffed as it pawed the ground, his harem grunting and squeaking in chorus with him.

Karel shook as his fantasy evaporated and he registered the group of wild pigs that had him in their sights. "Devil spawn!" he spat. "Here to trample the Garden of Eden, are you? Over my dead flesh will you spread your filth! You won't take them from me." He waved the pouch in the air. "They be mine. I know how to protect them!" He poured the contents of the pouch into his mouth and swallowed hard, the gems sliding down his throat as though they knew the way. "I'll get them back and you'll be long gone and dead, just like your sire!"

Karel set his feet as though readying for battle, but no stance could have prepared him for the blunt force of the herd as it trampled him. The tusks of the boar did the initial damage, slamming into him as it ran him down at full speed. Following closely behind, the rest of the herd added their snouts and hooves to the toll.

◆━◆━◆

The next morning Jezzie and Johannes emerged from their hideaway, the last of the food eaten and the bottle dry.

"That was the most awful thing to have to listen to last night," Jezzie said as she looked warily about.

"Aye. And it sounded like the wild boar feasted for hours. Bit of a mood-ruiner, wasn't it?" Johannes shook his head. "I don't think he made it. Nothing we could have done anyway."

"Don't you mean to say, 'nothing we *would* have done'? Not for the likes of him," Jezzie added. "But I wonder where he's got to?"

"There's a piece of him over there." Johannes pointed.

"Oh, and some 'round the corner here as well." After a moment of silence she added, "Did ye know that wild pigs eat flesh?"

"It's wild boar. They eat everything."

"Even friars fallen from grace," she said. "Oh look, there's another piece. His arm, I think." A silence again filled the space between them. "So, what do we do with him?"

Johannes shrugged. "I suppose we could gather up the bits. Maybe bury him in the churchyard? Throw him in the pits with everyone else?"

"Do ye think it'll be penance for me sins?" Jezzie asked.

He looked at her. "My sins are far worse than yours, given my usual clientele."

"I don't know. I think ye sin quite well," Jezzie gave him a sideways smile, "you know, well after all of this died down and we didn't have to hear it no more." She gestured to the remains scattered about.

Johannes blushed and kicked the dirt, unable to make eye contact for a moment or two. In the end, they did as he suggested, gathering up the remaining parts of the friar. Making use of the old, tattered gray cloak they found near one of his limbs, they dragged him to the church on the poor end of the village, being unwilling to put in the effort to move him all the way across town to be added to the mass grave site where nearly everyone else had been placed.

"This was his church, right? Here he should lie." Johannes pronounced the verdict like he was some type of church official himself.

"Well, I'm not opposed, but who's gonna dig the hole?"

He looked at her as if this was a new realization. "He's gotta go in a hole. Otherwise, he'll stink. And attract the pigs back."

"I don't wanna dig a hole nor do I wanna drag him to the far side o' town. That's too much work."

"Right. You only work on your back!"

"Oh, I'm much more creative than that!" They both laughed. "Ooooh, I've got an idea," she said with a sly smile. "I know where there be a hole, ready and willing. Just waiting. And once ye and I join the tail of the army, there'll be no one left but him to use that hallowed bit o' ground."

"Are you thinkin' what I think you're thinkin'?" He chuckled long and low.

It didn't take long to drag his body to the little building that concealed the hole in the ground. Rather than touch the dismembered sections again, they just wrapped him up in the cloth and poured the bits and pieces down the hole in the ground of the little latrine.

"I hate to say this, but being here, well, I gotta go," the man said to his companion.

"Don't stop yerself on my account! It's right there. Use it."

"On top of him?"

"He's dead! He won't care. Trust me. And honestly, he was so drunk I'm not sure he would've cared even before the pigs had their business with him."

"You're probably right. Give me a moment then, will you? I'll be most pleased to join you and we'll find that army together. I think we could do good business, you and me, teaming up."

She smiled at him. "I thought you'd never ask. Take yer time. I won't leave without ye."

Chapter 47

Trevor

"So, Hans is coming over to our little celebration this evening? Did I understand that correctly?" Trevor asked Everly, who just raised her eyebrows at him and shrugged. "Won't that be… awkward? Tell me, do roses and chocolates really make that much of a difference? I've never had anybody be terribly mad at me, but if that's a trick I should remember, then I want to know."

Everly put down her report and looked at him. "I think for some women it works. Not for all women. I think you have to know which kind of woman you're with."

Trevor blew out a whistle and then as he passed by Everly, paused and said, almost whispering in her ear, "Nylah doesn't strike me as the roses and chocolate kind. And to be honest, neither do you."

She gave him a look as he walked on. "Well, it doesn't mean I *never* like them."

"Really? Good to know. I'll have to tuck that away, just in case."

Everly laughed out loud. "It's their lives. They'll figure it out. They're over their biggest drama anyway. Nothing will top the events of two weeks ago." She sighed heavily. "I'm just glad we're through it all. Safe and sound."

"How's your report coming?"

"It's about done. I liked the part you wrote up. Very clean."

Trevor shrugged. "I tried to keep my imagination in check. And not have little papers of notes scattered all about it."

She smiled at him again. "I have to admit, figuring out they were poisoned was brilliant. Our little team is quite the trio. We have over a million followers. News stories world-wide. A half a dozen journal articles just from you and me. I've lost track of how many papers Gunter's masses of students are working on." She shook her head. "It's been an amazing few months, Dr. Trevor Payne, Junior."

"Oh no! I've been demoted in your eyes! I'm back to having… a title." He felt light-headed with happiness. "The traces of poison were so clear on their bones and in the clothing remnants. *La manzanilla de la Muerte.* The little apple of death. No way the fruit could have been imported. Not from the Caribbean. Not in the thirteen-hundreds. Whoever would have thought a Manchineel tree could have lived in a place like this?" He shook his head. "That would be a miracle."

"Sounds more like the work of the devil to me," Everly said nonchalantly, still focused on the report in her hand. "That part of the mystery, we'll never be able to explain. Just like that crazy wall. But there certainly isn't a trace of that tree left anywhere that we've found. It would be a terrible way to die, wouldn't it?" Everly looked distracted. "Even the smoke of the burning wood can blind you."

Trevor nodded. "My research on the tree said that the little apple-like fruits are supposed to taste sweet at first, but soon cause a burning and tearing sensation. People can't swallow after that. And then they start bleeding from the inside. I'd hate to be the scientist who found that out. Anyway, that looks like what happened to all our poor villagers. Now we know how they died. Almost the day they died. But we don't really know *why* they died."

Everly brought over a page from the printer. "I just got the test results from Specimen A. Remember that old guy who was, what did Nylah call it? Looked like he was trying to disco in a garbage disposal?

Yeah, him. No poison on his bones, but the scraps of the gray cloth—really high concentrations of the toxins."

"No kidding. Let me see that." Trevor took the paper from her hands. "And he had the gems, almost as if he'd swallowed them. That little bugger. I'll bet he's our murderer. Plotted the whole thing out most likely. Why, we'll never know, but I can just see it. He probably used that thick old cloak to keep himself safe from the poison while he turned *la manzanilla de la Muerte* into *el vineto de la Muerte*. He probably was the local vintner and gave Father B a poisoned barrel of wine that our poor Father B never suspected. Old bugger! Serves him right he got eaten like that. And then someone stuffed him down a toilet. Now I wonder just who would do that? Who would be left around to serve him justice like that?"

Everly put her hand on Trevor's cheek. "You have the best imagination for an archeologist. And I think you have just come up with a really good plot for your next fantasy novel."

Trevor looked puzzled. "It would have to be an historical thriller… not a fantasy novel. An archeological murder mystery! But I like the idea!"

Everly laughed at him. "C'mon. Nylah and Hans are expecting us to have a party tonight. And we have a lot to celebrate! We'll just have to accept that we'll never really know what happened in this village in the valley."

Under his breath Trevor said, "Don't be so sure, after all, we did hear from Gunther," but then he was caught by her words. "A lot to celebrate? Tell me, they aren't… are they?"

Everly shrugged. "Nylah doesn't seem like a roses and chocolate person to me either."

Trevor came up behind Everly again and once more whispered in her ear, "No, but is the devilishly handsome Hans a poisoned apple kind of guy?"

"You bad boy! C'mon. Let's get going."

Later that evening, four glasses glistening with bubbly clinked in celebration.

"Congratulations! It looks like you solved the mystery of the missing village! It is hard to believe… no plague." Hans had a broad smile on his face as he looked at the three of them.

"Right!" Trevor noticed that Nylah didn't have the same old blissful smile on her face she'd had all summer. And she wasn't standing quite as close to Hans as she usually did. She'd grown up a lot over the last few months. *Why can't joy cause us to grow up? It's always pain and disillusionment instead,* Trevor thought, but he tried to focus on the conversation at hand. He turned to Hans. "It wasn't an act of God, but an act of man. An act of betrayal and evil. You know, it might've been hidden for centuries, but truth will out in the end."

Hans looked like he faltered for a moment, but then smiled and raised his glass in toast. They all drank. "I like the truth that this is an excellent bottle of wine. German wines can hold their quality against any in the world."

Trevor gave him a tight smile and nodded. "We wanted to bring these poor people back to the daylight, to find out what happened to them. And today we have found out so much more. Ladies and gentleman, let me share with you a note I got from our good friend, Gunther Heintzelman. Hot off the press this is! It seems the ring he found on that young lady up in the fen was an important ring, historically. And it disappeared from the world during the plague. But using it, old Gunther was able to identify our mystery woman. Or shall I say, our mystery victim?"

"No kidding? So, who was she?" Everly asked.

"Well, according to Gunther's research, that ring was given in marriage to one Adelaide Trōst, daughter of a Duke nonetheless, who was married in January thirteen-forty-seven to a merchant by the name of Gerung Engelhaft.”

“An angel?” Hans said, surprise in his voice. “She was married to an angel! Engelhaft means ‘angelic’ in English.”

“A lady married to a merchant? Even an angelic one. Well, that must’ve been scandalous for the time,” Nylah said. “Were they some kind of clandestine, Romeo-and-Juliet-type of lovers?”

Trevor shrugged. “Maybe? Sure, let’s go with that. And among his many handsome qualities was that he was like the richest man in their world, so given the rising power of the merchants at the time, it was probably a step up for her. But she was young, younger than you, Nylah, not eighteen when she was married. And sadly, it was a brief affair: he died in the plague in thirteen-forty-nine, and she simply vanished. No one ever knew where she went or if she died and was buried in a mass grave like him. But the ring he married her with was quite distinctive. It had an upside-down diamond in the center, sticking up like a little pyramid. Gunther sent over some pictures.” Trevor proceeded to pull out his phone and show them.

“Why would anyone put a diamond upside down?” Hans asked.

“I don’t know, but it looks cool, even though it’s butt-end up,” Nylah said.

“Right, Nylah, it does. And blimey, but it’s a *nice* diamond too. Very high quality, so it wasn’t put, what did you call it? Butt-end up? To hide any flaws. They were rich enough to just think it was hunky dory.”

“Look at those bands, that intertwined gold. That’s really pretty,” Everly said. “Gorgeous even if it were a modern-day ring.”

“I thought so too. But the best part is the inscription on the inside.” Trevor pulled up another text from Gunther. “It says: *ieo vos tien foi tenes le moy.* Translated from Middle French, that means: *I hold your faith, hold mine.*”

Everly sighed. “Wow. He must have loved her. He must have loved her so much.”

"But then why did she end up out here?" Nylah asked.

"Up on that mountain, like as not we'll never know. But she came to this village because of her brother. You see, her oldest brother didn't follow in his father's footsteps and become the next very powerful Duke of Lotharinga. Instead, he became a priest. And his post? Our little valley village. And I would suspect that he is our architect of innovation. Cesspits. Latrines. Big garbage dumps outside of town to help keep the village cleaner. Brought his big city ways with him. Must've been a smart fellow. A real engineer."

Everly looked at the picture on his phone again. "So, after her husband died, she came out here to be with her older brother? Escape the plague and find family?"

"If you think that's interesting, take a look at this. There's a painting of her that still exists today." He tapped his phone and then showed it round to the group.

"Damn! She the very definition of bootylicious for a White chick! Like I mean, she looks like the very first Barbie doll!" Nylah exclaimed. "And where'd she get such perfect teeth? No orthodontists in the Middle Ages!"

"Yes," Everly said. "And she must have been awfully proud of them, because when did you ever see a painting with anyone smiling? I mean, they're all trying to do that Mona Lisa thing. But there she is, in a painting, showing those pearly whites."

"My guess is that they probably ran in her family." Trevor smiled. "May I introduce you all to Father Bernard Trōst." He retrieved and held up the skull. "Our very own Father B, a highly respectable man by all records. And not a mass murderer. Also, a man of exceptional dental hygiene apparently."

Everly shook her head in disbelief. "That's a great story. You know, in archeology, you don't often get the story tied up in nice little packages like that. We recovered her remains, what was her name again? And wait, you said victim?"

"Her name was Adelaide, beautiful thing. Beautiful name," Trevor said. "And then briefly, Adelaide Trōst Engelhaft. And yes, she was murdered. Buried on the top of that mountain. The toxin residues were on her bones as well. Isn't that sad?"

Nylah shook her head. "What in the world could have happened to her? What could she have done to have been murdered up on top of that mountain. And then buried there alone in the cold for seven hundred years." Nylah shuddered. "Gives me the shivers."

Everly sighed deeply. "We were able to help bring Adelaide back from that lonely grave on the mountain. She'll be reunited with her brother. It's so sad that she can't be reunited with her husband. But still, with her family. There's something really just so nice about that. And on a happier note: Father B has a real name now!"

"And the best part?" Trevor asked.

They all looked at him expectantly.

"Gunther's become something of a German celebrity over this. There's a real resurgence of interest in the German aristocracy. I think he's really excited. He sent me his speaking schedule. He's going to be touring all over Europe, telling the love story of Gerung and Adelaide, two lovers from different social classes who married despite the customs of the day—and then one died tragically in the Black Plague, while the other was ruthlessly murdered and hidden away for eternity on a lonely mountaintop! It's a real Romeo and Juliet kind of thing, with a bit of mafia overtones actually, the way he tells it."

"I wonder if that's how it really was between them?" Nylah asked. "It's easy to romanticize the story, but you know, real relationships are usually far more complicated and messier."

Trevor looked at Nylah, those parental feelings flooding him again. It was like he had a daughter that was growing up right before his eyes. "Right. You're so right, Nylah," Trevor said and then he noticed how uncomfortable Hans looked. The moment hung awkwardly.

"So, Everly," Nylah turned to her summer tent-mate, "it'll be back to Toronto for you? Will you teach the next semester or just write boring scientific papers about the dig? You could take a page from Dr. T's book? I'm pretty sure he's going to write the next best-selling novel about life and love, death, and murder in the Middle Ages. And probably something about a war between the specters of death: with death by poison beating out death by plague!"

"Oh, I like that idea, Nylah. That's very creative. So much potential!" Trevor said with a laugh. "Watch out! I might use that!"

Everly laughed but looked a bit unsure of herself. "Yeah, Toronto, I guess. I mean, I've got inquiries from Harvard, Berkeley, Stanford, Leiden, a few more. I suppose I could go a lot of places. But Toronto's always been home."

Trevor looked a bit shy for a moment. "You know, Everly, there's always an opportunity at Cambridge, I mean, I know it doesn't have the benefits of Toronto. Cambridge is terribly far away from fam… uh, people. You'd have to give up the snow, right? And the bitter cold. I'm sure you'd miss it. But for someone with your talent, there's always a position at my university. You could be a visiting professor. It's like trying it out. With no commitment."

Nylah burst out laughing. "You mean it's like 'swiping right'? Just dating the job? Checking it out to see if it's the real thing?" She gave Hans a sideways look but he seemed to be avoiding her gaze.

Everly blushed and Trevor actually became less awkward than usual. He felt full of confidence and calmness when he said, as he took Everly's hand, "Yes, if you want to put it that way. You can make sure it's the right thing for you. And if it is, then who knows? Maybe you could find your happily-ever-after in the most beautiful part of England." Then he started to wiggle again as he quickly added, "With a position that you, you know, love. And colleagues who you, maybe, love as well?"

Hans and Nylah exchanged glances, Hans looking surprised and Nylah looking delighted.

Before Everly could manage a reply, there was a sudden burst of shouting outside the tent.

"What the…?" a couple of them said as they all started looking wildly around.

Shouts of *"Achtung!"* and

"Sie sind hier, auf das Zelt!" and

"Schnell! Schnell!"

Suddenly the entry flap flew open and three armed men entered the tent.

Trevor, Everly, and Nylah leapt to their feet while Hans seemed frozen in place.

"They have guns!" Trevor shouted, his eyes wide open as he looked from gunman to gunman. "Since when do people in Europe have guns? What's happening?"

"It's a hold up, Dr. T," Nylah explained. She rolled her eyes and looked disgusted.

The men gestured with their weapons and shouted at them in German.

Slowly Trevor put his hands up, but he looked at Nylah, his voice animated. "A hold up? Like a robbery? Of an archeological site? How desperate are these blokes? I mean, all we've got are *bones*. And while they're interesting bones I can't imagine they would have much street value. You can't exactly snort them or smoke them."

The men waved their guns again and shouted at them in German.

"Yes, this is a hold up in any language. Trust me, I'm from New York. We see this shit all the time." While Trevor's hands were way above his head, Nylah's didn't even reach her shoulders.

Trevor shouted again, "I don't know what to do in a hold up! What do we do? I've never been held up before."

Everly's voice was trembling as she said, "I think we should do what they say."

One of the men barked at them again, with Trevor, Nylah, and Everly looking at the men with confusion and then at one another, looking for an answer.

Now Trevor looked at Everly and shouted at her, "But I don't know what they're saying. They aren't speaking bloody English. I have no idea what they want me to do. Why do they keep waving around those bloody guns?"

"These guys are amateurs. I think we can take 'em!" Nylah said as she stared at the ringleader, her eyes narrowing. The man took a step back, as if he was unsure about that one. "Yeah, we can take them. There's four of us and only three of them! Ten to one those guns are fake. Look for little orange tips."

"Nylah, are you crazy?" Everly managed to squeak out. Like Trevor, her hands were held high.

"I'm not crazy. I'm from New York." As she spoke she made an aggressive upper body lean towards the gunmen, who now all looked momentarily unsure of themselves and took a step backwards as if resistance was not what they had been expecting.

The ringleader looked at his compatriots and now yelled at them, unintelligible to their hostages, but the two henchmen stepped forward again, although a bit uncertainly.

"I'd give him my wallet if I had it on me. Not of much use in a tent though." Trevor moved to pat down his pockets, which stimulated a quick response of shouting and more gun pointing from the armed band. Trevor quickly raised his hands again and in a higher pitch, shouted, "I don't know what you bloody want! If you're going to rob an Englishman, speak bloody English!"

"They want the cross. And the gems." Hans' voice broke in as he started to rise slowly, his hands in the air, moving tentatively. "They don't speak English. Even their German isn't very good. They are not Germans. They are Gypsies."

"Gypsies? Like in B-movies?" Nylah said, incredulous. "And they've, what? Circled the wagons around us, I suppose? Next they'll start to sing with their tambourines? You can't call them Gypsies. I mean, that's so politically incorrect."

Carefully and with obvious respect and submission, Hans said something in German to the armed band and they relaxed slightly. Then he turned back to Nylah. "Today, in Germany, we call anyone Gypsy who is transitory. They have no permanent home. Refugees. People who are here but are not German and have no real employment. It has become a common term for migrants. Gypsies are a real problem in Germany." He gave a quick glance at the armed men.

"Whoa, back home we'd call *that* cultural appropriation!" Nylah shook her head.

"Uh, this might not be the right time for that, Nylah? huh?" Everly whispered urgently.

"They have said they do not want to shoot you, but they will if you don't give them the valuables. I suggest that wherever the cross and the rubies are, you hand them over."

"Geezh! Total amateurs!" Nylah said with disgust. "The artifacts aren't even here. They're at Brandenburg. I put it on the website, but I guess these bozos aren't into social media. Or watching the news. Or doing their homework!"

Hans translated again while everyone else looked at one another, with Nylah shrugging at her teammates. "What?" she said as she shrugged at them again.

Everly's voice was tinged with panic. "Right! We don't have the cross and gems. Oh my God, are they just going to shoot us? We don't have them! We don't have them!"

The lead thief listened to Hans and then shouted at the archeology team again, pointing his gun at Trevor, who shrugged at him and shook his head with incomprehension. The man yelled again and now moved over to Everly, grabbing her arm behind her and pointing his gun menacingly under her chin.

Everly whimpered and Nylah gasped, for the first time looking like she was taking this situation seriously.

Trevor jumped. "Wait! Stop! Okay?"

Hans translated.

The man loosened his grip on Everly.

"Right, right. Okay. No need for any of that now. We've photographed it, sure. Not the same as being in a museum now, is it? Right, but we can go ahead and give you what you want." Trevor cleared his throat. "Gentlemen, and I use that term lightly, if you'd let go of the lady and follow me." He beckoned with his raised right hand.

The man pushed Everly to the ground and Nylah ran to put her arms around her as Everly whimpered quietly. Looking at Nylah with wide eyes she said, "It's here?"

"What the hell, Dr. T? It's here?" Nylah looked incredulous, staring at Trevor.

The ringleader gestured with his gun and Trevor began to move over towards one of the many locked iron cases against the side of the tent that doubled as tables for the group. "After the failed attempt to take it from the university, I improved upon their security measures and decided it was safer out here." As he stood next to the third metal storage crate in the line, he began to lower his hands, resulting in much shouting from the gunman. He turned towards Hans. "Could you please tell them that I have to get the key out of my pocket. I mean, it's locked, right? So it needs a key. Can't open with my mind, now can I?"

"I can't believe you brought it back here!" Everly said, stunned.

Hans translated the highlights of Trevor's comments as Trevor slowly retrieved the key from his pocket, a rambling narration of his overly exaggerated movements accompanying every step of the process. Over his shoulder, Trevor muttered, "Looked like an inside job up at Brandenburg, right? So, we removed the target but not the temptation. World thinks it's up there, under lock and key." With a shaking hand, he opened the box and started removing smaller containers that held a variety of the artifacts they had unearthed.

One of the gunmen came over and eagerly ripped the box from Trevor's hand before he could set it down. He tore off the lid and cast it aside, nearly hitting Everly, who ducked. It brushed her hair as it passed by.

"Was ist das?" the man said angrily, as he smashed the box and its contents to the ground.

"Don't break it!" Trevor exclaimed as it hit the earth with a thud. He let out a frustrated sigh. "Right, early primitive tool. Already broken, but now broken a bit more. Okay." He turned to Hans. "Could you please tell them it's not in here. I have to get another key out of here. There's no need to destroy all the artifacts or toss them about! No need at all."

Hans translated, obviously trying to calm tensions in the two groups. At the bottom of the bin, Trevor was moving slowly and carefully as he pulled out a box with FRAGILE stickers all over it. "Now, just a reminder for the tosspots in the group, this is *not* the cross. Please don't break this. Not many of these from the era, you know." Gently, he set the box down on the floor and carefully removed the lid.

"Is that valuable?" Hans asked.

Trevor looked up at him. "Not unless you're writing a paper on food storage techniques in the fourteenth century. It's got a lid, see? Not many surviving lids to clay jugs from the day," he said as he pulled out a ceramic lid and set it gingerly on the grass. "You see, mice getting into your food was a big issue, although some thought it was the work of fairies and the like. You see, lids signified the more, shall we say 'progressive' of the population, the more science-minded. Those conservatives who clung to the old ways thought angels or fairies were taking their due share, giving a blessing to the family as it were. But unless mice back then had wings, *unlikely*, it was just vermin and those poor blokes often got sick from their lack of lids. Lids are good tools."

"I'm not going to translate that. I don't think they want a history lesson. They just want the cross and the gems." Hans was starting to look like he was losing his patience.

Trevor reached into the well-packed box and down into the ancient food storage pot and retrieved a key. "But they do want this. Or at least what this leads us to. Right."

The armed men seemed focused and interested now.

"Dr. Bergeron. Would you be so kind as to put the pot back in its box and back in the crate? Nylah, Everly seems a bit shaken. Maybe you could help her put things back? It's a metal box so it's going to protect the artifacts and such that are most valuable to us," he said with his face towards the women and away from the intruders. He gave them an intent look.

"Yes, Dr. Payne," Everly said, getting to her feet and dragging Nylah over to the metal storage crate. She slowly, carefully started to look busy while she quietly struggled to position the large metal boxes between Nylah and herself on the one side and the gunmen on the other.

Meanwhile, Trevor walked over to the main table, holding the key above his head in plain sight the whole time. All the gunmen carefully followed him and ignored the women. He removed the books and other objects and then pulled off the tablecloth, the winged unicorns crumpling in a pile on the floor. A bare metal folding table was left, its dull glint shining in the light of the electric lamps.

Now Hans was sounding really frustrated and impatient. "So, where is the cross! What is the key for?"

Trevor gave him a curious look.

"I think these men are serious, Dr. Payne. I don't think they are fooling around. I'm sure they know how to use those guns."

"Patience. All archeologists must have patience."

Hans looked from Trevor to the gunmen, and back to Trevor. "I don't think they are destined to be archeologists."

"They will be once they hold the cross." Trevor proceeded to start to pull the sides of the table apart. "Hans, can you help me here? Hard to do as just one person." Hans stepped up and took the other side of the table and between the two of them, they pulled the table apart, revealing a false metal bottom with a keyhole. "And that is what the key is for."

Everyone ducked down to look and saw the secret strong box that ran along the underside center of the table.

"I never noticed that before," Everly said, amazement in her voice.

"And that is what the tablecloths were for," Trevor gave her a wink. Then with a heavy sigh, he inserted the key and unlocked the box. With a terrible squeak and some amount of effort the top opened, revealing the golden cross.

Before Trevor could pick it up, Hans moved and retrieved it, a look of joy on his face. Then he looked intently at Trevor. "And the gems. They want the gems."

Trevor reached in and pulled out a little cloth bag. "Here you go, Hans," he said as he returned the intent look of Nylah's boyfriend and tossed the bag over to him. They fell on the ground at his feet.

Hans seemed to be caught off guard and two men looked at one another for a moment. Then Hans looked down at the object in his hands. "It is beautiful, but it is so light." He hefted it. "Gold should be heavier."

"Right. It's a relic from a small church in a tiny town in a part of Bavaria that remains undeveloped to this day. Why would you think they would ever have a solid gold cross? I mean, like the Queen of England had one. And the pope, but a priest in a by-water little church?"

"It's not *gold*?" Hans seemed devastated. "It's junk?" He translated the situation to the armed men, who yelled back at him angrily.

As the tensions ratcheted up another notch, Trevor said, "It's not junk! It's an artifact! It's priceless. And even made of gold, it would have more value *not* melted down. But that lot? That will burn and not melt. It's made of wood."

"*Holz. Der Müll,*" Hans said over his shoulder to the men, who angrily shouted again, at Hans, at their hostages, and at each other.

"The gems should do you well though, Hans. Why don't you take the goods you've got and leave the women. I mean, tell them," he gestured with a jerk of his head to the armed men, "to just take the money and run. Band on the run, you know? Before the bell starts ringing in the village square, those rabbits can be on the run. Hans—

robbery you can get away with. Murder, you can't. It follows you. Forever. Even across the centuries, right?"

It was a slow moment as Hans tore his gaze from a now very calm Trevor. He barked a few sentences to the armed men, who looked at one another in surprise. Suddenly they turned their guns on him and shouted at him, jerking their weapons to make Hans start moving.

"It seems I am to be their hostage. Mostly because they can understand me." He bent over and picked up the little bag with the gems.

Trevor nodded slowly. "Good luck then. I hope you survive, Hans. It gets dicey when you have your lot thrown in with the likes of them."

"*Ja.*" Hans nodded. "I will try to be careful." He turned to Nylah. "I love you, Nylah. *Ich leibe dich, meine liebschen.*"

The men barked again and Hans, still carrying the cross and the bag of gems, started moving towards them. Two of the gunmen grabbed Hans and shoved him before them, exiting the tent. The yelling continued outside. The ringleader stopped. With a sneer and an unintelligible comment, he turned around and raised his gun at the three remaining and sprayed the tent with gunfire, laughing all the while.

As soon as the man's face broke with that evil grin, Trevor shouted, "Everly! Be quick!" and he grabbed the edge of the table and pulled it on its side, falling to the ground behind its bulk. Everly pushed Nylah down into the open metal crate, and the girl crashed on top of the few cardboard boxes and artifacts remaining, with the open lid crashing down behind her, closing the case. Everly threw herself backward, sliding down between the tent wall and the metal crate next in line.

The gunman sprayed another round of gunfire, laughed again, then in the silence, heard his comrades yelling to him. He turned and ran to join them. There was another series of shots and then the sound of a car engine, first loud and then gradually dying in the distance.

A few moments of silence were followed by Everly's voice. "Trevor? Nylah?" In the quiet and with great effort, Everly un-wedged herself from in between the metal crate and the wall of the tent. "Nylah? Trevor? Oh my God!"

"I'm here," came a small voice from inside the closed crate. "But I'm stuck." The lid of the crate banged from her efforts inside.

Everly climbed back over the crate she had sheltered behind and, with some struggle, got the metal lid open. She helped pull Nylah out.

"Are you okay?"

Nylah grabbed her surgery site. "Yeah. Sore but I didn't break in two or anything." Blinking back tears she said, "Trevor?"

Everly nodded, also teary.

They both took a deep breath and held hands as they quickly made their way to the metal table, lying on its side, and riddled with bullet marks. Trevor lay on the ground behind the table, his arm covered in blood. He wasn't speaking or moving.

"Trevor! No! Trevor!" Everly fell to the ground and started examining him. "Nylah, get that ugly tablecloth and tear it into shreds. I need to make a tourniquet."

Nylah jumped to action, scrabbling to find shears that had been knocked to the ground by the spray of gunfire. She worked quickly to hand shreds of winged unicorn cloth to Everly.

Everly pulled a pocket knife out of Trevor's thigh side pocket and cut away his sleeve. "Oh my," she mumbled as she saw the wound and then she sighed with relief. "Just a scratch. Big scratch, but a graze of the bullet."

"He's unconscious," Nylah observed. "Does he have another bullet wound? Check the back of his head."

"Nylah!" Everly sounded exasperated.

"Well, c'mon, that would be really bad. And it would be a reason why he's not moving."

Together they checked the back of his head.

"He's got some cuts there, but I think they're from glass, not guns."

They proceeded to check his body. "No more blood. No more bullet wounds," Everly announced with relief.

"Then why is he out of it?"

Everly bent down to examine his face, putting her ear to his mouth to listen for breathing and her fingers to his neck to check for a pulse.

"Everly…" he whispered into her ear. "Are you alright? Is Nylah?"

"Oh my God, you're alive!" Everly shrieked and started kissing his face. "You're alive! You're alive!"

"Uh, Everly, if you're gonna resuscitate him, you usually put your lips on his lips," Nylah said.

Everly laughed and kissed Trevor on the lips. "Oh my God, you're alive!"

"I think I've been shot…"

"Yes," Everly said, tears running down her cheeks.

"Were you shot?"

"No."

"Was Nylah?"

"I'm all in one piece, Dr. T. Hell of a scratch from the corner of that metal crate she locked me in, but if I don't die of tetanus, I should live to tell the tale."

"Die of tetanus?" he said a bit weakly.

"No worries. Required booster before the dig. Hey, vaccines save lives!" Nylah looked at Trevor still lying on the ground and Everly holding his hand. "If you weren't shot, I mean like with a bullet actually in you, then why were you unconscious?"

Trevor looked at Nylah and then Everly. Then he laid his head back down and stared at the ceiling of the tent which was now pockmarked with little holes. "I think I fainted. I'm a muppet," he said dejectedly.

"You're a hero!" Everly smiled at him. "You maneuvered us over to be behind the metal crates, you sly dog you! Told me exactly what to do. You probably saved our lives."

He looked at Everly with a weak smile. "I knew you'd be smart enough to know why. Lids matter." The three of them chuckled. "I have a question." He still looked quite dazed. "Did you just, just… kiss me?" Everly smiled and kissed him again. When she pulled away a big smile grew on his face. "Blimey! Does this mean… does this mean you'll swipe right on Cambridge then?"

She sat back on her heels. "We'll see, Dr. Payne. We'll see. But for now, let's get you to the showers and get that bloody graze cleaned up. The first aid kits are there. I think we'll need to get you to a local clinic at least, see if you need stitches. And antibiotics probably."

Trevor looked at Everly. "Antibiotics? Did he shoot me with food poisoning? Or a rabid bullet?"

Everly shrugged. "I don't know, they just always prescribe antibiotics, don't they?"

Trevor glanced around at the tent. "My father won't be happy."

"That you were shot? I would hope not!"

"No. Not that. He'll say, 'That's all in a day's work,' if I know him. He'll be mad that on my watch there's twenty more holes in the tent than even his wonky brother-in-law managed."

Everly blinked and looked at Nylah, who shook her head in disbelief.

"But I did do one thing right." With his good hand, Trevor fished in his pocket and pulled out Father B's gold and diamond ring.

"How did you save this from being stolen?" Nylah asked, incredulous.

"I was wearing it, if I'm telling the truth. Backwards actually. I suppose it looks more like a modern wedding band that way, but I was, well, keeping it safe in the palm of my hand, as it were. They didn't seem too focused on any modern-day valuables we might have—just the artifacts. I mean, they weren't asking for our watches or the like, now were they? But when I had to fish a key out of my pocket, I slipped Father B's ring off, just in case."

"It fits you?" Everly asked.

"Like a glove. Like it's always been mine. Like a gift from a dear uncle." He looked up into Everly's eyes. "That sounds crazy right? I've got an excuse." He pointed to his arm. "I mean, I was just shot."

Everly laughed and said, "I don't know what to think about anything anymore, other than you are the most amazing man I've ever met, Trevor."

Trevor could feel the smile bloom on his face and if there was any pain from the wound in his arm, he couldn't feel it any longer.

◆━◆━◆

Everly got Trevor cleaned up as best she could. As she was placing a tight bandage on the wound, Nylah came in with her flashlight. "More bad news. I know we were going to take Dr. T to the local hospital, but news flash: we got no wheels. They shot up the car." Then she blanched and swallowed hard. "Oh shit! Hans! They took Hans. I was so caught up in our shared near-death experience that I totally forgot about him!" She started pacing, her hands in her hair and tears welling in her eyes. "And he said he loves me!"

"I think it's best you forget about him, Nylah," Trevor said.

"Harsh!" Everly whispered, signaling him to stop by subtly running two fingers across her throat.

"Not that! Not that!" Trevor shook his head. "He's fine. I'm absolutely sure they won't hurt him. Well, not absolutely sure after they think he double crossed them. They might shoot him and throw him in a river, but the rat bastard would probably deserve it."

"Double crossed them?" Nylah asked in surprise.

"Oh yes! I'm quite sure that the mastermind behind this little escapade was Hans himself. He was too cool, too calm. In fact, I wouldn't be surprised if he was behind the whole heist up at Brandenburg."

Everly nodded slowly. "I think you're onto something! Did you see how the gunmen yelled, like they were yelling *at him* when they found out the cross was made of wood and not gold? You're right! It was like he was their boss."

"I was dating the kingpin? This whole time I was dating the crime boss? And I didn't know it?" Nylah stopped pacing and looked frozen.

Trevor shook his head. "This doesn't necessarily end your career in detective forensics, Nylah. It's hard to see all the facts when they're too close to you. You lose your objectivity, you know. And while I'm not asking for any details… at all… I am under the impression that he was trying to work his way back into your good graces. Wanted to be close to you. Quite often in fact."

Nylah couldn't help but smile and then her look became quite serious. "Do you think he meant to kill me? Oh man. No wonder he didn't want the baby. He didn't really love me either. I was just a tool to help him get close to possibly valuable artifacts." She sighed heavily. "I really thought he loved me. Like really loved me."

Everly put her arm around Nylah. "I don't think he meant for any of us to be shot. I think he meant for his henchmen to get the valuables, be left here with us, and meet up with them later to fence the goods or melt down the cross and sell the gold."

"Right! I think Everly's right. I would bet a good bit that taking him as the innocent hostage there at the end was improvisation. So they could lay low and then the four of them could figure out what in the bloody hell to do next."

"And what about all that gunfire at the end? All the attempted murder?" Nylah asked.

Trevor shook his head. "Honestly, I don't think Hans knew what he was doing, and he chose the wrong partners. I don't think he's got a very good criminal mind, but I think he might have felt a bit desperate. I'm absolutely sure he's feeling desperate at this moment!"

"So, his partners got carried away. Watched too many American movies perhaps? Held deeply in the thrall of old-school masculinity and once they had those guns in hand, just couldn't resist the temptation to toy with them." Everly pushed her hand through her now very messy hair.

"Toy with them? And nearly kill us!" Nylah took few deep breaths and calmed down. "You know, I've had a couple of good professors before, but never two who saved my life. And not just once, but twice. Hans letting me down is one thing. Hans endangering the two of you? I'm done waiting for halftime. I'm gonna track that bastard down. He's going to jail for armed robbery, attempted murder, and criminal conspiracy."

With his good arm, Trevor grabbed Nylah's. "Hold on there, you American cowboy! We don't actually have proof yet. It's all speculation. It's just my gut instinct." Trevor looked at Everly for back up.

Everly said, "Yeah, but between your gut instinct and Nylah's determination, there won't be anyplace that man can hide."

Trevor shook his head. "I'd stay as far away from that young man as you can. Seems to me like third time's the harm with that one."

"Hell hath no fury like a woman scorned," Everly said. "I get your pain. I do. But Trevor's right, you know."

"Hell hath no fury like being shot at by your ex-lover's armed guards. That man is going down!"

Everly looked at Nylah sympathetically. "I don't know how you think you're going to find him in Germany. I'm sure he's on the lam and by tomorrow he could be anyplace in Europe."

"Oh, I'll find him. When he was so off-put about the pregnancy, I suspected that something was up. And well, I… I…"

"What did you do, Nylah?" Everly asked.

She glanced downwards and looked a little bit ashamed. "I slipped my luggage tag tracker into the sole of his favorite shoe. I know. Psycho girlfriend kind of move, but in my defense, I was high on pregnancy hormones. I wanted to know where he was going. And he loves those shoes. Wears them all the time. I have a map of all the places he's been for the last three weeks, trying to figure out if anything was going on. There was no other woman that I could find, but I can find him."

"Nylah! No! That'll be dangerous. Now he might have real motive to kill us. And the means to. You cannot track him down!" Everly said.

"Oh, I'm not going to bring him in by myself. Remember, I do the organizing. Not the dirty work. I'll be calling upon my new best friends to help me bring him to justice."

Trevor looked confused. "New best friends? Who's that?"

They were interrupted by the sirens of the police and emergency vehicles that started arriving on the scene en masse.

"What? How did they know to come? We're too far out for anyone to hear all that gunfire." Trevor looked amazed. "And our cell service is…"

"Fixed," Nylah said with satisfaction.

Trevor looked at Everly. "There's nothing that girl can't do, is there?"

"Nothing," Everly agreed.

"Oh no!" Trevor jumped up. "Another casualty." He walked over and picked up Father B's skull which was lying on the ground. It now had a neat bullet hole exiting the back of the head. "He got shot in the eye. Good heavens, when will the sacrifices of this good man ever stop?"

"What do you mean?" Nylah asked as she came over to look.

"Can't you see?" Trevor held up the skull with reverence. "He took a bullet for us. This man should be sainted. Even after death, he's taking one for the team."

Everly shook her head. "C'mon you dreamer, you. We are taking you to the hospital for some stitches. And some antibiotics."

"All right. But I'm bringing him along."

The End

Acknowledgements

No book project comes to fruition without the input, questions, corrections, criticisms, and hilarious ideas from that incredibly important chorus of loved ones supporting the work. One of the best parts of creating a story is sharing the initial germ of the ideas with dear friends, and I am appreciative of the fond memories of cocktails imbibed on the lawn with Erika Lusk and Katie Rosanbalm as they patiently listened to story ideas and even early dialogue. Their quick wit and keen insights glimmer in this story. What wonderful friends with whom to embark on this journey. Especially, I am ever-so-grateful for Erika Lusk and her willingness to read and re-read and give feedback while the story was a work-in-progress.

Creating a story as long and as intricate as Holy Orders requires some experimentation. Erika, along with Ruben Fernandez and Ethan Fernandez, had the joy of suffering through extensive test-approaches to plot line problem-solving and responding to rapid-fire idea propositions. I greatly appreciate Ruben's wry sense of humor, which permeates the story, and Ethan's input on the mindset of late teens/early twenties emerging adults as I developed the character of Nylah. Early feedback was also much appreciated from Alexander Fernandez, Pam Plaisted, Katie Rosanbalm, Linda Peterson, Michelle Abel-Shoup, Kathy Donnald, Bharthi Zvara, Don Cavellini, and Barbara Marcum.

Finished work feedback requires many hours of dedication and I'm so very lucky to have such a wonderful Reader's Circle who were willing to put in the time, complete with their editing pens, and dive into the story, marking it up with questions, ideas, and corrections. It takes a special talent to proofread a 500+ page work. Many warm thanks go to Alexander Fernandez, Katie Rosanbalm, Erika Lusk, Debbie Jepson, Laura Thomas Wood, Shannon Thielman, Ed Donnald, Amy Langenderfer, Patrick Market, Sarah Kotzian, Pam Plaisted, Patrick Plaisted, Susan Kermon, and Bekki Buenviaje —along with those

Reader's Circle members who wish to remain anonymous (you are no less appreciated!) I am most grateful for all your contributions to making this a polished work.

A special shout out goes to Denielle Hennis for her wonderful artistic eye and help with tweaking the cover design.

Many thanks also go to Michelle Abel Shoup, Kathy Donnald, Katie Brandert, Angela Rosenberg, Cheryl Noble, Melissa Green, Kimberly Allen, Adriana DiFranco, Dorothea Calhoun, and Dee Colello, who have all been so supportive as Reader's Circle members.

So much inspiration for this story is attributable to Shirley Scott, who taught me to speak German during four years of study and bravely led our cohort of high schoolers to Germany as exchange students. She gifted me with a love of the culture and the country that is imbued throughout this work. I'm so sad she didn't live to see its publication. As always, I appreciate the cross-Atlantic collaboration with my editor, Alison Williams. I also want to thank my publisher, Beach Reads Books, for being incredibly supportive of me as an artist and creative in getting the work out to the world. I hope that many readers get to enjoy the story.

As an Indie author, I appreciate the network of Indie writers and their readers. My most humble gratitude goes to the Next Generation Indie Book Awards, which has honored me not once, but twice, with naming my works as finalists in their national literary competition. As a new author, it is a spectacular encouragement to have your work be noted for its merit. Victory! was selected as a finalist in 2023 and Holy Orders was given that honor in 2024. Thank you to the judges who collectively read hundreds and hundreds of entries. I am so gratified that you like my work. Thank you for the honor.

Additionally, there are some people whom I have never had the pleasure to meet and who need to be acknowledged as well. In the book, Trevor Payne is quite the music aficionado and he gets caught singing snatches of lyrics by some amazing and inspiring poets. These include Kerry Livgren, who wrote Carry On My Wayward Son, which was sung by the band Kansas. Stan Jones penned Ghost Riders in the Sky, the version sung by Johnny Cash served as Trevor's favorite. Trevor doesn't sing but does refer to the song Band on the Run, written by Paul and Linda McCartney and sung by Paul McCartney and Wings.

Author's Note

Holy Orders has been quite a different project than my other novels. I chose to locate it in southern Germany since I have some familiarity with the country, having been an exchange student there and, at one time, being able to speak German quite passably. Creatively revisiting Germany brought back so many fond memories of my time spent there.

While the 2022 publication, Victory! required a good deal (read: five years) of research, Holy Orders took me on a wholly unexpected and even more intense journey. I spent as much time researching this book as I did writing it. Of course, the research needed to parallel the timelines of the story, so both modern day and the Middle Ages. It was fun to learn about archeology—from learning how different characters would spell "archaeology" to understanding the tools and approaches used at dig sites. I was surprised to discover the enormous challenges women face in finding the kind of rugged clothes a dig requires, leaving them to shuffle around looking like blocky Minecraft characters wearing ill-fitting and oversized men's clothes.

At times during the creative process, everything clicks. Writing Holy Orders was such an experience. I was amazed at how, once I started this story, the universe kept laying what I needed to know next at my feet. A favorite such memory is the stranger on a long plane flight, who held me a veritable prisoner as his overly large screen filled our tiny visual space with an hours-long BBC special on archaeological digs in England. Even though I couldn't hear a word, I opened my computer and took notes on landscape, tools, dig depth, safety equipment, site personnel, specimen processing—it was like some type of Writing Genie sent me a tutorial to help me really settle into the world of my contemporary characters.

My online research also took me to all kinds of places in the Middle Ages. I found a fashion revolution born of the power struggles between the church and the guilds. The entire ecclesiastical class of Friar was

538

assigned "math", which they used in order to serve as the clothing morality police of their time. Of course, the powerful and cunning merchant guilds clearly weren't having any of that hot mess of clerical interference in their craft. I found the ensuing struggle to be worthy of a novel in and of itself. It was amazing that for a brief shining moment, you could have found similar fashion from modern day red carpets donning those at the feasting tables of the high born. History might have been quite different in Europe had the cultural revolution that was rapidly spreading through the Holy Roman Empire and what we now call Italy and France not been outpaced by the devastation of the Black Plague. The pandemic of their time shuttered the world of the mid-fourteenth century just as things were about to get very interesting indeed.

My fashion research took me to museums in Prague to investigate the type and quality of seven-hundred-year-old clothing remnants from royal tombs. The history of jewelry making at the time provided several fun evenings of ooohs and aaahhs as I examined the actual rings Adelaide wears in the story. Both of those rings have been recovered from the time period and are described as they look today. The Sumptuous Laws of the time dictated which classes were allowed to wear what clothing, as well as the kinds of jewelry they were allowed to don. I suppose this is so completely American of me, but I delighted in learning how the rural people of Southern Germania were kind of forgotten, and as such did what they wanted, rather than hold tightly to rule of class, king, or clergy.

The politics of the day were fascinating: unlike other areas in what we now call Europe, it was the custom in Germania to continually divide one's estate through all of one's sons, making them all "Dukes", which resulted in sufficiently diluting the power structures of the nobility that it began to equalize with the power of the guilds. It also had the unintended consequence of empowering the small villages of the South to act as little universes of independence and freedom as compared to their northern neighbors.

I enjoyed learning when and why the people of the Middle Ages feasted and what lay on their tables, although I found that professional historians are not quite unified in their descriptions. And I have to admit some astonishment when I learned that neither potatoes nor tea were a part of European life until the sixteen-hundreds. "Tea" of the time was barley water, a leftover substance from cooking, akin to the pot liquor of the deep South in the U.S. from cooking up collard greens, but not nearly as tasty—and that's saying something.

The idea that so much can be learned from online research amazes me, even after my many hours immersed in websites and online directories, in stories, histories, debates, and fourteenth-century census documents. The fact that the information is available, in this case both in German and in English, is such a boon to writers. Given the fact that experts in the field don't hold unified views of history or meanings of archeological findings only enriches the possibilities for creative endeavors, such as storytelling. What a wonderful world where humanity is engaged in putting so much of what we've found, discovered, and learned out there to share with the curious, inquiring minds who want to learn more and possibly use that to create (or recreate) worlds. Thank you to all of those researchers for your dedication and ingenuity in preserving the past. I have endeavored to depict the world of medieval life, geography, food, clothing, travel, social structures, and customs, not to mention the experience of the black plague, as accurately as possible. Of course, the little town and the actual people named are simply constructs for the tale, both in the thirteen-hundreds and in the contemporary era.

About the Author:

Ci Ci Soleil is a two-time national literary competition medalist who writes engaging, complex stories that explore the thorny challenges of ethics and morals in daily life. Having lived and studied in Germany made locating Holy Orders in Bavaria a natural choice. A researcher and teacher by trade, Ci Ci enjoys imbuing her fiction with enough fact to blur the lines between what might have happened—and what really did. Born an urban Northerner, she has now planted her roots in the New American South, where she lives with her husband and two sons.

Connect with Ci Ci Soleil
www.CiCiSoleil.com